PIERCING
THE HEART OF
PEGASUS

A BLACKWATER FALLS STORY

Melodee Lane

PIERCING THE HEART OF PEGASUS

Melodee Lane

Published by houseBLEND Publishing
Atlanta, GA
Copyright © 2014 by Melodee Lane

www.MelodeeLane.com

ISBN-13: 978-0692343760
ISBN-10: 0692343768
Printed in the United States of America

For Information:

houseBLEND Publishing
Atlanta, GA
www.yourHOUSEblend.com

*For Zen, whose unquestioning support and patience
never once wavered;
for Laura and the Red Pen of Virtue,
and for Erin, whose belief gave me the confidence to shoulder on.*

Blackwater Falls owes its existence to you.

CONTENTS

PRELUDE 3

Chapter 1 - *blackwater falls* 5

Chapter 2 - *mystery man* 23

Chapter 3 - *mortification* 37

Chapter 4 - *on the lake* 55

Chapter 5 - *flashes* 79

Chapter 6 - *intruder* 97

Chapter 7 - *star-grazing* 111

Chapter 8 - *beverly's a bitch* 137

Chapter 9 - *movie night* 157

Chapter 10 - *leering letch* 169

Chapter 11 - *sacred mcstuffin possums* 187

Chapter 12 - *blue showers* 219

Chapter 13 - *board up the door* 235

Chapter 14 - *bored games* 251

Chapter 15 - *she's a wreck* 265

Chapter 16 - *music and doughnuts* 285

Chapter 17 - *more pause for prose* 299

Chapter 18 - *grey day* 315

Chapter 19 - *welcome party* 329

Chapter 20 - *off the map* 345

Chapter 21 - *breaking out* 359

Chapter 22 - *breaking back in…seriously* 375

Chapter 23 - *acoustic dreadnought* 387

Chapter 24 - *mordred* 403

Excerpt from GEMINI GATE: *PRELUDE* 421

Excerpt from GEMINI GATE: Chapter 1 - *solicitude* 423

PRELUDE

The night is muffled, almost empty, the way that only the hours after midnight can be. It's muggy and hot for early May, a premature summer night in the south. The only sounds are the crickets and tree frogs singing from the shadows toward the water. There's a lake not far away, down the little road that winds beside the small, tired convenience store with two faded gas pumps out front. The lights from the store windows and the ones illuminating the pumps and parking lot are harsh and slice through the liquid darkness, illuminating only stillness.

Inside the store, a young woman, twenty-something; her dirty blond hair is pulled into a haphazard ponytail at the nape of her neck. The faded blue polo shirt with the store's name on the breast pocket hangs limply on her thin frame as she lazily flips through a magazine on the counter. A sound outside draws her attention, and she looks up at the windows overlooking the parking lot. It had sounded like the sharp snapping of a large branch in the black woods just beyond the light's edge. Her eyes slide from the windows to a clock on the wall and back, slowly, her posture still slouched and bored. She flips another page and looks down at the magazine again. It's going dark, the scene fading back into shadows. The girl suddenly looks up again, alert, but her form is dissolving into the black, back into the black....just before the colors all run dark, she screams – until the sound is cut off abruptly. She's gone.

3

It had started like any normal Saturday. Aden slept in late, had cold pizza from the night before for breakfast. She drew a frown-y face on it with mustard and wolfed it down with a can of Diet Coke. Serious nutrition. Then, she pulled out her phone to check her texts. The only new message was from her Mom, reminding her, again, to call her at work when she'd made plans for the day and let her know where she'd be.

Her Mom has a Master's degree in Visual Communications, but she'd been working the deli counter down at the grocery store. Her other job is an Art Teacher at the local Elementary School on Tuesdays and Thursdays. Not a lot of job options in this part of South Carolina.

Blackwater Falls is a small town, population 4,876, in the extreme northwest corner of the state, close to the border with both North Carolina and Georgia. The town is situated a few short miles from the shores of Lake Jocassee on the fringes of the Sumter National Forest where the Appalachian Mountains slide down into the Jocassee Valley. Jocassee supposedly means "Place of the Lost One," according to legends of the Cherokee tribes that once lived here, long before the power company drowned their lands and created the man-made lake for the hydroelectric plant. As far as Aden was concerned, "Place of the Lost One" was succinctly appropriate for this lonely little corner of the world.

Deleting the text from her Mom, she mused silently about what she might do with her Saturday. She went to check the handwritten schedule on the calendar pinned to the wall above the desk in her bedroom just to make sure one more time. She had the whole day off of work. It was unusual, as she normally worked at least one shift at the jewelry store on the town square every Saturday and Sunday. They scheduled her work shifts around her classes at the high school, but every once in a while the rotation of the small staff was such that she got the rare weekend day completely free.

Puffing a slow exhale, she walked to the large plate glass window overlooking the turbulent river that wound through the never-ending woods on its way down to the lake. Her reflection in the glass stared back blankly; even tightly pulled back, her deep auburn hair glowed orange in a shaft of sunlight, and her blue eyes reflected even more pale than usual, as did her pale skin. She stepped out of the sun shaft so she wouldn't have to see herself and could concentrate on the world beyond.

Though she didn't have the view that included the magnificent set of falls that was visible from the living room and master suite of their house, the slice of river and surrounding forest outside her window calmed her. As always, it made her think of her dad, who'd chosen this site for their house and meticulously lined up its many windows to showcase the natural beauty surrounding it.

Her dad, Christopher Garrett, was an architect. He'd worked at an up-and-coming firm in Atlanta until he met Aden's mother, settled down, and had two kids –Aden and her brother. He began to seek out the "perfect" place for his "perfect" family and found this particular site sitting level above a rocky rise overlooking the river adjacent to the National Forest. The house he'd built here represented his soul in steel and wood and glass. Contemporary and modular, the house nestled comfortably within the Appalachian foothills and the forest surrounding it. Featuring several full walls of glass to bring the wonder of the river and the forest indoors, it felt like a tree-house, suspended on the edge of the ever-rushing river below. Or, at least, it had for that short time after they'd finally been able to move in, and before her Dad had died…but she quickly pushed those thoughts away.

The kitchen door banged loudly, startling her out of her reverie.

"Hey Aden! You here?" her brother yelled. *How could a 21 year-old still be so annoying?* She headed for the kitchen as she answered.

"Yeah, Drew. What's up?"

"Just wonderin' if the house was empty or not." he mumbled, his head stuck inside the refrigerator as he rummaged around for breakfast.

"Aren't you supposed to be at work already?"

"I switched shifts with Billy Ray. Said he couldn't sleep last night, so he went in early to open up. I don't have to go in until noon." Her brother was tall, like their dad, and had his super-thick light brown hair that curled in the summer humidity, but he had their mother's hazel eyes.

"Oh. He keeps some weird hours."

"Whaddaya mean?" Drew asked, between mouthfuls.

"He just switches a lot of shifts with you, and it's usually around his sleeping schedule."

Drew just shrugged.

"You working today?"

"No. Have the whole day off." she sighed.

"Lucky you. You don't look so happy about it?"

"I'm just trying to figure out what I want to do with my day." She turned to go back to her room, sat on the foot of her bed, and looked around for inspiration. She *should* be excited to have the whole day to herself, no obligations.

Her Mom would be working until late. She always worked as many hours as they'd let her – too many. She would come dragging home after the store closed at 11:00 p.m. most nights. She rarely took a day off. Aden thought it was because she couldn't stand to be here, in the house, for too long. It reminded her too sharply of Aden's Dad. Well, that and the whole money-to-live-on thing.

And Drew would be leaving soon for work. She looked at the clock. She hadn't realized how late it was, he'd better be leaving very soon.

"Drew! You'd better hurry up, or you'll be late," she called through the closed door. She only got a mumbled reply as he banged back out the kitchen door on his way to his room, up over the garage. The big, airy space over the detached garage had been their Dad's home office, but Drew had moved into it after he graduated high school and finally came to terms with the fact that he couldn't afford college right away. He'd been really looking forward to "getting back to civilization" as he called it. But like so many other things that abruptly ended the day their father died…

She was doing it again, allowing her brain to circle around, always coming back to gnaw at her most painful memory. She exhaled noisily and abruptly stood up, hands on her hips; she had "assumed the position," as her Mom always called it. Ready for action, just as soon as she figured out what that was.

Her eyes drifted back to the window, and she decided that she needed to get out of the house. She dug up her most comfortable shoes—a pair of dirty sneakers that slipped on like old friends—and shoved her cell phone into the pocket of her jeans. As she turned for the door, she hesitated for a moment, deliberating, then grabbed the yellow umbrella hanging behind the door with a shrug. They'd predicted afternoon showers or storms, and she had no idea where her feet might take her today.

Walking back through the kitchen, she saw that Drew had dumped a couple of plastic storage bowls into the sink but hadn't bothered to rinse them, let alone put them in the dishwasher that was two steps away. By the smell, they were overdue to be cleaned out. Wrinkling her nose in disgust, as much at Drew's laziness as at the odor, she rinsed out the bowls and put them into the dishwasher. Then, she quickly swiped at the counter with a sponge from the sink. This domestic activity made her think of her Mom, and she dug her phone out of her pocket and sent a quick text message to her to let her know that Drew was on his way to work, and she was going for a walk. Aden promised to let her know where she ended up.

As she pushed out the kitchen door into the paved courtyard between the house and the garage, Drew was backing his car out of the bay furthest from her. The battered old gray Honda was idling choppily, and it stalled just as he pulled free of the garage and into the driveway. He looked to be muttering darkly under his breath as he started it up again. The starter reluctantly caught, and the engine coughed back into life with a puff of smoke from the tailpipe. He caught sight of Aden as he sat revving, silently coaxing the engine, and rolled the window down as far as it would go (only about six inches) to speak.

"Hey, keep the house locked up, even when you're inside, okay?" he yelled. She stepped closer in order to hear him over the revving engine. "Radio's sayin' there's been another disappearance, just down at Devil's Fork."

"Devil's Fork? Inside the park?" That was only about a four-mile hike down the river—a few more miles by the winding mountain roads.

"Yeah, that convenience store just at the main entrance on the highway. The girl who worked the night shift last night is missing. The owner got there this morning and found the place deserted. Her car was still outside, and her purse was locked in the back office."

"Who? What's her name?" she shuddered involuntarily. This was the third disappearance in two months within Oconee County, and definitely the closest to home.

"Didn't hear. I wasn't payin' much attention 'til I heard Devil's Fork State Park." He revved the engine again, trying to keep the car from stalling, then took notice of the umbrella she was holding. "You going out?" He frowned.

"Yeah, just goin' for a walk."

"By yourself? Can't you call Cadence or somebody to hang out with?" His hazel eyes darkened under worried brows.

"She's out of town this weekend with her mom. They went up to Charlotte to visit her grandmother." She shrugged.

"Well I don't think you should be walkin' around all by yourself out here," he started.

"I'll be fine. I'll stick to our trail by the river, and I won't go far. I've got my phone."

"Yeah, but you know how crappy the reception gets every step you take away from the highway. Maybe you should—"

"Aren't you running late?" she reminded him. He glanced quickly at the clock in the dashboard—one of the few things that still worked on the car.

"Crap, yes, just be careful, okay?" He ran a hand through his thick mop of hair and scowled. "Stick close to the house and keep the doors locked."

She waved a half-hearted promise as he backed into a turn and straightened out to drive down the winding, woody half-mile of driveway. Ducking back inside, she grabbed her house key from its hook beside the refrigerator, then locked the door behind her as she headed around the house toward the river. A slight breeze blew tendrils of her auburn ponytail across her neck, which felt like spider's webs.

The back of the house was almost entirely glass, with large sliding doors opening onto the narrow deck, which were all that separated the house, anchored into the bedrock of the cliff, from the steep drop-off down to the perpetually rushing water below. The deck had two graceful staircases that turned the short distance from each corner of the house down to the slate and gravel pathways leading along the banks of the river. Her Dad's plan had been to landscape the paths a little further along each year in both directions, leveling and installing gravel, slate, and rough-hewn steps where necessary and planting hedges and flowers along the path. Although, the original paths now petered out within sight of the house, and the neat, bordered pathways gave way unexpectedly to red, uneven, hard-packed clay that was covered in drifts of last year's fallen leaves.

She was surprised by the state of the path, now overgrown and uneven. It had been worn smooth in the first couple of years they'd lived here. She and Drew had frequently wandered this meandering track when they'd first moved in, not knowing anyone and living just far enough out of town to make socializing inconvenient anyway. They had explored for miles up and down both sides of the river, sometimes joined by their Dad, who liked to exaggerate the excursions into "day hikes" and would push further on into the wilderness of the state park surrounding their property than they would have gone themselves. After the accident, she and Drew sought the solace of the woods both together and individually, and frequently, as a means of escape from the house where grief seemed to well up out of the air and threaten to engulf them. But then Drew had gotten his driver's license and inherited their grandmother's old Honda. That was when these paths had become Aden's own. Her Mom was always working, and Drew had a means of transport out. Aden's only means were the paths by the river.

She used to trek out here after school every day, and every weekend, with her battered backpack full of sandwiches, water bottle, and camera. She'd pick a direction and walk until her legs got tired, sometimes down to the park, where the entrance to Devil's Fork State Park sat beside the river's noisy confluence into the lake. Thinking of the park brought her back to the present and the news of the latest disappearance. She couldn't remember, exactly, the last time she'd been out here. With school, an ever-increasing load of homework, and her job at the jewelry store, she just hadn't had as much time as she once did.

Rounding a bend that followed a loop in the river, she came upon one of her old "rest stops." She had several places along the trail where she might stop to rest, eat, read or just watch the river. This was the first one you would come to going upriver, not really far enough from the house to merit a rest, but it was far enough away to ensure solitude within the leafy folds of the forest. Here, the river wound its way around a harder outcrop of what looked like granite on the opposite bank, and the resulting kink caused a comparatively quiet little bay, complete with a small sandbar that changed shape, and sometimes color, with each visit. There were noisy falls further upriver, and also downriver by the house, but here it was much quieter, as the water was forced to slow. The path wound down to just above water level, and there was an old downed pine tree and a couple of rocky outcroppings that offered ample seating. The rocky grit of soil that made up the bank here looked dry, so she plopped down on the ground with her back against one of the smaller rocks and stretched her legs out toward the green water.

The ever-present sound of the water meandering past was soothing. It made a peaceful backdrop to the chatter of birdsong and the soft whisperings the breeze made as it moved through the heavy, green foliage surrounding her on all sides. She stretched her arms up over her head and watched a squirrel on the opposite bank gracefully bobbing along a tree limb stretched out over the water. She watched the furry little guy *or girl* bounce unerringly closer, balanced with ease on the narrowing branch, and she wondered if it was looking for a way across the water. *How far can squirrels jump?* she wondered. It didn't look like it could possibly make it across from where it was. It stopped as the branch dipped further under its weight. The squirrel sat back on its haunches, seeming to consider its position and twitching its face every so often. Aden remained perfectly still, watching and waiting. *It's not like I have anything else to do.*

She closed her eyes for a few moments, but when she opened them again, the squirrel still sat, considering the end of the branch with twitchy concentration. Just then, a large, black bird landed a few feet away at the edge of the water. She watched as it examined the ground with beady black eyes, turning its head slightly as it hopped along. Glancing back at the squirrel, it seemed to be watching the bird too; its fluffy tail stirred in the breeze, and it sat up, as though sniffing the wind for news or encouragement. At the same moment, the bird that had been slowly heading in Aden's direction, suddenly took flight with a loud caw. The squirrel disappeared back the way it had come, around the tree without so much a twitch.

Aden sighed, disappointed, and then rolled her eyes. *So stupid to feel a pang of loneliness at the parting of wildlife.* She huffed softly and sat up, thinking of continuing upriver for a while until she reached the spot where she could cross to the other bank over the rocks. Her Dad and Drew had told her a million times not to cross there alone; the footing *was* pretty treacherous sometimes, but she'd done it a hundred times before. She'd cross over and continue back downriver on that side to the huge old tree that had fallen, creating a bridge just below her house. Then, she could get home just in time to be really hungry for dinner. Satisfied with her plan, she reached for the umbrella she'd dropped at her side and took one last look around. She froze.

Somebody was there; watching her from the path across the river. He was half-hidden in the foliage, but Aden could see enough to know that she didn't recognize him. Tall, with piercing green eyes and dark hair: that was all her brain registered before her suddenly-racing heart delivered the adrenaline to her startled system. She gripped the umbrella as her only weapon and shoved herself up, running back down the path toward her house as fast as she could.

Drew's unheeded warning to stay close to the house kept echoing in her head as she stumbled along the uneven terrain. *What if that was The Guy, the one who had kidnapped three people?* Still running, she dug into the front pocket of her jeans for her phone and then tripped over an exposed tree root. She caught herself before she fell flat, and squatted, panting as she listened for the sounds of pursuit. She finally managed to get the phone out of her pocket and stared at the small screen, willing it to show that it had a strong enough signal to make a call, but she had known she was too far from the highway for that. She took off again for a few minutes before slowing to a jog. She already had a stitch in her side. It'd been too long since she'd run like this. Of course, she had been sprinting flat out, up and down steeply rolling hills. The original adrenaline rush had been used up on the rough terrain. Just at the top of the next rise was a tall, looming rock that hung over the river on her left. She sat down with her back to it to catch her breath, facing away from the river and hiding from any watching eyes. Semblances of sanity began to return with the oxygen that gathered in her lungs and blood stream.

It was just a guy, she told herself. *Just somebody out for a walk.* She tried to quiet her panting to listen for any approach, even though she was starting to feel a little foolish.

But what was he doing way out here? she argued with herself. The marked trails that led from Devil's Fork State Park into the National Forest on the other side of the river sloped around toward the east and followed another, larger waterway back toward the lake. Not very many hikers made their way this far off the marked trails.

But it does happen, she told herself. The fact that he didn't seem to have any hiking or camping gear with him when she saw him was a little odd though. Unless he'd come from miles and miles upriver, the best way into the forest where he'd been would have been to hike the unmarked paths coming from Devil's Fork. The woods had gone quiet again, except for the rushing water and the breeze sighing through the branches. She tried to hold her breath and listen, but she still did not have control of her lungs. She decided that, silly or not, it would be safer all around if she went back home and locked the door behind her. She stood up, still clutching her umbrella as if it were a lifeline. She sighed looking at it, bright yellow—almost glowing in the comparative gloom of the forest surroundings. It might as well be a neon sign pointing her out to anybody within sight. Whoever he was, he was probably still back there where she'd left him on the other side of the river anyway, laughing his head off at her hysterical departure. And, well, it was still a better weapon than the cell phone, the only other item she'd brought. She gripped the umbrella in both hands as she stepped out from behind the rocky outcrop and continued down the path towards home.

Seriously, you are completely paranoid, she told herself as she pushed on. She wasn't running anymore, but she wasn't dawdling either, keeping an eye out both behind her and on the other side of the river for any movement. She could just hear traffic on the two-lane highway through the trees to her right; she was nearing the house. She finally rounded the final bend and surveyed the yard and surrounding woods quickly as she panted her way around the house. It occurred to her that the closest entry-point to where she'd seen the guy by the river was their driveway. She'd been picturing him coming either upriver or downriver from some other spot, but with no gear, he could have just as likely come right by her house. She shuddered and danced impatiently as she dug in her pocket for the door key. She had a hard time getting the key into the lock because she was frantically searching the yard and all the shadowy corners and depths of the woods pressing in by the garage.

She finally managed to open the door, dart inside, and lock it immediately, as though she'd been closely pursued. As she stood gulping air in the kitchen, her eyes were drawn to the big, open family room with its expanse of glass overlooking the river. She examined the woods on the opposite bank, searching for any sign of movement…or a face with startling green eyes staring back. Though she knew it was impossible to see inside the house during the day due to the tinting on the glass, she still felt exposed and hesitant to go any closer to the glass wall. Sitting down on a bar stool at the counter, she laid the umbrella aside, dug her phone out of her pocket and dialed her Mom's number.

What the heck am I going to say to her, though? She scrutinized every inch of woods visible through the windows waiting for the call to connect. *Hi Mom. Just saw a guy in the woods. Almost peed my pants and ran all the way home.* She sighed as the line finally began to ring. No, that would just scare her. She didn't need anything else to worry about. Aden was fine, after all. Her Mom's voice mail picked up immediately, as it usually did when she was working.

"Hi, this is Janet," her voice chirped. "I can't get to the phone right now, so please leave a message." Aden held the phone away from her ear, waiting for the obnoxiously loud beep.

"Hi, Mom. Got back from my walk. I'm home now. Just thought I'd check in. Love you."

She pressed the button to end the call and put the phone back in her pocket. Normally, she would have left it on the counter or put it back on its charger in the bedroom, but she was still jumpy and thought it couldn't hurt to have it nearby. She'd seen too many silly horror movies where the victims were attacked just after they'd reached what they thought was a safe location and let their guard down. Then, she had a jarring thought: what if she'd left one of the other outside doors unlocked this morning? Could the guy have beaten her back to the house?

Stop it. She silently scolded herself. There was no good place to cross the river back to this side for another half mile past the house. *He'd never have beaten me back here. Plus, it was just a guy. He didn't have "Serial Killer" tattooed on his forehead or anything; could have been just anybody.* Anybody just walking in the woods. Miles deep into the woods…

She shrugged off her paranoia, but got up to check all the doors anyway. The rarely-used front door in the deep foyer just off the kitchen was locked. She slipped into her mother's bedroom on the opposite side of the house from her own. The big glass slider that led from the room out onto the back deck was locked as well, and secured with the security bar built into the floor. She let the heavy drapes fall back into place and padded out to the living room. Here, the large glass wall was actually made of three huge glass sliding doors that could all slide back and stack beside each other to open up almost the entire expanse of the wall to the deck outside. The lock on the big door's handle was locked, but she saw the security bar on the floor wasn't down in the locked position, so she quickly snapped it into place.

The only other entry point was a door leading out from the unfinished space upstairs. There was a temporary wooden staircase outside that led to a small landing on the side of the house to give access to the door. Of course, the temporary stairs and landing had been there over five years now. The upstairs space had never been finished, and they only used it for storage. It was going to become a game room with another guest bedroom and bath up there, but when her Dad had died, the funds and the plans had just dried up. Aden's Mom had a door installed at the top of the iron and wood staircase that curved gracefully up from the family room, and it now remained closed all the time. Though it was silly, because they hardly ever went upstairs, she felt compelled to check it anyway. Glancing back at the woods across the river first, she climbed the stairs and pushed the door, creaking loudly, open into the second story floor space. The heat and the smell of raw wood and dust hit her immediately; instead of an upstairs living space, it felt like an attic. *Which is what it's used for now*, she supposed. She picked her way among the boxes strewn haphazardly across the big, open space, her footsteps echoing weirdly on the bare plywood floor. She reached the door and ensured that it was indeed, locked up tight.

She was coming down the stairs, using the higher vantage point to search new areas outside the glass wall when her phone rang, startling her in the silence of the house.

13

She really needed to calm down.

"Hello?"

"I can't begin to tell you how incredibly bored I am right now," a girl's voice drawled.

"Cadence! Oh, I'm so glad you called. Can you talk?"

"Well, that's why I'm calling you, yeah." Cadence laughed. "Miss me much? What's up?"

"Well, I do miss you, but I just really needed to hear another voice for a few minutes."

"That's flattering. Thanks," Cadence said slowly.

"No, sorry, it's just that something really weird just happened, and I'm still kind of freaked out."

"Well, what is it?!"

"Okay," She took a deep breath and plopped into her favorite corner of her favorite sofa. "I went for a walk up the river, you know, on our path and I'd decided to sit down for a minute, just taking in the scenery, when suddenly there's this guy in the woods across the river from me, staring right at me." She paused just long enough for Cadence to interject.

"A guy?"

"Yeah, I didn't recognize him," Aden continued. "He was just standing there staring at me. So, oh, I forgot to tell you there's been another disappearance, too. A girl working at the convenience store down at the Devil's Fork convenience store is missing, same as the others, purse, car, everything left behind. Drew had an uncharacteristically caring moment this morning telling me about it; he'd heard it on the news and warned me to stay in the house with the doors locked."

"Do you know her name? The missing girl?"

"No, I haven't caught the news myself yet."

"That's just right outside of town." Cadence sounded worried for the first time.

"I know, right? So I'd been thinking about how she'd gone missing just a few miles downriver from my house when I saw this strange guy in the woods. Scared the crap out of me."

"Did he say anything?"

"No, he was just staring."

"What'd you do?"

"Well, I ran all the way back home and locked myself in. Of course, now I feel like an idiot."

"Why would you feel like an idiot?"

"I totally overreacted. It was just some guy, not a three-headed monster."

"Yeah, but that's creepy that he was that far out in the woods."

"Well, that's why it creeped me out at first."

"So have you seen him again?" Cadence asked.

"No, I've been watching the trails out back." She scanned the woods for the hundredth time. "Wish you were in town this weekend to keep me company."

"I wish I was home, too. Gran's idea of a good time is tooling around Wal-Mart double-checking the price of practically everything in the store. I love her, and I'm happy to see her, but I'm bored stiff." Cadence sighed, theatrically.

"What are Grace and Patience up to?" Aden asked. Cadence, Grace and Patience were triplets, known around town as the Kendall Triplets.

"Well, Patience disappeared a few hours ago. Said she was going to the mall with a girl who lives across the street from Gran, but I'm sure there were boys involved somewhere—I saw her 'borrow' one of Grace's new lipsticks." Aden just laughed. "And Grace," she continued, "is upstairs reading. I swear she's already read that book twice, but apparently, she's bored too."

"Well, I know the feeling. I have the whole day off with absolutely nothing to do."

"How could you be bored? You were just scared to death."

"Well, I was bored before I spotted the guy out there," she said lamely, feeling sillier by the minute.

"So did you call your Mom?"

"I left her a message when I got back home, but I didn't say anything about the guy." She paused. "She's got enough on her mind, and she'd just want to come home, and that'd be a hassle with her boss...." She trailed off, shrugging as though Cadence could see her.

"Well, is Drew there?"

"Nope, he's working."

"So you're there alone, with weird dudes running around the woods. Aden, you really need to start learning how to drive," she admonished.

"Wouldn't help me right now; I wouldn't have a car to drive, anyway." They'd had this discussion a few hundred times over the past couple of years. Ever since Aden's fifteenth birthday had come around—the age at which Learner's Permits were the golden ticket for every other kid that age in South Carolina. Aden just wasn't interested.

"You're going to have to get over it sooner or later, you know," Cadence said quietly.

"Why? There's no law that says I have to know how to drive a car." She was pretty sure she'd said those words before, too.

"What happened to your Dad was a fluke, an accident," Cadence said even softer. "I know that you—"

"Look, when I can afford a car, I'll go get my license, okay?" she interrupted her. The cold pain sliced through her abdomen, though she tried to shake it off.

"I'm sorry, Aden. I don't mean to hurt you," Cadence said, quietly. "But you're stuck in that house all by yourself out in the middle of nowhere. If you could drive, though—"

"I know; I could be...hanging out at the mall down the highway with all of Patience's popular friends," she teased, trying to lighten the mood.

"Or you could go out to Lookout Point like Patience did twice with Luke Stephens." She snickered.

"Luke Stephens? Isn't he in college?" she asked, a little taken aback.

"Yeah, but they're not really dating, she says." Cadence had lowered her voice again, Aden guessed so that Grace wouldn't overhear. "I suspect he dumped her when he wanted to take their relationship a little further than she was ready for."

"Wow, TMI," Aden smiled wryly. "Much more information than I needed on that one."

"Just trying to get your mind off the woods, you know."

"Well, thanks for that," she said earnestly. "Just talking for the few minutes we have has helped."

"Glad to be of service," Cadence said. Aden could hear the grin in her voice. "So do you think you're gonna be okay?"

"Yeah, think I'll make it. I'm all locked in tight."

"Okay, well I'm gonna go, but I'll call you back later, okay?"

"Sure."

"And you can call me if you need to, you know, sooner."

"I'm a big girl now," she shot back. "Got my big girl panties on and everything." Cadence giggled at that, but then became serious.

"Well, don't go out again, okay?"

"I'm not."

"Seriously," she emphasized. "I mean it. Just stay put."

"Where the heck do you think I'm gonna go?"

"Just checkin'."

"Thanks…but you sound like my Mom."

"Okay, I'll stop then." Aden could hear her impish grin in the sound of her voice. "So go clean your room."

"Stop it."

"Don't forget the dishes," she added.

"I mean it," Aden was trying to keep from laughing. It wasn't really that funny, but it had been an emotional hour or so.

"And finish your homework."

"Okay, really?" She smiled, "Are you finished?"

17

"Yep. I'm all done." Cadence laughed. "You be careful. Keep your phone with you."

"Yes, mother," Aden sighed, shaking her head. "Hey, thanks for listening to my drama."

"I'll call you back tonight after I help Gran with dinner, okay?"

"Yep."

"Okay, but call me if you need me."

"Alright already. Good bye!"

"Bye."

Aden was smiling and shaking her head as she hung up. It was true; just the few minutes she'd spent talking to Cadence had made her feel better. It seemed to put a little distance between her and the fear she'd felt earlier and brought her back to normal. She'd watched the window the entire time she'd talked, slumped over the arm of the couch. She stretched, and her stomach rumbled. She glanced at the large wall clock, 1:56. Though she'd had such a late breakfast, all the running around had made her hungry already. So instead of the early dinner she'd originally planned to follow her leisurely walk, she'd have a late lunch.

Tearing her eyes from the woods outside, she went into the kitchen and made a salad. As she munched on the first few bites, she rummaged in the pantry by the kitchen door for a can of soup and heated up a bowl of that as well.

As she ate, she realized just how quiet it was; the simple act of chewing lettuce seemed to echo throughout the house. Taking her lunch into the family room and setting it on the coffee table, she grabbed the remote and turned on the TV. Of course, there wouldn't be anything worth watching on a Saturday afternoon. She flipped channels until she found a vaguely interesting show about Ancient Greece on the Discovery Channel. She sank back into the couch and munched away while the soup cooled on the coffee table. By the time she'd finished lunch, Ancient Greece was wrapping up, and she flipped channels again and landed on a movie, a romantic comedy she'd already seen, but her other choice was a horror movie (normally her first choice, but not today). She could still see the pathway on the other bank of the river if she sat up very straight. She didn't want to keep continually scanning the path, so she resisted the temptation by lying down on the couch so the large, padded arm blocked her view. She forced herself to concentrate on the movie's heavily clichéd plot.

It seemed just moments later that she startled up from a deep sleep, blinking rapidly into the gloomy shadows of late afternoon. She sat upright, looking around and listening for a repeat of the loud thump that had roused her from her nap. The wind had picked up outside, and judging by the darkening light, a storm was blowing in. It had probably been just a branch or a pine cone hitting the house in the wind, her sleep-numbed mind slowly reasoned. She sighed and stretched, glancing at the clock. 5:47. Wow. She couldn't remember the last time she'd taken a nap that long. A completely different movie was playing on TV now, and she searched for the remote to channel surf some more. She wasn't really interested in watching more TV, but it was good background noise. There were more muted thuds and bumps as another wind gust blew up through the trees. She decided that any channel would suffice since she wasn't really watching and set down the remote.

Picking up the lunch dishes, she made her way into the kitchen to add them to the dishwasher load. With that done, she fished the phone out of her pocket. There was a text from her Mom acknowledging that Aden was back from her walk and wishing her a happy afternoon. Another wind gust swooshed through the trees outside, followed closely by thunder. She went around the house switching on lights, as the storm had brought on a premature dusk, and then reclaimed the TV remote and switched it to the evening news that was just coming on. The latest disappearance was, of course, the lead story, and without any introduction, the middle-aged broadcaster looked gravely into the camera.

"Yet another abduction in Oconee County overnight, the third since mid-February, has residents worried, demanding answers from local officials. The overnight disappearance of twenty-four-year-old Cindy Bradford, a clerk at Hodges' Bait & Convenience Store on Jocassee Road at Devil's Fork State Park, is similar to the previous disappearances in that police don't have much to go on." The picture cut to video showing the front of Hodges' store. A reporter stood talking to a sun-browned older man in a worn baseball hat.

"We're standing just outside the entrance to Devil's Fork State Park near Blackwater Falls, and I'm here with Vernon Hodges, owner of Hodges' Bait & Convenience Store. Vernon, can you tell us how you learned of this latest kidnapping?" he stuck a microphone in front of the old man's chin.

"Yessir," he drawled, "I got a call 'bout four in the mornin' from the Sheriff's office. Said a deputy drivin' by noticed the lights still on and found the store sittin' empty."

"So it was a Sheriff's deputy who discovered the disappearance," the reporter prompted.

"That's right." The old man nodded, looking a bit annoyed.

"You say the deputy noticed the lights still on. Your store is normally closed at that time?"

"Yessir. We close at 1:00 a.m. on Friday and Saturdays. Not too much late night traffic

19

goes through here. So Ames, the deputy, this is part of his regular route, and he noticed the lights still on when they shouldn't be." The reporter nodded. "By the time I got here, they'd cordoned off the whole place, and the search had started in the woods."

"I understand," the reporter looked down at a notepad in his hand. "That is Ms. Bradford's car over there." He pointed at an older model Chevy in the background. The old man nodded. "And her purse was found locked in the back of the store?"

"In the office, yessir," the old man confirmed.

"And I understand that there is a videotape from your security system?"

"We have cameras in the store. It shows Cindy going outside into the parking lot. Looks like she heard somethin' and went to go see about it."

"She just walks out? Does it show anything else?"

"Not that I saw. The police have it now, lookin' it over."

"Did they find anything else?"

"Not that I know about. Ever-thing's here 'cept Cindy." The old man looked grimly at the reporter. "But you see, they're still lookin'." He pointed to the obvious police presence behind them both. "Maybe there'll be somethin' this time that'll lead 'em to find her. We're prayin' fer that."

"Yes, we're all praying for that. I'm Gene Halsford, with the Channel 7 Live Eye, on location in Oconee County." He signed off. The grim-faced anchor came back on then, in the studio.

"Thank you, Gene. The scene at Devil's Fork State Park is still active, and search parties are fanning out in all directions looking for any clues that might lead them to find Cindy Bradford. Road blocks have been set up in the area, so avoid travel in the vicinity if possible." He turned slightly and addressed a second camera in the studio. "This latest disappearance follows two others within the past few months. Nineteen-year-old Shonda King's white Ford Escort was found abandoned, it's hood open, on the side of Rambling Ridge Drive in Oconee County on February thirteenth. Ms. King had reportedly been on her way home from a friend's house the evening before, but she never made it. Then on April twentieth, forty-eight-year-old Raylene Marcus disappeared from the beauty salon adjacent to her home on State Road 42 outside of Blackwater Falls. Her husband and teenaged son were both at home at the time and didn't notice anything out of the ordinary until late that afternoon, when Mrs. Marcus failed to return to the house after an appointment in the shop next door. Investigations into both of those disappearances are ongoing, and police are asking anyone with any information to please call the number on the screen." The scene switched to video again, showing a small crowd on the steps of a public building as a familiar man in a suit and tie stepped toward a podium and microphone.

The anchor continued speaking, "Blackwater Falls residents came to the Town Hall today to hear what Mayor Max Dixon, Jr. had to say about the safety of his town following the last two disappearances." The video showed Mayor Dixon step to the podium, and the camera pushed in closer on his face.

"Thank you all for comin' out here today," he began, and then paused. Aden sat up and turned up the volume. Mayor Dixon was Cadence's step-dad. Aden hadn't seen him in person since before the last two disappearances had occurred within his jurisdiction. Cadence had mostly hung out at Aden's house lately, getting away from her siblings. She thought he looked really tired.

Mayor Dixon sighed and continued. "I don't have any new information about any of the missing persons cases. I can tell you that Sheriff Richey and his department have worked tirelessly these past few months, and every local, county, state, and now even national authority that can be called in, has been brought in, and no resources are being spared to locate the missing women and bring the perpetrator or perpetrators to justice." He paused again, scanning the crowd.

The camera's angle pulled back, showing some of the people standing on the steps behind the mayor. There were a few more middle-aged men in suits, and one woman with a phone to her ear and a clipboard in her hands. Beside her stood a tall figure wearing a dark t-shirt and jeans looking away from the camera, and out of place among the officials. "We will continue to pursue every avenue. In the meantime, we urge you to remain vigilant. Keep all vehicles locked ..." Aden didn't hear any more of what he was saying. In the background, the tall figure turned toward the camera, and she lunged for the remote. She hit the rewind button for just a second, and then hit play.

"Thank God for TiVo." she mumbled under her breath as she watched the last few seconds of the newscast replay. Then she hit pause again and stared at the TV screen. On the screen, staring back at her was a dark-haired young man, his green eyes and sharp facial features highlighted in a frozen burst of camera flash. It was the face she'd seen across the river today. She was sure of it.

A lright, we're gonna divide y'all into two groups today," the big uniformed man drawled loudly, wiping the back of his neck with a white handkerchief. "Group one will fan out around the east side of the lake, and group two will go west." The crowd of tense and restless volunteers shuffled and mumbled quietly in the shimmering sun as they surveyed the long expanse of lakeshore they could see from their location. "Remember to stay just a few feet from each other and search the grids just like we did yesterday. There's a lot of underbrush out there where just anything could be hidin'."

"Anybody searchin' across the road? Up the river?" a rough-cut younger man interrupted from the crowd. "We searched 'round the lake yesterday." The crowd grew still again. "She was mos' likely driven off in a car. She could be anywhere."

"That's right," the uniformed man said slowly, raising his voice just a bit for emphasis and staring down the younger man intently. "She *could* be anywhere, just like the other two victims, so we're gonna search everything for miles around here looking for anything that might lead us to them." His muddy brown eyes slowly surveyed the crowd again. "Now, it's hot, so make sure you take water with you. We don't wanna have to rescue any of y'all, too, and keep your eyes open. Most of you have hunted; look for signs of passage." He stopped and sighed. "Let's find 'em and bring 'em home."

The crowd quietly started to disperse into the two directions he'd indicated, groups forming up as men and women checked their water bottles, adjusted hats and sunglasses, and hefted the sticks they would use to literally beat the bushes as they searched.

"People are a lot more scared today, Dave." The mayor had watched from the shadow of a drooping pine tree as the Sheriff had addressed the volunteer search party. Sheriff Dave Richey removed his sunglasses to wipe his flushed face and greying temples with the handkerchief before he replied.

"Hey Max, didn't see you'd come out here." He put his sunglasses back on and pocketed the handkerchief as he surveyed the scene.

"Any word yet from forensics?" the mayor asked, unknotting the loosened tie from his neck and slipping it into a trouser pocket before unbuttoning his collar.

"Not yet. They lifted several dozen prints and a whole truckload of swabs, assorted artifacts, and just plain trash that they have to sort through. It'll be a while." He looked sidelong at the mayor. "Everybody's gonna be more careful on this one." The mayor raised an eyebrow in response, and the Sheriff continued. "The first disappearance was a random tragedy. The second could've been just a horrible coincidence, but three now...that ain't coincidence."

"The media are already calling it a serial case," the mayor said quietly, screwing up his tanned face into a scowl and rolling up his shirtsleeves.

"What do you want to call it, Max?" the sheriff asked, just as quietly.

"I want to call it solved, Dave, quickly. We gotta find this guy."

"You know I got every man on it already."

"I know." The mayor sighed and squinted up into the bright sky. "I called Kim a couple a' weeks ago. She flew in yesterday." The sheriff's dark eyebrows ticked up a notch at the news.

"She here in an official capacity, Max?"

"No." Max shook his head and didn't meet Dave's eyes. "Not yet."

Sherriff Richey said nothing.

"She's just here as a favor to me, takin' a look around," Max said, then more hesitantly, "You'll give her full access?"

"I already got the state guys crawlin' up my back. What's one more?" The Sheriff didn't look happy.

"She's here to help, Dave."

"I know," he sighed. "Guess we need all the help we can get."

Max remained silent, so Sheriff Richey strode briskly toward a group of deputies hunched over a map.

"All the help we can get," Max whispered to himself.

Aden sighed deeply as she spritzed the glass display case, wiping it down for the hundredth time. The small jewelry store on the town square was empty today, as it often was on Sunday afternoons; the only sound was the soft jazz music dripping from the speaker system overhead.

The only customer she'd seen today was Mrs. Carmody, who came in every Sunday after church to have her small collection of diamond-clustered rings cleaned. Even then, Mr. Keith, the store's owner, had uncharacteristically bustled over to take the rings from Mrs. Carmody and took them into the back room to clean them in the ultrasonic cleaner himself. After she left, fingers weighted down with sparkling clean diamonds, he'd slipped back into his office at the rear of the store. Aden could just barely hear the clacking of the keys on the keyboard of his ancient computer every now and then. She wiped at a non-existent smudge on another glass cabinet as she slowly walked around the store's showroom.

Outside the windows, there were a few people out on the square. A young family was walking a dog in the tree-lined park in the center of the square. The small fountain at the park's center was a silent spray of rainbow hues through the plate glass window. Two elderly, leather-faced farmers were sitting at a table outside the coffee shop, each bent over sections of newspaper. A young woman slowly walked down Main Street, browsing the windows of the small shops as she talked on her cell phone, and two young boys with skateboards were half-heartedly trying to teach each other tricks on the wheelchair ramp beside the courthouse stairs. They all looked hot. The early heat wave had settled over the valley in a smothering preview of coming summer. Aden was thankful once again for the new air conditioning system Mr. Keith had installed. When she'd first started working there last fall, the store's ancient AC unit would blow warm air more often than cool, and the store would become oppressive in the early afternoons when the sun shone through the big front windows. She could barely believe it was almost summer again. Just one more week of school was left before summer vacation. A week of final exams, she moaned inwardly, and spread the cleaning cloth on the glass to lean her elbows on the counter. She was deep into a summer vacation daydream when a figure walking by the store front drew her attention, and she stiffened.

Dark hair, not quite black, raked back from a face of strong, masculine angles. He was looking straight ahead, so she saw him in profile; his dusky brow drawn down against the sun's glare, above intense green eyes. His straight nose pointed to lips curled down into a half frown and further to a chin with a slight cleft and strong jawline. His shoulders were bunched as though he was angry, and the sleeves of his dark blue t-shirt were tight around masculine, but not overly-muscled arms. In just a few, long strides he had passed out of sight, and Aden flew around the counter to the shop's glass door. She pressed her head against the door's window trying to see further down the street without stepping out, but she couldn't see him. Hesitating only a moment, she pushed the door open slowly, trying to keep the bell above the door from ringing, and peered out in the direction he'd gone. He continued down the square at a quick pace, facing straight ahead and slowing only for a passing car when he crossed the intersection. Aden watched him all the way down Main until he turned onto Abbott's Ferry Road and out of sight.

She inhaled deeply, realizing she'd been holding her breath. She stared at the street corner where he'd turned in the distance while her mind raced. She wondered if Cadence was home yet. Cadence lived on Abbott's Ferry, in the rambling Victorian in the middle of the block, but she couldn't call because she was at work.

Aden slipped back inside and eased the door closed, watching the doorway to the back rooms. Her phone was in her purse, which was in the drawer of the worktable just outside Mr. Keith's office. Maybe just a quick text, she thought as she walked slowly back through the showroom. Just at that moment, she heard a distinctive squeak come from Mr. Keith's chair as he rose from it, and she startled, guiltily. Stretching his arms above his head, he emerged from the back room and looked around the empty shop.

"Guess everybody's out at the lake today," he mused aloud.

"Guess so," Aden shrugged back. He walked slowly to the front windows and peered out, sighing.

"Alright, why don't we shut down a bit early?" he smiled at Aden.

Normally, she would have protested; leaving early meant a smaller paycheck, but not this time. She shot him a grin and ran to the back for her purse. With a hasty thank you thrown over her shoulder, Aden was out of the shop and jogging down Main Street, leaving her bemused employer shaking his head.

She had her phone out, dialed, and to her ear in record time, silently urging Cadence to pick up and praying she had gotten home from her grandmother's by now, but the familiar voicemail message played almost immediately. Sighing dramatically, Aden dropped the phone back into her purse and sped even faster down the street in pursuit of the stranger.

She sprinted the two short blocks down Main Street and rounded the corner onto Abbott's Ferry, slowing to scan the sidewalks and the deep, shaded yards for any sign of the guy she was following. The huge, old trees lining the block at regular intervals had grown to intertwine their branches above the road, creating a sun-dappled, green tunnel. They also served to screen the yards in the distance, making it hard to spot anyone walking on the sidewalks behind their trunks. Aden speed-walked to the middle of the block, slowing to survey the rambling gray Victorian where Cadence and her family lived. The deep porches were empty and the door to the detached garage out back was firmly closed. Sighing, she continued on, searching for any sign of his passage until she reached the next intersection. Stopping to swipe the hair from her now-sticky neck, she looked both ways down the intersecting street but saw no one. Not even a dog or a squirrel stirred in the gooey humidity. She sighed, weighing the options. He'd had a couple of minutes' head start, and he could have easily slipped inside any of these houses or outbuildings. She could wander around the neighborhood for hours and not find him.

She pulled the phone from her purse again to check the time. Drew had dropped her off at work on his way to his job at the garage, and she was supposed to walk to the garage after her shift had ended at the jewelry store and wait for him to finish up and drive her home; but because she'd left work early, now she had even more time to kill. Cadence wasn't home yet, and none of her other friends from school lived close by. She sighed, turning back the way she came, and slowly retraced her steps back to the town's square, still searching for any sign of the mystery man.

Smiling at the two old men at the table outside as she passed, Aden stepped into the coffee shop that stood on the opposite corner from the jewelry store where she worked. There were only three other customers, all engrossed in reading material or laptops. She smiled again at the thought of such urban culture reaching into this quiet corner of South Carolina. The girl behind the counter was familiar, having graduated from the high school just last year, but Aden couldn't remember her name. She stepped up to the counter and browsed the chalkboard menu above the girl's head. She might as well get something for Drew, too, to try to make up for her snarky-ness yesterday. She opted for two iced vanilla lattes and sat at a nearby table while she waited for the girl to make them.

Someone had left part of a newspaper in one of the chairs, so Aden smoothed it out on the table. The front page headline screamed "THIRD DISAPPEARANCE," and the photo underneath showed the convenience store at Devil's Fork surrounded by police vehicles, officers, and crime scene tape, with the lake sparkling through the trees in the background. Off to one side stood a small knot of people, bystanders and gawkers, by the looks of them. Aden caught her breath and brought the paper closer to her face with narrowed eyes.

"You've got to be kidding me," she whispered. One of the other customers looked up at her questioningly, but Aden didn't notice. There, on the front page of the paper, standing just a bit apart from the crowd, was the guy she'd followed just a few minutes earlier. She was shaking her head unconsciously – who was this guy? She was sure she'd never seen him before that moment by the river yesterday, and then he'd been on TV, walking through town, and now on the front page of the bleeping newspaper.

"That's some crazy shit, ain't it?" the drawling voice was so close that Aden jumped. Startled, she looked up. A man was leaning over her shoulder, only inches from her face, grinning. "Sorry, stuff. Crazy stuff." He chuckled. Aden blinked rapidly a few times, leaning away from him and took a deep breath as he sat down in the next chair.

"Billy Ray," she breathed, trying to calm down. "You scared me. I didn't see you come in." Billy Ray worked at the garage with her brother. A self-confirmed bachelor in his late twenties, Aden had never seen him outside of the garage that his Dad owned on the outskirts of town. She could smell the ever-present reek of oil and cigarettes as he crossed one ankle over his knee and leaned back in the chair.

"Sorry, I didn't mean to scare 'ya. Just saw you in here and thought I'd come say hey." He smiled. He was a big man, solid, with a head full of coppery red hair that he always wore spiked up in front. Today, there was a smudge of grease on his forehead. "Did you know any of those girls?" he asked, motioning toward the newspaper Aden had dropped on the table.

"No, no, I don't know any of them. It's awful, though," she answered, looking toward the counter to check on her order.

"Yeah, it's awful. Got ever'body in town all in an uproar." He sighed, still smiling a little at Aden. "You know, Drew and I worked on Shonda King's car a week or so before she went missing. She was that first girl."

"Really? Drew never mentioned that."

"Probably didn't know. He'd come in late that day, had an appointment or somethin'? He just saw the car, not the girl."

"Wow," was all Aden could think to say.

"She was kinda shy. Didn't stick around, even though we were just changin' her oil and checkin' hoses and belts, that kinda thing. She came back and picked it up from Dad later that night." Aden just nodded politely and looked back to the girl behind the counter. She seemed more interested in the idle gossip that Billy Ray was giving out than she was in making the coffees. Aden tried to catch her eye; she just wanted her coffees and to get out of this awkward conversation.

"Shonda was real sweet," the girl chimed in. "I knew her from school. Well, I didn't really know her well, but I knew of her. She was always so quiet. I couldn't believe anybody would ever want to hurt her." A few of the other customers in the shop were now listening, too. She continued, "You know, my boyfriend, Shaun Bowman, he drove by her car that night, sitting on the side of the road. He didn't know it was hers. Said it was empty when he drove by. The hood was up, but nobody was in it." She looked around, noticing her audience. "He just thought it was weird, but we didn't know 'til the next day what had happened."

Billy Ray abruptly stood and went to the counter to place an order, leaving Aden blinking stupidly at his back. She got up and went to stand at the opposite end of the counter, under the hand-lettered "PICK UP" sign, before he could sit back down and start talking again. Billy Ray was okay most of the time, but he'd spooked her a little, and she just had too much on her mind at present to keep up a polite conversation. The girl behind the counter took Billy Ray's order and then walked toward Aden, two cups in hand.

"Here 'ya go, two iced vanilla lattes." She smiled a friendly smile, and Aden returned it before she turned to leave.

"Y'all be careful out there, now," Billy Ray said behind her. She half-turned her head and nodded but kept walking through the door without seeing who he was talking to.

Outside the shop, she paused at one of the tiny café tables on the sidewalk to put a straw into one of the drinks and then turned down Main to make the trek out toward the garage. She didn't see Billy Ray's truck parked anywhere nearby, and she hoped he hadn't walked into town, too. Well, really, she hoped he wouldn't catch up with her walking down the road back to the garage. She decided to take a more circuitous route, just in case, and turned down the next side street away from the main drag.

She felt a little guilty about her aversion toward him. He'd always been polite to her when she'd see him at the garage, but beyond the usual greetings and pleasantries about the weather, she couldn't imagine anything they'd have to talk about. Besides, the mystery man who kept popping up all over town this weekend was consuming her thoughts, and all other thoughts would soon turn back to him.

She had to find out who he was. Somebody had to know him. And why in the world did Cadence pick this weekend to go visiting her Gran? There were too many things happening at once and nobody to talk it all out with. She thought about trying to call Cadence again, but her hands were full. She'd wait until she got to the garage. There would be plenty of time before Drew was able to leave and drive them both home.

Walking slowly, she managed to make it to the garage with only about forty minutes until Drew was supposed to get off work. Good timing. Sometimes, she'd have to sit around the front office and read for an hour or more waiting for him to finish up his shift. As she crossed the street toward the garage, she saw that Billy Ray's beat up black truck was parked beside Drew's Honda at the side of the building. She walked slowly by the three-bay garage front, all three doors open today, looking for Drew. She wasn't allowed in the garage area. Big Bill, the owner was strict about who was allowed in the garage bays. She saw Drew in the middle bay, leaning way over into the engine compartment of a car.

"Hey, Drew, I brought you something," she called. He straightened up, wiping his hands on a filthy, red rag from his back pocket, and came out to greet her.

"Hey, thanks. I could use a drink." He smiled and, taking the top off the cup, drank it down in a few big gulps.

"You didn't even ask me what it was before you started gulping," Aden laughed.

"Long as it was cold, it didn't matter," he answered, upending the cup again to shake out the last few drops from the rattling ice. "I've got a few more minutes before I can cut out," he finally said.

"Okay, I brought a book. Come get me when you're ready."

She walked into the front office where there were a few battered chairs and a rickety table holding magazines that looked at least a decade old, in front of a stained and much-used counter. Behind the counter, at an even more beat-up desk, sat Big Bill Payne, the owner. He was on a phone call, but nodded at Aden as she came in.

Though there was an old window A/C unit in the office, it was almost as warm inside as it was outside. Sighing, Aden sat in the chair in the corner and pulled a paperback out of her purse, setting it aside on the next chair. Then she pulled out her cell phone and texted Cadence. She would have called instead, but she didn't want to disturb Mr. Payne. He continued to growl into the phone, ignoring her.

Hey, are you home yet? Aden sent the message and waited only a second.

No. On the way. Cadence answered.

Call me when you get home?

7:30-ish okay?

Aden sighed, and then sent: **Guess so.**

She frowned as she tucked the phone back into her purse. There was so much to tell Cadence, yet it was Sunday evening, and she'd have to do some studying for all the finals coming up next week. *Crap.*

"Bad news from your boyfriend?" Aden was startled again by the voice. She looked up at Billy Ray, who'd come out of nowhere, once again.

"What?" She was confused and a little annoyed at being startled again.

"Just looked like you weren't too happy with whoever was on the phone." He smiled.

"Oh, no, just…" She shrugged. "It was nothing." *None of your business,* she thought testily. How could such a large man keep sneaking up on her like that?

"Well, Drew should be done soon." He walked through the door to the garage bays without waiting for her to answer, which she wouldn't have done, anyway. She sighed. *What a weird day.*

At home that night, she'd hurried through the dinner her mom had brought home from the store's deli counter and fell across her bed after quietly closing the door. It was 7:43 before her phone finally rang.

"Oh my God, I can't believe you're finally home," Aden said in greeting.

"So nice to hear from you, too," Cadence said.

"Sorry, it's been a really weird day. A weird weekend, actually. And I wish you had been here."

"Well, it's good to be needed, I guess," Cadence softened.

"So, how was your trip?" Aden asked. She wanted to get the news of the trip taken care of so she'd have time to analyze everything that had happened with Cadence before it got too late.

"You know you don't want to hear about my trip." Cadence chuckled. "It was nice. Good to see Gran. Patience and Grace were, well, the same as always, but we didn't kill each other. So what's the big news that you're just dying to tell me about?"

Aden sighed, "I don't even know where to start."

Over the next ten minutes, Aden spoke rapidly, detailing everything that had happened since they'd talked the day before, after Aden saw the stranger in the woods. She talked in great detail about the guy she'd seen in town, on TV, and in the newspaper, detailing his eyes, the color of his hair, his build, height, and chiseled features. Finally, Cadence broke in.

"So, he sounds kind of cute. Are you, like, stalking this guy?" she teased.

"Really? I tell you I see the guy from the river on the TV, right behind your step-dad by the way, walking around town, and then again on the front page of the Herald, and all you can say is he sounds cute?" Aden was exasperated.

31

"I'm just kidding. Jeez. Calm down," Cadence answered. "But you did seem to notice a lot about his looks."

"Of course I did! He scared the bejeezus out of me, and then I keep seeing him. I want to know who he is."

"Okay, we can just ask around. You can't be the only one who's noticed a new guy in town. Oh! Speaking of which, I have to tell you what happened when we got home. Daddy Max's ex-wife and son were here at the house. I didn't even know they were coming; isn't that weird?" She paused, "Oh, hold the phone!"

"What?"

"You said this guy has dark hair? And looks a couple of years older than us?"

"Yeah?"

Cadence giggled. "No, it couldn't be."

"*What?* What are you laughing at?"

"Um…well, it just occurred to me that Maddox, my sort-of step-brother I just told you about?"

"Yes…?" Aden was getting impatient.

"Aden, Maddox is 19, almost 20. He's tall, has dark brown hair, green eyes, great body, if he wasn't my step-brother, I'd be drooling all over him."

"That's great, but….wait, are you saying that I might have been seeing your *step-brother* all weekend?" Aden was incredulous.

Cadence laughed. "Could be. Sounds like him."

"Holy crap. But it can't be him. I've been thinking this guy could be the kidnapper."

"Well, he is kind of quiet and moody, but then, the only time I've seen him is with his Dad's second wife and all three of us daughters. It's probably a little much for him to take, you know?"

"But why would your step-brother have been so far up the river?"

"I don't know, but it makes sense that he would have been standing near Daddy Max in the news footage. He and his Mom would have just gotten into town around that time, I

32

think. They were probably meeting him at the court house when he had to do that press conference. I'm telling you, the more I think about it, it's got to be Maddox."

Aden sighed loudly and closed her eyes. "So you said they just got into town. Where are they from?"

"After Kim divorced Daddy Max, she and Maddox moved to Virginia. Kim's with the FBI, a profiler, I think."

"So Kim is Maddox's Mom?" Aden was trying to keep it all straight. "Well, if they live in Virginia and just got to town this weekend, I guess it couldn't be Maddox who's kidnapping people."

"Nope," Cadence agreed.

"Oh my God, my head hurts." Aden sighed. "So you really think I've been stalking your step-brother all this time? For no good reason, apparently."

"I don't *know*, but it sounds pretty likely." Aden could hear the suppressed grin in Cadence's voice. "I mean, there aren't that many guys around our age in this town that we don't already know, so odds are…."

"Odds are, I'm a lunatic," Aden finished.

"Well, there *were* some unusual, extenuating circumstances," Cadence offered.

"Yeah, but at the end of the day, I'm still the weirdo jumping to all sorts of crazy conclusions."

"No worries. With everything going on in town right now, you're allowed to be a little jumpy."

"I guess." Aden sighed. "So why are Maddox and his Mom in town anyway?"

"Like I said, Kim is a profiler with the FBI. I guess Daddy Max asked for her help to catch the kidnapper."

"Wait, Kim is Max's ex-wife, right?"

"Yes, keep up. You already asked me that."

"Did not. I asked if Kim was Maddox's Mom."

"Ugh! She and Max were married just after high school and had Maddox about a year later, but then they divorced, and Kim moved to Virginia to work for the FBI. Max and my Mom had been high school sweethearts, before he met Kim. You know that my real Dad skipped out on Mom when he found out we were triplets. After Mom divorced him and moved back to Blackwater Falls, she and Max met up sometime after that and fell in love all over again."

"That's some story."

"I know, right? And you'd think that Kim and my Mom might not be very friendly toward each other, but they seem to get along just fine."

"Adults are weird."

"Seriously, so anyway, Kim is here because Daddy Max asked for her help with the case, and I guess Maddox tagged along. He hadn't seen Max since he was here last summer."

"Maddox was here last summer?"

"Yeah, he visits every summer, why?"

"Because I don't remember you ever mentioning him before. Not specifically, I mean, I knew you had a step-brother. So why haven't I met him?"

"I dunno." Cadence sounded thoughtful. "I guess you were never over here at the same time he was? He doesn't hang out with us anyway. Keeps to himself when he's here, especially after he could drive."

"Huh. I just thought I would have run into him at some point over there."

"I'd be happy to introduce you," Cadence offered.

"Well, that might be a bit awkward after my panic by the river," Aden said sourly. "Maybe I should just steer clear. How long will they be here, anyway?"

"Dunno. I didn't even know they were coming. But they're staying at the motel out by the highway, not at our house. Maddox usually stays with us when he comes, but this time, I guess he's staying there with his Mom."

"Well he's definitely been getting around town," Aden grumped.

"What else is there to do around here? You expect him to sit in a motel room?"

"No, I guess not," Aden conceded. "Well, I hope his Mom can help them figure out who the kidnapper is, and soon."

"Me too," Cadence agreed quickly. "Listen, I've gotta go get some studying in. Mrs. Bremer's History final is supposed to be brutal."

"Ugh. Me too. I've got Mr. O'Connor's math final first thing in the morning."

"Oh," Cadence sympathized. "Good luck with that. I don't have math finals until Wednesday."

"Yeah, good luck on yours, too." Aden sighed, "And thanks for listening to all my paranoia, *and* talking me down."

"No worries. It all worked out in the end. See you tomorrow in Language Arts."

"Yep, see you then. Bye." Aden ended the call and fell back onto her bed.

Cadence's step brother. She'd been all worked up over Cadence's step brother from out of town. Good grief.

Sighing, she pushed it out of her mind and rolled over to grab her math book.

CHAPTER 3
mortification

"I just don't understand how someone with such a heavy Southern accent could be so picky about dangling participles," Cadence groaned, following Aden to her locker just down the hall.

"Well, we only have to sit through just a few more classes, and Mrs. Fowler is history. Speaking of which, how'd your history final go today?"

"Okay, I guess." Cadence shrugged, leaning against an adjacent locker. "Keeping the names and dates straight wasn't too bad, but all those essay questions about insights and intentions of people who died centuries ago are just brutal. I'm praying for a B."

"I can relate. I'll be lucky to pass math at this point," Aden frowned. Cadence just giggled.

"Seriously? You've never gotten less than a B in your life." Narrowing her blue eyes, she shook her short, blond head in frustration.

"Not true. I got a C in math just last semester," Aden corrected her. "It's my worst subject, and Mr. O'Connor just hates me."

"Why would you think he hates you?"

"He never cuts me any slack," she started. "He always calls on me to answer questions when I don't have my hand up, and he *knows* I have no idea what the answer is. I've gone to him for help after class and told him point blank that I don't understand the day's assignment; he blows me off and tells me to read the book. He wants me to just read the math book, and somehow that's supposed to help." Aden shook her head in disgust.

"Sounds like he's just a lazy teacher." Cadence waved to someone passing by in the hallway. "Maybe you needed a tutor."

"Well, it's too late now. Guess I'll just have to see how I did on that final and move on."

Aden swung the locker door closed and spun the lock.

"Oh, hey, I almost forgot!" Cadence suddenly slid the book bag off her shoulder and began rummaging in it frantically. "I brought something for you."

"O-kay…" Aden raised an eyebrow and glanced around at the thinning crowd making their way through the hall.

"Here it is." Cadence grinned, holding a photo out in front of her. She waited and then cocked her head. "Well?"

Aden sighed loudly looking at the photograph Cadence held, "Okay, yes, it's Maddox that I stalked all weekend."

"He's really cute, though, right?" Cadence teased. Aden just stared her down, refusing to be baited.

"So do you know what he was doing in the woods by my house?"

"No, I haven't seen him since we got back from Charlotte." Cadence's smile had vanished. "Are you mad at me?"

"For what?" Aden asked, surprised.

"I dunno, you just looked…"

"Embarrassed," Aden admitted. "That's how I look. Stupid and foolish and childish—"

"Why in the world would you be embarrassed?"

"Because I was stalking your step-brother, imagining him to be a serial criminal?"

"Well, you didn't know who he was." Cadence appeased her. "And he *was* way out in the woods by your house."

"You're a really good friend, but that doesn't change the fact that I'm an idiot who jumps to all kinds of crazy conclusions." Aden started walking slowly down the hall with the dwindling stream of students, Cadence by her side. "When's he going back to Virginia?"

"Um, I dunno. Why?" Cadence smiled again. "Would you like to meet him?"

"No!" Aden nearly shouted. "Oh my God. I want to be sure I don't run into him ever again." Cadence stopped in the middle of the hall and looked perplexed. Sighing, Aden explained, "I'd be mortified! What if he recognized me from the woods—the crazy girl who ran away, terrified? Then the one who chased after him through half the town?"

"Um, you said he didn't see you when you followed him in town," Cadence pointed out. "He only saw you in the woods."

"Okay, so I'm only a *little* weird."

"You say that like it's some *new* information." Cadence smiled as she pushed open the door, freeing them from the school building for the day. "Why would you care what he thinks anyway?"

"Well, I mean, he's your family member. I can't have your family thinking I'm crazy."

"And so it has nothing to do with the fact that you think he's gorgeous?"

"What?! I don't—"

"Come on." Cadence smiled slyly.

"Why are you trying to push me on him, anyway?"

"Admit it. He's gorgeous."

"Okay, he's fairly good-looking, but I don't see what that has to do with anything."

"Who's good looking?" Cadence's sister Patience interrupted. She'd walked up unnoticed as the girls were walking toward the buses.

"Absolutely nobody," Aden insisted, annoyed. Patience was one of her least-favorite people: nosy, stuck-up, gossipy. She could never understand how the Kendall triplets could all be so different from one another. Where Cadence was blond, funny, generous, and fun to be around, Patience's hair was several shades darker, just like her personality. Their sister Grace was somewhere in between, both in looks and temperament. Though Aden liked Grace, definitely more than Patience, she was more serious than Cadence most of the time.

"Oh, come on," Patience cooed. "We all want to know who the infamous ice queen has thawed out for!" she laughed meanly toward her friends, a short distance away. "I mean, we all figured you're a lesbo; you've turned down every boy who's asked you out."

"Patience—" Cadence lashed out.

"I didn't realize you were so interested in my love life," Aden answered. "I'm sorry that you're so sad and pathetic that you have to butt into everyone else's business to make yourself feel better."

"Trust me, lesbo, I don't give a cat's fart about you." Patience's eyes flashed as she swept her dirty blond hair behind one shoulder. "I just thought somebody should warn the poor soul you've set your sights on. That's all." She smiled sweetly as she turned away.

"You should get back to your little minions now, Patience," Cadence growled out loud enough for the nearby group to hear, "Nobody else can put up with you."

Patience ignored her sister and walked away laughing. Her group of friends followed, shooting condescending looks, and a few hissed "lesbo" comments toward Aden as they left.

"Oh my God, how could I end up with such a bitch for a sister?"

"Seriously. You said she wasn't always like that, right?" Aden stopped beside one of the idling buses.

"No, she wasn't always evil, but I have no idea what made her turn to the dark side."

"Any ideas as to why she hates me so much?" Aden asked. "I seem to bring out the evil in her."

"I think it's because Darren Trimble asked you out, and Patience liked him."

"But I didn't go out with him," Aden pointed out. "And he and Patience went out for a few months right after that."

"But he asked you first."

"Whatever." Aden shook her head in exasperation. "I'll talk to you later."

"Yep." Cadence waved as Aden climbed aboard the bus for home.

Later that evening, as Aden poked around the kitchen looking for some inspiration about what to make for dinner, her phone rang.

"Hello?"

"Hey sweetie, how was your day?" her Mom asked.

"Good, I guess. How about yours?"

"Not bad. I feel like I haven't seen you in a week, though. Have you already eaten?"

"No, I was just looking for something to make."

"Well, do you feel like Italian?" She could hear the smile in her mother's voice.

"Um, sure? But we don't have any—"

"Drew is on his way to pick you up. I'll meet you both at Provino's at seven-thirty."

"Wow. You're getting off work early?"

"Yes, they'd changed the schedule, and I just thought we could use a nice dinner out."

"Sure, sounds great." Aden smiled. She couldn't remember the last time the three of them went out for dinner together.

"Okay, then I'll see you both there."

"Okay, bye." Aden hung up.

Wow. Dinner out with the family. She wasn't sure how to feel about that. It hadn't happened very often lately. She'd eaten with her Mom on occasion, on her rare free hours, and she'd eaten with Drew a bit more frequently after he got off work, but even less frequently, she'd eaten with one or the other at a restaurant. Most of the time, eating out was a luxury their small family couldn't afford. Well, it's not that they couldn't afford it; they weren't destitute or anything. But it was just much cheaper to eat at home, with the groceries their Mom brought home from her job.

Her mom was waiting in the tiny entryway of the restaurant when she and Drew got there; she rose quickly from the plush bench with a smile and a hug for each of them. Slim and shorter than either of her children, Janet Garrett had natural auburn highlights in her shoulder-length brunette hair and the hazel eyes she'd shared with Drew.

"This is such a cool idea, Mom." Aden hugged her back. "So what's the occasion?"

"No occasion. Just dinner out with my favorite kids," she answered, gesturing to the bored-looking girl at the hostess stand. Aden and Drew exchanged a glance as she turned away to follow the girl to their table. Clearly, something was up.

The restaurant was quiet, with only a couple of other diners seated in the large, dim room. They were led to a table by the large window that overlooked a tiny walled garden, beyond which ran a picturesque creek.

"I'm starving," Drew grimaced as he studied the menu. "I didn't get to finish my lunch today." Answering his Mom's raised eyebrows, he continued, "Mr. Payne left early again today, and then Billy Ray spent most of the afternoon next door flirting with that blond receptionist. Then, just as I'm eating lunch, this old farmer limps in asking for help because his truck's broken down. So by the time I got Billy Ray back to the shop, and then drove the guy back to his truck and got it running, lunch was cold and gross.

"Sorry about that," Mom said over her menu. "Maybe a big plate of lasagna will help."

"Maybe two plates," Drew muttered.

Aden shook her head as she closed her menu; she always ordered the Shrimp Fettuccini Alfredo, anyway. Then, she glanced around the dining room. A young family with a baby in a high chair was quietly wiping up a spill at the booth in the corner. Three women were laughing at another booth, and there were two people at the large, group-sized table at the back --- Aden gasped. It was Maddox, and he was with his Mom, she guessed.

They had papers and files spread across the large table between them, plates and glasses pushed to the side. As she stared, Maddox looked up and met her gaze. A warm, electric current rose through her body in a flash, coloring her neck and cheeks in one of the uncontrollable blushes she hated. Her eyes felt locked to his; she couldn't look away. He broke the connection, turning his eyes back to the paper he held. Aden's blush deepened as she grabbed the menu again to hide.

"Someone you know?" Her Mom smiled, and Drew looked up.

"No, don't look!" she hissed from behind the menu. They chuckled at each other. "And no, I don't know him. That's Cadence's step-brother, Maddox…and his Mom, I guess."

"Well, he's really good looking." Her Mom smiled, raising her own menu again.

"Yeah, what a hottie," Drew teased in a stage-whisper.

"Oh my God, grow up, both of you," she hissed back, dropping the menu. "I've never met him. I've only seen a picture that Cadence had at school one day."

"Hmmm, the step-brother," Drew teased, ominously.

"Seriously, how old are you?"

"Alright, Drew. Don't embarrass her," their Mom interrupted. "I wanted to have a nice dinner."

Aden stared at Drew, but he had already moved on, impatiently waving over the waitress, already on her way to their table.

As they ordered drinks, and Drew insisted that they were ready to order entrées as well, Aden peeked out of the corner of her eye towards Maddox. He was still head-down in the papers on the table; neither he nor his Mom were talking.

"So what's up, Mom?" Drew sat back in his chair, oblivious to the abrupt awkwardness of his question.

Janet looked surprised. "What do you mean?"

"I mean what's up? What's going on? What's happening with you?"

"Um." She raised her eyebrows again. "Not much. I've been working a lot, and I haven't been able to spend a lot of time with you guys, and since I was off work earlier than usual today, I thought we could have a nice dinner and catch up."

"That's nice." Aden smiled. Most of her attention was still directed surreptitiously toward Maddox.

"So what about you, Aden? What's new?" her Mom prompted.

"New? Not a thing." She arranged her silverware meticulously as she spoke. "We're in the middle of finals at school."

"And how are those going?"

"Okay, I guess. Everything's fine except for math, but I think I'll pass." She shrugged.

"You think you'll pass?" her mother asked, surprised. "Is it that bad? Can I help you study? We can get you a tutor—"

"Mom, it's the end of the year. I already took that final," she sighed.

"Well, why didn't you tell me sooner that you were having trouble?"

"I'll probably end up with a high C or *maybe* a low B if Mr. O'Connor's feeling generous. It's not a big deal."

"Your grades are a big deal. You need to be working toward some scholarships." Her mother reminded her. Drew shifted in his seat, uneasy over this subject.

"Okay, so enough about me." Aden's attention was pulled away again as conversation opened at Maddox's table. She didn't look directly over and couldn't make out any of the words as they spoke quietly across their table.

"If you're having trouble at school—or work," she directed toward her son, "You know you can talk to me about it, right? Ask for help." She looked at both of them. "I'm sorry I've been working so much lately. I know it puts a toll on both of you. I haven't been there, but that's going to change."

Aden and Drew both looked up at this unexpected news.

"I've been keeping an eye out for a better job ever since I had to take the job at the store," she began. "You remember the education conference I went to a few months back, with the principal?" She didn't wait for an answer. "They were exploring new initiatives around keeping the arts in schools. With all the budget cuts, art programs are usually the first things to go. Athletic programs are seen as more necessary –" she stopped herself. "Sorry, I won't get up on that soapbox again." She took a deep breath. "Anyway, they're creating a new position at the district level to oversee the rollout of some new programs across several schools, and I've been offered the position."

"Wow, Mom that's great!" Aden enthused.

"Yeah it is! Congratulations!" Drew got up to hug his Mom. "Is it full time?"

"Yes, full-time, Monday through Friday," she hesitated. "The job is located in Spartanburg, so it's a bit further away."

"That's not so bad, though. " Drew sat back down.

"Well, at least I'll be home nights, now." She smiled.

"When do you start?" Aden asked.

"Mid-June. I'm working out a couple of weeks' notice at the school and the store. I just told Mr. Case the news before I left the store tonight."

"How'd he take it?" Drew wanted to know.

"Okay. He's not thrilled that he'll have to interview for a replacement, but he's known all along that I was looking for another job. He's been very supportive," she added, "He's a widower, so he's always looked out for me, giving me all the extra hours he could." They just nodded. "Fortunately, the new job will pay a bit more than my two current jobs do. Not a lot more, but it'll be enough to take care of some bills—and I'll be able to be home more often."

"That's great news, Mom." Drew smiled. "Maybe I should take your example and start looking again for a new job, myself."

"You know," she immediately warmed to the subject, "I saw that they're offering summer classes now over at the college."

"I know. I've looked into it." Drew's mood soured a bit.

"Well, maybe you could do the community college thing for a year or two, get the core 101 classes behind you and then transfer to another school with a good legal program—"

"I know, Mom. We've talked that into the ground. I just don't think I have enough saved yet."

Aden's attention shifted back to Maddox's table, though she refused to actually look in that direction. Mom and Drew's conversation faded slowly into the background of her focus as she strained to hear anything being said at the big table in the back of the room. *Eavesdropping*, she chastised herself. *What the heck was she doing?*

Then, she realized she really just wanted to hear his voice. Would it be deep, like his eyes? Smooth or rough? *Oh God. She was fantasizing about his voice. Crap.* She rolled her eyes, firmly telling herself to cut it out. *Talk about embarrassing…she was becoming a stalker. Crap, crap.*

"—why you're rolling your eyes like that, Aden. You should be making some decisions about your future, too." Her mother's voice intruded into her thoughts.

"I know, Mom." She snapped her attention back to her own table…mostly.

The waitress came with their drinks and dinners, and it was enough to break the tense atmosphere. Backing into their neutral corners, they discussed the latest zombie TV show.

Aden very intentionally ignored everything outside their own table. At least, she tried to. Her attention was immediately stripped away when Maddox suddenly stood, but he just made his way slowly down the short hallway to the restrooms while his Mom stayed rooted to her spot, engrossed in her files and papers. Aden studied him, indirectly. *He's tall*, she thought to herself. Taller than she'd remembered. And the view he presented as he walked with his back to her—Aden shook her head minutely and turned her attention back to the fettuccini in front of her.

After dinner, Drew ordered a large dessert for each of them.

"So, that's Cadence's step-brother over there?" their Mom asked.

"Yeah, I guess his Mom and Mayor Dixon were married. She's with the FBI, and Mayor Dixon asked for her help with the kidnapping cases," Aden spoke barely above a whisper.

"FBI. Cool." Drew nodded. "Maybe I could join the FBI instead of trying to become a lawyer…I could probably talk to Ms. Dixon over there." He grinned at Aden, who glared at him silently.

"I heard they're thinking the cases are related, now." Their Mom frowned. "So much for the security of small towns and everybody knowing everybody."

"I still can't believe the last one happened so close to our house." Aden shivered.

"I know," their Mom nodded. "I want to remind you both again to be careful. Keep an eye on your surroundings; don't go off on your own—"

"Don't take candy from strangers." Drew grinned again.

"I'm serious, Drew. I worry about you two. I can't help it, it's a Mom thing." She kicked him lightly under the table. "The women who are missing right now didn't think they were in any danger, either, until they were. I'm just saying, I want you to use your head, and don't do anything stupid until they catch this guy."

"And *then* we can go back to being stupid," Drew whispered.

Though Maddox and his mom were at the restaurant before Aden and her family had gotten there, they lingered at their table as Aden's mom paid the bill—after fighting with Drew over who would pay. Drew left the tip on the table as a compromise and stood, ready to leave.

Aden glanced at Maddox directly for the first time since she'd first entered. He was speaking quietly into his phone, leaning away from his Mom with his hand to his forehead, covering his eyes. Like he was talking to a girlfriend. Aden sighed, annoyed at the stab of disappointment that thought brought with it. *Stalker*, she chided herself, and followed her family outside.

It's the sounds. Always the sounds that come first. Crickets. And dripping water, growing louder, more present. The darkness begins to recede back to the edges. The girl. There she is. She's gagged. A dirty orange and purple cloth is tied tightly across her mouth, pinning her disheveled blond ponytail against her sweating neck. Her breathing is ragged through her nose, through her sobs. Her hands are behind her back, handcuffed around a metal pole sunk into the concrete floor. There's a moan – it's somebody else, not the blond. Then a sensation of blackness trickles in. He's coming. His tread is slow and heavy, deliberate. The girl's eyes go wide, staring as she tries again to stand. Uselessly. The slow footsteps stop close by, and the girl's sobs become a muffled scream. He can smell the urine on the floor beneath her, and he's euphoric. He's taken them. All his. He'd thought about this for so long. Dreamed and planned. Watched and waited. His time has finally come. And he's just getting started.

At lunch the next day, Cadence found Aden in a shady spot by the gym eating a granola bar.

"Thought you'd be out here." She smiled as she dropped her heavy bag on the thin grass. "I saw Patience holding court in the cafeteria."

"Hail to the queen." Aden saluted. "Where were you this morning? I waited by your locker."

"Oh, slept in a little bit. Talked my Mom into it since I'd already taken that final. What am I gonna miss?"

"Nice." Aden nodded. "So we had family night last night. My mom took us out to dinner, announced that she has a new full-time job in Spartanburg."

"Wow, that's awesome!"

"Right? She was really happy. Already gave notice at the store." Aden bit her lip, hesitating. "So we went to Provino's, and Maddox and his Mom were there."

"Really? Did you go say hey to them?"

"Be serious," Aden sighed.

"I am serious, and why am I just now hearing about this?"

"Well, after dinner we went home and watched some TV together. Then, I studied and went to bed. It wasn't any big news, anyway." Cadence cocked her head to the side. "What? We were there. He was there. We all ate dinner."

"Okay, then. Are you working tonight?" Cadence shrugged. Aden was surprised by the sudden change of subject.

"No, I'm off 'til Friday, why?"

"Grace and I are going to the lake this afternoon with some friends. Wanna join?"

"Love to." Aden smiled. "I've been rattling around my house a little too much lately, but I'll need to get home early to study. Can you pick me up?"

"Of course. Wasn't gonna make 'ya walk."

"Thanks. Sounds like fun."

They sat back in the grass, enjoying the very slight breeze for the rest of the lunch hour, and then met up again at Aden's locker—as they did most days—after school was out.

"Okay, I'll pick you up at 3:30," Cadence announced her predicted arrival time. "Did you already check with your Mom?"

"Yeah, I texted her. I'll be ready at 3:30, assuming that old bus makes it up the hill again." She smiled at the familiar bad joke, and they chatted all the way out to the parking lot where Cadence turned one direction toward the battered old Monte Carlo she shared with her sisters, and Aden turned the other direction toward the noisily idling buses.

At 3:27, the doorbell rang, and Aden ran to open it, turning immediately back toward her room and yelling over her shoulder, "Hey, come on in. I've just gotta find my other shoe."

"Okay, come on in for a sec." Cadence said to someone else. Aden wondered which of their friends were joining Cadence and Grace on the outing as she ran to dig for the mate to a light blue flip flop. She could hear Cadence inviting someone over to the big windows to see the falls on the river below, just as she located the shoe.

Grabbing her trusty backpack, stuffed with towel, sunscreen, and water bottle, she shoved her sunglasses onto the top of her head as she walked out of her room. And there he was. Maddox was standing in her living room.

"Um, sorry. I couldn't find my shoe," she stuttered lamely.

"Aden, this is Maddox, my step-brother visiting from Virginia." Cadence grinned from behind him. "Maddox, this is my best friend, Aden." Maddox had turned from the window to face her and stopped abruptly. "We invited Maddox to join us because he doesn't know anybody in town, and we thought he was probably going out of his mind spending all his time with his Mom."

48

"Hi." He smiled. "I saw you at the restaurant last night." His voice was perfect. His green eyes seemed to twinkle, *And running stupidly through the woods by the river.* Or maybe that was just in Aden's head.

"It's so nice to meet you." Aden smiled back. "Cadence has told me about you."

"Good things, I hope." He smiled lazily at Cadence. "We never really get to spend any time together when I'm here, it seems." *Holy crap.* His smile hit her like a physical force.

"All good things," she forced out, a half-beat too late.

"Well, let's get going," Cadence chirped happily. "We're meeting Grace and them at the lake. Couldn't all fit in one car," she drawled, winking behind Maddox's back.

"Who all's coming?" Aden asked, biting back her annoyance with Cadence.

"Kelly, Rob, and Greg are riding with Grace, and Tina and Bunkie and Trey are supposed to come later."

"Bunkie?" Maddox asked.

"Yeah, his name's Bob, but everybody calls him Bunkie." Cadence shrugged as she walked out the door.

Aden locked the door behind her and turned to see a dark blue Audi Sedan parked in her driveway.

"It's Maddox's ride," Cadence said before she could ask. Maddox slid silently behind the wheel and waited for the girls to get in.

"It's Maddox's Mom's ride," He corrected dryly, as Cadence opened the back door to get in. As Aden started to follow her, he cleared his throat, frowning slightly. "I'm not a chauffeur; one of you has to sit up front."

Cadence clicked her seatbelt and grinned at Aden. Aden glared back and prayed that Maddox wasn't watching them in the rear view mirror. She climbed into the front seat, vowing revenge one day soon. She couldn't believe Cadence would be so obvious, so embarrassing. She'd never forgive her for this dirty little trick. Glancing to her left, Maddox's arm rippled as he buckled up. Okay, she would thank Cadence for this. Maybe.

"Where am I going?" Maddox asked as they reached the highway at the end of Aden's meandering drive.

"Left," Cadence answered, "Back toward town." Maddox pulled out without comment.

He was a good driver, if a little on the speedy side, and he drove with a purpose as though he was ready for the trip to be over. As Aden racked her brain for a non-lame subject of conversation, the silence stretched out uncomfortably.

"We haven't seen too much of you at the house this trip, Maddox," Cadence finally prompted from the back seat. "What'cha been up to?"

"Not much," he answered, glancing at her in the rear view mirror then focusing back on the winding road.

"Sooo…you gonna expand on that or just leave us guessing?" Cadence pushed. He glanced at the mirror again and sighed.

"There's just not that much to do around here." He focused on the road once more.

"Well, it's good that you're going to the lake with us then." Cadence smiled. "And maybe we can do some hiking while you're here. Remember how we used to go trekking off into the woods when you'd come here for summers?" Aden swore she saw Maddox shoot a tiny glance her way before he answered.

"I remember trying to get away from my three whiny sisters and how they'd follow me everywhere I went—even when I tried to lose them in the woods," he said without expression.

"Oh, and the time Grace *did* get lost—we'd been chasing you, and she tripped and fell, but we didn't know it and kept going. You called Daddy Max on that walkie-talkie he gave you that year," Cadence reminisced, laughing. Maddox didn't answer. "…and he came and found her, and then we all got into trouble."

"You three were always trouble," Maddox said.

"Did you come here every summer?" Aden ventured.

"Not every summer," he answered, and she thought he'd go silent again, but he continued, "I was here most summers for a few weeks, and a lot of my holidays were spent here."

"So you know the town pretty well then," she stated. He turned his head and looked at her before answering.

"I guess so." He made another turn, un-prompted by Cadence. "Have you lived here long?"

"I've lived here about six years," Aden answered.

"I don't remember meeting you before this summer," Maddox stated without looking away from the road.

"No, we hadn't met before," Aden answered, and as the road twisted out before them, she added, "Guess I just don't get out much."

Maddox didn't answer and made another un-prompted turn toward the state park.

"Oh, don't go in the park entrance," Cadence piped up. "Keep going past it."

"We're not going to the beach?" Aden asked, twisting around. The beach was the narrow strip of sand that had been trucked in and dumped on top of the red clay shore at the designated swimming area of Devil's Fork State Park.

"Nah, we're meetin' everybody at the old chimney," Cadence answered. The old stone chimney was all that was left of a cabin that had crumbled away at least a century before. It stood in a clearing beside the lake dotted with picnic tables.

"Wish you'd told me sooner. The trail from the pull-off on the road there is pretty overgrown this time of year. I would've worn different shoes." Cadence just glanced quickly at Maddox and winked at Aden, grinning from ear to ear. "Cadence—" Aden began, then bit back her annoyance with a long sigh and turned back to the front.

"Always trouble," Maddox mumbled quietly. Aden couldn't stop a small smile but turned to look out the side window to hide it.

The already curvy road became increasingly more serpentine as they drove around the lake. Around one of the sharp bends was a pull-off where a couple of cars were parked, surrounded on all sides by the dark green of forest.

"Here we are," Cadence announced, and Maddox pulled over and parked the car.

"It's so overgrown you can't even see the lake from here," Aden said, unbuckling her seatbelt.

"No worries. I'll blaze the trail and go find Grace." Cadence announced, springing from the car and jogging into the trees with a big smile for Aden as she left. Aden watched her go in disbelief.

"I feel like I should maybe apologize," Aden said, sighing.

"I was just thinking the same thing." He half-smiled back at her, "Think she'd miss us if we left now?"

Aden felt the electric warmth creeping up her neck at the thought of leaving with him, just the two of them.

"Well, I don't know about you, but I'd never hear the end of it." Aden chuckled.

"Guess we're committed then," he agreed, still slightly smiling. The heat zinged again as he said "committed." *Crap. Down, Stalker!* She thought lamely and opened the car door to get out.

Inwardly sighing at her impractical flip-flops, she grabbed her backpack and began picking her way carefully along the dubious path. Maddox followed silently, a towel draped over his shoulder. Aden could hear laughter through the trees, but couldn't see anything but underbrush and tree trunks.

"You can go on ahead; I'll be there in a minute," Aden offered over her shoulder after stumbling as a fallen branch, hidden under layers of pine needles, poked the side of her foot painfully.

"I could carry you," he offered. Aden almost stumbled again at the thought. She chuckled to hide it.

"I'm fine, just a little slow, and it's right through there." She pointed ahead.

"I'm not in any big rush." He gestured for her to continue. She smiled and picked her way in silence.

When they broke through the confining trees into the clearing, the gray-weathered, stacked stone chimney loomed in their path. Rounding it, they found that most of the group was already in the murky water splashing around. Cadence sat at one of the picnic tables where a girl in a bikini was laid out on its surface, tanning in the sun. Aden felt a stab of insecurity looking at her that she wouldn't have felt if Maddox weren't here. She took the sunglasses from the top of her head and put them on, then walked to an empty table nearby and climbed up to sit on its top, her feet resting on the bench. Cadence waved but didn't join her. Maddox just stood, surveying the lake.

"Have you been here before?" Aden asked.

"Yeah, but it's been a while," he answered without looking at her. The lake was wide here, deep and green, reflecting the surrounding forest. The beach and the more crowded park areas were hidden around a large, rocky bend. Just past the lake's opposite, wooded shore, the green-covered mountains rose up quickly into the heat-shimmered blue of sky. A fishing boat was anchored in a small inlet on the farther shore, and a pontoon boat slowly rocked its way past, out in the lake's middle. "Your house is over that way, isn't it?" he asked, pointing across the lake at the quickly mounting forest.

"Yeah," she answered. "Actually, there's a trailhead just over there that leads around and follows the river right up by my house." She watched his face closely as she spoke. He was still looking at the lake, though, so she could only see his profile, but she thought she caught a small reaction there at the end of her statement. He seemed to be thinking, then turned to her.

"Does it go near the main park areas over there?" he asked, nodding toward the beach and other areas they'd passed on their drive here.

"Yeah, it sort of curves around away from the lake and crosses the road just above the main entrance." She gestured with her hands as she spoke, and he watched them with a small frown. "We passed it. The trail crossing with the big fence posts on either side of the road."

"Yeah, I've been up that one," he said, still looking away over the lake.

"Like this past weekend?" She held her breath and waited. As he turned to look at her, he looked distracted for a split second, then understanding dawned, and he almost smiled.

"Yes, when I saw you across the river," he said quietly. "I will apologize this time. I didn't mean to scare you."

The heat swept over her, and Aden lowered her head, knowing she must be five shades of red at this point.

"I'm so embarrassed," she admitted with a small laugh, looking away from him.

"Why?" He sounded sincerely puzzled as he sat on the bench beside her feet.

"For running away like I did. I felt like an idiot." At least, she felt like one now. "I thought I was all alone out there, miles from anybody. I'd just heard about the disappearance here and was thinking how that was so close to my house…and then I saw you." She looked at him for the first time. "And I kinda freaked out." She shrugged.

"Again, I'm really sorry I scared you," he said seriously. "I didn't expect you to be there, either." She waited for more, but he was staring off into the distance again.

"Well," she hesitated a moment, still intimidated by Kelly's small bikini (and great body) displayed on the nearby table, "shall we hit the water?"

"Sure. You go ahead; I'll be there in a minute." He stood and looked back toward the chimney, dropping his towel on the table.

"Okay." Aden smiled. As he walked back toward the tree line, she quickly stripped off her t-shirt and shorts. The two-piece bathing suit she wore underneath was dark blue, and though not as revealing as the racy white one that Kelly wore, she felt she could hold her own. Her figure had filled out in all the right places over the past year, leaving her thin frame curvier than it had been. Plus, there was no way Kelly could get near the water in that white suit – not only would it probably become see-through despite whatever lining it contained, but the perpetually muddy water would turn it a permanent pink-brown. Cadence and Kelly both waved as she continued to look their way. "Goin' swimming?" she asked loudly.

Kelly just waved, but Cadence stood and walked over.

"Hey, where's Maddox?"

"Dunno. Back to the car maybe?" Aden was still annoyed with her. "Listen, no more of your moronic match-making, got it? It's unbelievably embarrassing, and I can't believe –" Cadence started laughing, interrupting Aden's angry diatribe. "Really? You think this is funny?"

"I think you two are adorable together."

"And I think you've lost your mind. You're supposed to be on my side."

"I *am* on your side, silly."

"Seriously? He thinks I'm a complete and total freak; I'm mortified to be around him, and you're doing everything in your power to make it worse."

"You don't look mortified," Cadence giggled. "Actually, you're looking pretty hot."

"Angry, you mean."

"And he doesn't think you're a freak."

"Like you'd know that." Aden turned in a huff toward the lake. "I mean it. Cut it out. You're done."

CHAPTER 4
on the lake

Cadence's laughter followed Aden to the water, but Cadence walked away to sit with Grace and a couple of the guys at another table right at the water's edge. After saying hello to Grace and her apparent admirers, Aden kicked off her flip flops and stepped down into the water. It was surprisingly cool. She walked as quickly as she could across the slimy mud bottom until she got deep enough to pick up her feet and swim. She swam out to where several heads were already bobbing in the water.

"Hey, Aden." Trey grinned as she neared. His longer, sandy hair was darkened and slicked back from his handsome, tanned face.

"Hey, guys," she answered. Though she knew this group, she wasn't particular friends with any of them. They all greeted her friendly enough, welcoming her to the group.

"So that was Grace's brother you were talking to, right?" Tina asked, her arm around Bunkie's shoulder as he held her up in the water. They were both more tanned, toned and muscled than Aden would ever be.

"Maddox, yeah," Aden smiled.

"He's hot." Tina nodded her dark head.

"Hey!" Bunkie frowned, playfully splashing her.

"Chill out, Bunk, you're not the *only* hot guy on the planet." She splashed him back, laughing.

"Oh, now you're gonna get it," he teased, throwing off her arm and dunking her under the water. She came up spluttering and calling for war. Trey laughed and feinted toward Aden to pull her into the fray, but she held up both hands in surrender.

"Hey, I'm totally neutral here. Just a bystander, thanks."

Trey laughed as Bunkie pulled him under from behind, and Aden took the opportunity to escape. She swam out deeper, keeping her face out of the water, since she was still wearing her sunglasses, then turned and paddled lazily along the shore, away from the still-frothing group.

The water was warm at the surface but quickly cooled in the muddy depths, and currents of even colder water would slice through the warmth on occasion. Aden didn't particularly like swimming in the lake, or anywhere that she couldn't see what was underneath her. Today, with the horseplay behind her and the wake of the passing boat churning up the muddy bottom, she couldn't see more than a few inches down. It made her uneasy to think of the fish that could be swimming around her, and she couldn't be on this lake without thinking of the Indian burial grounds and the remains of buildings from a small town swallowed by the rising waters when the electric company built the dam to create the lake. It always creeped her out, and she shivered before striking out with much more energy toward a large, half-submerged rock down the shore. It appeared to be a boulder shorn from the larger hill behind it. It looked like a good spot to sit and dry off, away from the group for a bit.

As she neared the rock, a large figure appeared above it on the rocky hill and abruptly jumped into the water in her path. She spluttered in surprise and backed away instinctively. Maddox came up smiling right beside her, hair slicked back, looking like a mischievous water god fallen from above.

"Did I scare you again?"

"Were you trying to?" she asked, blowing water from the lenses of her sunglasses.

"No, not really." He kicked toward the half-submerged rock that had been her destination, and she followed. It was just big enough for the two of them to climb part of the way out of the water and sit side-by-side.

"You shouldn't go so far away on your own," he mused. "You're supposed to swim in groups."

"I'm not that far away," she said, but looking back the way she'd come, she couldn't see anyone. She could still hear them, but they sounded further than she'd have thought. Maybe the water and the rocks were playing tricks with the sound.

"It's a good thing Trey saw which way you'd gone," Maddox said, following her gaze. "When I got back, you'd disappeared."

"I was just trying to get away from all the ruckus for a minute," she said, trying not to look at his glistening abdomen so close beside her. He nodded.

"We should probably head back over there soon, or they'll think I got lost, too."

Aden sighed, "It's so nice here. Quiet." She smiled. "And this rock is so warm."

Maddox smiled, too, and actually laid back on the gray veined granite, arms above his head, and closed his eyes. Aden could feel her own eyes opening into round circles, and she swallowed louder than she'd meant to as she gazed at him. She wished she had her camera. He looked so much better than any male model she'd ever seen on the stupid clothing store commercials, and she wanted to freeze the image, and this moment, forever. The sight of him froze her heart, her mind, and her entire body ached to touch him. *Oh God.* She closed her eyes and inhaled deeply. *Get a grip on yourself.* Exhale. *That's it.* She turned her face up to the warmth of the sun and tried to breathe through the fantasies invading her mind. She felt her sunglasses start to slide backward and opened her eyes as she reached for them.

She caught her sunglasses in the same second she realized that Maddox's eyes were open. He was watching her. The green of his eyes was as deep as the shadowed recesses of the forest around them, with glints of the golden sun reflecting back. She could fall into those eyes and—a laughing scream, closer than before, broke the moment. Aden blinked rapidly, and Maddox sat up.

"Do you always swim with your sunglasses on?" he asked, expressionless.

"Only on sunny days," she answered. She wasn't sure where that had come from, but she was still having a hard time thinking. The planes of his dripping chest, his thighs. *Stop it. Seriously. Control yourself.*

"Well, we should get back." He looked toward the sound of another loud shriek.

"Yeah, I can tell they're totally missing us." Aden nodded, sarcastically. She didn't want to move. Taking a deep breath, she slid into the water and began paddling back the way she'd come. Maddox swam beside her silently. She watched him, without looking directly, as his arms sliced through the water effortlessly. She could tell she'd never beat him in a race.

Rounding the outcrop of the rocky shore, they saw that most of the others had left the water and were setting out a picnic on one of the tables. Only Tina and Bunkie were in the water, and they were standing in the shallows, talking quietly.

"Crap. I didn't think to bring anything to eat." Aden frowned. "I thought we'd be over at the beach, and I'd planned on grabbing a hot dog at the stand or something at the store."

"Cadence and Grace packed a ton of sandwiches and chips," Maddox said, "I'm sure they'll share."

"There they are!" Grace said loudly, elbowing Cadence beside her. "We wondered where you two had gotten to," she shouted suggestively.

"Oh God," Aden winced. "Not her, too. This is brutal."

"Sorry," Maddox sighed. "I'll take care of it."

Aden wondered what that meant as they climbed out of the water and retrieved their towels. She quickly dried off and pulled her T-shirt on over her head before following Maddox, still shirtless, thank the gods, to join the rest of the group.

"Cadence, Grace," Maddox said quietly, "Can I speak with you in private for a moment?" and he turned, giving Aden an apologetic look, as he walked back to the table where Aden's backpack rested. The two girls, grinning, followed with a wink in Aden's direction.

"Hey, Aden," Kelly called, "Help yourself. Grace and Cadence brought enough for an army."

And it was true. There was a large, soft-sided cooler stuffed with sandwiches, a large tote stuffed with individual bags of chips, and a rolling cooler full of bottled water and sodas.

Aden grabbed a sandwich and a bottled water and went to sit at the third table by the water. Trey was already there, and Bunkie had joined him as Tina went to grab some food.

"Anything good up there?" Bunkie asked, eyeing the sandwich in her hands.

"Dunno yet. Tons of it, though." Aden smiled and sat down. She had been anxiously watching Maddox, trying to catch any hint of the conversation going on over there, but Maddox faced away from her, and his sisters both stood casually, smiling and nodding. Aden realized that Trey had been talking to her. She turned toward him.

"Sorry, what?"

"I asked how long Maddox would be in town," Trey repeated.

"Oh, um, I really don't know," Aden shrugged.

"So what kind of sandwich is that?" Bunkie asked, pointing at the one lying in front of Aden still unwrapped.

"Jeez, Bunk, Tina will be back in just a second." Trey rolled his eyes at his friend, "Or you could go get your own, you know."

"Looks like ham and cheese." Aden half-smiled at their banter, but most of her attention was elsewhere.

"Do you have big plans for the summer?" Trey asked.

"Haven't even thought about it yet," Aden admitted, wrenching her attention around to the guy at her side. "You?"

"Not a lot, I guess. My parents are taking us all to Arizona for a couple of weeks. My aunt and uncle live out there, and I guess I have a new, little cousin." He shrugged.

"Do you have brothers and sisters?" She couldn't remember if she'd ever asked him before. She didn't hang out with Trey and his group often, but she needed to get her mind off of Maddox before she embarrassed herself any more.

"Yeah, I've got one of each." He grinned at her interest. "My brother graduated already. I think he knows your brother, Drew." That he knew her brother, and his name, surprised her. "And my sister is a year younger than me," he continued, warming to his subject. "I haven't been to Arizona since I was little. My aunt and uncle usually come here on vacation because my grandparents live here, too. But I guess since they have a new baby, it's our turn to go see them." He stopped as Tina sat down opposite him. She gave him a look before distributing the food she'd brought to Bunkie. "Sorry, I didn't mean to get into a big story."

"Well, I asked." Aden smiled, mystified by the glance she'd caught.

"I haven't seen you in a while, Aden," Tina said, unwrapping a sandwich. "How are you doing?"

"Just studying for finals, working, you know, same old, same old." Aden smiled back.

"How long have you known Maddox?" she asked before taking a large bite.

"Just met him today, right before we got here, actually," Aden answered. Tina almost choked.

"You're kidding. Seriously?" she mumbled around the food in her mouth, behind a polite hand. Both Bunkie and Trey were staring at her, too. She shifted uncomfortably on the seat.

"I'm serious." She laughed half-heartedly, "I met him at my house when they picked me up to come out here."

"Oh," Tina said finally. "I just assumed you guys went way back, I guess. You know, 'cuz you and Cadence have been tight since…forever."

"Wow, I thought you two were together," Bunkie said, mouth unashamedly full, glancing at Trey.

"Nope." She forced an uncomfortable laugh. "So how long have you and Tina been going out now?"

"Almost five months," Tina answered for him when he hesitated. "We started going out the week after Christmas."

"Yeah, but Bunk liked her a lot longer than that. He waited 'til after Christmas so he wouldn't have to buy a present," Trey laughed. Bunkie just looked at his friend, amused. "Said he wouldn't have known what to buy anyway." Tina just rolled her eyes and sighed good-naturedly.

"See what I have to put up with?" She shook her head. Aden grinned.

Everyone looked up as Cadence joined them, sitting on Aden's other side.

"Hope these sandwiches are edible," she said, taking a dubious bite. "We're out of mustard."

"They're good. Thanks for makin' 'em." Trey saluted her with a sandwich.

"Yeah, we owe you," Tina said seriously. "I didn't realize you were bringin' enough for the whole crew."

"Forget it. Not a big deal." Cadence shrugged. "Besides, we invited you. We're the hostesses," she finished with a flourish.

"We could've helped though, if you'd have let us know." Aden elbowed her playfully.

"Oh, just eat," Cadence directed. "I thought we could take a little ramble up the path after we eat, you know, let the food digest a bit before we jump back in the lake."

"Okay." Bunkie shrugged, looking to Tina for confirmation. Aden glanced at her flip flops with chagrin but didn't comment.

As conversation picked up around her, Aden glanced around to see that Maddox sat at the farthest table with Grace and Greg, Kelly, and Rob. As she watched surreptitiously, Rob tried unsuccessfully to get Kelly's attention while she spoke animatedly with Maddox.

After they'd re-packed all the food in the coolers and stowed them back in the car, the group came together in preparation to walk up the path. Aden had intended to beg off, citing unfortunate footwear, but she saw that Kelly also wore flip flops and was already clinging to Maddox's arm for support. Cadence noted the flirtation also, with a tiny, sad nod at Aden. Suddenly, she wouldn't have been left behind for anything.

"Do we have a destination in mind?" Rob asked, eyeing Kelly and Maddox.

"Where does this lead, anyway?" Tina asked. "I don't remember. It's not steep, is it?"

"Nah, it winds around, over to the river, before it heads up the mountain over there," Rob answered her.

"How far up the mountain does it go?" Kelly asked, still clinging to Maddox. Rob just shrugged and turned away, but Maddox glanced at Aden with an inscrutable expression before looking quickly away. At least he looked uncomfortable and seemed to avoid meeting Kelly's gaze, even if he wasn't shaking off her possessive grip.

"I just hope it's not steep or anything," Tina said. "I'm not dressed for that."

"Jump on," Bunkie said, turning his back to her and holding out his arms. "I'll take care of you." Tina giggled as she jumped onto his back, and he manfully led the way into the trees. Grace and Greg followed, Trey held out both his elbows to escort Aden and Cadence on either side. Shrugging, they each took an arm and started up the path. Maddox followed, frowning, with Kelly at his side, and Rob brought up the rear with an even deeper scowl than Maddox.

"Where's Patience and the posse today?" Trey asked Cadence as they walked.

"Not sure. She swiped a couple of sandwiches when Grace and I were gettin' 'em ready and left. I didn't see who picked her up."

"I saw her and Lauren at the movies the other night. They were talking to some older guy, like mid-twenties lookin'. They all walked in together." Trey shrugged.

"I know, she's always after older guys." Cadence rolled her eyes. "Mom would kill her if she knew."

"She needs to be careful," Trey said, concerned, "That guy just looked like he was up to no good."

"Grace and I could tell her that all day long, but she won't listen to us. Never has." Cadence shook her head. They walked on in silence for a bit before Trey spoke again.

61

"So have either of you seen that new comedy with Will Ferrell that just came out?"

"No, is that what you saw the other night?" Cadence asked.

"Oh, no. I went to see Tae Kwon Death with Bunkie and Keith Anderson," he answered.

"Was it any good?" she asked.

"Yeah, it was pretty good." He nodded and walked on a bit. "You guys wanna go check out that Will Ferrell movie sometime?"

Cadence leaned forward to look at Aden and stumbled slightly. Trey's arm held her up as they stopped walking. Kelly, with Maddox in tow, passed them by with a contented smile. Maddox looked from Cadence to Trey, and then to Aden as he passed, turning his head as he went, seemingly to study her face. She wished she could read his.

"Um, sorry. Thanks for catching me." Cadence smiled and looked to Aden again, eyebrows raised slightly in question. Rob passed them then, still looking surly. "I think that movie looks like it'll be pretty good." Her gaze still questioned Aden.

"Sure." Aden nodded, trying to look anywhere but at Maddox's retreating form. "That sounds like fun."

"Cool." Trey grinned at her. "How 'bout Saturday night?" Cadence's brows shot up even higher as she grinned at her friend.

"Um, I get off work at 9:00. If there's a later showing that would still get us home by 11:00 or 11:30, that should work," Aden answered. She'd been hoping to see Maddox this weekend, somehow, but that was looking less and less likely, anyway. "How 'bout you Cadence?"

"Yep, I think I can do that." Cadence nodded thoughtfully. "Can you drive though?" she asked Trey. "I don't think I'll be able to get the car on Saturday."

"Of course." He grinned. "I can go pick up Aden and then swing by your house on our way to the theater." He offered his arms again, and they followed after the group. "It must suck to have to share a car with your sisters." They chattered on as Aden was lost in thought and the glimpses of Maddox ahead of them through the trees.

When they reached the river's noisy confluence into the lake, they rested on the rocks strewn about in the shade of the massive trees before heading back to the chimney. Trey stuck close to Cadence and Aden as both the girls watched Maddox trying to politely extricate himself from Kelly's grasp. Kelly, however, hung on obliviously, and Rob hung back and glowered.

"I think Rob's gonna explode," Trey said quietly on the trek back. Cadence and Aden walked with him again, but without arms linked this time. "Somebody should warn Maddox."

"Maddox can take care of himself." Cadence smiled. "But Kelly should watch out."

The threesome in question led the group back down the trail and was mostly out of sight, as Maddox set a much faster pace. He'd stood and practically jogged into the trees as soon as it was suggested that they start back. Kelly had jumped up after him, but was slower in her flip flops and was instead accompanied by a murderous-looking Rob.

"She's asking for it. She and Rob have gone out a couple of times. I don't think it's exclusive, at least to Kelly, but she doesn't have to make him miserable," Cadence continued. "She's ruining everybody's day." Aden couldn't argue with that.

When they finally cleared the trees back at the chimney, Kelly was at one table gathering her things and Rob sat at another, facing away from her toward the lake, with his arms tensely crossed. Aden looked around for Maddox and saw him floating on his back far out on the lake.

As she didn't want to sit with either Kelly or Rob, she took a seat at the table by the water and looked out over the lake. And Maddox. Trey joined her without speaking, and Tina and Bunkie soon came over.

"Wanna go back in?" Bunkie asked Tina, nodding toward the water.

"No, I'm dry now. I don't wanna get all wet again," she said.

"But it's hot out here," Bunkie complained. "You'll dry off quick."

"It's getting late. We should be going soon, and I don't want to get the car all wet."

"It's my car." Bunkie fake-pouted, "I don't care if it gets wet."

"Nobody said you couldn't get back in the water." She shook her head. "It'll just be getting dark soon, and I need to get home and study."

"So, no swimming," Bunkie pouted.

"Good Lord, you're a mess." She smiled. "I must love you." She got up and ran full speed into the lake, followed by a laughing Bunkie.

"Those two are somethin' else." Trey smiled at Aden, who just shook her head and gave him a small smile back. "You goin' in?"

"I might in a little bit," she answered. "I'm gonna go get some water first." He nodded and went to follow his friends into the water. Aden caught Cadence's eye as she stood talking to Grace and Greg.

"Hey, is there any water left?"

"Yeah, we put the cooler back in the car. It's unlocked." Cadence answered.

Aden went slowly through the trees toward the road, enjoying the quiet. Tina was right; it was going to be getting dark soon. The sun slanted heavily through the trees, and the shadows stood out longer this time down the path. As she reached the car, the atmosphere seemed to change. The road was deserted, and the woods had gone silent. She couldn't hear the sounds of her friends behind her, and even the very slight breeze had died in a humid vacuum. She began to feel uneasy, the skin prickling on the back of her neck. *Or maybe it's just sweat*, she thought to herself. *Must be a hundred degrees out here.* She stopped and looked around as something cracked on the opposite side of the road. Sounded like a branch. It echoed in the silence, and she almost shivered at the sensation that someone was over there. Watching her.

Shaking her head, she climbed into the back seat of Cadence's car where the cooler sat on the floor. Even in the furnace-like heat of the car's interior, she nervously watched the road and the woods beyond it as she grabbed a dripping cold water bottle and stepped back out of the car. From this vantage point, she spotted a vehicle parked just a bit further down, pulled off into the trees. It was mostly obscured, but it looked like a truck. She thought it odd, since they hadn't seen anybody else all day. *I'm just creeping myself out again*, she thought, *I should get back.* Turning for the path, but still watching behind, she ran into Maddox as he emerged, jogging out of the trees. A small scream squealed out before she recognized him.

"Sorry," she inhaled deeply, "I didn't hear you coming." Maddox barely registered her existence as he intensely scanned the surrounding woods, looking and listening for... something.

"Did you see anyone?" he asked quietly, finally looking at her, searching her face. Aden was stunned by the intensity, her unease ratcheting up again. She shook her head.

"But I thought I heard someone across the road," she almost whispered. "I felt like—" she stopped as his eyes zeroed in on a spot above her head, in the woods behind. "What is it?"

He didn't answer at first, his body had gone rigid. Then, he abruptly reached for her, and putting his arm around her shoulders, he began walking quickly back toward the lake. Aden's head swirled. She registered his arm around her, pulling her tight against his chest, still wet from the lake. But overriding that sensation was fear, a certainty of danger behind them.

"Maddox, what is it?" she asked again, trying to keep up with his pace.

"Probably nothing," he muttered, but his expression said otherwise. His green eyes smoldered darkly under angrily-lowered brows. "We should get back to the group."

"Yeah, I got that," Aden huffed. "What did you see back there?" he stopped abruptly at her question, and she would have fallen if he hadn't held her so tightly. He glanced back the way they'd come and seemed to be listening for pursuit.

"You said you heard something." He ignored her question and searched her face.

"I thought I heard someone walking in the brush across the road." She nodded. "I felt like I was being watched." She felt silly for saying it, except he was so intensely serious. "Oh, and there's a truck parked in the trees just up the road."

"A truck?" He started to turn back, then stopped himself. "What'd it look like?"

"I could only see the bumper. I'm not positive it *was* a truck, but that's what I thought."

"So could you see what color it was? Any bumper stickers? License plate number?" he grilled her.

"Just a chrome bumper." She shrugged lamely, wishing she had more to tell him. He looked from her to the path behind them, then back at her as he seemed to make a decision.

"You go on ahead. I'm gonna go back and grab a water. Be there in a minute." He smiled, but it didn't reach his eyes.

"You're going back to look at the truck." Aden tilted her head. "So let's go."

"No I'm –" He stopped, looking at her strangely again. "I just forgot my water because you were so spooked, but that's what I came up here for." Aden knew he was lying, but she was bewildered.

"You knew something was going on up there before I ran into you." Her eyes narrowed. "You were practically running up that path, and you barely noticed I was there. You were so focused on the woods."

"I knew you were…there." She waited for more but was disappointed. His attention was up the path behind them.

65

"Come on." Aden pulled him back toward the road.

"No, really. You need to get back to your friends," he insisted.

"And are you coming?" she asked, but he hesitated. "I thought not. And you don't need to be skulking around in the woods by yourself either. So are we going to go check out that truck or are we going back to the lake?"

He sighed loudly, holding up his hands in surrender. "Fine. We'll just go take a quick look." Aden smiled back at him. "But you stay right beside me. Got it?"

"Where do you think I'm gonna go?" she muttered.

She followed him closely as he made his way quietly back up to the road. He paused at the edge of the trees, searching the surrounding woods and listening. The sluggish breeze had picked up again in the late afternoon heat, and the birds chirruped lazily in the trees. It was like someone had turned the volume back up since they'd been here last. Aden stepped around Maddox, looking toward where she'd seen the truck. He grabbed her hand as she went by, but followed. She slowly walked around their parked cars and out onto the hot, faded road. She couldn't see the truck. Frowning, she walked toward the spot. Maddox took the lead, still holding her hand.

"It was right here." She pointed. They could both see the path the tires had made as a vehicle had swung off the road and pulled into the trees, but the tracks also showed that it had backed out again. Maddox was silent as he searched the ground all around the area, making sure Aden was always close by.

"Nothing," he finally sighed.

"It was probably just somebody out for a walk, and I totally blew this whole thing out of proportion," she said doubtfully. *Not that she hadn't done that before,* she thought to herself. But this still felt different. And Maddox had known—no, Maddox KNEW something. He watched her carefully, but didn't comment. "So are you going to tell me why you came running up the path in the first place?"

He stared, searching her face again, then looked away into the trees. She ached to know what was going through his mind.

"Come on, we should get back," he finally said, gesturing for Aden to walk ahead.

"You say that a lot," she observed, standing her ground.

"Well, I'd gathered that going off alone with me was compromising your reputation. I'd worked to try and fend off the rumor mill already once today."

66

"Yes, you and Kelly looked so cute together," Aden commented drily.

"Well, what do you think they'll be saying after the two of us have disappeared for the second time?" he ignored her jab.

"I don't particularly care what they think," she said stubbornly.

"And I don't believe that for a second." One side of his mouth curled up almost in a smile, and he raised one eyebrow. *Gorgeous. He was so flippin' gorgeous.* And right – she *did* care what the others were thinking. But she cared so much more about what he might be thinking.

"Why won't you answer my question?" She watched his smile disappear and instantly wanted to take back her words. Almost.

"This just isn't the best place or time for that conversation." He shrugged, frowning again, and picked his way back to the road. Aden followed reluctantly. *Not the best place or time? What the—?*

He led her silently back to the path and gestured for her to take the lead. She looked up at him for a moment, then, sighing, passed him by and stomped down toward the lake. Emerging from the back side of the chimney, she saw that everyone was back in the water except for Kelly, sunning herself again on the farthest table, and Grace and Greg were looking quite chummy walking hand in hand down by the shore.

Without a glance at Maddox, she walked to the table where she'd left her backpack, stripped off her shirt and shoes and stalked into the shallows. She heard a splash to her right and turned to see Maddox take a running, shallow dive. Determined to ignore him, she turned away and paddled lazily along the shore. He surfaced at her side.

"I'm sorry if I made you mad." He backstroked slowly, keeping up with her as she paddled, exasperated. "I wasn't sure how to answer your question."

"Words help," she bit out. The corner of his mouth quirked slightly.

"Look, I know it sounds lame, but there are just things…well, I'm not good at talking to people for starters." It was her turn to stare, stonily. He sighed. "What do you want to know?"

What didn't she want to know? Just as she framed the first question in her mind, they were interrupted by the splashing arrival of Trey.

"Hey guys!" He swam up smoothly. "We're gonna swim around the point. There's some rocks over there that make for some good jumping and diving."

"Yeah, I was over there earlier." Aden smiled, though she was irritated at the interruption. Cadence swam up next.

"So, are you comin'?" she asked. Maddox looked at Aden for her answer.

"Sure. Lead the way," she said sourly. Cadence looked confused by her tone, but smiled as she swam off. Tina and Bunkie just waved as they swam by, a bit further out.

"Okay then," Trey said, and he turned reluctantly to follow the other three around the point.

Maddox was still looking at her, waiting, as he treaded water beside her. She just sighed and stared back. He was right; this probably wasn't the time or the place. There were so many things she wanted to know about him. The questions piled up in her mind, but she wasn't sure she knew where to start, or where her questions might lead them. She was suddenly afraid she'd push him away if she pushed him for answers.

"Aden?" he prompted softly. It was the first time he'd said her name. She closed her eyes and took a deep breath, deciding.

"We should go with them," she finally said, opening her eyes, but she continued to tread water, in the same spot beside him. He frowned and looked surprised.

"Are you sure?"

"You've been saying we should stay with them all day." She smiled tentatively. He smiled back, though he still looked concerned. "Come on. We'll talk later."

He followed as she swam around the point and joined the others, exploring the half-submerged boulders and watching as Trey and Bunkie climbed up to jump off the highest perches they could find. Aden and Maddox were both quiet as the day wore away, and though she didn't seek him out, she kept finding herself beside him, laughing at the antics of the others, if not fully joining in.

As the sun blazed down to sink almost to tree level, Tina reminded everyone of the late hour, and of the tests awaiting them at school the next day. They made their way back around the point to find that Kelly and Rob had gone already. Apparently, Kelly had called someone to pick them up after Grace, who'd driven Kelly, Rob and Greg to the lake, asked her to wait for Cadence to get back.

"So they couldn't wait?" Cadence asked, incredulous. "We weren't gone that long."

"Actually, we probably were gone for a while," Trey said quietly. Grace just smiled at Greg and shrugged. She obviously didn't mind the wait.

"So were they speaking to each other when they left?" Tina wanted to know.

"Sort of," Grace winced. "It wasn't pretty though."

"Too bad for them," Tina said. "Guess she sort of brought it on herself, though." She glanced toward Maddox, standing off a bit and staring at the lake.

"Well, we'd better get you home," Bunkie said, hugging her with one big arm.

"Yeah, you need a ride, Aden?" Trey offered suddenly. Aden looked up, surprised speechless. Cadence and Grace both spoke at the same time, saying that she was riding with them; she wasn't leaving yet, and talking over each other while surreptitiously eyeing Maddox.

"Well, I mean, I rode in with Bunk, but there's plenty of room, and he wouldn't mind." Trey smiled.

"I don't mind taking you home," Maddox said quietly. He'd appeared at her side again. "If you want to ride with me, that is." Aden glanced up at him only to be lost in his gaze. She blinked herself free and smiled at Trey.

"Thanks, Trey, but I'm gonna stay a bit and help Cadence and Grace get everything packed up." She realized a little too late that there was nothing left to be packed up, but…oh well.

"Okay," Trey shrugged, smiling as big as ever. "You guys all be careful gettin' home, then."

"You too." Aden smiled, thankful he was so cheerful.

"Oh, before I forget," he said, turning back to her, "Should I pick you up at the front or the back of the store when you get off work Saturday?" he grinned, and she swore she saw a mischievous sparkle in his blue eyes as he watched Maddox's reaction. She was trying so hard to be nonchalant that she missed what that reaction was.

"Oh, um, I'll be out front."

"Cool. See you then." He grinned and turned to follow Tina and Bunkie. He stopped to have a quieter word with Cadence on his way, then ran to catch up.

"I can't figure him out," Maddox muttered. Aden turned a quizzical look up to him. "One minute, I'm convinced he's after you, then the next, I'd swear he's after Cadence."

"Maybe we're both so hot he just can't decide." Cadence laughed as she joined them.

"He's just a nice guy." Aden shrugged, "Maybe he's not 'after' anybody."

"Uh-huh." Maddox nodded dubiously.

"What's it to you anyway, big brother?" Cadence challenged him with a wink. He gave her a withering look, refusing to be baited, and slung his towel around his neck.

"So ladies," he said louder, "Are you ready?"

"Oh, I told Grace I'd ride with her." Cadence smiled. "That way, you don't have to drive all the way back into town after you drop Aden off. She and Gregory look like they might need a chaperone." She waggled her eyebrows to try to cover her mischievous look. It didn't work. Maddox shook his head, sighing.

"Is that alright with you?" he asked Aden quietly.

"Um, I guess. If you don't mind." They watched as Cadence practically pushed Grace and Greg toward the chimney and the path beyond.

"I'll talk to you tomorrow, Aden!" Cadence called back over her shoulder, and then they were gone. Aden stared after them for a second, listening to the crickets as they began to stir in the darkening woods. The sun was sinking fast behind the mountain.

"What a day," she mused. Maddox huffed an agreement, looking out over the now-still lake mirroring the orange, pink, and red-clouded sky. She followed his gaze. It was all so quiet and peaceful now.

"You wanna go?" he asked finally. *No*, she thought, looking up into his eyes, but it would probably be weird for her to say that out loud. She'd just met this guy a few hours ago.

"Guess I'd better. I have a test tomorrow, too, and you probably have much better things to do than chauffeuring your sisters and their friends around town."

"Oh yes," he agreed, nodding. "There are so many exciting possibilities for a Tuesday evening's entertainment here in 'Backwater' Falls."

"You mean Blackwater Falls." Aden laughed.

"No, I meant Backwater," he assured her, smiling.

"Oh, I'm slow today." She shook her head, laughing. He watched her, an amused glint in his shadowed eyes.

"So what test do you have tomorrow?" he asked, still watching her closely.

"Um…" she frowned and blinked. He really shouldn't look at her that way. "Physics."

"So are you good in school?" He took her by surprise again. She just shrugged.

"Okay, I guess. I struggle a bit with math. How 'bout you? Last year, I mean, when you were still in school," she babbled.

"Math was my best subject." He smiled. "And I was finished two years ago." Aden looked confused, so he continued. "I graduated a year early." He shrugged, self-consciously, looking away from her. *Oh crap. Cute* and *smart.* She wondered why he wasn't in college but wasn't sure if she'd offend him by asking.

"Alright, I'd better get you home before I get you in trouble." She smiled and nodded, though she was sad to be leaving now.

They were quiet as they walked up to the car, sitting alone on the road now. They both looked into the shadowy woods opposite the car and exchanged a half-amused glance over the roof before climbing in. The million questions resurfaced in Aden's mind, but she wasn't about to spoil the easy mood that was between them now.

"Thanks so much for driving today," Aden said as he smoothly backed the car into the road. "I live pretty far out, and I appreciate your willingness to drive back up the mountain again."

"It's not that far." He shrugged. "Whoever's made it out to be a big deal has just lived in this tiny little burg for too long."

"You really don't like it here." Aden turned her back to the window so she could face him as he drove.

"Do you like it here?" he asked, turning the tables again instead of answering.

"No." She shook her head, "We moved here from Atlanta. I guess it's just more… exciting? …to live in the city, I mean." He smiled. "I mean, I was a kid, and we didn't go out much or anything, but at least when we did, there were interesting things to see and do."

"Your house here is beautiful, though," he said, in a quiet way that made her suspicious that he knew her history. "Right there on the river."

"Yeah, but it's still 'Backwater' Falls." She smiled. He glanced at her and grinned before returning his attention to the winding road. *God, he is gorgeous.* "So what about you?

71

In Virginia, right? That's where you live with your Mom?"

"Yeah." He nodded, his smile slipping away, "I've been looking around for my own place, just as soon as I know where I'll end up."

"End up?" Aden frowned, confused. He sighed, looking apologetic.

"Sorry, another conversation that would take more time than we have tonight." He looked genuinely concerned that she'd take his answer the wrong way. She wasn't sure just how she felt about it. Her head had been spinning since she first saw him standing in her living room earlier in the day. "Isn't this the highway ramp coming up?" he asked. *Crap*. They were almost to her house already.

"Yeah, that's it." She couldn't help the spiral of disappointment that came with the thought. She wasn't ready to leave him.

They drove in silence for a couple of miles as thousands more questions invaded Aden's head.

"You're gonna have to tell me when we're coming up on your driveway," he broke the silence. "I should have turned the stereo on before now, sorry." He turned it on and lowered the volume. "Guess I just had so much on my mind, I didn't notice."

"I was just thinking the same thing." Aden smiled, "About all the thoughts in my head, not the music." She rushed to say. "I don't mind the quiet."

"You're pretty easy to be around," he said suddenly. She felt the blush crawl up her neck; luckily, it was dark out. "I'm glad Cadence introduced us."

Aden grinned through the electric warmth of his simple statement. "Me too. I had fun today." *Did that sound casual? Not too stalker-like?* "Well, most of today," she amended.

"It was a crazy afternoon." He smiled at her, and even in the dark, she lost her breath. *CRAP! The driveway was coming up fast. Damn it.*

"My driveway's right around this next curve," she told him reluctantly. *Could he hear that reluctance?* "There's lanterns on the posts on either side that should be lit." *If they weren't burnt out again…maybe they'd be dark. They'd miss the driveway and just keep on driving into the night…*

"Okay, I see it," he said, slowing. *Damn.* He turned in and crept up the narrow, winding way toward the glow of lights surrounding the house.

"So I was thinking," he said as the house came into view, "I know I owe you some answers. Today was just kind of…"

"Bizarre," she offered, smiling half-heartedly.

"Exactly." He smiled back, pulling into the courtyard between her house and garage and stopping. He put the car in park and turned to face her. "I was hoping we might start over, go out, get to know each other like normal people." He smiled. "Assuming my whack-job step-sisters will allow it, of course."

Aden's head reeled. *Was he actually asking her out? On a date?* She blinked stupidly at his shadowed face as he watched for any sign of her answer. His smile began to fade.

"Of course, I'd completely understand if everything that's happened today—"

"No!" she said suddenly. "I mean, yes." She sighed at her own moronic tendencies. "If you're asking if I'll go out with you, the answer is yes." Her face must be glowing red in the dark by now. He just stared. "Oh my God, I'm a moron," she said, shaking her head in embarrassment. He chuckled quietly.

"Well, I *am* asking if you'll go out with me, and I don't go out with morons."

She sighed, looking at the dark house. She'd forgotten to leave a light on. Looking up at the rooms above the garage, she saw the curtain twitch back and lights were on. Drew was home, at least.

"So I heard you making plans for Saturday, right?" His expression said he was asking more than just if she was free.

"Yeah, Cadence and I are going to see a movie with Trey." She emphasized Cadence's name.

"So are you free on Friday?"

Oh my God, we're actually making a date. "Um, I have to work Friday night, too, but I get off at 9:00."

"I could be there at 9:00." He smiled, tilting his head. "So it's a date." Aden stared at him in awe. He'd smoothed his dark, wet hair back away from his face, which in all its angled symmetry couldn't draw her awareness away from the intensity of his eyes. Even in the dark, she felt the force of them, their gaze on her had a physical strength. Did he have any idea the effect he could have on people? Could he feel what he was doing to her? *She* was feeling it so intensely she couldn't imagine he'd be completely clueless. Then he turned and looked toward the house.

"Is there anybody else home? It looks pretty dark."

"My brother Drew is here. He lives up there, over the garage." She tossed a thumb over her shoulder.

"But nobody's in the house?" he asked, frowning a bit. Aden shook her head. "I should walk you to the door at least—there's some crazy stuff going on in this town lately." He turned off the car's engine and climbed out. Aden met him at the front of the car, and he walked with her to the kitchen door. She unlocked the door and reached in to switch on the kitchen lights, peering in from the doorjamb. "Do you want me to go in with you, take a quick look around?"

"No," she sighed. "It's fine. I'm fine."

"Aden?" Drew called from the top of the garage stairs, "That you?"

Like he hasn't been watching us this whole time. "Yes, I'm home, thanks."

"Do you want me to come down and help you turn some lights on in that dark house?" This was code for: *I see that guy about to follow you into that empty house, and you'd better not think I'm going to allow that.* He was trying to embarrass her.

"Actually, that'd be great," Maddox called back, stepping toward the stairs. "With all the disappearances and everything, I think one of us should at least check the house before she goes in alone, and it'd probably be more appropriate if it was you."

Seriously? More appropriate? She stared at Maddox.

"Well, it would." He shrugged. "We've got enough tongues wagging in this town already, and we just met, for God's sake." *Okay, good point, but...*

"Hey, I'm Drew, Aden's brother." Drew had arrived and stuck out a hand. Maddox shook it.

"Maddox Dixon. I'm Cadence's brother." He smiled.

"I know you from somewhere..." Drew went into the kitchen, and Maddox followed. Aden winced and groaned inwardly. Here it came; Drew would bring up her obsession with Maddox at the restaurant the night before.

"Richey Vargas' graduation party." Maddox smiled, "Think I met this whole town at that party."

"That'd be it. Were you in our class?" Drew looked stymied.

"No, I was just in town and got invited. Didn't have anything better to do, so I dropped by. Ended up spending half the night there. It was one rockin' party." They bumped fists over the kitchen island.

Another enigma. Maddox knew her brother, had met him two years ago. He was Cadence's step-brother. How could she have been so unaware of his existence until this week?

"Were you there for the infamous 'wardrobe malfunction?'" Drew asked, ducking into their mom's bedroom and looking around.

"I was there, but I didn't see it," Maddox called after him. He turned and gave her the most blinding smile. "I was helping carry out some guy who'd passed out in the pool. Somebody was taking him home."

"Matt Conroy!" Drew laughed, coming back out of the master bedroom. "Don't think he'll ever live that down." He walked into the foyer, and Aden could hear him check the deadbolt on the front door.

"Funny, doesn't seem to match the story we got from you the next day about that 'boring' graduation party," Aden teased.

"Oh, I went to a dozen of 'em. You have no idea what we're talking about." Drew waved her off and went to check her room.

"I should go," Maddox said, and she thought she heard reluctance in his voice, or maybe that was just spillover from her own emotions. He pushed away from the kitchen counter where'd he'd been leaning and headed for the door.

"Okay, perimeter's secure," Drew announced, emerging from Aden's bedroom.

"You haven't checked upstairs," she pointed out.

"There's nothing up there," he said incredulously.

"Exactly where I'd want to hide if I was a murderous lunatic." She shrugged. Drew sighed and headed for the stairs in the den as Maddox chuckled behind her.

"I know. I'm truly a moron. I just love picking on him." She smiled, but she was thinking of the other day when she'd checked upstairs, herself...after running away from Maddox in the woods. Of course, she hadn't known it was Maddox.

"Stop saying that. You're not a moron." He stepped closer, and Aden could feel the warmth of him, though they weren't touching. Growing serious again, he said quietly, "Promise me that you'll be careful whenever you're here by yourself."

She was staggered; her breath had hitched to a stop, along with her heart, as she was drawn into his eyes. He stood motionless just a breath away, his eyes locked on hers. She wasn't sure how long they stared at each other before Drew slammed the upstairs door behind him and stomped down the stairs. He was making a point; he could see Aden and Maddox clearly from the stairs. Maddox inhaled sharply and took a discreet step backwards into the kitchen.

"It was good to see you again, Drew," Maddox said loudly.

"You too, man. You still play guitar?" Aden glanced to Maddox in surprise again.

"A little bit, when I can." Maddox shrugged. "We should get together and jam if you've still got those drums."

"Let's do it. You can reach me through Aden." He smiled mischievously at his sister and walked toward the kitchen door.

"Guess I'm gonna need your number, then." Maddox smirked at her, "You know, to reach your brother."

"A-ha." She nodded, biting back a smile, "Then I guess you can just get it from your sister."

"Wow." Drew shook his head in disgust and walked out the door. "Good night, you two." He called in a tone that let them know he'd be watching.

"Oh my God." Aden closed her eyes. "My brother, ladies and gentlemen." She opened her eyes and looked for Maddox. He was already waiting by the door.

"I think that's my cue." He smiled, nodding toward the garage and her slowly retreating brother behind him.

"You really care so much about what people think?" she asked, and he smiled a half-smile.

"Only certain people." His smile widened, "The important ones." She thought that through while she watched his lips. "Good night, Aden."

Before she registered that he was leaving, he was out the door. She rushed to follow and stopped short as he opened the car door and turned to face her.

"Maddox—" she stopped. What could she say to him that wouldn't sound pathetic? "Drive carefully." It was all she'd come up with on the spot. It was so lame, but he smiled readily enough.

"Thanks." He sank into the car. "Lock that door behind you."

"I will. Good night."

"'Night." He smiled his brilliant smile and pulled the door closed. He waved her back inside before turning to head back down her driveway. She glanced up at Drew's windows and saw the curtain twitch slightly again.

"Good night, Drew!" she shouted. There was no answer as she backed into the kitchen and locked the door behind her.

CHAPTER 5
flashes

Aden floated through the next day at school. She remembered taking the Physics final, but the rest of the day was sort of hazy. Her thoughts were all about the previous afternoon and evening. Actually, they were all about Maddox. His face, his body, his voice, his eyes… Yes, she was pathetic, but she couldn't bring herself to care.

Cadence was waiting by Aden's locker at the end of the day as usual, but today, she was practically dancing in excitement as Aden approached.

"Details, girl!" she practically squealed. "I want details."

"Hi, Cadence, it's so good to see you today." Aden smiled politely and turned to open her locker.

"I'm serious! I want to hear everything!" Cadence whined, "Or I won't tell you about my conversation with my brother last night." Aden looked at her with sudden interest.

"You didn't talk about me, did you?" she asked anxiously. "Please tell me you didn't embarrass me again."

"Well you're trying to jump to the end of the story," Cadence complained, "You have to start at the beginning."

"You mean the beginning, as in when you blindsided me by bringing your brother to my house without telling me," Aden grabbed her book bag from the locker and slammed it shut. "Or the part where you so blatantly tried to set us up all day long?" She dug her phone out of a pocket in the bag and turned it on. "Or the part where you—" she stopped talking as her phone chimed several times, indicating she had text messages waiting. That was uncommon for this time of day. She froze, staring at the phone.

"What? Is it him?" Cadence beamed.

Hi. Got your number from Cadence. Hope you don't mind.

Was wondering how you did on your Physics final. Feeling guilty for keeping you out late. Hope you got to study.

If you have more tests this week, I'm a pretty good study partner.

"Kinda makes me wish I did have more tests," Aden mused as Cadence read over her shoulder.

"Oh my Lord," Cadence gushed. "Okay, tell me everything. Start with the first time you two wandered off in the lake yesterday."

"There's really not that much to tell," Aden hedged, dropping the phone back into her bag and heading for the door.

"Spill it."

Aden sighed, "Well, I was swimming down the shore by myself when Maddox suddenly appeared. We sat, we talked, and then we swam back to where you guys were."

"Oh come on!" Cadence whined. "What'd you talk about?"

"Nothing important, really. Just, you know, commenting on the surroundings, how I was swimming with my sunglasses on. Stupid stuff." Aden shrugged.

"Ugh, fine," Cadence huffed. "What about when he followed you to the car later on? You two were gone for a while."

There really wasn't time before her bus would leave to tell Cadence about the watcher in the woods or the truck or the fact that Maddox knew more about what was going on than he'd let on. It was all so strange, and she hadn't processed it herself yet. Plus, she really wanted to talk it out with Maddox first. It just didn't feel right to tell Cadence yet.

"I went up there to get a bottle of water," Aden said, shifting to get through the door. She grabbed her sunglasses from the bag and put them on as the wet heat hit them.

"I know that part—" Cadence stopped and turned back to where Aden had frozen on the sidewalk, staring. "What?" She turned around to follow her gaze.

A familiar dark blue Audi was parked at the curb in the student parking lot. It was drawing a small crowd of onlookers as Rob stood by the open driver's window, having an intense conversation with the driver. Kelly was trying to pull him away by the back of his shirt. Aden and Cadence glanced at each other, then ran to the car, fighting through the growing crowd.

"So why don't you get out of the car, then, Big Man?" Rob sneered and backed away from the door, giving it room to open.

"Rob! Stop it! Just come on," Kelly begged, picking up his discarded book bag from the ground and simultaneously trying to pull him away.

Aden and Cadence pushed through the crowd just as Maddox slowly stepped from the car and faced Rob.

"Rob, man, calm down," Maddox was saying.

"You don't tell me—" Rob just snarled.

"I didn't come here to see Kelly," Maddox explained so quietly Aden had to strain to hear. "She saw me sitting here and waved as she walked by. That's it."

"Then what the hell are you doin' here?" Rob screamed.

"He came to pick up his sisters from school, you Neanderthal!" Cadence shouted, pushing her way around the front of the car to stand by Maddox, followed by Aden.

"So what's wrong with your car?" Rob gestured meanly to where Grace was climbing out of the car just down the lot and heading their way. Maddox saw Aden for the first time and sighed loudly, giving her a small, apologetic shrug.

"Actually, I came to see Aden," Maddox said, his gaze penetrating her sunglasses. Realizing that the crowd's attention was now on her, she couldn't stop the blush from rushing to her cheeks.

"Oh, please," Rob sputtered, noticing the crowd for the first time. "You both told everybody yesterday that you'd just met. You're not going out or anything."

Maddox turned his gaze on Rob and stared him down as Kelly continued to try to coax him away.

"I can't believe you're doing this!" Kelly finally screeched at Rob. "Stop it right now and get your ass in your car!"

Aden felt the focus leave her as everyone turned toward Kelly's shriek, and she stepped closer to Maddox.

"Hold on," he said quietly, never taking his eyes off a still-sputtering Rob. He took her hand and gently pulled her to stand behind him, then warned Cadence to back away. His quiet stance said he was ready should Rob decide to make good on the threats he was spitting out. Rob's face was a fiery red, and Aden couldn't tell if it was all anger or embarrassment at the spectacle this was becoming. He glanced around wildly before stepping back toward Maddox.

"What's wrong, Big Man? Afraid to fight?" He gestured Maddox forward.

Maddox continued to stare him down, unmoving, "I don't fight without reason." He tilted his head slightly as he said it, and either that or his comment seemed to enrage Rob even more.

"I'll give you a reason," he said, and he launched himself at Maddox, fists swinging.

Maddox took a casual step forward to meet him, cocked his arm back, and launched it forward so quickly it was a blur as he connected with Rob's face. Rob connected with a weak gut-shot as he slumped slowly down to the pavement.

"Rob!" Kelly screamed, running to where he lay on the pavement.

Maddox slowly turned and found Aden as the crowd surged around the car to converge around Rob and Kelly. He seemed immune to the shouted comments around them, both positive and negative, as he walked toward her. He stopped bare inches away and stared down into her eyes with a concerned expression.

"I'm so sorry," he paused, "I *thought* this would be easier than texting." He shrugged and had a tiny smile on his face.

"Are you okay?" she asked, tearing her eyes from his gaze to inspect his hand. His knuckles were already bruising a bit, and one had a small scratch. He flexed his hand and huffed.

"Fine." He frowned down at her, "I wish Rob hadn't come at me, though. Schoolyard fights aren't my thing." She raised her eyebrows in surprised amusement.

"So what is your thing?"

He smiled a smile so brilliant it took her breath away but didn't answer.

"Rob's okay." Cadence rushed up, out of breath. "They're walking him to his car, and Kelly is driving him home." Aden and Maddox just looked at her. "His eye's already swollen. He probably won't be able to see out of it for a couple days."

"I am sorry about that." Maddox frowned with a sheepish expression.

"Oh, am I interrupting?" Cadence asked, looking from one to the other with an impish smile. "Aden, you *will* call me later," she ordered seriously. She pointed at Maddox with mock solemnity. "You take care of her." Grace pulled up alongside them then and grinned at Maddox through the open passenger window.

"K.O. Bro!!" she laughed. "It's so good to have you in town." Cadence climbed in beside her, and they both waved as Grace pulled away.

"So much for starting over and meeting like normal people." Aden grinned.

"Yeah, we seem to make a scene wherever we go." He shook his head. "I feel like I'm always apologizing to you, and now I owe you another one." He glanced around the parking lot.

"You already apologized, and besides, this was all Rob."

"Not about that, though I am sorry about that, too." His lip curled into an impish smile. "I'm also sorry for making you miss your bus." He nodded with his head at the last bus pulling out of the bus lane.

"Darn." She grinned. "Now I'm gonna have to find a ride." She leaned back against the side of his car as she gazed up at him.

"And there's still more," he admitted, playfully shaking his head. She looked at him, confused, and he moved to stand in front of her, his hand propped on the scorching top of the car, seeming oblivious to the heat as he blocked her in. "I'm sorry for making such a public spectacle and calling so much attention to you. I'm afraid the whole school knows that I came to pick you up today."

"Another few minutes, and it'll be the whole town." She smiled up at him, his face, his body, his lips only inches away. His gaze swept her face, and his free hand came up to slide her sunglasses up onto the top of her head so he could see her eyes. His gaze penetrated her soul. He touched only her hair as his hand skimmed back to his side, though she could feel every inch of him. The air hummed with heat and lightning in the small space between them.

Maddox inhaled a long, slow breath and took a small step backward, dropping his arm and putting more space between them. Aden's breath came out in a disappointed rush; she hadn't realized she'd been holding it.

"Do you have to work today?" he asked, raking a hand through his hair.

"Um, no." She couldn't think straight. She'd been so sure he was about to kiss her. "I'm off 'til Friday."

He nodded, glancing around the rapidly-emptying lot.

"Do you have a lot of studying to do? I don't want to interfere with your finals."

"No, I actually took the last one today." She smiled uncertainly. Her head was swirling.

"Oh," he said, nodding, still looking away. "So, do you wanna go home, or can I give you a ride somewhere else?"

"Um…" She didn't want him to take her home. Her house was empty, and she couldn't let him stay with her there all alone. She wasn't ready for him to leave. "I don't really have anything to do at home. Did you have any plans this afternoon? You know, besides kicking Rob's butt."

His lip curled up in the half-smile she was coming to love.

"Clearly, I didn't think this whole thing through. We could…go get an iced coffee or something?"

"How very metropolitan of you," Aden teased.

"Do you have a better suggestion?"

"No, iced coffee sounds great."

At the coffee shop on the square, they had their choice of tables.

"How's your hand?" Aden asked, sipping on her iced caramel macchiato.

"It's fine." He shrugged.

Aden couldn't help but notice that the two girls working behind the counter were checking out Maddox, giggling together and continually sneaking peeks at their table. One of the girls was in Aden's Language Arts class, and the other was the older girl who was working the last time Aden came in.

"Looks like you have a couple of new admirers." Aden smirked.

Maddox just looked at her thoughtfully and didn't answer.

"Let's see, that's Kelly, these two girls, at least half the girls in the school parking lot today, judging by the looks I caught. You're a popular guy," she teased.

"It's just that I'm new in town." He shrugged, "You know, sort of new, anyway."

"I don't think that's it." Aden shook her head.

"So what about you?"

"What do you mean?" She frowned, confused.

"You seem to have a few admirers, yourself."

"I do not—what are you talking about?"

"Well, there's Trey for starters, and I caught Rob checking you out a couple of times at the lake."

"You're making that up." She squirmed.

"I'm not." He shook his head, smiling that half smile. "Aren't you going out with Trey on Saturday?"

"Cadence and I both agreed to see a movie. It's not a date."

"Are you sure?"

"It's just a movie with friends, end of story." She shrugged. "I mean, I'm going out with *you* on Friday, right?"

"Just friends?" He smiled and searched her face.

"You tell me." Her thoughts were scrambled by his gaze. He watched her for a moment before speaking.

"So what would you like to do on Friday?" Of course, he wouldn't answer her question.

"Um, I'm not sure. I don't get off work 'til 9:00, and as you know, they start rolling up the roads around here about then."

"Well, I'd originally thought we could see a movie, but you'll be doing that Saturday." He stared at her intently. "I know a place up the mountain. It's a quick drive, an easy hike, even with flashlights, and the view is amazing."

"Sounds cool." She nodded. She'd have to ask her mom if she could extend her 11:00 curfew, or it might be a short trip. She sipped her coffee and watched the intermittent traffic go past outside as she thought about how to bring up the truck in the woods and

Maddox's part in that whole situation. It had been so bizarre. The more she thought about those events, the more she thought she must have dreamed parts of it. She glanced at Maddox to find that he was watching her behind his own coffee cup, with an odd look.

"What?" she asked, self-consciously.

"You look as though there's something you want to ask me." He frowned.

"How would you know that?"

"Just the way you're chewing that straw into oblivion, staring off into the distance, and the way you looked at me. You've obviously got something on your mind." He shrugged. "So just ask."

"It's been my experience, in the brief time I've known you, that you don't answer questions," she said pointedly.

"Well, you could give it a try, anyway." He smiled. "You never know. I might be in a talkative mood."

Aden huffed a small, sarcastic laugh, shaking her head, "Good one."

"So what do you want to know?"

"What *don't* I want to know?" she hedged. "I'm not even sure where to start."

"You look a little scared." His small smile was kind. "How 'bout I just start at the beginning?"

Aden raised her eyebrows, confused.

"My birthday is July thirteenth. I'm named for my Dad, Charles Maddox Dixon, III. I live in Virginia with my Mom. My favorite color is blue, but it used to be green; I have no idea why. Let's see, my July birthday makes me a Cancer – what?" he laughed. Aden had closed her eyes and was shaking her head dramatically.

"Really?"

"What? I was starting at the beginning." He laughed. "So I guess that's not what you wanted to know."

"Well, I am interested to know those things, but I really wanted you to tell me how you knew about the person in the woods yesterday." She watched him carefully as he turned to frown out the window. "You did know something was wrong, didn't you?"

"Yeah, I did." He sighed, meeting her gaze.

"But there was no way you could have seen…or heard, from the lake?" Aden prompted. "So what made you come running up that path?"

He glanced around at the other tables and then searched her face before answering.

"I knew you'd gone to the car, alone." She watched him decide whether he was going to tell her the truth. The choices waged in his suddenly intense gaze. "And in nothing but a t-shirt over that bathing suit…"

"I was at the lake," she pointed out defensively.

"I just meant that it would have been hard not to notice you." He sighed, looking around again. Another couple had come in and were placing an order at the counter. Then, he leaned in and spoke even softer, so that she could barely hear him. "I knew there was somebody up there, and I knew that he was watching you." He sat back suddenly, taking a deep breath. Aden waited. He looked pained as he leaned back in, staring at the table top. "And I knew that it was perfect for him, with no witnesses around, you'd have been gone without a trace…unless I got to you first."

"But how?" Aden shook her head slowly, suddenly terrified. The feelings she'd had yesterday rushed back, and the skin prickled down her spine.

"Look, this is gonna sound crazy." He sighed again, still looking at the table. "I, um…" He looked at the ceiling and then straight into her eyes and took a deep breath, "Sometimes I see things. In my mind, I mean." He groaned. "I could see what he was seeing, hear what he was hearing. Sometimes, I can even hear what they're thinking." He stopped and dragged a hand down his face. "I knew what he was trying to work himself up to do."

Aden stared, shocked speechless; he wasn't kidding. She could tell that he was serious, but he was telling her that he could, what? Read minds?

"I know this sounds completely nuts. I don't know if I'd believe me, either," he rushed, leaning further towards her, pleading with his eyes. "I've never told anybody. I mean, my Mom knows, but—I know how this must sound. I'd imagined that if I told you any of this, you'd walk away laughing. Or run away screaming. Or just generally get as far away from me as you could." He sighed. "I would totally get that. I just wanted you to know the truth. I'm a freak. There it is." He sat back in his chair, looking defeated. Aden stared, unmoving.

Outside, she seemed frozen in place, but inside, her mind and emotions were whirling. He was seriously telling her that he could read minds. Like, for real. That he knew the person in the woods yesterday was watching her and was going to…what? Attack? Kidnap her? *Oh my God, was it the kidnapper? And he'd saved her.* Maddox had run to her rescue. *Maybe. If this wasn't some weird joke.*

"So you're telling me that you can read minds," Aden whispered. She couldn't bring herself to say it any louder. He nodded, searching her face.

"Sort of. I mean, I can't 'read minds' really…I just get these, like, flashes." He stopped, frustrated.

"Flashes," she repeated.

"I know. It's crazy." He shrugged, sighing once more, "I don't really know how to explain it. I'm usually not doing anything on purpose. It just sort of happens."

"So…" she started, frowning, "You can read my mind?"

"Oh, no!" he shook his head, trying to smile. "I've never tried…I mean, I have to really concentrate to make a connection."

Aden watched him dubiously as his expression became more pleading.

"I've only ever connected with bad guys." He stared at the ceiling a moment, "Yeah, that didn't come out right." He brought his elbow up onto the table and laid his head in his palm. "Okay, can I start over?"

Aden nodded very faintly through a confused frown. She wasn't sure if he was trying to be funny or serious, or if he expected her to be taking this as truth. He looked so serious, so embarrassed, so hesitant.

"Okay," he sighed louder than before, "You know my Mom works for the FBI, right? Cadence would have told you that?" She nodded once. "Well, she works in the profiling division, do you know what that is?" Aden nodded again. "Okay, so they predict as much as possible about an UnSub, I mean an unidentified subject, given their apparent habits, modus operandi, etc.…crap, modus operandi is-"

"M.O., I know what it means. I get what your Mom does," Aden assured him. She wasn't sure what this had to do with his claim to be a mind reader.

"Okay, great." He searched the wood grain of the table top for the thread of his story. "So, she is really good at her job. I mean, phenomenally good at her job. That's how she ended up in the FBI. She's practically infamous for getting into a suspect's head. She knows what to look for, where to look for it, and she can predict a motive in the most random of cases. She can tell them an approximate age, race, sex, sexual orientation, religion, educational background and come up with a profile before any of her colleagues know there's a pattern to look for."

He looked up at her before continuing, "They all think she's a freak, that she has some ability beyond the norm…and they're right, even if they don't know that. She gets flashes of the suspects. What they're doing, what they're thinking sometimes. She can 'see' through their eyes, and she can hear their thoughts, literally, and since I was about twelve, I started picking up on them too." He took a big breath. "Only the big cases. The ones that would take her away for days or weeks at a time. I knew when she was really worried, and I just wanted to help, mostly so she could spend more time at home, with me, but as I grew older, the flashes came more often. It was always the bad guys, whoever she was chasing at the time. I could never 'see' anybody else, not that I tried." He looked like he was in pain.

"Are you okay?"

"I'm fine, sorry," he assured her, "I've never tried to explain this to anyone before." She just nodded. "So when my Mom is working on a case, we both see these 'flashes' of the suspect, sometimes." He stared out the window without seeing anything for several moments.

"Is that why your Dad asked you both to come down here now? To help with the disappearances?" Aden whispered.

"Yeah, he knows about my Mom. It's part of the reason they got divorced." He hesitated, "He was never really sure the…flashes were a real thing. It undermined their relationship." He stopped and stared at her.

"But he called her, now."

"Yeah." He shrugged. "He called her now."

"Does he know that you—" she couldn't finish her thoughts.

"I think so. I think she's told him."

"But you never did. Tell him."

"No, it never came up." They stared at each other as questions and thoughts whirled on both sides of the table.

"So you think it was the kidnapper? In the woods yesterday?" She shuddered.

"Yeah, it was him," he said quietly, watching for her reaction.

"And you saved me," she stated, frowning. There were so many questions circling her mind, but this seemed the most innocuous response. He just shrugged. "And we saw his truck." Her eyes grew big.

"No, *you* saw his truck," Maddox pointed out. "I just saw some tracks in the underbrush."

"He was *right there*," she continued, wide-eyed. "So close." He just watched her, waiting.

"Oh my God. Was he watching us? All of us? At the lake?"

"I don't know," he said, still watching her closely. "I only know that he was watching you when you went up to the car."

"Oh my God," she panted. "You saw him?"

"Well, I didn't see him exactly. It's more like…feel him." He winced at her. "I know. It's weird. I was in the lake, floating pretty far out when I watched you head for the path behind the chimney, and I knew you must be going to the cars. I was concerned that you were going alone, when I got this flash of someone watching, waiting. I started swimming back to shore because I knew you were in danger. I must have looked like a lunatic." He chuckled darkly. "Suddenly lunging from the lake and running up the path after you."

"But you saved me," she said matter-of-factly. "Even when no one else knew I needed saving, including me."

He stared, frowning.

"Thank you," she said, out loud. They were the first words either of them had uttered in a tone loud enough to be heard by neighboring tables, though all the neighboring tables were empty.

"You're welcome," he answered, in the same tone, staring into her eyes. "So does this mean you believe me?"

She raised her eyebrows and contemplated her answer. "Well, I knew you weren't normal the moment I met you." She smiled slowly.

He winced at her comment, almost imperceptibly, and searched her face.

"But who the hell needs normal?" She smiled, and his whole body relaxed. "It's so overrated."

He raised his coffee cup as though to make a toast. "To not normal," he saluted, still half-hearted.

"Not normal." She grinned and tapped his cup with hers.

They sat for several moments in companionable silence, watching as another customer came in and flirted with the girls behind the counter as he placed his order. When their eyes met over the table again, it was as if reality had shifted for both of them. He'd shared his deepest secret, and she was still there, waiting to hear more.

He wasn't convinced that she was convinced...not fully. Neither was she, for that matter, but she was still at the table, still waiting, still looking at him like she had before he'd started talking like a lunatic. It was more than he would have imagined.

"So you're not running away, yet," he observed carefully.

"Nope, still here," she stated. "Were you *trying* to run me away?"

"No, just afraid that you would." He shrugged. "So I would imagine that you have a million more questions for me?"

"Eventually," she conceded. "Right now, I'm just sort of...processing."

He nodded. "So the running might start later."

"Maybe, but I doubt it," she said seriously. "If I was going to run away, it probably should have happened by now." She frowned. "Maybe I'm just not normal."

"Wait, *you're* not normal?" He laughed. "Who's the one connecting with psychopaths? Oh yeah, that's me."

"As long as I'm not included in the psychopath category?" She smiled.

"Definitely not," he said seriously.

"Good to know." She smiled, and he finally smiled back.

"I can't believe I just told you all that."

"I know. Maybe it was the caffeine. I'll have to remember that," she teased, "You know, for next time."

"*Next* time, what?" he hedged.

She shrugged. "Next time you decide to open up, answer questions, and admit to whatever other super powers you're hiding."

He rolled his eyes and stood, holding out a hand to help her up. Her heart leapt into her throat as she took his hand and stood.

"I have no idea what you're talking about," he said in a superior tone, but his lip curled up on one side as he said it. She felt the eyes of the girls behind the counter follow them—*no, him*—out.

"So, do you want to take a walk?" she asked, still not ready to relinquish him.

"Here? In the square?" He glanced around as she shrugged one shoulder. "Normally, I'd say sure, but we don't know who that guy is, or where he is." Aden shuddered as he spoke. "He's already seen you once, and I think it'd be better if you kept a low profile for now."

"You think he'd come after me?" She looked around wildly for suspicious characters.

"I really don't know, but now that you've come to his attention at least once, I think it's better to be on the safe side." He led her back to his car, and they climbed in. "Do you know if Cadence is home?"

"Hold on." She sent a quick text, and Cadence answered quickly. "Yeah, she's helping her mom clean out the pantry."

"Wanna swing by there for a bit?"

"Sure." Aden hid her surprise. She was under the impression that he didn't like spending time at the rambling Victorian filled with his pesky little sisters. She texted a heads up to Cadence, and they pulled up just a few moments later. She was waiting on the front porch.

"Hey guys! I am so glad you came over. I was becoming buried in Mason jars." She drooped her body dramatically.

"So is your Mom okay with us interrupting you?" Aden asked.

"Yeah, once I told her it was the two of you together." She grinned, without shame.

"No," Aden said sternly. "I will not stay here if you're going to keep doing that."

"Ditto," Maddox chimed in.

"Oh fine, whatever. You're so sensitive." She laughed, leading them up the steps to the deep, wrap-around porch. She led them to the rounded jut-out at the corner of the porch where the wicker rocking chairs and cushioned settee sat beneath a quietly whirring ceiling fan. With the huge ferns hanging from the eaves, the shade from the huge old oaks in the yard, and the fan's efforts, it was at least ten degrees cooler. "So what have you two been up to?"

"Just had iced coffee and stopped by here," Aden said, dropping into the chair beside Cadence. She knew Cadence's plan had been for her to sit on the settee beside Maddox, and though she'd rather be there, she didn't think she could stand the inevitable looks and comments.

"Have you or Grace heard from Kelly or Rob?" Maddox wanted to know.

"Yeah, Grace talked to Kelly. She's pissed at you, by the way, for hitting Rob."

"Kelly's pissed at Maddox?" Aden's eyebrows shot up.

"Yeah, apparently Rob's the love of her life now, and she's somehow blaming Maddox for the whole fight scene."

Maddox just sighed and frowned at the yard.

"Oh, don't. Seriously, everybody saw that he came after you." Cadence waved off his frown. "It's what she gets for going so far to make him that jealous anyway. That was just stupid." Maddox continued to glare. "And you did warn him, after all, before you laid him out with one punch. That was epic, bro." Maddox turned his glare on her, and she smiled back, unconcerned.

"I hate this town," Maddox muttered, just as the big mahogany front door opened, and Cadence's mom came out, bearing a tray of glasses.

"Anybody want lemonade? It's fresh-squeezed." LeighAnn Dixon was a tiny, blond woman with a large voice. Her daughters took after her. "Maddox, Aden, I'm so glad you dropped by. Cadence was driving me to distraction, telling me over and over again about that fight in the parking lot and then talking incessantly about the two of you."

"I'm so sorry about that fight, LeighAnn. I hope it doesn't cause any more trouble," Maddox said sheepishly. "I honestly tried to stop it."

"Now, don't you worry about it. I've already heard from Cadence and Grace, and Patience, who wasn't even there, and Mrs. Anderson who drives one of the buses, and Mrs. Brooks across the street. Anyway, everybody has said the same thing: he swung at you first." Apparently, that was all she had to say on that matter because she sat beside him on the settee and handed out glasses of lemonade as she changed subjects. "And so I guess you were there to see Aden, is that right?"

Aden and Maddox shared an uncomfortable glance before he answered.

"Yes, ma'am. We met at the lake yesterday." He sounded so comfortable, confident. Aden felt like melting into the spaces between the woven wicker of the chair in which she sat. Mrs. Dixon just smiled as she rose to go back inside.

"Well, you couldn't do any better. Aden is a lovely, smart, and level-headed girl, and we just love her."

"Well, that's not a weird thing to say at all, Mama. Thanks for the awkwardness," Cadence answered while Aden stammered. Maddox just smiled as Mrs. Dixon closed the door behind her.

"That was high praise," he said, chuckling.

"Then why do I feel about two inches tall right now?" Aden scowled.

"Is Dad home?" Maddox asked to change the subject.

"Are you kidding? It's a week day. We won't see him 'til supper time."

"And you guys eat late, too."

"You could probably call him," Cadence suggested.

"No, I'll catch him later. Mom and I will be here for dinner again."

"Yeah, I heard my Mom on the phone with her earlier; she's probably already on her way. I just hope we're not in for another endless lecture." She rolled her eyes to Aden. "The parents ganged up last night and started in about how we should all be careful, and smart, and travel in packs, and stay alert, and not get kidnapped, and it just went on and on and on."

"Well, you three didn't seem to be taking it very seriously," Maddox said.

"Well, we're not morons," Cadence huffed. "I mean, Patience can be a little flaky."

"But you're all acting as though this is just something else happening on the news, instead of something that could actually happen to you." He held up a hand to stop her from butting in. "This is a tiny little town, and the three of you know practically everybody. There is every possibility that you know the kidnapper. It could be somebody you talk to every day." He glanced at Aden. "You have no idea how close this guy might be."

"Yes, I get it," Cadence sighed. Maddox turned to Aden with lifted eyebrows and an apologetic look.

"Tell her." Aden nodded.

"What?" Cadence narrowed her eyes, looking from one to the other.

"I didn't know if you were ready. I was going to ask if you'd already told her."

"Told me what?!" Cadence whined, "Spill it!"

Maddox and Aden explained what had happened at the lake the day before, leaving out Maddox's flashes. He hadn't mentioned it and was obviously talking around it, so Aden didn't bring it up. Cadence's eyes grew larger as they spoke.

"So why am I just now hearing about this?" she demanded of Aden. Then, she turned on Maddox. "And why didn't you tell us all last night when we were discussing the kidnapper?"

"It's just been a bizarre 24 hours." Aden shrugged. "Seriously, I just haven't had a chance to process everything, and there hasn't been a great time to talk with you, since it happened."

"And I didn't bring it up last night, because I hadn't had a chance to discuss it with Aden. It seemed wrong to tell everyone about it when I hadn't really spoken with her to know how she'd feel about that."

"So you didn't think it was important to let us know that a psychopath might be watching us?"

"He'd already left before we got back to the lake," Maddox pointed out.

Cadence blinked slowly as she studied one face and then the other.

"There's something not quite right about all of that. Something you're not telling me."

"I'm telling you that you're all in danger," Maddox said. "The only similarities between the three victims are that they're female, local, and petite-framed. That describes you, your sisters, and Aden."

"Those are the only similarities?" Aden asked, to change the subject.

"Yeah, the first victim was 19, five foot one inch tall, African American, went to the community college and lived with her grandmother. She was taken from her car on a back road one night. The second victim was 48, five foot even, Caucasian, brunette, and disappeared while working in the salon adjacent to her house, where she lived with her husband and teenaged son. The last one was 24, five foot two, blond and also disappeared from work, at the convenience store in Devil's Fork State Park. She and her two year old son live with her sister and her kids."

"How do you know all that?"

"He remembers everything." Cadence rolled her eyes again.

"I've been helping my Mom catalog some of the documents. There's not much else to do around here."

"Okay, fine. Keep your secrets," Cadence said, rising. "For now," she finished, and she narrowed her eyes at both of them. "I have to get back in and organize ten thousand mason jars in a dark pantry."

"Why are you so convinced there's a secret?" Aden asked innocently.

"Because I know you two, and you're hiding something." She opened the front door and paused. "So, Aden, are you staying for dinner?"

"Oh, no, I have to get home." She looked at her phone. "Sorry, if you give me a ride home, will you be late for supper?" she asked Maddox.

"No, they eat really late around here."

"She knows that we usually wait for Daddy Max to get home. She's just being polite." Cadence still surveyed them with narrowed eyes. "I'm watchin' you two." She warned before closing the door.

Aden took a deep breath and let it out slowly. "Alrighty then."

"Come on. I'll take you home."

I t was a quiet ride through town. The radio was on this time, but neither was really paying any attention to the music.

"Will anybody be at your house when you get there?" he asked after several minutes.

"Yeah, Drew should be home from work any time now."

"Cadence told me that you're there alone a lot; that your Mom works a lot of hours, and Drew's gone during the day."

"Yeah?"

"I don't like the thought of you all alone in that house," he admitted. "Not right now, anyway."

"I'm careful. I keep the doors locked."

"And you sometimes go for long walks along the river." He glanced at her quickly before turning back to the road.

"Yeah…That won't be happening again soon," she huffed. "I know you didn't intend to, but seeing you out there scared the crap out of me that day." He seemed to think about that for a while.

"It really scares *me* that that creep was watching you; that you were on his radar at all, that it's possible you might *still* be on his radar." Aden watched as he glared at the road. She wasn't sure what to say, but then, he continued. "So, will it totally creep you out if I pick you up from school again tomorrow?"

"Creep me out? Really?" She grinned. She was thrilled.

"I don't want to seem like a stalker, myself, but I do have a lot of free time, and I could keep you company so you're not at home alone." He looked concerned. "And you know, I don't want to push myself on you, but I could be your ride wherever you wanted to go. Cadence said you don't drive…and I could bring her out to your house, or you to hers, or whatever."

"So you and Cadence talked about me?" she asked, trying not to feel defensive.

"Well, it's Cadence." He shrugged. "You know how…enthusiastic she is."

"So what else did she tell you?"

He glanced at her before answering. "She told me over and over again about how cute she thinks we are together and that we should be a couple."

"Ah-huh, and what did she say about *me*?" It was Aden's turn to be suspicious. She knew there was so much more that he wasn't saying.

"It was Cadence. She's your best friend. It was all good." He shrugged.

"*What* was all good?" she insisted. He just sighed.

"She told me about how you'd moved here in your 5th grade year and that you became friends because your names almost rhymed, but I'd heard that story before, you know." He glanced at her warily. Aden gestured for him to continue. "She told me a bit about your family…that you have an older brother who'd graduated a couple of years ago," he sighed, reluctant to continue, "and she told me about your Dad's accident. Though, I'd already heard about that before now, too."

Aden waited.

"And she told me how your Mom has been working more than one job to make ends meet. Then, she explained that you have a fear of driving, and that you wouldn't even go near a car for several months after the accident. I'm really very sorry about your Dad."

"Thanks," she murmured, eyes cast down. "So what else?"

"Well, isn't that enough?" He smiled kindly.

"Not for Cadence. I'm sure there had to be more."

"Not really." He shrugged, and he looked sincere. Aden just raised an eyebrow and waited. "Seriously, that was about it outside of all the reasons that she feels you and I should be together in a relationship."

"Sorry, I don't mean to be so weird. I just never know what Cadence might say next…

about anything. She's never felt embarrassed in her life, so she doesn't understand how anyone else might be."

He just smiled. "Don't worry. All your secrets are still safe. Everything she told me I basically already knew from previous visits…nothing I couldn't have found out just by reading old newspapers."

Aden cocked her head. "How is it that we never met before?"

He shrugged. "I dunno. I don't know that many people here, though. I've always been kind of shy."

Aden laughed. "You are not!"

"I am, really. I mean, I've gotten better about it as I got older, but I'm just not ever going to be that outgoing, life-of-the-party kinda guy." His lip curled up in that smile.

"I just can't believe we didn't meet before, somewhere along the way."

"I'd seen you around a couple of times, but I guess we were just never introduced."

"You saw me? When?" She wanted to know.

"I don't even remember. I just know that Cadence had pointed you out to me once or twice, and I think I was at the house one time when your Mom brought you over."

"Really?" She was stunned. "Then why can't I remember you at all before yesterday?"

"I don't think we ever actually met." He shrugged it off. "I was just Cadence's shy step-brother who stayed at their house a couple weeks during the summers."

"But you'd think I would have noticed you…" Aden frowned.

"Well, now we've met." He grinned, making her heart instantly pick up speed. "It's our second day of being acquainted, and the whole town is already talking about us. You scared?"

"Nope." She smiled, then it fell. "Not of you, anyway." Maddox's smile fell, too. "Sorry. It just keeps hitting me at odd moments that the kidnapper was right there." She shuddered. "I really didn't mean to trash the mood."

"No, I'm worried about him too. That's why I warned you that I'm going to be kind of a pest for a while, at least until he's caught."

"I really appreciate that you're willing to do that." She looked forward, through the windshield. "For a practical stranger you just met yesterday."

"But you're not a stranger. Cadence has told me everything," he teased.

"Well, even more reason for me to thank you for still being willing to help me out." They were on the highway, almost to her house. Once again, she wasn't ready for him to go. "So are there any leads on this guy? Anything at all?"

"Not much. He doesn't leave any evidence. Like yesterday, no clear tracks that we could analyze, no cigarette butts, no food wrappers, nothing." He glared at the road. "My Mom went back there earlier today and did a more thorough search. She couldn't even find any tracks of where he'd gone into the woods or come back out, nothing. Even the faint tire tracks where the grass and underbrush had been bent over were hard to find."

Aden sighed, frowning. Then, she slowly smiled. "So, it looks like you might have to stay here for a while then."

He laughed. "Yeah, well, that asshole will screw up eventually. He's only human, and we'll find him," he promised grimly, slowing to turn into her driveway.

"Does your Mom think those other women are still alive?" she asked quietly.

"We think so, but we don't know for sure." He glanced her way as the car slid slowly around the curves. "But we're working on the assumption that they are. And that this is still a rescue mission." Aden shuddered again, remembering the feeling of being watched with malicious intent, and she knew there was more to his answer than he was telling her, again, but they were discussing an FBI investigation, after all. She was sure there were things that he wouldn't be able to tell her, even if he wanted to.

"Are you sure nobody's home?" Maddox asked, parking the car in the courtyard.

"Don't think so, but I'll check." She frowned, digging for her phone. She'd missed a text from her Mom. "Mom's on her way home. Should be here any minute."

"And Drew?" he asked, surveying the windows of the house and garage on either side of the car.

"He probably won't be home for another half an hour or so. His shift would have just ended, and he'll have to clean...what?"

Maddox's frown had become a glare as he stepped out of the car, leaving the door ajar.

"So you're sure your Mom didn't beat us here?"

"I can call her, I guess…what is it?" She was already dialing her Mom's number while opening the car door with her other hand.

"Those blinds moved when we drove up." He gestured with his head toward the house. "Stay in the car."

"Are you sure?" She was instantly afraid; he just nodded. "Oh, hi, Mom," she said into the phone, forgotten at her ear. "Are you home yet?" She watched as Maddox walked toward the front foyer door. "My Mom's almost here," she called to him. He slipped under the grand portico for just a moment and then walked back toward her, only to detour to the kitchen door.

"These doors are locked," he said quietly. "Please get back in the car." She complied, and he sat in the driver's seat, with the door still open, listening and watching. "I'm going to go walk around the outside of the house," he started, but Aden was already shaking her head vehemently. He ignored her. "Stay here and lock the doors. If you see anything, lay on that horn."

"Maddox, no! We should call the police."

"Yes, do that. I'll be right back." He slammed the door behind him, keys in hand, and locked the doors as he walked away. She watched him in a state of total indecision: she didn't want to stay here in the car while he was out there, and she didn't want him to be out there either. Oh wait—she was supposed to be calling the police. She fumbled with the phone in her shaking hands and dropped it, with a half-squeal when one of the garage doors began rising. Her Mom pulled around the corner and, with a questioning look at the Audi in her driveway, parked in the garage. Aden met her at the door before she could get out of the car.

"Aden, who—"

"Mom! We just got here, and Maddox thinks somebody might be in the house. He saw something in the window as we pulled up. We have to call 9-1-1!"

Her Mom glanced at the house, "What? Somebody in the house?" She pulled out her own phone and dialed as she spoke. "Whose car is that?"

"It's Maddox's, well, his Mom's, actually. I was at Cadence's, and he gave me a ride home…You know, Cadence's step brother," she explained at her Mom's blank look. "He's walking around the house, looking for…I dunno."

"Yes, hello?" her Mother said into the phone. "This is Janet Garrett at 2613 Highway 178…yes, I need police for a possible intruder in my home. Yes, 2-6-1-3. No, I've just pulled into my garage, my daughter was here before me and thought they saw someone in the house before they'd entered. No, we're both in the garage; oh, and my daughter's friend is here, he's walking around the house now…ok. Yes, I'll hold, thank you." She switched the phone to her other ear, looking at Aden. "So you haven't been in the house?"

Aden shook her head. "No, we just pulled up, and Maddox was asking me if anybody else was home because he didn't want me going in alone, and then he saw the blinds move in one of the windows."

"Are you positive Drew's not home?" her mother asked.

"I'll call him now." Aden dialed and danced impatiently waiting for Drew to pick up. "Drew, where are you?…He's at work," she said to her Mom, then into the phone: "Mom and I just got home, and we think there may be somebody in the house. No, she's on the phone with the police already. We're fine. We're in the garage, we hadn't gone in…okay. See you then." She pushed the end button and looked around for any sign of Maddox. "Drew's on his way home."

"Yes, I'm here," her Mom said into her phone, nodding as though the person on the other end could see her. "No, we're still in the garage. Nobody's gone into the house." She nodded again. "Yes, we're going to wait here. Do you know how long…okay…yes… alright." Her Mother put an arm around Aden's shoulders and lifted the phone away from her mouth, while keeping it close to her ear. "They're on the way. The operator will stay on the line until they get here."

Aden barely heard her, straining to see or hear any sign of Maddox.

"So Maddox drove you home?" her Mom asked, overly nonchalant.

"Yeah, we met yesterday." Aden shrugged. "He was driving Cadence to the lake, and they came by to pick me up." Her Mother was still nodding, and Aden wasn't sure if it was at her or the police operator. They both jumped a little as they heard footsteps coming around the side of the garage. Maddox came into view with his own phone to his ear.

"Yeah, okay, I'm gonna go now, Aden's Mom is here," he said, and he hung up without saying anything further. He surveyed the front of the house diligently as he joined them in the garage. "Hello, Mrs. Garrett, I'm Maddox Dixon. I'm so sorry you had to come home to this."

"It's nice to meet you Maddox, and thank you." She smiled.

"The sliding door on the back deck is open about two feet. I didn't go inside, and I couldn't see or hear anyone. I didn't see much else. Could you guys have left that door open?" Aden and her Mother looked at each other with wide eyes.

"No, that door was closed. We all left early this morning; nobody had been out on the deck," her Mom said, questioning Aden with her eyes as she spoke.

"No, she's right. I don't think that door's been open for several days," Aden whispered. "And last time I checked, I'd put the security bar down on both the back door and the one in your room, Mom. That was Saturday."

"I haven't opened it since then," her Mom said, shaking her head emphatically. "I know I haven't, and Drew rarely ever comes in except to raid the refrigerator—yes," she said suddenly, into her phone. "It looks like the sliding door on our back deck is open, and it shouldn't be. Right…okay." she turned the phone away from her mouth again, keeping the speaker to her ear as before. "They're just a few minutes out now."

"My Mom is coming, too." Maddox said, not taking his eyes off the house. "She's FBI," he explained for Aden's Mom's benefit. Mrs. Garrett frowned in confusion.

"FBI? Isn't this a bit below her pay grade?" she asked.

Maddox flashed a brilliant smile, "Guess she's worried that I'm here, and she's heard about your family, of course." His brief glance at Aden questioned whether she'd told her mother about the incident at the lake the day before. Aden shook her head once. She didn't think her mother was any the wiser. Maddox frowned, and she knew they'd discuss it sometime later. The wail of a siren, definitely getting louder, interrupted any further silent conversation. Maddox watched the house and surrounding woods with intensity, his eyes constantly scanning back and forth.

An hour later, Aden sat on the couch in her den between Maddox and Drew. Her mother and Maddox's mom sat on the second couch with Sheriff Richey between them; he looked more tired than Aden had seen even her mother after back to back shifts. The first police car had come, followed by two more soon after, and policemen swarmed the property. Aden's Mom kept asking anyone who stood still long enough why so many of them would have responded to this call. Clearly, it looked like overkill from the perspective of someone who didn't know her daughter may have been targeted by a kidnapper. That's the only explanation Aden herself could come up with, that Maddox had told his Mom, and she'd called in the cavalry.

There were countless police officers inside and outside, searching, fingerprinting, and going through the house with what looked like a black light, all determined to search and dust and illuminate every square inch. They'd been told to stay where they were, in the garage, for what seemed like forever in the stifling heat watching as more and more people came and went. Maddox's Mom had arrived, and introductions were made all around. Kim Phillips Dixon was a striking woman. Though not overly tall, she commanded attention. Maddox's piercing green eyes stared out of her attractive, more feminine face and complemented her professionally coiffed brown hair. She'd excused herself and disappeared inside the house with the other lawmen. Now, finally, they'd been allowed inside and were waiting to hear what had been found.

"Alright Sheriff, this is quite the circus. What's going on?" Janet Garrett demanded.

"Mrs. Garret, who has access to your house? Particularly the door that leads into your second story from outside?"

"What?!" she nearly screeched. "Nobody. I mean, me and my kids. We all have house keys that fit every door in the house. My husband had it keyed that way."

"It appears someone gained entry through that door into the second floor, and they left through the sliding door there." He pointed toward the back deck a few feet away. "There's no sign of forced entry on either door, but both the inside and outside doorknob on the door upstairs as well as the security bar and handles on the door down here have been wiped totally clean of fingerprints." He cleared his throat. "We've been all through the house, and we can't find any other evidence that anyone has been here. Now, maybe y'all scared 'em off when you pulled up, but there's nothing obvious that's missing. All your electronics, medicine in the bathrooms, food in the kitchen, and jewelry and computers in the bedrooms are all still there. Now, we'll need y'all to go through and verify that there isn't anything missing or that there isn't anything that they might have left behind that we've missed because we thought it must be yours. We need you to make note of anything at all that's out of place, out of the ordinary, doesn't belong."

"I'm sorry; I just don't understand," Janet Garrett said. "There are so many of you, taking this so seriously, so quickly...and don't get me wrong, I do appreciate it, but I can't say that I understand this kind of response to a possible intruder or break-in..." Kim Dixon exchanged a look with Sherriff Richey, and he leaned back on the couch, sighing. She took up the explanation.

"Janet, I'm guessing that Aden hasn't shared her experience at the lake yesterday?" Aden's Mom looked from Kim to Aden and back and shook her head slowly.

"Apparently not," she muttered.

"Mom," Aden started, but Maddox grabbed her hand and squeezed it.

"It's my fault, Mrs. Garrett. I asked Aden not to speak with anyone until I'd had a chance to fill my Mom in on what happened...because someone was at the lake yesterday, in the woods, and he might have been targeting Aden. Now it's just a theory—"

"What??!!" Janet shrieked. "What happened? What's going on? Aden?"

"Janet," Kim interjected quietly, "Maddox has been assisting me with certain aspects of the kidnapping case so he's familiar with…certain markers of the perpetrator. While the group was at the lake yesterday, Aden had gone back up to the cars alone and Maddox followed, thinking there was safety in numbers. While they were away from the others, they became aware that there was someone else in the woods across the road from where they were—"

"And you think it was the kidnapper?" Janet interrupted, eyes huge.

"We're not positive, but we're just not taking any chances. The kids never got a look at whoever was following them, and they left soon after." She shot a reproachful look at her son. "So when Maddox called me and said there might be an intruder in your house today, well, we probably overreacted, but we're not taking anything lightly right now. Until this guy is caught, everybody is in danger, and everybody is under suspicion."

"Aden?" her Mom looked stricken. "Why didn't you tell me?"

"Mom, it really wasn't…I mean, I heard somebody in the woods across the road, and I felt like, maybe, I was being watched, but then Maddox was there, and we went back to the lake where the group was, and I honestly haven't had a chance to talk to you yet. By the time you got home from work, I was in bed, and then this morning….well, it was morning." Aden shrugged. "We were all in a hurry to get where we were going. I was going to tell you tonight, Mom. I just didn't get the chance."

Janet shook her head at her daughter, eyes still wide. "So you thought there was a possibility that the person in our house was the kidnapper," she stated quietly. Sheriff Richey just cleared his throat again.

"It's possible, but we don't have any evidence to prove that," Kim answered. "The door upstairs is unlocked, and the doorknob has been wiped clean of prints inside and out. Normally, there'd be prints or smudges from you or the kids. Same thing with the door that was left open down here. The safety bar and the handles both inside and out on that door are pristine. Somebody obviously wiped them all clean."

"There's not evidence of much of anything here," Sheriff Richey said, sitting forward again to put his elbows on his knees. "It does appear that someone gained entry upstairs and then left through that sliding door, there." He pointed again. "But we don't know who, and we don't know why. We're going to need your help over the next few days to keep an eye out…Go through the house now, while we're here, room to room, and let's make sure nothing's missing or out of place."

He rose, and everyone else followed. "Now Drew, Deputy Harris over there is going to go with you to your rooms above the garage, and Agent Dixon will accompany Mrs. Garrett and Aden through the house." He looked pointedly at Maddox. "And everyone else will go on outside for a while."

Aden watched as Maddox followed several people out into the driveway; then, she followed her mother up the stairs. They would start there.

After spending several minutes in each room of the house, they reconvened on the couches.

"Nothing," Kim told Sheriff Richey as he came back into the house. "They can't identify anything that's missing or anything that isn't as they left it. Except for the doors, of course."

"So they probably scared 'em off when they got home, just like we said two hours ago," Sheriff Dave Richey scoffed.

"Maybe," Kim conceded with a sigh.

"This goes against the other three cases," the Sherriff said under his breath. "There's no evidence that they were stalked in their homes."

"No evidence that we've found," Kim pointed out. "And the second victim *was* taken from her home. Or, well, the salon adjacent to it, and all the crime scenes were wiped absolutely clean… just like these doors."

"We don't have the manpower to bring this kind of response to every –"

"I know. It was a hunch," Kim interrupted. "An abundance of caution. We can't afford another victim."

"We?" His eyebrows shot up with a tiny sneer. "The rest of us live here. These are *our* people who are disappearing. You're not the only one who wants this to be over, and we don't get to go home to Virginia afterward. We have to live with it."

"Oh, so do I." Kim met his glare without flinching. The Sheriff sighed unhappily and turned away. He gave a few more directions to the dwindling number of deputies in the kitchen and left, shoulders slumped in exhaustion.

Kim joined her son and the Garretts on the couches.

"I am so sorry that we had to meet under these circumstances, but I'm very glad to have met you all." She said, sinking into the couch. "I've heard very nice things about you from the Kendall girls and LeighAnn and Max of course."

"Well," Aden's Mom seemed at a loss for a moment. It had been a long and stressful day. "We're very glad to meet you too." She opened her mouth as if to say more, but then sat back and looked as though she were fighting tears.

"Mom," Drew said, going to sit beside her.

"I'm so sorry, Mom." Aden began, tearing up.

"We should go," Maddox said from where he stood behind the couch, directly behind Aden. Kim stood.

"If there's anything I can do," said Kim, sincerity ringing in her voice, "Please do let me know. I've left my card on the kitchen counter."

"Thank you," Janet said, slowly registering that they were leaving. "I really do appreciate everything you've done here today."

"I just want to be sure that you're all safe." Kim smiled.

"And are we?" Janet asked, frowning. "Is Aden Safe?" Her lip quivered. "What can I do? What should we…"

Kim sat back down. "I think you should call a locksmith. Today. Have every lock in the house changed, and you might consider changing the codes on your garage doors, too."

"Mom!" Maddox rolled his eyes. Janet looked shell-shocked on the couch.

"I can do that." Drew spoke up. "I'll call them right now."

"And I see that you don't have a security system. Consider installing one, monitored, with cameras." Kim directed.

"I don't know that I can afford—" Janet started.

"I understand." Kim nodded. "I know what it is to have a single income and a tight budget, but just changing the locks will help, and make sure none of you comes or goes or stays here alone whenever you can help it. Switch up your schedules as much as you can. If you have anyone who can come and stay with you, or friends of the kids, there's always safety in numbers. This perpetrator is an opportunist. Don't give him any opportunity."

Janet nodded vaguely. Her very demeanor screamed just how inadequate she felt.

"So, change the locks, don't get caught alone, don't stick to our regular schedules, make it hard for anybody to get to us," Aden summarized, watching her mother with concern. "We can do that."

"With your permission, Mrs. Garrett, I can take Aden to school and pick her up in the afternoons. The bus schedules are widely publicized," Maddox said, "and I can take her to Cadence's house so she's not here alone, and even to work and back..." his voice trailed off. "Just an idea."

"No, that would be great," Janet said nodding. "If you could take her to school and pick her up, Drew and I leave for work a few minutes before the bus gets here in the morning, and she's here for hours before we're able to come home. It would be a blessing, if you wouldn't mind." She finished with a questioning tone.

"I don't mind at all," Maddox said earnestly, avoiding Aden's surprised stare.

"Good." Kim nodded, standing again. "This guy is someone in this community. Be suspicious of everybody, every day. Be aware of your surroundings."

"Mom." Maddox shot her another look.

"You're right. We're leaving." She took a few steps and paused, "I meant it when I said to please let me know what I can do to help."

"Oh, thank you so much again for everything you've done already," Janet gushed, following her through the kitchen. "When this is all over, we should have lunch."

"Or a big bottle of wine." Kim smiled.

"Several bottles." Janet nodded, and they both laughed. "Are all the police and sheriffs and everybody gone?"

"If not, I'm taking them with me," Kim promised. "Lock all those doors and don't worry. He won't be back tonight."

"And tomorrow?" Janet asked, sobering.

"I really don't think he'd be stupid enough to come back here." Kim didn't look entirely convinced of her own statement, but Janet let it go and walked her to the kitchen door.

Aden had risen, watching her Mom and Maddox's placate each other in the kitchen. Maddox stood nearby, watching her.

"Was it him? Do you know?" Aden asked quietly. Maddox's eyes bored into hers as he shook his head.

"We're not sure, but it'd be quite the coincidence if it was just a run-of-the-mill thief we scared off before he'd had a chance to take anything."

"But you're not sure," she hedged; she wasn't sure why. She needed answers, but she knew she wouldn't get any tonight.

"What time do you have to be at school in the morning?" he asked.

"8:30. I can be a little later tomorrow because of the exam schedule messing up all the classes this week." She shrugged.

"I'll be in your driveway at 8:00," he said.

"You really don't have to do that," she said, frowning. "Sleep in. It's only two more days, and then I won't be riding the bus again until Fall."

"I'll see you in the morning," he insisted, moving to the sliding doors. He pulled them shut and locked the handles, pulling on them to make sure the locks held. Then, he went to the security bar on the floor and deliberately set it in place. "I'm going to check upstairs."

She watched as he took the stairs two at a time and lithely disappeared behind the second story door. She heard his tread as he went to the door on the side of the house and then back again. She met him at the bottom of the stairs.

"All locked up," he said grimly. "Will you please go into your Mother's room and check that the door in there is locked?" Aden sighed but turned into her Mom's room to do as he asked. When she came back out, he was returning from the foyer. "The front door is secure, and I've checked all the windows in the house except for any in your room and your mother's. Will you please check them? Make sure they're all locked up tight?"

"No, I'm throwing all the doors and windows open to the night breeze." She smiled.

"I'm serious, Aden." He frowned.

"Yes, I know. I will," she promised, "But it looks like the cops checked all of that already."

"And what if one of the cops was the kidnapper?" he asked. "Or an accomplice? We haven't ruled out an accomplice yet. You've had dozens of people coming and going in this house today."

"Yeah, cops," she pointed out sarcastically.

"Doesn't matter. Don't. Trust. Anybody." He glared at her.

"I trust you," she said quietly.

"Why?" he asked frowning.

"You saved me," she said, shocked, "Twice."

He just shook his head. "You should be suspicious of everybody and everything. Only trust yourself."

She huffed and turned for the kitchen where her Mom had just followed Kim out the door. Maddox followed her outside. All the official vehicles were gone; only the Audi stood in the courtyard, and Kim was climbing into the passenger's seat. Aden's Mom stood by the open car door with an exhausted look on her face.

"So I'll see you in the morning," Maddox said, digging car keys out of his pocket.

"You know you don't have to do that." Aden sighed.

"I know." He grinned a lopsided grin and climbed behind the wheel. He waved once before the Audi disappeared down the driveway.

"I'm starving," Janet said, going to the garage and entering the code to close the still-open door. "And I'll have to figure out how to change that code, I guess."

"The locksmith will be here tomorrow at 11:00," Drew announced from above them. He'd apparently gone to his rooms above the garage for the call. "It's the earliest I could get him, and every other locksmith in town couldn't be here before that, so I booked it." He loped down the stairs toward them. "I also ordered a pizza. It should be here shortly."

"My boy." Janet smiled. "Okay, let's go on inside."

CHAPTER 7

star-grazing

The next day was another blur for Aden. She'd hardly slept at all, startling at every breath of wind or tiny creak in the house. She thanked God that she'd already taken all her finals because she truly was barely conscious. Maddox had been in her driveway when she opened the door at ten 'til eight, and he'd driven her to school in almost silence. He had tried to ask her about how she was feeling but soon gave up. Aden wasn't a morning person on the best of days. After the week she'd had, she was practically catatonic.

Before she knew it, she was at her locker with Cadence at the end of the day. An oversized trash container stood in the hall as they were supposed to clean out all their lockers today. Aden removed a torn and yellowed schedule and a magnetized mirror from the door of her locker and threw them in the trash. The mirror had been printed with a bubble-gum font reading "JUNIOR YEAR." Maybe she could find one for Senior Year over the summer. She grabbed her book bag, strangely lightened since all her textbooks had been turned in, and slammed the locker shut.

"Are you okay?" Cadence asked dubiously.

"Fine," she mumbled, tossing the bag over her shoulder.

"Are you ready to talk about last night?"

"Last night?" Aden asked. "Somebody was in my house. Good thing I was at yours, instead."

"Aden," Cadence was concerned, and it was a rare experience for her. Her seriousness broke through Aden's haze.

"Sorry, I'm fine, just really, really tired." She rolled her head on her neck. "It's been a totally chaotic week and I haven't slept too well."

"I know. Do you want to spend the night at my house tomorrow?"

"Um, I'm going out with Maddox tomorrow after work." She blinked. "Maybe Saturday?"

"I know that you're going out with Maddox tomorrow night, you zombie." She rolled her eyes. "But you could still come back to my house and spend the night after. The whole weekend if you want."

"Thanks." Aden smiled. "Really, but I can't leave Mom and Drew in that house alone right now."

"Aden," Cadence hesitated, "It's not your Mom or Drew this guy is after."

"We don't know *who* he's after." Aden frowned. "The second victim was older than my mom by several years, and I wouldn't want my brother to be the first male victim, either. There's safety in numbers, Cadence. I have to stay home with them."

Cadence held up her hands, palms outward. "Okay, it was just a suggestion. I'm worried about you."

"Don't," Aden mumbled, pushing through the door to the heat outside. "I can take care of myself." Her eyes sought and found the blue Audi at the curb, and she sighed. "Cadence, I'm sorry."

Cadence was already several steps away, heading toward their car in the lot where Grace waited. She turned and tilted her head. "Please take care of yourself, Aden. Get some sleep."

Aden nodded and waved as Cadence turned again to leave, then her attention was drawn back to the green gaze locking her in place from inside the Audi. She followed its gravitational pull, and Maddox stepped out of the car as she neared. He looked concerned as he walked around to meet her at the passenger door.

"Are you okay?"

She nodded, sighing again. "Everybody keeps asking me that."

"With reason," he said, opening the passenger door for her, "You look exhausted."

"Thanks," she murmured sarcastically.

"Don't get me wrong—you look amazing for everything that you're going through this week," he said, lip curling up on one side. "You never answered me this morning. Did you get any sleep last night?"

She shook her head, and he closed the door and went around to the driver's seat.

"Cadence offered her room if you'd like to go take a nap. LeighAnn is taking Grace and

Patience shopping, and Cadence has a piano lesson, so you'd have the house to yourself for a while."

"I don't want to sleep," she said, "Maybe coffee?"

"Sleep would be much better for you."

"I just don't think I'd be able to." She ran a hand through her hair.

"Okay then, why don't we get out of town a bit? I was saving my special spot for tomorrow night, but we could scope it out today—you'll get a better sense of the view in the daylight anyway. It's really cool at night, but incredible in the daytime."

"Sounds good." She tried to smile. "I really do appreciate you keeping me company."

He just smiled and pulled the car away from the curb.

They drove for a little over half an hour, winding around mountain passes before he pulled the car into a scenic pull-off area and parked. The view beyond the low stone wall was expansive. They got out of the car, and he led her to a small, indistinct trail leading off one side of the small lot.

"We're not going to look at the view?" she asked, pointing.

"Yes, but there's a better vantage point." He smiled, taking her hand and leading her away and up the winding trail. The trail forked in several places as it snaked further up the mountain and was very steep and rocky in some places. She was glad she'd worn sneakers to school today. After climbing for another twenty minutes, Maddox pulled her up the side of a small, vertical rock face onto a plateau that seemed to float in space. Aden wobbled a bit as she stood up and looked around.

"Wow." She grinned, her breath taken away for an instant. "This is spectacular!"

The vertical column of solid stone stood up and out from the mountain on three sides. The 'back' side was anchored into the hill by a huge, wind-gnarled tree. Beyond the edges of the rock's drop off was an expansive view of blue-hazed mountains and deep, green valleys marching into the distance below. From their perspective so high above most of the horizon, the sky was huge and blue, interrupted only by thin, white clouds. It was cooler up here, and there was an ever-present breeze that gusted from time to time to shriek through the ancient rocks, sounding almost human.

Aden stood and took it all in for several minutes before speaking again. Maddox remained quiet behind her.

"This feels almost magical," she whispered between gusts of wind. "I mean, I've been all through the mountains of course, and I've seen a lot of beautiful views, but there's something about this place. Something...else." She shook her head in amazement.

"Can't you just imagine a Cherokee shaman standing here, chanting with his arms raised to the heavens when the wind cries like that?" Maddox asked quietly. A slow smile lit her face as she looked at him, and she nodded.

"I can totally see that."

"Close your eyes," he suggested, smiling.

"I don't think I can." She winced, looking toward the steep drop off. "I'd feel like I was falling and probably lose my balance and find a way to go over the edge for real."

He stepped up behind her and spoke quietly, "I wouldn't let you fall," and he wrapped his arms tightly around her waist from behind. "I've got you. Now, close your eyes."

Aden's head swam with the heat of his body against hers, the smell of him, the strength of him. If he hadn't been holding her, she surely would have swooned. She turned her head to the side and looked up to meet his intense gaze, his eyes only inches from hers. She had to remind herself to breathe.

"Go on. Close your eyes," he whispered, and she did, however reluctantly.

At first she was only aware of him, but slowly, the sounds and gentle caresses of the wind penetrated her awareness. She breathed deeply and marveled at the sweetness of the rarified air. Beyond the arms holding her steady, she could feel the ancient stone under her feet, implacable in its resistance to the wind and rain and time. The way the wind rushed around the pinnacle of rock on which she stood made her feel as though she was standing on a solid piece of sky, above the world. Apart from it.

"Pretty cool, right?" he said, and she could hear the smile in his voice. She nodded, eyes still closed.

"I think I can hear a hawk somewhere below us, and song birds that I hadn't noticed earlier, and even some faint sounds of traffic on the road that I don't think I heard at all before I closed my eyes and really listened." She opened her eyes and blinked, smiling; dropping her arms to rest on top of his, still holding her steady. "At the risk of being too clichéd, do you come here often? Because I'd come here all the time if I could."

"I'm glad you like it." He chuckled softly and released her, stepping back, to Aden's immense disappointment. "And yes, I come up here as often as I can when I'm in town."

"How'd you ever find it?"

"I've probably explored just about every trail in the area by now." He shrugged. "Not much else to do when you're trying to escape three annoying little sisters."

"Well, thank you for bringing me to one of your secret places." She grinned.

"It's nice up here today," he said. "Do you want to sit here for a while?"

"On the top of the world? That sounds nice." She laughed. He walked to the immense tree and found a perch among the bulbous roots and patted the space beside him. Aden sat, leaning back against the sun-warmed rock. It was surprisingly comfortable. She stared out into blue space, breathing deeply. "Magical," she sighed, contented, and closed her eyes.

When she opened them again, she gasped, blinking furiously. The matchless blue of the sky had darkened a bit as the sun had sunk toward the mountains. Her head was pillowed on Maddox's shoulder as he held her in place beside him.

"Sorry, I was trying not to wake you," he said at the same moment that Aden spoke.

"Oh no, I'm so sorry!" She abruptly sat up, looking around.

He just chuckled. "You weren't asleep that long."

"The sun's moved," Aden said, whipping out her phone to check the time. "Holy crap!"

"It was only like an hour and a half." He smiled and stretched his arm behind her. "And you obviously needed it."

"Oh Maddox, I'm so sorry!...and your arm is probably asleep and totally numb by now."

He flexed his arms and rolled his head on his neck. "I'm fine," he assured her. "I got to spend time in one of my favorite places just contemplating life with a pretty girl at my side." Aden turned her head away to hide her blush. "Besides, I didn't have my arm around you the whole time. It was just since you almost slumped over." When she turned back in shock, his eyes had a mischievous glint.

"Oh, crap." She buried her face in her hands. "So tell me, did I snore or burp or talk in my sleep or anything else really embarrassing?"

"Nope. Just sleeping." He smiled kindly. "It's not a big deal. You were asleep on your feet when I picked you up at school. It's a miracle you made it up here, really."

Aden peeked out from between her fingers. "I still can't believe I fell asleep."

"Feel better?"

"Yeah," she sighed, dropping her hands. "I guess I should have let you take me to Cadence's. Now, I've messed up the ambiance of your favorite spot with an awkwardly embarrassing memory."

"I don't feel awkward or embarrassed."

"Well, you wouldn't." She frowned and watched his lips curl into that smile.

"As much as I would enjoy sitting here to debate the horrors of an afternoon nap long into the evening, we probably should start heading back."

"Right," Aden said, standing and stretching. She was stiff. As she stretched her limbs, she marveled again at the view and the magic of this spot. She didn't have to try as hard to hear the chanting Cherokee in the wind.

"Do you want a milkshake?" Maddox asked, breaking her reverie.

"What?" She turned to him in confusion, and he laughed.

"There's a small store we'll pass on the way home that makes great milkshakes. I'm thinking of stopping in for one."

"Sounds great, but it's almost dinner time," she pointed out.

"We'll just have our dessert first." He shrugged, unconcerned, and she laughed.

By six o'clock, they were winding back around and over the mountains toward Blackwater Falls, milkshakes in hand. Aden's head was filled with the memory of being in Maddox's arms, and she had a small smile on her face as she reminisced.

"Penny for your thoughts?"

She blinked and looked at him, so gorgeous she couldn't believe she was getting to spend so much time with him.

"I enjoyed being on top of the world with you," she answered enigmatically, her smile broadening.

"I enjoyed being there with you, too." He smiled back before returning his attention to the road.

They drove on for a while, each lost in their own thoughts as the sun slipped lower. It wouldn't be dark for a couple of hours yet, but the sky was already deepening into gradients of orange, pink, and red.

"So tomorrow's your last day of school," Maddox stated. Aden just nodded and waited for him to continue. She knew he would. "Do you have plans for the summer?"

"Nope, just working at the jewelry store, cleaning jewelry, wiping counters, arranging jewelry, wiping counters, selling the occasional piece of jewelry, wiping counters," she droned, and he smiled. "How 'bout you? Got big plans…after your Mom catches the bad guy here?" She couldn't bring herself to say 'back in Virginia.' That thought brought an ache.

"Everything's kind of up in the air right now," he answered. "Guess I've got a lot of decisions to make."

"Is that good or bad?" Aden couldn't tell from the strange look on his face. He seemed to contemplate the question for a while.

"We're almost to your house," he said, instead of answering. "Why don't you text and see if your mother or Drew is home yet?"

Aden just shook her head and sent the texts. "Why don't you answer questions?"

"I answer questions all the time." He grinned.

"Not mine." She just stared at him. "Not when they're about you."

"Sometimes you just ask hard questions," he said grimly, "I don't have all the answers."

Aden's phone chimed. "My Mom is home already." He just nodded, and they drove in silence until the light posts at the end of Aden's driveway came into view. "Thank you, for today," Aden said quietly.

"You're welcome. It was a good day." He nodded, turning into the driveway. "So, 8:00 again tomorrow?"

"Yeah, if you still insist on taking me to school."

"It's just one more day." He shrugged. "I think we can both hunker down and power through."

"Hunker?" She smiled. "You've been in the Carolinas too long, son," she said, exaggerating her southern accent.

"Aw, now that's some sexy talk," He drawled right back with a wink, and they both laughed. All the lights in the courtyard were on as they pulled up, and Aden got out. Maddox had put the car in park and was getting out to walk her to the door when it opened, and her mother stepped out.

"Oh, hi Mrs. Garrett." He smiled, and she waved.

"Hey Maddox. Thank you so much again for bringing Aden home. It's one less worry in my day."

He waved her off politely. "How are you? I mean, you had to come home to the empty house today...um, sorry that didn't come out right." He looked embarrassed for the first time since Aden had known him. Not that it'd been just a couple of days.

It was Janet Garrett's turn to wave him off. "No worries, I appreciate your concern. I had taken off a little early so I would get home before dark. Oh, and let your mother know that we had the locks changed earlier today. Drew took off a couple of hours to be here with the locksmith, which reminds me: Aden I have a new key for you." Aden nodded and reluctantly walked toward the door. "Maddox, can you stay for dinner?" her mother asked. Aden stopped in surprise and turned to him, hopeful.

"I'd love to, but I can't tonight."

"Next time, then. We'll see you tomorrow?" He nodded. "Good night." She slipped back inside the door, pulling it most of the way shut behind her.

"Are you sure you can't stay?" Aden pleaded.

"No, I would, but I promised my Mom I'd help her with more paperwork tonight."

"Doesn't that get her in trouble? That you're so involved with her cases? I've been meaning to ask."

He chuckled, shaking his head. "You and your questions. She only shares the paperwork or information with me that she would be able to share with any assistant, so no, I don't get her in trouble...except maybe with the Sheriff here." He frowned. "He doesn't like me being on 'his' crime scenes."

"Oh," was all she said.

"That's it?" he laughed. "Just 'oh?'"

Aden just nodded innocently. "See, I asked a question, and you answered it. Easy, wasn't it?" she grinned.

"Good night, Aden." He grinned, turning for the car.

"Good night, Maddox." She called and went inside. She smiled as he sat in his car and waited for her to close the door before pulling away. She waved once and shut the door.

It was over before she knew it. Her junior year was done, and she waited at her locker, now empty, for Cadence. She'd pulled out her phone and checked for texts from Maddox or her Mom, but there was nothing. She searched impatiently down the hallway looking for the bouncing blond head. Cadence had ridden with Maddox and Aden to school this morning, chattering away the entire trip, and Aden had seen her sitting with Tina, Trey, and Bunkie at lunch – she was burning with curiosity at that unusual turn of events. Did Cadence like Trey? She'd ask her if she would ever show up.

"Aden! Are you coming?" the voice came from behind her, toward the door to the parking lot. Cadence leaned into the door waving frantically. "Come on!"

"O-kay," Aden said to herself and went to join her.

"We're going to the lake! Like, thirty of us. Trisha Corbett's Dad paid for tons of food and drinks and a DJ from Greenville!" she was flushed with excitement.

"Cool. Sounds like fun." Aden smiled. "You'll have to tell me all about it."

"Well you're invited too, silly!"

"Um, Cadence, I have to work."

"Oh, crap!! I forgot!! That sucks!!" she screamed, pushing through the door to outside. "You can't call in sick or something? Just this once? It's the last day of school."

"He already let me off this whole week for finals. I have to be there." She shrugged. It would have been a more disappointing moment if she couldn't see Maddox over Cadence's shoulder, waiting for her. And he was taking her out tonight! Much better than a party at the lake, in her opinion. "Cadence? Cadence!" she shouted, grabbing Cadence's arms to gain her attention. "Are you going to the party with Trey?"

Cadence laughed, "Well, I think he really likes you, but I'm trying to change his mind." She winked. "He's cute, and he's a nice guy. I'm cute, and I'm a nice girl." She shrugged.

"And he's been working out and looked pretty good at the lake earlier this week?" Aden grinned.

"Well, he does seem to be growing up nicely."

"Growing up nicely? Really?" Aden shook her head.

"What?"

"Never mind. Listen, I could very easily get sick by tomorrow night so you don't have a third wheel at the movies," she suggested. Cadence stared at her, suddenly still.

"I hadn't even thought of that!"

Aden faked a cough. "I'm already feeling a bit under the weather, and you know how I looked yesterday. I'm probably coming down with something, and I'll just want to go straight home after work tomorrow. I can feel it."

"You're the best!" Cadence hugged her fiercely. "She's the best!!" she screamed to Maddox behind her. "Love you! Call you later," and she ran off across the parking lot with a small wave to her step-brother.

Aden was still chuckling and shaking her head as she reached the door Maddox was holding open for her.

"What the heck was all that about?" he asked, brows raised.

"Cadence likes Trey. She's going with him to the lake right now with about thirty other people for an epic end of school party."

"Oh." He frowned. "Sucks that you'll have to miss it."

"It's okay." She shrugged, and it was—she'd rather be with Maddox. "Anyway, I told Cadence that I'd been feeling a cold coming on, and I don't think I'll be up to joining them at the movie tomorrow night."

"So Cadence was just being appreciative then?" He shook his head, "So the two of you have cooked up a date that poor man doesn't even know about yet."

"Well, he'll figure it out," Aden pointed out, "and he's a big boy. He doesn't have to go if he doesn't want to."

"Okay." He smiled her favorite smile, still shaking his head, and closed her door.

It didn't take long to reach the jewelry store on the square. Maddox pulled up to the curb at the front door, and Aden grabbed her bag to jump out, but paused and turned back.

"You can pick me up over there by the park. I'll meet you there at 9:00."

"I'll be right here," he said. "I wouldn't want you to hurt yourself running across this road in those heels." Aden looked at her feet. She was dressed nicely for work and wondered if he'd noticed. "I really like the heels."

"Oh, I brought jeans and sneakers to change into." She smiled, holding up the bag. "Crossing the road is a snap, but climbing back up that rocky trail in these shoes would be deadly."

"Perfect. I thought maybe you'd changed your mind about going back up there." He smiled. "Or that we'd have to detour to your house for you to change."

"Nope. I've been looking forward to being back on top of the world." She grinned, watching as his lips curled up in response.

"See you at 9:00," he said, and the tone of his voice and the look in his eyes melted her soul. Unable to form words, she just grinned like an idiot and stepped out of the car. She felt his gaze on her as she walked into the store and toward the back hallway to stow her bag away. Just before she would have left his line of sight, she turned. He still sat at the curb, and he smiled before pulling slowly away. She sighed and turned back to the hallway.

The store seemed empty. Nobody was out front, which was strange, and she didn't hear any sound coming from Mr. Keith's office.

"Mr. Keith? Anybody home?" she called. Then, she heard the distinctive squeak of the chair in his office.

"Aden!" he said, sounding out of breath. "You startled me. I didn't realize it was time for your shift. I'll be right out." The door to his office was slightly ajar as she approached the hallway, and he bumped it closed as he rounded the desk in his small office.

Aden put her things away and returned to the showroom, immediately grabbing the glass cleaner and a dry rag from under the counter. There were smudges and smears all over every glass case. Apparently, no one had wiped them down all day. She got to work making the surfaces sparkle again. As she wiped the diamond case, she noticed a 'hole' in the display where a large diamond ring, probably the most expensive in the store, had stood for months.

"Did somebody buy that big diamond solitaire with all the baguettes around it?" she called. There was no answer; he must not have heard. She imagined he would be very happy about such a large sale.

Mr. Keith emerged from his office straightening his thinning brown hair. He was in his early 30s and obviously spent some time at the gym. He liked to wear his dress shirts tight across his muscled chest and arms. The brightly colored ties that he preferred over his neutral button downs always seemed too tight on his beefy neck. Not that much taller than Aden, he commanded attention with his impeccably tailored clothes and shoes and, of course, the large rings he wore.

"Hi, Mr. Keith, did you sell that big diamond solitaire with all the baguettes?" She smiled.

He blinked at her for a moment, never one for quick action. "Oh, yes. I sold it earlier in the week."

"Wow, congratulations," Aden said warmly. "That was a beautiful ring, and a great sale for the store."

"Thanks," he said. "How did your finals go? We all missed you around here."

"They went well. School's all done for another year. Did I miss any other exciting news while I was buried in books?"

"Not a thing. Beverly called out on me Tuesday and Wednesday, and I had to get Mrs. McConnell to fill in." He sighed. "She's a sweet old lady, but she runs off customers. Wish she'd hurry up and get that hearing aid."

Aden nodded in understanding. She'd worked shifts with Mrs. McConnell before. She was hard of hearing and tended to shout everything. She'd been talking about getting a hearing aid for years. On the plus side, Mrs. McConnell knew her diamonds, maybe even better than Mr. Keith.

"We had a good week though, in spite of all that. It's graduation gift season," he said. "Sold lots of watches and pearls."

"Think it'll be busy tonight?"

"Nah, last day of school—all the teenagers will be out partyin' and their parents will be home worryin'." He smiled. "Everybody else just knows to stay off the roads and let you young'uns take over for a bit. Spread your wings." Aden's eyebrows had lifted, and she laughed.

"I didn't know adults schemed like that."

"I'm just teasing you. I forget how young you are sometimes." His eyes roamed the store as he spoke. "I'm glad that you're here though. Would you mind re-arranging the merchandise in the cases this afternoon? Beverly had done them last, and they just don't look as nice as when you did them a couple of weeks ago."

"Wow, really?" She beamed. "I'd love to." Arranging how the merchandise was displayed was the only creative pastime in the store. Because of that, Beverly, who had seniority over her at the store, usually got the assignment. "What would you like featured in the front window case?" she asked.

He stared at her for an uncomfortable moment as he deliberated in his slow style. "You know what? You've been here several months now. Why don't you decide?"

"Well, I was thinking...Beverly has had everything so segregated in the front window – pearls one month, sapphires the next. It makes sense to group items inside the store so customers can find what they're looking for if they've come in for something specific, but for the front case in the window, shouldn't we try and showcase the depth of our inventory? Mix it up a bit."

He stared at her for another over-long moment, blinking slowly. Then he nodded. "I like it. Mix away." Aden was thrilled. The long stretch of hours in front of her suddenly seemed more interesting. "Don't forget to take pictures of the finished cases so we can put it all back together again when we take everything out of the safe in the morning," Mr. Keith ordered. Aden nodded and got to work.

He'd been right that there were very few customers. The whole square seemed deserted all afternoon and evening. She had rearranged every jewelry tray and display in every case of the store, beginning with the large front window display and working her way to the back of the store. She realized that it was getting dark outside the big display window and glanced at the clock on the wall. It was after 8:30 already, and she hurried to take the Polaroid photos with the ancient camera Mr. Keith kept. Glancing outside again, she saw the unmistakable outline of an Audi parked in the lot across the street. She smiled and hurriedly began to clean up the discarded and unused trays and ring holders.

Mr. Keith had only emerged from his office twice since she'd arrived, and he didn't have much to say about her progress either time. She hoped he liked what she'd done.

When she'd finished putting away the empty display cases, she replaced the flat brushes that were used to brush the velvet linings and wiped down every glass surface in the store again. She glanced up: 8:39. She sighed and went to the back to retrieve the heavy industrial vacuum cleaner. She started at the front door and vacuumed her way through the small store and into to the back hallway. Mr. Keith's door was closed.

"Mr. Keith?" she tapped lightly, "Would you like me to vacuum your office?"

"No, thank you," he mumbled through the door. Sighing, she put the machine away and tidied the tiny back room. Going back into the front showroom, she saw that the Audi still sat in the same spot; a silhouette across the empty street. She glanced at the clock. *8:47, almost there.* She paced slowly back and forth, checking her handiwork in the cases. She was pleased with it. *Don't look at the clock. Don't look at the clock.* She looked: 8:50. Five more minutes, and Mr. Keith should unlock the big safe in his office and come out to help her transfer most of the contents of the cases to the safe for the night. She heard his chair squeak as he got up and a moment later he came out stretching. She waited quietly as he walked around the store, peering into each case, nodding and grunting. He came to the front case last and stared down into it for a long time. Then, he went to the door and looked in from the sidewalk outside for several minutes before he came back inside.

"The store looks really great," he told her nonchalantly, his face almost expressionless, "and that front window display is eye-catching." He stared at her. "From now on, you're in charge of merchandising the displays."

"Oh my gosh, really?" She beamed. "Thank you Mr. Keith."

"You're welcome. This is good work. I can tell that a lot of thought went into every case." She just nodded.

"Alright, let's get this place locked up. I would imagine you have a party to go to?" He smiled at last.

The inventory was locked in the safe in record time, and Aden went into the small bathroom to change. When she came out, Mr. Keith was in his office, and the lights had already been turned out in the showroom.

"Good night, Mr. Keith. See you tomorrow."

"See you tomorrow, Aden. Be careful."

Aden made her way to the front door, but it was locked already. She was surprised by Mr. Keith, right behind her, with the key to let her out. She hadn't heard him, and it had startled her. *Maybe I should get my hearing checked.*

"Good night," he said as he opened the door to let her out. Maddox sat right outside the door in his Audi, waiting. "Boyfriend, I take it?"

"No, just a friend." Aden shrugged. Mr. Keith looked the Audi over with a disdain she didn't understand before retreating into the store and relocking the door.

Aden climbed into the car with a big sigh.

"Hi, there." He smiled, and her heart melted in one moment.

"Hi, there." She smiled back.

"I like the displays," he said. "They look a lot better."

"Because you can see so much from here," she teased, "or from across the street for that matter. Were you there all day?"

"Nope, not all day, and I could see what I needed to." He smiled and pulled away from the curb.

"Well, thank God Mr. Keith liked them. I worked on them all day." She stretched in her seat. "But he said I'm now in charge of all merchandising in the store."

"Wow, that's pretty cool." He grinned. "Are you tired?"

"Nope. Just working out the kinks." She yawned and giggled. "There's nothing that'll wake a girl up faster than a brisk climb to the top of the world."

"Top of the world it is, then." He smiled.

"So how was your day?" she asked. "The part when you weren't stalking me, that is."

"It was good." He laughed. "And at least I warned you that I'd be stalking you."

"Yes, you're a very polite stalker," she admitted.

"Thank you."

"So what'd you do today?" she was curious how he spent his days.

"I worked with my Mom today while you were in school. Then, after I dropped you off at work, I went to the lake and checked on Cadence and Grace."

"You spied on them?"

"No, I breezed through the party, made the appearance of the concerned older brother to make sure everybody was keeping their hands to themselves—what?" Aden's jaw had dropped. "It's in my job description. Then, I tracked down Patience at another party. I did some laundry, and then I came back here."

"So you're now in charge of taking care of all the females in your life?" she asked. "And laundry? Really? I can't get Drew to put his in a basket, let alone *do* something with it."

He stared out the windshield and didn't answer.

"I'm sorry, I was just kidding," she began, but Maddox cut her off.

"No, it's okay. It was just an observation I hadn't seen in myself, but you're right. I guess I do spend a lot of time taking care of people."

"That's an admirable trait." Aden shrugged. "It's a compliment."

"Well, thank you, Miss Garrett." He said, finally smiling a genuine smile.

"You're welcome, Mr. Dixon." They drove in easy silence for a while, the darkness making the confines of the car feel more intimate.

"So this is our first real, official date," Aden observed, looking out her side window to avoid his gaze. "The first time we've spent together that you haven't been tricked into, or felt obligated to be there."

"Obligated?" He started, then he shook his head and rolled his eyes. "I enjoy spending time with you." His lopsided smile grew larger as he continued. "But it is nice that, for just a few hours, we can hang out without all the distractions we've been dealt this week."

"That's what I meant."

"First dates are usually much more awkward than this, though."

"So you've been on so many you can make that observation?" she asked. "Wait, never mind. The answer to that could get awkward. Forget I asked."

Maddox just grinned.

They reached the scenic pull-off and parked the car. Maddox produced two flashlights from the back seat and gave her one. Then, he eased into the straps of a backpack, and they started off up the trail. It was slower going at night, but much more thrilling. The trail ahead was delineated into the few feet they could see in the light from the flashlights, since there was pitch blackness outside of that illumination.

"I hope you can find the right trails in the dark," Aden said after a long while following him ever upward.

"It's not the first time I've been here at night." He smiled, taking her hand and helping to boost her up onto the plateau. Aden turned and gave him a hand to help him up, though he didn't really need it. Then she turned to view the gulf she'd seen the day before. It had grown somehow.

The vast horizon of mountains and valleys she'd looked down on in the daylight disappeared and melded into one large, dark expanse dotted with tiny lights. Looking up, she could see more stars than she could remember seeing before and looking down, the darkness that hid the mountains and valleys was dotted with more tiny clusters of light. The wind was quieter than it had been yesterday, and the tiny puffs of breeze produced whispers instead of screams as it travelled through the rock crevices.

"Hello, world." She muttered, hugging her arms tight to her torso. Maddox chuckled quietly. He was taking things out of the backpack and arranging them on the stone's flat surface: a down comforter, a lantern, a couple of pairs of binoculars, some cheese and grapes, and bottled waters. Aden watched, amused.

"Looks like you've thought of everything."

"I have my moments." He shrugged. "Come sit down."

He'd laid the comforter out with the lantern burning just off one corner, giving off a broad, warm light. The cheese, grapes and water were in easy reach, and the binoculars stood ready. She sat Indian-style on the comforter next to him.

"This is nice." She smiled. "I had wondered what an official Maddox Dixon date might look like."

"So?" he raised his eyebrows.

"Very impressive." She fought a grin. "This will be very difficult to beat."

"I didn't realize there was a competition?"

She giggled, suddenly nervous. "There's no competition," she said, gazing into his eyes. But she could only hold his gaze for a second before she had to turn and look at the stars instead. *Coward.*

Maddox handed her a pair of binoculars and took up the second pair himself. Aden scanned the horizon, bringing the tiny points of light into focus: headlights, street lamps, glowing windows in businesses and homes. Then, she turned her gaze to the heavens and lost herself looking at the stars. She'd never done this, looked at the stars with binoculars or a telescope. Her Dad had a telescope, and she guessed it was in Drew's rooms now, but she'd never been interested. This was a whole new universe.

"I have a telescope back home. It's much better for stargazing." Maddox said, seeming to read her thoughts.

"This is breathtaking, though." She smiled, still searching the sky.

"Yes it is," he breathed beside her. She dropped the binoculars and turned to see that he was looking at her. "I've never brought another soul up here with me."

"Really? I'm honored." She smiled. The heat of his gaze could have melted the rock on which they sat. He smiled as he reached up to catch a wayward lock of her hair and tuck it behind her ear.

"Your hair is beautiful in this light," he said and his hand, relinquishing her hair, brushed slowly down her cheek. Aden nearly gulped before she caught herself, frozen by the dance of fire in his eyes. *So gorgeous it almost hurts to look at him.* She wasn't sure what to say, and she was too busy memorizing every detail of his face, his voice, his touch, and his words, to say anything anyway. His hand dropped only to search for hers lying on the comforter between them, and he held it tight. He closed his eyes and breathed deeply before lying back to look up at the stars, his free hand thrown up above his head. *Wow.*

Aden watched him for a moment, then laid back beside him, hands still clasped. The unbroken arch of glittering stars seemed closer than ever before. Her hand was warm, almost tingling, enveloped in his. She breathed a slow sigh of contentment and gazed at the heavens as they lay side by side. She didn't know how long they'd lain in silence, staring at the stars and listening to the night breeze in the rocks, when his sudden exclamation startled her out of her reverie.

"Look! Over there!" He pointed, excited.

"What?" She was startled and looked at him, instead of toward where he was pointing.

"A meteor! Over there, heading toward Pegasus!"

Aden followed his pointing arm and saw the small, bright arc of a shooting star just before it burned out in the atmosphere in front of them. A childhood superstition made her close her eyes and make a quick wish: *I wish that Maddox would kiss me.*

"Did you see it?" he asked, grinning like a little boy.

"I did." She nodded, smiling. "Very cool."

"It pierced the heart of Pegasus," he said, lying back again. Aden glanced at him with a raised eyebrow. "The constellation, Pegasus?" he prompted.

"I've heard of Pegasus, the winged horse. But I'm not so sure I knew it was a constellation," she admitted.

"It's that triangle over there," he said, pointing. His finger traced a line between the stars as he showed her, "and there's a star for the head…" he trailed off, looking at her. "Anyway, the meteor burned out right in the middle of the constellation." He shrugged, looking embarrassed.

Aden tilted her head looking at him. She could imagine what he would have been like as a little boy, with all that wonder in his eyes. "Piercing the heart of Pegasus." She smiled, nodding slowly. "More magic at the top of the world."

His eyes searched her face as he raised up on his elbow, face to face once again. *Gulp.* Aden felt the familiar heat rise up from her collarbone, but only as a vague notion. His eyes bored into hers from a scant few inches away, and for Aden, the world around them fell away into blackness. There was only Maddox. His hand still clasped hers between them, and his eyes melted her consciousness until it was just him there with her, outside of space or time.

His free hand came up to caress her jawbone ever so lightly before he caught her chin in a light grasp and gently pulled her face to his. His lips touched hers hesitantly for a second, and then they both leaned in toward each other, deepening the kiss. Aden's whole consciousness sang with the long-awaited contact. But then he was pulling away. *No! Wait!* Aden's eyes flew open as he disentangled himself from her and stood, facing away into the darkness. She was left stunned, speechless, staring at his back.

He took a deep breath and let it out, then another before running his hands through his hair and turning to face her again.

"Aden, I'm—" he started, and sighed again. "We shouldn't—"

"Look, I get it," she ground out, scrambling to stand.

"No, wait." He grabbed her hand and pulled her down so they were both sitting again. "I want to try to explain."

"Don't bother. I'm just your annoying little sister's friend, you're only here temporarily, and then you'll be gone back to Virginia. That it?"

He frowned, "You're not just my sister's friend," he started, "but I *am* here temporarily, and I *will* be going back to Virginia soon." He searched her face—for what, Aden couldn't know. "And I don't want to hurt you."

"It hurts me when you pull away like that. Just shutting down, shutting me out, so suddenly," she ground out, looking away from him. "Like none of this means anything to you."

"Aden, I'm sorry." He gently squeezed her hand, the one he still held between them. She turned reluctantly to face him, and his gorgeous face wore the same pain she felt. "This does mean something to me." He took a breath, and his blazing eyes bored into her soul. "You mean a lot to me."

Aden almost gasped on a sob, somewhere between joy and pain.

"This is all happening so fast." He frowned, searching for the words to make her understand. "We've only known each other four days. It's crazy—I feel like I've known you so much longer than that…and then other times, I feel like there's so much I don't know about you, and I can't wait to find out." Aden stared as the words poured out. "All the time we're spending together…it's not enough, and when we're apart, I think about you constantly. I worry that you might be in danger from that punk-ass lunatic running around this town, and I want to protect you. I want to make sure you're safe. But more than that, even if that lunatic didn't exist, I just want to be with you."

Aden softly exhaled a breath she didn't realize she'd been holding. "Well, here we are."

"Yes, here we are. For now," he said softly. "But we're going to catch this guy. Could be tomorrow, in another week, maybe two…and I'll have to leave."

Aden stared at him for a moment and then shrugged. "I know that. So what?" She was angry, she was joyous, she was sad, all at the same time. "Let's enjoy the time we have."

"And when I have to go?"

"We'll deal with it. A whole lot can happen between now and then." She sighed, "Maybe we'll be sick of each other in another few days." He raised an eyebrow. "Or you might fall for Kelly, or some other girl in town."

"Funny."

"I appreciate that you're trying to protect me, but you can't protect me from you. It's too late." She smiled. "I fell for you that first day at the lake. So stop pushing me away."

130

Maddox stared, blinking slowly, and she could almost hear the warring emotions inside his head as he tried hard to look impassive. She waited, and his eyes softened almost against his will as a tiny, lopsided smile transformed his features.

"Carpe diem," he whispered, reaching for her and pulling her into a long, slow kiss. *Seize the day indeed*, she thought as her heart and her soul reached out for him. She didn't know how she would manage to let him go when the time came, but she wouldn't have missed this kiss for anything. The world fell away, and it was just the two of them, together. The electricity she'd felt on occasion when she was with him before were tiny sparks to the lightning ravaging her senses now – his lips on hers, on her face, her jaw, her throat scourged all her confused emotions away in a blinding, blissful jolt. His hands slowly moved up her back to gently hold her face on either side as he pulled away, and Aden opened her eyes to see his mere inches away. He touched his forehead to hers and took a long, slow breath. "Wow." He grinned.

"Wow," she agreed, smiling back. He pulled her into a lingering embrace as the world slowly crept back in. Too soon, he sighed and released her.

"It's getting late. I should get you home."

Aden frowned. She wasn't ready for this night to end. She wasn't sure she'd ever be ready. Reluctantly, she rose and helped him gather everything up. "We didn't even touch the food."

"Are you hungry? We can nibble in the car on the way home."

Much too quickly, he had everything stored in the backpack. He held out a hand, and she took it as he helped her down the dark path, putting his arm around her occasionally and drawing her in for a quick embrace before the path narrowed to single-file again. Aden barely noticed the terrain as she floated along in pure happiness. When they reached the car, he opened her door for her, and she paused to look back up the mountain for a moment.

"Don't worry, it's not going anywhere. We'll be back," he promised. Aden kissed his cheek and climbed into the car. He was smiling as he closed her door and climbed into the driver's seat. A couple of miles into the drive, he reached for her hand. "So," he began, "How did the 'official Maddox Dixon date' measure up?" He looked a little anxious. "I mean, there were some rocky moments there, but I enjoyed being with you."

"Wouldn't have missed it for anything in the world." She squeezed his hand, smiling.

The winding drive home passed too quickly, and before she was ready, they were coming up on the light posts framing her driveway. He squeezed the hand that he'd held the whole way, and she smiled at him. Suddenly, he was frowning at the road ahead.

"What's wrong?" Aden asked, at the same time she saw the taillights of a vehicle, reflected in the Audi's headlights. It was parked on the side of the road about fifty yards past her driveway. Their nearest neighbor on that side was more than half a mile further on. As they watched, the brake lights flashed, and the vehicle pulled onto the road, turning on its headlights after a moment and accelerating quickly away. "That was a truck," she said, suddenly afraid. Maddox sped up in pursuit.

"Here, call my Mom," he ordered, handing her his phone. "She's on speed dial, number 1." Aden dialed, and Kim Dixon picked up after the first ring.

"Mrs. Dixon? This is Aden. Maddox and I are following a truck that was parked on the side of the road just past my driveway. It pulled away quickly as we slowed to make the turn."

"Tell Maddox to turn around. I'm calling the highway patrol, and they'll pick up the chase."

"She said to turn around. She's calling the highway patrol." Maddox was already shaking his head as Aden turned on the speaker on his phone.

"We'll lose him."

"We don't even know who it is," Aden pointed out. "Everybody drives a truck around here."

"Tell him to take you home and check on your Mom." Kim's voice demanded from the phone.

"I can at least get the license plate. Otherwise, the cops won't have anything to follow," Maddox nearly shouted at the phone.

"There's a patrol only two minutes out," Kim's voice said.

"This guy's long gone in two minutes," Maddox growled.

"Where is he? I don't see him up there?" Aden leaned into the windshield, searching the winding road ahead. Most of the road was visible as it wound up the side of the mountain, but it was dark. Maddox growled.

"I mean it Maddox. Break off the pursuit now," Kim's voice commanded.

"Looks like I've lost him anyway," He ground out. "I have no idea where he could have gone, but we can see the highway ahead, and it's empty."

"Get Aden home. Then, call me back," she said, and the line went dead. Aden hung up their end of the call.

"Where could he have gone?" Maddox asked. "Did we pass any turn-offs? Somewhere he could have pulled over where we wouldn't have seen him?"

"There are a couple of driveways we passed. They're easy to miss in the daytime, let alone at night."

Maddox muttered under his breath.

"Sorry, I wasn't paying enough attention while I was on the phone."

"It's not remotely your fault," Maddox said. "I had my eyes on him until he rounded one of the curves. Then he was just gone." Maddox slowed as another turn-off appeared ahead. Headlights rounded the curve behind them as he turned into the gravel road and stopped. They couldn't see anything on the drive ahead of them as it wound almost instantly into the darkness of the trees. They both turned around in their seats to see the car pass by on the highway behind them. It was a small, compact car.

Sighing, Maddox backed out onto the highway and headed back toward Aden's house.

"I'm sorry. I should never have taken off after that truck and put you in danger that way."

"Are you kidding? Like we should have just watched it drive off into the night?"

"I should have realized sooner the danger I was putting you in, putting us both in." He frowned. "All I was thinking was that he was *right there*, and if I could just get a license plate number or identify the truck somehow..."

"I know. Me too," Aden assured him. "But we still don't know it was him. It could have been anybody."

Maddox smacked the steering wheel with the palm of his hand. "I can't believe I lost him that quick!"

"I can't believe we can't have one day without some kind of drama." Aden rolled her eyes.

"I really wanted today to be different – to take your mind off of everything for a while."

"You did." She smiled, grabbing his hand. "Thank you so much for letting me in."

"You know, the paths, the mountain, that plateau...it's all public. I didn't exactly 'let you in,'" he teased.

"I don't mean the place. I meant thank you for letting me get a glimpse inside your enigmatic head."

"Enigmatic??" He was surprised. She just shrugged and let it stand.

"I had fun tonight, even the crazy parts." She smiled.

"Me too." He laughed. They were turning into her driveway. Maddox grew somber again and scanned the woods on either side as he drove up to the house and parked. Every exterior light on the house was lit. "Sit tight a sec," he said, getting out of the car. He walked around and opened her door.

"How very gallant of you," Aden teased, loving every second. As she climbed from the car and reached out to hug him, the kitchen door flew open, and her mother came out, phone to her ear.

"They're here," she sighed into the phone, sounding relieved. "Yes, thanks so much Kim. Okay, I will. Good night." She ended the call and came to hug Aden and Maddox together, one in each arm. "I'm so glad you're safe."

"My Mom called you already," Maddox stated. "I'm so sorry Mrs.—"

"Now, you stop that," she interrupted. "You don't have any reason to be sorry. You're giving up all your time here to help keep my daughter safe. It's not your fault we have a psychopath running around the county, and you don't go apologizing for trying to help."

"Is everything okay here?" he asked her. "Did you see anybody?" Janet was shaking her head.

"No, nothing unusual here. I was out for a while myself—got home a while ago," she glanced at Aden quickly, "so I'd be sure to be here when Aden came home. There was nobody parked on the highway then that I noticed, and everything's been quiet." Aden saw the glance her Mom threw at her when she mentioned that she'd been out. She wondered where her mom had been.

"Well, we were worried about you, too," Aden said. "We were hoping that we could at least get a license plate number before we came back."

"It's okay. Kim already explained. You're both here, and you're safe. That's all that matters." She smiled. "So, did you have a good time tonight?"

"We did." Aden hugged her again briefly. "How about you?"

"Oh, fine. Fine." Her Mom nodded. "I haven't had that many weekend nights off lately, so it was fabulous just not being at work." Aden knew there was more she wasn't saying but let it go, for now. "Well, thank you again, Maddox, for bringing Aden home safely and for looking out for all of us."

"Speaking of which, is Drew home?" he asked, glancing up at the windows above the garage. "I'm still uneasy about you two being alone up here with that guy still out there."

"He's not home yet, but don't worry. The house is all locked up tight, and he'll come dragging in before too long. We'll be just fine. Really."

Maddox didn't look convinced, but he knew he had to let it go.

"Well, good night. Thank you again." She smiled at him. "We'll see you again soon, I hope?"

"I hope so." He nodded. "Good night." Janet smiled broadly and retreated back inside.

"Jeez. I think she likes you." Aden smirked.

"You say that like it's a bad thing," he teased, reaching for her hand. He pulled her into his chest in a tight embrace. "Be safe tonight."

"You too," she admonished. "Don't go getting yourself hurt chasing after bad guys."

He released her just enough to see her face, but still held her close. "Can I see you tomorrow?"

Aden grinned, nodding and tilted her face up to meet his in a kiss. The world spun away again for a brief moment. When he pulled away, sighing, reality rushed back in.

"Um, I have to work tomorrow until 5:00."

"Didn't you take any time off for end of school celebrations or anything?" he chided.

"No, I need the hours." She shrugged. "Plus, I didn't know I'd *have* any plans to need off for, at the time."

"Such a responsible girl." He shook his head.

"You say that like it's a bad thing." She grinned.

"Can I pick you up from work, then?"

"That'd be great." She smiled. "I'll see you then."

"See you then." He released her and waited until she'd closed the door behind her before he left.

C ome on, Drew! You're making us both late!" Aden shouted. She was standing in the courtyard at the bottom of the garage stairs. Drew emerged a moment later, pausing long enough to lock the door behind him before he stumbled down the stairs.

"Okay, let's go." He followed Aden into the garage where his beat-up Honda stood. "Did you open the garage door?" he asked. She nodded impatiently. "Just making sure I didn't leave it open last night."

"What time did you get home anyway?"

"I dunno. Around 1:00, I guess. Billy Ray took me to a party at one of his friend's houses. I knew a few of the people there, and I got to talkin'. Next thing I knew, Billy Ray had ditched me. I had to find somebody willing to drive back to the shop so I could get my car to come home."

"Nice," Aden winced. "I can't believe he'd just leave you there."

Drew shrugged. "Probably picked up a girl."

"I don't know how you hang around him. He gives me the creeps."

"Ah, he's not so bad." They drove in silence for a few minutes. "So, looks like I can get you to work on time, but I'm gonna be a few minutes late."

"Just tell old Mr. Payne that his son ditched you last night and you were late getting home as a result."

"Like Mr. Payne would give a …rip," he caught himself. "How are things going with you and Maddox?"

"That's changing the subject."

"I hear you two have spent quite a lot of time together this week."

137

"So?"

"So, I just want to be sure he's treating you right."

"Why would you think he would treat me badly?"

"I don't, Jeez. Just checkin' on my sister." He shook his head, dramatically. "So are you two like an item?"

"An item?" she grimaced. "We're just hanging out. Getting to know each other."

"So how long will he be in town?"

"I don't know. Why are you being so nosy?"

"It's not nosy. I care, so sue me."

"I'm fine. Maddox is great. I enjoy spending time with him, and I appreciate your concern." She smiled, with a teasing glint in her eyes. "Oh, and he's picking me up at the store when I get off, so I won't be coming to the garage."

"Must be love." He smiled and ducked a half-hearted fist to his arm. He pulled up to the curb in front of the jewelry store and stopped. "Have a lovely day."

"You're so immature." Aden shook her head, but she was smiling. "Thanks for caring." She jumped out and waited for him to pull away before heading to the front of the store. Only then did she realize the sidewalk wasn't empty.

"Oh, hey Beverly." She took in the dark storefront. "Mr. Keith's not here yet?"

"No, third time recently, too." Beverly surveyed her from head to toe. "Last week, I waited for almost fifteen minutes in the heat before he showed up."

"That's weird," Aden said. "Hope everything's okay."

"He's fantastic, I'm sure," she said sarcastically, "but my hair and makeup are wilting in this humidity." Aden didn't answer, looking up and down the street for an approaching Mr. Keith. Of course, she realized, she didn't even know what kind of car he drove or from which direction he'd be coming. He'd always already been here when her shift began, and she left before he did. "I haven't seen you here in a while. Thought maybe you quit."

"I took the week off for final exams," Aden said simply. Beverly's annoyance factor was higher than usual today.

"Oh, you're in school?"

"We've talked about my classes before, Beverly, about the school and how popular you were when you went there," Aden said, her face expressionless.

Beverly just smiled, "I was the queen. Homecoming. Head cheerleader. Student Council..."

"Yes, you told me." Aden glanced up and down the street again then checked the time on her phone. "It's only 9:06. I'm sure he'll be here in a sec."

"And how would you know that?" Beverly looked suspicious.

"I don't. Call it wishful thinking. He's just not usually late." She frowned.

"I just told you he was late three times in the last couple of weeks." Beverly huffed, still looking her up and down.

"Ladies. Won't you come in?" Mr. Keith had opened the door behind them. He must have entered through the back. "The safe is already open, so let's get to work. Beverly, Aden will show you the new merchandise layout. It's really impressive."

Beverly paused on her way through the showroom to glare at Aden. Aden was a little shaken at the pure malicious intent she saw on the woman's face. "I'm sure it's quite impressive," she almost hissed.

Mr. Keith didn't seem to notice, but hurried back into his office. Aden followed, and with a few re-directions to Beverly, they got the cases laid out. Aden stayed as far as she could from the other woman within the small confines of the showroom. Beverly didn't try to speak to her anymore, and Aden was grateful. She'd had just about enough of the grating suspicion and disparaging looks. She spent her time polishing the glass cabinets and minutely tweaking the placement of every merchandise tray in the cases. She would jump to help the few customers that had come in that morning, just to break the monotonous tension. A few minutes before 11:00, Aden's attention was drawn to the window. Maddox was sauntering slowly by, checking out the front window. He looked up at her and winked before continuing down the sidewalk.

Just the sight of him made her heart soar, and she was still smiling several minutes later when an older gentleman came in.

"Good morning ladies, I was told to ask for Aden..." he said, glancing at Beverly momentarily, but turning to smile at Aden.

"I'm Aden," she said, mystified. "How can I help you?"

"Ah, I knew it'd be you. I just met a young man over at the coffee shop, and during our conversation, I mentioned that my anniversary is coming up. He directed me to you for your help in finding a gift for my wife. He told me to look for the prettiest girl on the square." The man's eyes twinkled mischievously in a face that looked younger than the stoop of his shoulders and the cut of his clothes.

Aden's laugh came with a blush. "You're very kind, Mr. ...?"

"Vinings." He inclined his head like in an old movie. "Julian Vinings."

"It's very nice to meet you, Mr. Vinings."

"Oh please, call me Jules. Mr. Vinings makes me feel so old."

She smiled. "Jules. What kind of jewelry does your wife wear?"

Beverly watched with mounting malice as Aden showed the new customer several pieces. They conversed and laughed like old friends as he deliberated. It was close to an hour later when Aden was gift wrapping the exquisite pair of pearl and diamond earrings and ringing up the sale.

"Aden, I am so happy that young man directed me to you. Thank you for your patience with an old man, and my wife will thank you as well, I suspect, when she sees this gift. It will be a special day." Aden smiled and walked with him to the door.

"You're very welcome, Jules. Please stop back by any time."

He smiled and waved before leaving, and Aden waved back as she pulled the door closed.

"Please come back any time, Jules," Beverly simpered, in a twisted imitation. "God, you're a flirt."

Aden stared at her and took a long, deep breath. She decided to ignore her again. A few minutes later, Mr. Keith emerged from the back.

"I heard the sounds of sales out here. How's it going?"

"You heard the sound of flirting, you mean." Beverly laughed. "Aden made a spectacle of herself."

"Aden made polite conversation with every customer that's come in this morning," Aden said sternly, in Beverly's direction. "And Aden has made three sales today, including the pair of pearl and diamond earrings from the window."

Mr. Keith looked from Aden to Beverly and back. "Everything…okay out here, ladies?"

"Just a little healthy competition." Beverly shrugged, smiling.

"And how many sales have you made?" he asked. Her smile dropped instantly. "Or is that not the kind of competition you meant?" She looked away, but didn't answer. He sighed, "Aden, why don't you go ahead and take a lunch hour? I'll see you back at 1:00."

"But, I was only scheduled for a half-hour lunch today," she reminded him.

"You've earned it. Take the extra half-hour." She caught an unpleasant undercurrent in his demeanor that made her suddenly uncomfortable. She nodded quickly, thanking him as she ran to grab her purse and practically jogged out the front door.

She'd brought a sandwich from home that she'd planned to eat in the park, but now she had an extra half an hour to kill. She headed for the café a block down the street. She shook out her hands at her sides as she walked, trying to shake off the bad vibes from the jewelry store.

"Hey Aden! Wait up!" She turned to see Maddox running to catch up from behind her.

"Maddox! What are you doing here?"

"Stalking you, of course." He smiled, but then frowned in concern. "Are you okay?"

"I'm fine. Have you been hanging around out here all day?"

"Not all day. I've checked in every now and then." He searched her face. "Is that too weird?"

"No," she shook her head for a greater effect. "It's not you. I'm sorry. I'm so glad to see you." She was; just having him near made her feel better.

"What's wrong?"

"Just work. People at work. It's been a weird day." She tried to smile, but he just looked more concerned.

"Did Mr. Vinings come in to see you?" he asked.

"Jules? Yes, he was the highlight of the day. Until now." Her smile this time was genuine.

"Jules." He grinned. "So I guess you two hit it off." Aden nodded. "So did something else happen?"

"It's just co-workers." She shrugged. "I was headed to the café. Can you join me?"

"I'll have to consult my busy schedule…" he whipped out his phone and pretended to check his calendar.

"Shut up. Come on." She grabbed his hand and started walking.

After their order was delivered to the table, Aden filled him in on her day while they ate.

"Beverly sounds like hell on wheels." He frowned.

"More like a bitch on stilettos," Aden mumbled, making Maddox laugh loudly.

"Sorry, that was just kind of unexpected coming from you."

"I can take care of myself." She frowned.

"No argument here." He held up his palms in surrender. "So it sounds like your boss was going to reprimand her while you were gone. Maybe it'll be better this afternoon."

"I hope so. I've never seen a clock tick so slowly in my life." She glanced at the clock on the wall. "And of course, now it's racing past. I've got to be back in a few minutes."

"I almost forgot. Cadence wants to know if you'll come to her house after work to help her get ready for her date with Trey."

Aden laughed. "And what about you? What will you be doing?"

"Hey, I've got an opinion. I can help navigate the finer points of a wardrobe." His light, bantering attitude was just what Aden needed.

"Thanks for lunch, oh, and for the referral this morning. Jules was a great customer."

"My pleasure," he said, following her outside.

"How did you two meet anyway?" Aden asked, walking slowly back toward the jewelry store. "He mentioned the coffee shop?"

"Yeah, it was a little crowded, and he asked if he could sit at my table. We were just conversing politely, and he brought up his upcoming anniversary and how he felt he'd disappointed his wife with last year's gift. So I sent him to you."

"What did he get her last year?"

142

"A mixer or something, some kind of kitchen appliance?" Maddox shrugged. "He said she'd been talking about wanting one. But apparently not for their anniversary."

"Anniversary gifts should be romantic." Aden nodded. "He got her a really nice pair of pearl and diamond earrings. She should be happy with him this year." She stopped on the sidewalk, sighing, just before they reached the jewelry shop. "Four more hours."

He pulled her into a hug. "That's not so long, and I'll be waiting right here at 5:00. Promise we'll find some way to salvage your day."

"Thanks," she said, releasing him. "I'll see you later."

He smiled, and she trudged into the store.

Beverly didn't look up from where she sulked behind the counter. Mr. Keith must have been in his office again. The afternoon went faster than Aden would have thought. Beverly took her lunch hour when Aden returned. Several more customers came in, mostly to browse, but she made another couple of sales. When she came back from lunch, Beverly completely ignored her presence and actually helped a few customers.

At 4:30, Aden saw Maddox walk by again; this time, he was across the street. He was carrying a bag from the shipping/copier place down the block. She thought he must be running errands for his mom, and she watched him, smiling, until he was out of sight.

"How many men are you stringin' along?" Beverly asked, with a quick glance toward the back.

"What?"

"Well, I saw you go to lunch with that hunky dark-haired one that just walked by again, but he's not the one who dropped you off." She tried to make her smile genuine and polite. It didn't work.

"I'm not stringing anybody at all."

"So you wouldn't mind if I got to know Mr. Dark and Handsome a little better, then? I've seen him around the square several times. He's a hard one to miss."

Aden knew she was just trying to get under her skin, and she wasn't going to give her the satisfaction. "I don't keep his social calendar, so you can give it a try, I guess. How old are you again? Like 29?"

"I'm 23," she seethed, "and I don't mind 'em a bit younger, especially when they look like that."

Aden just shrugged, as though completely unconcerned, and went back to wiping counters. A few minutes later, Mr. Keith emerged from the back.

"How's it going out here ladies?"

"Just fine," Beverly answered. Aden just smiled.

"Will you watch the store for just a minute?" he asked Beverly. "I need to talk to Aden about her schedule." Beverly just nodded as Aden followed him to the counter in the back where they rang up sales. Normally, he had his big calendar in hand where he would hand-write the employees' schedule in pencil before entering into his archaic computer for the official printout. Now, he stood with one hand on the counter and the other on his hip, looking at her for an awkward moment.

"So, do you have plans this summer I should know about?" he began. "Vacation? Family obligations?"

"No, we have no plans that I know about right now," Aden answered.

"What about your social life? Friends? Parties? Boyfriends?"

"Um…I don't know of anything that would affect my work schedule."

"Oh come on, I know you all hang out at the lake, right? Maybe drive up into the mountains?" He smiled. Aden wasn't sure what he was getting at.

"Well, yeah, but I do those things on my days off. There shouldn't be any scheduling conflicts."

Mr. Keith just nodded, staring at her. She glanced at Beverly, who was hanging on every word across the small showroom.

"So where do you kids hang out these days?" he asked. "We used to go to movies and the state park and hike different trails. Where do you all go?"

"Um, same places, I guess. There aren't that many choices around here, locally."

He stared at her, knocking his knuckles against the counter a few times. "So what about tonight? It's Saturday. You're probably going out, right?"

She shrugged. "I guess." He seemed to become more perturbed with her responses, but she wasn't sure why he would need to know specifics about her social life. She thought they were discussing the work schedule. "Do you need me to stay late?"

"No, no. Mrs. McConnell is coming in." He smiled. "I was just making small talk."

"Okay." She smiled and hoped it didn't look as awkward as she felt.

"Alright." He nodded. "Good." With another rap or two on the counter, he went back to his office.

Mrs. McConnell came in just a few minutes later and after stowing her big bag in the back, exchanged pleasantries with Aden and Beverly. At 5:00, Aden clocked out.

"See you tomorrow, Mr. Keith." She called.

"Have a good evening," he answered through his closed office door.

"Thanks." She searched the front window for Maddox as she walked to the front, but didn't see him or his car. She smiled to Beverly and Mrs. McConnell as she walked out.

Maddox was leaning against the wall just out of sight of the jewelry store window.

"Hi." She smiled.

"See? It's over. You made it." He smiled back. "Ready to go?"

She nodded, and they started walking, hand in hand, the couple of blocks to Cadence's house. She resisted the urge to glance inside the jewelry store window as they walked by it. She was sure Beverly would be watching.

Cadence met them on her front porch.

"Oh my God, I thought you'd never get here." She said loudly as soon as Aden and Maddox came into view. "I feel like I haven't seen you in forever." She said, hugging Aden. Aden just laughed.

"I just saw you yesterday."

"That was at school. I meant, we haven't really had a chance to talk in a while." She ushered them into rocking chairs under the whirring fan. "Seriously, I've had to get all the news from my Mom and Kim and Daddy Max, and you know they don't tell us everything."

"What's to tell?"

145

"What?!" Cadence shouted. "Um, your house was broken into. There was some strange truck parked by your driveway. You two went on a date last night?" she looked incredulous. "And we haven't talked about any of it."

"You already grilled me about last night," Maddox pointed out.

"Yeah, but I need Aden's point of view," she huffed, as though it was too obvious. Aden and Maddox exchanged a smile.

"So what do you want to know?" Aden asked, settling back into the chair.

"Well, let's start with the date." She grinned.

"Okay, that's my cue. I'll be inside," Maddox sighed, getting up.

"We won't be long," Cadence promised, then turned to Aden before he was through the front door. "Okay, so how was it?"

"It was really nice." Aden smiled. "I had a great time." Cadence gestured with her hands for more information. "Um, I guess Maddox told you where we went?"

"Well, he won't tell me specifically, but he described the place. Guess it's a big, secret location."

"It's breathtaking. The view goes on forever, and the wind in the rocks sounds almost human." Cadence grimaced. "No, it's really cool. I just can't describe it right. Maddox brought a blanket and lantern and some grapes and cheese, and binoculars. We did some stargazing. Oh! And there was this meteor." Aden took a deep breath. "It was just a really beautiful night."

"Hello? The kiss?" Cadence waved impatiently. Aden laughed. She'd known that was the part Cadence really wanted to hear.

"So what did Maddox say?"

"About the kiss?" Cadence grinned.

"The date in general...and the kiss." Aden laughed.

"He talked about it the same way you just did, with stars in his eyes. He said you are beautiful in lantern light and that he couldn't help but kiss you, but he wouldn't say much of anything else. Kept telling me it was none of my business."

"Well, I don't know what to say about it all either. It was...awesome. I just don't know the right words to describe it." She shrugged. "I can't believe I just met him a few days ago."

"I *knew* you two would hit it off." Cadence beamed. "You owe me big time."

"Well, I've wanted to kill you several times this week for helping me to humiliate myself, but I guess I *do* owe you one," she conceded. "So let's go get you ready for *your* big date."

For the next hour and a half, Cadence modeled various outfits and hairstyles. She and Aden would put an outfit together and then traipse down the stairs to get Maddox's opinion. To Aden's surprise, he was quite opinionated, but she suspected some of it was just to tease his sister. Finally, they all agreed on a teal sundress with sandals. Aden did her makeup and hair, sweeping her blond locks into a casual up-do, and escorted her downstairs.

"Okay, this is it. The final reveal." Aden called before they entered the dining room where Maddox sat, working on his laptop. Maddox smiled and rose when they came in, making Cadence turn around as he inspected her with a serious expression.

"Well, I still think you should wear a sweater or a scarf or something," he critiqued.

"Oh my God, it's like a hundred degrees outside, and you said that about every outfit. You'd have me in a turtleneck if you could." Cadence rolled her eyes.

"Seriously, you look very nice. Trey is a lucky man," Maddox said, giving her a hug. "What time is he picking you up, anyway?"

"He should be here any minute."

"Oh! Well I've got to hide then. I'm supposed to be sick, remember?" Aden asked.

"Come on. We can go up to my room," Maddox said, picking up his computer. Aden was intrigued. She'd forgotten all about the bedroom at the end of the upstairs hall that had never been occupied when she was here. She'd known for years that it belonged to Cadence's step-brother, but she'd never actually been inside it, never thought much about it. She followed him up the stairs and down the narrow guest hallway.

"So, I guess this end of the house at the back was originally servants' quarters, according to LeighAnn," He explained. "It used to be three small bedrooms and a bath, but Dad and LeighAnn remodeled it into a guest wing with two bigger bedrooms and a bathroom in between." He ushered her into the bedroom on the left. The pale gray walls contrasted with the cheery white trim of the baseboards, crown molding, and window trim. The queen-sized bed was draped in a darker grey comforter with a few orange accents. An iPod deck and speakers took up one of the shelves on the massive bookshelf on one side of the room, while the other shelves were crammed with books and miscellaneous personal items. Most were from days gone by: a dirty baseball and battered glove, an old, broken compass, a few scattered sea shells, what looked like a rock collection, and even one of the pairs of binoculars he'd brought along the night before.

"Yeah, most of that stuff's been sitting there for years." He shrugged self-consciously and grabbed a t-shirt from the upholstered chair in the corner and tossed it into a hamper in the closet.

"It's too clean in here. You're never allowed to see my room," she complained.

"Well, I've been staying mostly at the hotel with my Mom. And of course, most of my belongings are at home in Virginia. It isn't this clean when I'm staying here for any length of time." The thought seemed to sober him.

"I feel better then, I guess." She laughed. Just then, Cadence stormed up the stairs and into the doorway.

"He's here! Maddox, you've got to answer the door and let him in; nobody else is home."

"Patience is here, I saw her earlier." Maddox frowned. "And why don't you answer the door yourself? He's your date."

"I can't answer the door! I have to make an entrance." She rolled her eyes. "Don't you know anything?"

"It's not like a dance or something," Maddox mumbled, heading for the hallway.

"Men!" Cadence huffed, following him into the hallway. "Just go down and answer the door."

Maddox mumbled under his breath all the way down the stairs. Cadence and Aden stood in the upstairs hallway, just out of sight as the doorbell rang. Maddox opened it immediately.

"Oh, hey Maddox," Trey said, a little surprised.

"He should have waited a few seconds," Cadence whispered, "Oh my God."

"Hey Trey, come on in." Maddox waved him inside. "Cadence will be down in a minute."

"Thanks. How are you doin'?"

"Just fine. You?"

"Doin' alright I guess."

The exchange was awkward even at a distance, and Aden pushed Cadence toward the stairs. *Go on*, she mouthed silently and moved to where she could peek down the stairwell.

"Hey, Trey." Cadence called, regally descending the staircase.

"Oh, hey, Cadence. Wow, you look nice." He smiled.

"Thanks, so do you."

Maddox stood behind Trey and rolled his eyes.

"So Aden's still sick huh?" Trey asked.

"Yeah. Just a summer cold she thought, but she wanted to stay home and rest," Cadence said smoothly. "I hope you don't mind that it's just us."

"No, not at all. You ready to go?"

"Sure, let's go." She squinted at Maddox who obediently opened the door as Trey and Cadence turned to go. "Thanks, Maddox," she said sweetly.

"Behave yourself." He shook his head slowly. Cadence winked and pulled the door closed behind her. Maddox watched them through the window until they were in his car and turned as Aden came down the stairs. "She's a force of nature."

Aden laughed. "Gotta love her."

"Trey is a brave man." He grinned. "So, what do you want to do this evening?"

"I'm not sure." She bit her lip as she deliberated. "We could hang out at my house for a while. Drew said he was hanging out there after work today. We could watch a movie or walk up the river?"

"Sounds good." He agreed.

Dank. Dark. The air is wet and cool. There is slow breathing to the left, ragged sobbing to the right, and a silent figure curled on a filthy mattress on a cement floor directly ahead.

149

Excitement. Satisfaction…and indecision. I can…oh, so many things I can do. The scene swivels to the left, to a figure curled tightly into a dark corner. The dark one, my milk chocolate beauty, my first living doll. Should I have just a taste…? Oh, I could. I can. I can do anything I want to her. But not yet.

The scene swivels again to the right. A blond woman is chained to a post sunk into the floor and quietly sobbing. Barbie's sobs are glorious and darkly exciting. A step towards her, and a long sigh…but I must wait. All in good time. The brunette doll on the mattress is quiet. Her submittal is an ache, inviting me to…but no. The long, slow anticipation is a constant arousal, almost peaking. But I am in control, patient. Control.

Mine. All mine. But it's not right yet. Not finished. On a wall to the left, there are shackles and chains bolted into the concrete, awaiting fragile wrists and ankles. I can almost see the slender figure, arms and legs stretched out and away from a torso of pale, soft skin, and huge, terrified blue eyes staring out from a fall of auburn hair. Deep breaths. Not yet, but soon. Soon. My collection will be complete. And I can begin to play.

"Maddox! What is it?" Aden gasped. She was shaking his arm. "Hey!"

"Sorry," he mumbled, dropping his face into his hands and wiping hard, as if to erase thoughts from his head. He desperately wanted a long, hot shower. "I'm really sorry. How long…" His voice trailed off, and he raised his head and looked around, taking deep breaths. He was sitting on the back deck of Aden's house. Late afternoon sunlight slanted through the trees to the noisy river passing below.

"Are you okay?" The fear on her face almost mirrored the face in the vision, and he closed his eyes, shuddering.

"I'm fine. Really." He breathed deeply. "I'm so sorry." He opened his eyes. She was still crouching beside his chair, grasping his arm. He tried to smile. "I just need a minute."
"Was it a vision?" she asked just above a whisper.

He nodded slowly. "Where's Drew?" he'd been out here with them earlier.

"He got a phone call. Remember?" Aden still frowned, concerned.

He did remember. The three of them had gathered on the deck talking and laughing. They'd eaten sandwiches and lingered in the shaded, cooling air. Drew's cell phone had rung, and he'd jumped up and left them with a grin and wag of his eyebrows. Had to be a girl on the line.

"So he was gone before I…blanked out?" she nodded.

150

"You're okay?"

"Yes, I promise. I'm fine." His smile was almost convincing. Then, he suddenly pulled her onto his lap into a tight embrace. "And so are you. You're safe. I swear it." There was a menace in his voice that she'd never heard.

Aden clung to him as desperately as he seemed to hold her. Her heart was still racing, and she burrowed as close to him as she could, reveling in his nearness.

"What did you see?" she whispered. His arms tightened around her, but he didn't answer for a long moment.

"I saw…what he was seeing. What he was thinking." He shuddered, and a trickle of fear ran down Aden's neck. His eyes were shut tight against the memories. "I need to call my Mom."

"Maddox." She waited until he looked at her. "What did you see?"

He stared at her for a moment, and she could tell he was deciding whether or not to answer. He watched her carefully as he slowly began to speak.

"The three women are alive, I think. They're in a concrete room." He paused. "He's a collector. Thinks of them as dolls." His lip curled up in disgust, and then he took a deep breath before continuing, "And his collection's not finished." He paused again, searching her face with a concern that turned the trickles of sweat on her neck suddenly icy. "I think…I think he's coming after…"

"Me." She finished quietly as the ice spread through her veins. His arms tightened again.

"I swear to you, Aden," he said with a sudden fury, "he will not touch you."

"Are you sure it's me he wants?"

"I can't be positive, but he was thinking about…red hair."

"My hair isn't really red," she said. Maddox started shaking his head as she continued, "Wait though, there are other red heads in town."

"I know. Like I said, I can't be absolutely sure." He frowned. "But he saw *you* at the lake, and somebody broke into *your* house, and a mysterious truck was parked by *your* driveway."

"But—"

"He won't touch you. I swear it," he vowed again. "We're going to find him. Stop him."

"Well I don't want you near him, either." Aden frowned. "You're not a cop, you know. And who knows what this maniac is capable of?"

"It's not me he wants to 'collect,'" he ground out, furious.

"But what will he do if you get in his way?"

"Will you stop worrying about *me*?" He was exasperated.

"No, I won't." She frowned back. "Not until this is over." She stood, regretful that she couldn't sit still any longer; she'd much rather have stayed on his lap, but she couldn't contain the nervous energy pulsing through her limbs. She shook out her hands and arms at her sides and walked to the railing overlooking the river, pacing from one side of the deck to the other. Her eyes scanned the darkening woods, shadows stretching out on every side as the sun sank behind the mountain. It would be full dark in just a few more minutes. She shuddered. *What if he was out there, watching?*

Maddox came up behind her and grasped her shoulders to stop her pacing.

"I'm sorry I scared you."

"It's not you I'm afraid of."

"I know, but we were having a nice evening until I…had to go and spoil—"

"So did you flash into that creep's head on purpose?" she challenged.

"Of course not."

"Then stop apologizing for things that aren't under your control." He released her shoulders, and she turned to face him. "You wanna go inside? It's almost dark and I feel…I dunno, like he could be out there watching us."

"He's not. Not right now, at least." Aden just stared at him as he slowly examined her face. A slow smile lit a mischievous glint in his eyes as they softened. "Right now, it's just you and me." He leaned in slowly, and his lips met hers as his arms wound around her waist. Her fear was gone in an instant. She felt like a silly little girl, with all the danger surrounding them, all she could think in that moment was of him. There was just him. Holding her. Caressing her face. Looking at her with that adorably uneven smile. *He is so stinkin' gorgeous.*

A door slammed, knocking her from her reverie, and Drew called from the kitchen.

"Sorry 'bout that! Had to take that call though." He grinned, coming through the door onto the patio a moment later.

"Important business?" Aden sighed, stepping out of Maddox's embrace. He gently pulled her back, draping a casual arm around her shoulders.

Drew eyed the two of them for a second, then shrugged. "Yeah, I guess you could say that."

"Oh good grief, just say it was a girl." She rolled her eyes as Drew smiled. "We were going inside. It got dark while you were, um, on the phone."

"Okay, I was thinking about watching a movie."

"You're not going out?" She was surprised. Drew didn't meet her gaze as he answered.

"Decided to stay in, but I did invite someone over. Hope you don't mind." That was a first. Drew had never invited anyone to the house that she knew of. He glanced at Maddox in a way that suddenly made her suspicious. Maddox's carefully blank face confirmed that something was up.

"Okay, what's going on?"

"What?" Drew shrugged, leading the way inside and turning on lights as he went. "You know Mom would have a fit if I left you here with Maddox—alone."

"I know the rules, thanks, and I know there's something else going on with you two." She eyed them both, brows raised. Drew looked to Maddox and raised his hands in surrender.

"I'm gonna go make popcorn. Why don't you guys pick out the movie?" he asked, and he scurried into the kitchen. Aden rounded on Maddox, arms crossed.

"What?" he asked innocently. She just stared, one eyebrow still raised. He sighed. "It's really not a big deal."

"What's not a big deal?"

He gently pulled her to sit on the couch beside him. "I asked Drew to hang around tonight." That surprised her. "We don't know what this guy could do next."

"I can't believe he would agree. It's Saturday night." She frowned.

"He's your brother. Your house was broken into on Wednesday. On Friday, there was a

153

truck parked—"

"I know. We just went through all that."

"He's worried about you, too. He was asking me what I knew about the case, and I told him everything I could." She wondered when they'd had that conversation.

"So he invited a girl over? Right into ground zero of this guy's weird…" She shook her head as her voice trailed off in search of the right word for what was happening.

"Obsession?" he offered grimly, and she nodded once. "There's safety in numbers."

"So you had this planned already?"

He shrugged. "I'm going to do everything that can be done to make sure you're safe."

"But do you have to keep me in the dark about it?"

"Sorry. It wasn't really a secret."

"You just didn't tell me." She frowned; he sighed.

"I really am sorry." The sincerity of his gaze made her annoyance feel suddenly childish.

"Maddox, I really do appreciate everything you're doing, the time that you're spending—"

"Hey, do you guys want some white cheese on this popcorn?' Drew interrupted from the kitchen behind her. Maddox chuckled.

"That sounds good," he answered. "Is that a car I hear?"

"Yeah, it's Natalie." Drew shrugged. "I was giving her directions earlier on the phone." Maddox nodded as Drew went outside to greet her.

"Natalie," Aden repeated. "I think he's been out with her before."

A moment later, Drew came back in with a tall, pretty brunette in his wake. "Come on in," he said, "This is my sister Aden and her boyfriend Maddox. Guys, this is Natalie."

"Hey there. It's so nice to meet you, Aden. I've heard so much about you." Natalie smiled.

"It's nice to meet you, too." Aden smiled back. She wasn't sure what else to say; she hadn't heard anything about Natalie before now; at least, nothing she remembered anyway, and she wasn't sure if Natalie had any idea about the large red target on the house in which she stood.

"Hi, Natalie. I believe we met last summer." Maddox smiled.

"We did, briefly. You're the mysterious brother of the Kendall triplets, right?" It was all Aden could do not to react. Yet another person in town who knew Maddox already. Seriously, she was going to have to get out more often from now on.

"Well, I am their brother, dunno about the mysterious part." He smiled.

"So Aden, how'd you get past this guy's notoriously cold shoulder?" Natalie teased good-naturedly. Aden just raised her eyebrows in confusion. "Every summer he came to town, he'd cause a ruckus among all the single ladies trying to catch his attention, but I never heard of him giving anybody the time of day, until now."

"Okay well, that's an exaggeration –" Maddox started, holding up his hands.

"You want something to drink, Natalie?" Drew interrupted. "We were gonna do popcorn and a movie."

"Cool. I'll have whatever you're having." She smiled at him, and Aden could see more than friendship in her demeanor, though she seemed to try to hide it. "What are we watching?"

"Dunno yet. Did you guys pick something out?" he asked Aden and Maddox.

"Not yet," Aden answered.

"Excuse me, I need to go make a quick phone call before the movie starts," Maddox said, heading back for the deck.

"We were thinking maybe a comedy would be good?" Aden continued, watching Maddox from the corner of her eye. She knew he was calling his Mom to fill her in on his flash. She hoped his Mom wouldn't want him to leave, or worse, for her to come here for more questioning.

"I love comedies," Natalie answered.

"Come on in, and let's get comfortable," Aden said, leading the way to the couches in the den.

By the time Maddox returned, apologizing, they'd selected a movie and had it cued up to play.

The movie was a great distraction for Aden. She and Maddox had curled up on one couch, while Drew and Natalie were on the other. She leaned back against Maddox's warm chest as he slowly brushed his fingers through her hair. There were several times she almost fell asleep, but the movie was a good one, and she laughed enough to stay awake.

When the credits rolled, she glanced at the other couch. Drew was asleep, breathing deeply, his arm still draped around Natalie where she lay in front of him. Natalie was awake but seemed quietly content to stay where she was.

"Who's got the remote?" Maddox asked.

"I think Drew had it," Aden said, starting to get up.

"He's asleep. I'll get it." Natalie said quietly. She rose up on one elbow and looked around, spying it on top of the cushions at the back of the couch. "Aha." She grabbed it and tossed it gently to Aden. "Sorry, your remote looks totally different than mine."

Maddox had caught the remote before Aden had even registered it sailing towards her, and he turned the cable on and the volume down. Either the movement or the noises had awakened Drew, and he sat up, sniffing and stretching.

"Great movie." He grinned.

"You missed half of it," Natalie pointed out.

"Yeah, but I enjoyed it anyway." He yawned. "What time is it?"

"Almost eleven," Maddox answered. "I should get going." Aden sighed, disappointed. "I'll be back tomorrow," he whispered in her ear, causing goose bumps to pop up on her arms.

"Should we…um, go take a look around?" Drew asked. "I'm gonna walk Natalie to her car, anyway."

Natalie looked confused.

"I was going to, before I left," Maddox said, looking out the big glass doors to the darkness beyond. "I don't mind following Natalie home either, if it's not too weird, I mean."

Aden jumped up and began locking the big glass doors and putting the security bar down.

"Ahhh, what's going on?" Natalie asked.

"Just taking precautions," Drew answered. "That last kidnapping was too close to home. We're just making sure everybody gets home safe."

"Oh," she sounded surprised.

Maddox double-checked the locks Aden had just locked as she went into her Mother's bedroom to check those doors. Drew checked the front door in the foyer and met Maddox at the bottom of the stairs to the second floor.

"I'll go," Drew said, heading up.

"This is some production," Natalie observed, frowning.

"Somebody broke in here earlier this week," Maddox explained as Aden emerged from the bedroom.

"Oh my God, you're kidding!" Natalie exclaimed, rising from the couch. "Drew didn't mention it."

"It wasn't a huge deal." Aden smiled. She could imagine what they all must look like to somebody who didn't know. "They didn't take anything. We think Maddox and I scared him away."

"You were here?" her eyes were huge.

"Well, we pulled up and saw somebody in the house so we called the cops and waited outside."

"Holy cow!" her huge eyes tracked Drew coming down the stairs. "So did they catch him?"

"Not yet," Drew answered. "But I had all the locks changed since then. We're just being careful."

"Wow," she said. "I'm glad you're all okay."

Drew smiled back, then glanced to Maddox, who was all business.

"Why don't you ladies wait here for just a moment while Drew and I go check outside?"

Natalie looked at Aden, who just nodded as the men headed out the kitchen door into the courtyard, pulling the door shut behind them.

"I can't believe somebody broke in here," Natalie said, concerned.

"Me either." Aden gave her a half-hearted smile.

"Looks like you've got your own personal protector, though." She smiled in return.

"Yeah, I do. I don't know what I would have done if Maddox hadn't been with me the other day." She shuddered.

"You two make a cute couple."

"Thanks. So do you and Drew."

Natalie smiled. "I like to think so anyway."

"How long have you two been going out?"

"I dunno. Off and on for a few weeks lately." She shrugged. "We went out for a few months back in high school."

"Oh." Aden frowned; she should have known that. Now, she remembered where she'd heard the name Natalie before. Drew had complained bitterly to her one night about a stalker ex-girlfriend… "Maybe it just wasn't the right time back then."

"Well, we both had a lot of growing up to do. That was back in Junior year."

"I just finished Junior year." Aden said, wincing a bit.

"No way! I'd have sworn you were older." She seemed sincere. "You seem to have your life together so much more than I did at that age."

"Not so much," Aden mumbled, "But it's good that I can give off that impression, I guess."

Natalie smiled. "Well, you have two men in your life who adore you." Aden raised a brow in question. "Your brother and Maddox, of course."

"I am lucky, I guess," Aden conceded.

"Drew talks about you all the time. He's so proud of you."

"Seriously?"

Natalie nodded. "I'm serious." She laughed. "And then there's Maddox Dixon...kudos on hooking that one, girlfriend." Aden laughed with her.

"What's so funny?" Drew asked through the partially open door.

"Natalie. She's a hoot," Aden said, still laughing.

"Okay then. All's quiet out here," he said, holding the door open in invitation. The girls walked outside.

Natalie's car was parked beside Maddox's in the courtyard.

"Where's Maddox?" Aden asked, looking around.

"Checking the perimeter," Drew answered in a demeanor so serious it made Aden giggle. "What?"

"Nothing. I'm glad I have both of you." She surprised him with a quick hug.

"Aww, you guys are so cute." Natalie hugged them both. "Thanks for inviting me over."

"No big deal," Drew said. "Thanks for coming out here."

"It's not that far." Natalie shrugged. "I had a good time."

"Me too." He smiled. Aden stepped away from them, heading for one corner of the house to look for Maddox.

"Where are you going?" his voice came from behind her, and brought a smile to her lips.

"I was looking for you." He had come around the opposite corner and veered around Drew and Natalie, now standing between the cars. "Everything look okay out there?"

"You wouldn't still be standing here if it didn't." He pulled her gently toward him and wrapped his arms around her shoulders. She peeked toward Drew and Natalie, but their attention was wrapped up in each other. "Thanks for having me over tonight."

"Apparently, I wasn't the one who invited you," she said, alluding to the plan he'd hatched with Drew earlier.

"On the contrary, you did invite me." He laughed. "Standing in my Dad's foyer."

"Hmmm," she conceded, "so I did. Well, I'm glad you came over."

"Me too." He leaned down for a long, slow kiss. Aden's hyper-awareness of her brother and Natalie faded into the background until she forgot there was anyone else in the world but Maddox. He ended the kiss, but put his forehead to hers. "Stay safe."

"I will," she promised. She would have promised him anything at all with his eyes probing her soul the way they were. "You be careful, too."

"Of course." He smiled, melting her concerns away.

"You're gonna follow Natalie home?" she asked.

"Yeah. Are you okay with that?"

"Why wouldn't I be?"

"Just making sure." He shrugged. "I want to be sure she makes it home okay – just in case anybody's watching your house." He stopped, frowning.

"It's okay. I'm the one who asked why she'd walk into the big red target. I get it."

"Well, I just, you know, I want to be sure you're not the jealous type." He grinned. "You have absolutely no reason to be jealous, you know."

"Don't I?" she teased, "I mean, I keep hearing about all these other women pursuing you…" He cocked his head to the side, and she laughed. "Don't worry. I know I'm extremely fortunate to have you protecting me, but I'm not the crazy jealous type."

"Protecting?" He frowned. "You know why I'm so protective of you, don't you?"

"Hey Maddox," Drew called. "You following Natalie home or do you want me to?"

"Point taken," Maddox called back over his shoulder. "Guess I'm going now." He smiled to Aden. "Lock that door behind you and keep your phone beside your bed. Call me if you need anything."

"Anything?" she teased, hugging him tighter. "I just need you." She bit her lip. The words had slipped out before she thought, but he smiled her favorite smile and kissed her forehead.

"I just need you, too," he whispered. Then he was gone, striding toward the cars. Aden smiled triumphantly and followed him.

"Good night, man," Drew was saying, "Thanks for seeing her home."

"No problem. You guys keep safe." Maddox climbed behind the wheel of his car and motioned to Natalie to pull out ahead of him. He started his car and waited as Natalie pulled her car around. Then, he waved to Aden and Drew before he followed her down the driveway.

"He's a good guy," Drew said quietly.

"She's a great girl," Aden answered. Then, they went inside together.

Aden awoke the next morning to the buzzing of her phone, vibrating on the nightstand. *Ugh, go away!*

We kissed! The text read. It was Cadence of course.

OMG! Spill it. Aden sent, then rolled back over with a pillow over her head. She knew Cadence would be typing furiously, and probably would send several screens of text, not leaving out any detail. She dozed as her phone buzzed a few more times, and she reached for it when it grew quiet again.

The date had gone really well. Trey took her to dinner and then to the movie. They'd had great conversation over dinner, then he held her hand halfway through the movie. After the movie, he drove her home, and they sat in his car in the driveway for a while talking. He walked her to the door and kissed her on her front porch before leaving.

Of course, Cadence's version was much longer, punctuated with 'OMG's and 'I can't believe it's and 'Guess what's? Aden was really happy for her. She sounded as happy with Trey as Aden was with Maddox, and that was pure bliss. She smiled and sent Cadence a long text of congratulations. Then, she put the phone back on the nightstand and buried her head in the pillow again.

A moment later, the phone buzzed insistently. It was ringing this time. Groaning, she rolled over and answered it without opening her eyes.

"Seriously Cadence, can I call you back when I get up?"

"Oh, sorry!" It was Maddox. "Cadence said she'd been texting with you."

Aden's eyes flew open. "Maddox. It's okay, she *has* been texting. I just hadn't gotten out of bed yet."

"I can let you go—"

"No!" She glanced at the clock on the nightstand. 10:42 a.m. Normally, she would have slept in until noon, but that was before Maddox. "I'm up, or, well, getting there."

"Seriously, go back to sleep. Call me later."

"No, I'm totally awake." She said, yawning. He laughed. "What are you up to?"

"Well I'm…um," he sounded embarrassed. What the heck was he doing? "I'm standing in your driveway."

"What?!"

"But I'm getting back in my car, and I will come back la—"

"Don't you dare leave!" Aden shouted into the phone. She jumped from the bed and raced into the kitchen, only to come to a skidding stop and turn back for the bathroom. She had to at least brush her teeth…and her hair. "I'll be out in just a minute." She hung up.

Five minutes later, she opened the door and peeked out. He was leaning casually against the side of his car talking to Drew.

"Good morning." Drew laughed at her. She froze. She must look really bad. Or she forgot her pants or something; she glanced down. The t-shirt and shorts she'd slept in weren't glamorous by any means, but they weren't too embarrassing. Maybe.

Maddox just smiled her favorite smile. "I really could have come back later."

"I was up." She shrugged, glaring at Drew as he snickered.

"You're never up before noon if you can help it," he teased.

"Okay, so I was *awake*." She frowned at him. "It's summertime, and it's my day off, so sue me."

"What's going on out here?" their Mom called from the doorway. "Oh Maddox! Good morning."

"Good morning Mrs. Garret."

"Why are you all standing in the driveway? Come on inside."

Drew led the way into the kitchen. "We were waiting for Sleeping Beauty to make her appearance."

"How long have you been here?" Aden asked Maddox quietly.

"Not long," he whispered back.

"Aden, always so good of you to join us," her Mother chided, "Before lunchtime, I mean."

Aden rolled her eyes. "We can go sit on the deck." She glared at her mother and brother. "It's still shady this time of the day."

"Like she would know," Drew stage-whispered, and Aden whacked him on the shoulder as she went by. Maddox waited while she lifted the security bar and unlocked the big sliding door, then he helped push it aside a few feet and waited for her to go out first. Always the gentleman.

She pushed the door shut again behind them with a warning glance at her family, still in the kitchen. Maddox had taken a seat in one of the reclining chairs, so she sat in the one beside him.

"Sorry about that," she mumbled. "So really, have you been here long?"

"No, I'd been texting with Cadence, or I should say she'd been texting me, about her date last night. I was…in the area, so I pulled into your driveway to read it all and text her back. Then, she said she was texting you, so I pulled on up to the house." He shrugged sheepishly.

"In the area," she repeated, frowning. "And how long were you 'in the area' this morning?"

"I warned you that I'd be stalking you," he reminded her with a small smile.

"That's not an answer."

His smile faded, and he stared into her eyes for several minutes before he finally spoke,

"I swear, I'm not this creepy normally. I promised I would keep you safe, but I don't want to make you feel uncomfortable either." He looked pained.

"Oh my God, you're not creepy." She rolled her eyes again. "And I'm not uncomfortable," she sighed. "I just absolutely hate the idea of you having to spend any amount of time just hanging around…putting yourself in uncomfortable situations on my behalf."

"Will you stop worrying about me?" he groaned.

"Nope." She smiled back. He was trying not to smile, looking out at the sunlight dripping through the green canopy.

"Do you want to go walk by the river?" he suggested. "Or did you have something else you'd like to do today?"

She sighed, stretching. "We can do that. Let me go get dressed real quick."

When she emerged from her room a few minutes later, Maddox was in the kitchen with her Mom, packing a backpack with food.

"Aden, I put in the last of those strawberries and that cheese you like," her mother said. Aden was still surprised by just how much her mother seemed to like Maddox and encouraged the time they spent together.

Maddox had stopped and stared as her Mother was speaking. "Wow. I really like that color on you."

Aden blushed immediately, looking down at the plain green t-shirt she wore. "Um, thanks."

"You're welcome." He smiled. "Cadence was wondering if we could meet her and Trey at the lake later this afternoon."

"Sure, I guess."

"Are you sure it's safe?" her mother frowned.

"Mom," Aden sighed.

"I won't let her leave my sight," Maddox said, "And we'll all stay together the entire time." Aden's mom didn't look entirely convinced, but let it drop.

"Is there water in there?" Aden asked, pointing to the backpack.

"A couple of water bottles, and I put in some lemonade." Her mom smiled. "Hope it's not too heavy."

Maddox lifted it with one hand from the counter, weighing it briefly. "Just fine." He smiled back at her. "Are you ready?"

Aden grabbed a banana from the bowl on the counter, peeled it, and took a bite. "Now, I am."

"Oh, you didn't get to eat any breakfast," Maddox said, dropping the backpack back onto the counter.

"This is breakfast," Aden said, holding up the banana. "And you're carrying a backpack full of food. Come on. Let's go." She tossed the banana peel in the trash and led the way to the back deck. Maddox followed, shouldering the pack. "Let's go upriver. It's a prettier hike."

"Lead on," he replied.

Aden struck out up the path and thought about how she'd come this way just over a week ago and seen Maddox for the first time. She smiled, listening to the birds quietly chirping in the still forest. There was no breeze, and she knew that the heat would be far worse out from under the canopy of the trees. Maddox followed her quietly.

When she came to the spot where she'd first seen Maddox, across the river, she stopped.

"This is where I saw you last Saturday."

He looked across the river and then looked at their surroundings. "It looks so different. I wouldn't have recognized it."

"Really?"

"Well, I guess I really don't remember much except for seeing you." He smiled.

"Yeah, I'm sure I made quite the sight," she soured. "You know, you never told me how you came to be all the way out here."

He shrugged. "I'd gone with my Mom to the convenience store down at the lake. She was investigating the scene." He dropped the backpack to the ground. "I'd had a quick flash the night before; I saw the scene right before he took her, so I was looking around, trying to keep an open mind, so to speak." He smirked. "And I got a sudden urge to check out that path. Told my Mom I was following a hunch; she was busy at the scene anyway. I just felt drawn...I know that's weird, but I just followed the path up the river."

166

"Did you see anything?"

"Not until I saw you." He smiled.

"So what did you do, anyway? After I ran off?"

"Turned around and walked back to the crime scene."

"So you walked right by my house. Did you see me again?"

"No, I saw the house, of course, and I kept looking for you—or anybody else, but I didn't see anything." He shrugged.

"It's just so weird." Aden frowned. Maddox looked at her, concerned. "I mean, Cadence and I've been friends for years, but I'd never seen you before last Saturday. Then, you feel compelled to follow that path up the river last weekend, and I hadn't been out here in months and months. It's just weird that we both ended up right here at the same moment."

"Fate?" he suggested.

"And then when I saw you standing in my living room that day…" her voice trailed off, and she shook her head. "It's just all so bizarre."

"Good bizarre, I hope."

She blinked and smiled up at him. "Of course. I'm so happy I met you; I just can't get over how it all came about."

"Definitely not normal." He smiled back. "So, are you hungry?"

She tilted her head and stared at him for a moment before shaking her head slowly. She picked up the pack and went to sit on a rock beside the water.

"Sorry, I wasn't dismissing what you were saying," Maddox said, joining her and helping to spread out their picnic. "I've thought about it a lot over the past week myself, and not just how we met, but how quickly I found myself wanting to know more about you, wanting to spend time with you. None of that's exactly *normal* for me."

Aden was nodding in agreement. "Me either."

"It still worries me a little," he admitted, watching her reaction. "We're moving pretty fast, emotionally, and when we catch this guy—"

"You'll be leaving. I know." He looked unhappy when she said that, and she reached for his hand.

He smiled and squeezed her hand back. "So we've got about an hour and a half before we'd need to get going if we're gonna meet Cadence at the lake."

"Okay. I'll drop the depressing stuff."

He smiled again and offered her a strawberry. "Someone very wise told me once that we should enjoy the time we have." She took the strawberry with a grin. She couldn't believe how lucky she was to be here with him and have him looking at her like that. ... *at ME! He's so incredibly gorgeous.*

Shadowed. Cracked linoleum and the smell of old garlic...Facing a faded, green door. Where the door's panels were worn and scraped, red-brown paint showed through at the edges. The door opens onto a wooden stairway descending into darkness. Listening for sounds from below, it's silent at first, and then a stifled sniffle floats up from the darkness. The sound evokes glee and evil images. The anticipation has built even more. Barely contained. Almost time though. And I will touch and taste and grope and rip and slash and....deep breath. Control. Breathe.

CHAPTER 10
leering letch

"M addox?" Aden asked quietly. Her hand gripped his arm again.

He blinked several times, squinting against the bright sunlight. The river slid quietly past on its ancient route as Aden waited beside him. He sighed, scowling and closed his eyes again. "I'm so sor—"

"Save it," she interrupted. "Could you see him?"

He shook his head. "No, I just see what he sees." She waited. "There was a door that opened onto stairs going down…like a basement. I think he has them in a basement." He was already searching his pockets for his phone. He dialed his Mom and told her, in a bit more detail, about what he'd seen while Aden listened intently.

"Well, at least it narrows it down to houses. Older homes, I think. That linoleum and the old paint on the door…yeah…and it's not like an abandoned house. I smelled food. Garlic…I don't know…No, that was it…Okay." He glanced at Aden and smiled. "Yes, I will. We're going to the lake to meet Cadence…okay…bye." He reached out tucked a stray lock of hair behind Aden's ear. "My mom says hi."

"Did they have any new leads on their end?"

"No, nothing." He sighed. "Looks like you'll have me around for another day."

"Silver linings," she mumbled, smiling.

They hung out by the river for a while eating, tossing stones into the murky water, and talking of lighter subjects before they packed up to go meet Cadence.

Maddox pulled into the parking lot in front of the convenience store at the Devil's Fork State Park entrance where he'd arranged to meet Cadence and Trey. "Can I get you anything from inside?"

"No, I'm fine," Aden said, waving as Trey and Cadence pulled into the space beside them in Trey's car.

"Hey guys!" Trey waved back, through his open car window.

"Let's go to the Chimney," Cadence suggested, leaning across Trey toward the window.

Maddox backed out and led the way. When they got to the pull-off, there was a pickup truck parked at the very end. Seeing it gave Aden goose bumps, and she glanced quickly at Maddox, who was checking it out as well. He shot her a questioning look as he parked.

"There are probably hundreds of pickup trucks in this county." Aden shrugged, getting out of the car.

Maddox kept a watchful eye on their surroundings as he grabbed the backpack from the back seat. It had been restocked with snacks and drinks, sunscreen, and other lake necessities. He grabbed the two beach towels and draped them over his shoulder.

"It's so good to see you!" Cadence came over and hugged Aden tightly.

"Um, thanks. Great to see you, too." Aden laughed. "But we did just see each other yesterday."

"Hey, does that look like the truck you saw here last time? Or in your driveway?" Cadence asked.

"I really don't know." Aden shook her head. "I never got a good look at either one, and like I just told Maddox, there are hundreds of trucks around here, all the time."

"Cadence told me your house was broken into and that you might have a stalker?" Trey asked, concerned.

"Oh…yeah," Aden stuttered. "I mean, somebody did get into our house, but they didn't take anything."

"That's just crazy." Trey shook his head. "You're being careful, though, right?"

"Oh, sure." She nodded. "We're all taking precautions and being careful." She glanced at Maddox, who was studiously surveying their surroundings.

"Guess the whole town's on edge with all these kidnapping cases." Trey frowned. "You girls especially should be really careful, don't go out alone if you can help it,"

"Well, we're all here together today," Cadence said brightly. "Who's up for a swim?"

Cadence had brought a couple of inflatable rafts, so they roped them together and swam out to where the water currents were cooler and took turns floating, swimming, and dunking each other with the rafts acting as a home base.

Aden was having a great time laughing and playing with no thought of kidnappers, disappearances, stalkers, or break-ins. She hadn't felt this carefree in over a week.

"I think I need more sunscreen," Cadence said, examining her upper arms held out of the water.

"Hey, who's that?" Trey asked quietly, pointing back to the shore. A man sat silently at one of the picnic tables, watching them. "How long's he been there?"

"He's been there for a while," Maddox answered. "Came walking from around the point over there and then sat down."

"That looks like Billy Ray Payne," Aden said. "Drew works with him at his Dad's garage."

"Will you go with me to go get the sunscreen?" Cadence asked Trey.

"We can all go," Maddox said, keeping an eye on the shore. "I'm a little waterlogged, and I could use a drink of that lemonade we brought."

As they neared the shore, Billy Ray lit a cigarette and blew a stream of smoke into the lethargic breeze. He dipped his head in greeting as the group pulled the rafts out of the water.

"Hey, Billy Ray," Aden greeted him awkwardly. The way he was staring was unsettling, but then again, he unsettled her every time they met.

"Hey, Aden. Thought that was you out there." He took a drag from the cigarette and looked her up and down through squinted eyes.

"This is Maddox, Cadence, and Trey." She indicated each as she said their name. "Guys, this is Billy Ray. Drew works with him at the garage," she repeated, trying to be polite. Billy Ray's eyes slid to Cadence's form next. Maddox stepped forward with his hand out, blocking Billy Ray's view of the girls.

"Maddox Dixon, don't think we've met," he stated, unsmiling. Billy Ray took another drag before taking his hand slowly.

"Oh, you're the mayor's kid, right?" Maddox didn't answer immediately, and Trey stepped up beside him, muscled arms crossed. Aden and Cadence had both begun donning their t-shirts and wrapping the towels around their waists to cover up, over at the nearby table where they'd left their things. Billy Ray's insolent gaze followed them.

"Have you done any fishing around here?" Trey asked him, obviously trying to divert his attention. Billy Ray grinned and turned his eyes slowly to Trey as he blew a couple of smoke rings.

"Yeah. Fishin's pretty good the farther you go away from the crowds over there at the beach." He squinted at Trey. "You new here or somethin'?"

"Just haven't had a chance to fish around here in a while." Trey squinted back, unmoving. Billy Ray rubbed his chin and nodded once.

"Hey, Aden!" he called. "Come here and tell me about that break-in at your house. Drew didn't have too much to say about it."

Aden reluctantly rejoined the guys. Billy Ray looked to be enjoying the tense atmosphere and pointedly ignored Maddox and Trey as he lounged back on the table.

"Well, there's really not that much to tell." Aden shrugged. Maddox put his arm around her when she reached his side, and Billy Ray's squinting gaze watched every movement. "Somebody was in the house when Maddox and I got home, but they ran away before they took anything."

"Drew didn't tell me you'd gone and got yourself a boyfriend." Billy Ray smiled, but it didn't look friendly.

"Do you and Drew often discuss each other's family? And their private business?" Maddox asked, steely-eyed.

"Settle down there. Drew and I been friends for a long time. Guess I just think of Aden as a little sister, too. Keep my eye out for her, you know?" he eyed Maddox.

"Hey, I'm starving," Cadence said from behind them. "Let's go get something to eat."

"So that's your sister, right?" Billy Ray asked Maddox, nodding toward Cadence. "You gotta keep an eye on 'em. 'Specially now, while there's some asshole out there helpin' himself to women."

"We appreciate your concern," Aden interceded. Trey and Maddox were looking more unfriendly by the moment, and for all his words of concern, Billy Ray's gaze made Aden shudder involuntarily. "It's good to see you, Billy Ray." She took Maddox's arm and led him away to the other table where she quickly gathered their things into the backpack. Cadence and Trey followed. Maddox swung the backpack over one shoulder and hugged Aden close to his side with his free arm as they headed for the cars. Cadence and Aden tried to make normal small talk, but it was hard as Billy Ray's gaze followed them into the trees.

They were all subdued when they reached the cars.

"Does anybody else think that was just over-the-top creepy?" Cadence asked quietly.

"Maybe we should check out his truck." Trey suggested to Maddox. "That dude—"

"Shh! I think he's coming," Aden whispered as a dry twig snapped loudly behind them. "So where are we going?"

"We could go to the square," Maddox said, loud enough for anyone in the vicinity to hear. "Maybe hit the deli or the coffee shop?"

"Works for me," Cadence said brightly, and winked surreptitiously. At that moment, Billy Ray came sauntering through the trees, hands in his pockets, kicking old leaves and twigs as he slowly approached the road. He smiled and waved as he walked to his truck and got in. He didn't start the engine.

"Ok, let's go then. Cadence, you've got your phone?" Maddox smiled nonchalantly. She nodded. Aden watched Billy Ray out of the corner of her eye sit unmoving in his truck as they pulled away. Trey and Cadence followed. "Call Cadence for me," Maddox said, glaring into the rear view mirror, "We're not going to the square."

Aden turned the phone on speaker as Cadence answered stating, "He's still sitting back there."

"Good. Let him," Maddox answered, leaning toward the phone Aden held between them. "Where would you ladies like to go?"

"Well, normally, I'd say let's just go home," Cadence said, "but Patience and the Bitch Squad are there this afternoon."

"We can go back to my place," Aden suggested. "Hang on the deck or by the river?"

"Okay, Lead on. We'll see you there." She hung up.

Aden ended the call and began dialing again. "Mom? Hey, would you mind if I brought some friends over this afternoon? ...Yeah, just Maddox and Cadence and Trey...oh!" Maddox glanced over at her surprised tone, "Well, we'd probably stay out on the deck, or if you guys wanted to be out there, we could watch a movie or go down by the river.

Umm, would it be a problem if they stayed for dinner with me? ...Okay...thanks Mom. See you soon."

"So your Mom has company?" Maddox surmised when she'd hung up.

"Yeah." She frowned. "Mr. Case from the store where my Mom works."

"Is that bad?" Maddox processed her expression.

"Well, no...I guess. It's just different."

Maddox started to say something then hesitated. When he spoke again, she knew he'd deliberately changed the subject.

"So, what do you know about Billy Ray Payne?"

Aden looked at him for a moment, deciding whether she would pursue what he'd been about to say before he asked about Billy Ray.

"I don't know much, really. Billy Ray's Dad owns the garage in town where Drew works. Billy Ray's a year or two older than Drew, and they used to hang out sometimes, but I haven't heard Drew talk about him lately."

"What about his mother? Siblings?" Maddox asked.

"Um, the mother's not in the picture. Not sure where she is—it just never came up, and I don't think he has any siblings, not that I know about anyway. It's just him and his Dad."

"Do you know where they live?"

She shook her head. "No, never asked. I always see them at the garage." Maddox was quiet for several miles. Aden seemed deep in thought and started texting on her phone. "I'm warning Cadence that my Mom has company. You never know what might come popping out when she's surprised." Maddox chuckled, nodding. Then, she noticed that he kept checking the rear view mirror. "What are they doing back there that's so interesting?"

"What? Oh, I'm not watching Cadence and Trey. I'm making sure we're not followed."

"Oh, right. Do you see anything?"

He shook his head. "No, I don't think he followed us. Has Billy Ray ever been to your house?"

174

"Umm, not that I know of, but it's possible he's been up in Drew's room without me knowing about it." She glanced at the side mirror. "But he didn't hear us say that we were going to my house anyway."

"I know. Just wondering."

"Is he a suspect?"

"Everybody's a suspect right now," he answered quietly. "But he does raise some suspicion."

"He's always been a little odd." Aden shrugged.

"What do you mean?"

"Well, you met him. He's just…I don't know. He's always been polite to me, but the way he looks sometimes…and the things he says, well, he's just always kind of creeped me out." Maddox was quiet, frowning at the road ahead. "I thought you and Trey might be getting ready to jump him back there at the lake. You both looked pretty intense."

"The words he said were innocent enough." Maddox glared darkly, "But the disrespectful way he looked at you and Cadence…it's like he was looking for a fight."

"No, he pretty much always looks that way. When females are around, anyway." She shuddered.

"Well, somebody may have to teach him some manners," he glowered. Aden looked at him, surprised.

"You did the right thing, walking away."

"This time."

When they pulled up to Aden's house, there was an unfamiliar BMW in the driveway. Trey pulled in behind them and parked.

"So, your Mom and Mr. Case?" Cadence chuckled, getting out of the car.

"Cadence—" Aden rounded on her, but she held up her hands.

"Oh, stop. I'll behave myself." She smiled innocently. "I like your Mom, and if she's found a new boyfriend, well, more power to her." Maddox glanced from Cadence to

Aden for a moment before following them inside.

"Hey, Mom, we're here." Aden called as she entered the kitchen.

"We're in the den." Her mom called back. She rose from the sofa as the group entered.

"Don, I think you've met my daughter, Aden."

"I have, but it's been a while." Don Case smiled, rising to shake her hand. His dark hair was graying just at the temples, and his blue eyes smiled from an attractive face. "You have a beautiful daughter, Janet." Aden blushed as her Mother introduced the others.

"This is Cadence Kendall, Aden's best friend and her brother, Maddox Dixon." Janet hesitated, looking at Trey, whom she'd never met.

"Mom, Mr. Case, this is Trey Miller, our friend from school," Aden said, awkwardly.

"It's nice to meet you." Janet smiled at him.

"It's nice to meet you, too Mrs. Garrett," Trey answered, glancing around.

"We're gonna go hang out on the deck for a while, I think," Aden said, motioning the group to follow.

"Wow, this is a really nice house," Trey said as they stood at the deck railing, looking down on the river.

"Thanks. My Dad designed it." Aden said quietly.

"Great job." Trey looked suddenly embarrassed. "I, uh, I'm really sorry about your Dad. I didn't mean to—"

"Don't worry about it." Aden smiled. "So, can I get you guys anything? We've got some flavored waters, tea, lemonade…there might be a Coke or two in there if Drew hasn't gotten to them." Everyone declined. "Well, I thought we could hang out and have dinner here, if you all want to do that." She continued, "We could grill some burgers, and there's stuff to make a salad."

"That sounds great to me." Cadence looked to Trey.

"I'd love to. Lemme just let my Mom know," Trey said, taking out his phone and sending a text.

"And can you stay for dinner with me?" Aden asked, putting an arm around Maddox's waist.

"I thought you'd never ask." He hugged her tight, grinning.

"Oh my God, you two are so adorable together!" Cadence clapped, beaming.

"So when did you guys officially get together?" Trey asked.

"Well, I don't know how official anything is, but we've been hanging out this week," Aden answered. She felt a little guilty since she'd opted out of the movie plans she'd made with Trey just last night.

"You both just seemed pretty adamant at the lake on Tuesday that you weren't together." Trey shrugged. "I was just wondering. Didn't mean to be nosy or anything."

"We'd just met that day," Maddox explained. "We've gotten to know each other better since then, and it's official that I like spending time with her." His eyes were doing that smoldering thing as he looked down at Aden.

"Cool," Trey said, looking out at the trees.

"So did you and Cadence have a good time last night?" Aden asked. "I'm sorry I couldn't go."

"Yeah, it was great." Trey smiled, looking suspiciously from Aden to Maddox. "I'm glad you're feeling better."

"Just needed a good night's sleep, I guess." She hoped the guilt she felt didn't show on her face.

"Aden, can I see you for a sec?" her mom asked from the doorway, so Aden stepped inside. "Don and I are going out for dinner." She glanced at Mr. Case, still sitting on the sofa. "What are your plans?"

"Um, would it be okay if we just grilled some burgers here?"

"Sure. All four of you are staying for dinner?"

"Yes, if you don't mind."

"Okay, Drew will be home in a while."

"Mom, we don't need a chaperone. We're just eating dinner."

"Okay, but he'll still be home in a while. I wasn't sure what your plans were, and I don't want you here by yourself." She hugged her daughter fiercely. "Make sure you stay here, on the deck or inside, and stay together."

"We will; I promise." Aden rolled her eyes behind her mom's back. "And you have fun at your dinner."

Her mother smiled. "Thank you. See you later."

"Bye," she called to Mr. Case as he got up, waved, and escorted her mother out the kitchen door. She opened up the window wall to the deck all the way. The sun was dipping behind the mountain again, and the air had cooled off.

"Everything okay?" Cadence asked.

"Yeah, my Mom just left on a date." It was so surreal for her to say those words out loud, and it obviously showed in her friends' reactions to her expression.

"Are you okay with that?" Cadence raised her eyebrows. "I mean, she looks really happy."

"You're right. She does." Aden nodded and took a deep breath. "I'm happy for her." Maddox and Trey both smiled quietly.

"It's so cute that they waited until she wasn't going to be working there anymore," Cadence bubbled. Aden didn't answer, still lost in thought. "So, should we get dinner started? I'm hungry."

"Sure." Aden smiled again, coming back to the present. She lit the gas grill at one end of the deck so it could heat up and went inside to the kitchen. "Cadence, will you grab the plates and stuff and set the table for me?"

"Sure. Are we eating inside or outside?"

"Whichever you guys want." Aden shrugged. "If you want to eat at the table on the deck, there's a tablecloth and some candles in that cabinet over there."

Cadence, assisted by Maddox and Trey, whirled around the kitchen, setting a nice table in no time.

"Is it okay if I light a few more candles around the deck?" Cadence asked. "There are several in this cabinet."

"Go for it." Aden was patting the burgers into shape. "Hey, can somebody grab the

178

lettuce and peppers in the fridge?"

"I've got it." Maddox stepped up. "You want both these peppers?" he asked, pointing to the green and red bell peppers on the shelf.

"If you guys are all okay with that?" Everyone nodded. "Onions? Anybody not like onion? I don't think we have any tomatoes, not sure what else is in there."

"Where's a cutting board?" Maddox asked. Cadence knew where it was and got it out for him, also handing him a knife. She took a second knife, and they began chopping.

"Okay, I feel left out. Can I get drinks or something?" Trey asked.

"That'd be great." Aden smiled. "I'll have some of the tea in the fridge." Trey began fulfilling drink orders, and soon, the burgers were ready for the grill. Aden pulled a pink polka-dot apron from a drawer and began putting it on, but Maddox grabbed her hands to stop her. With a flourish, he tied the apron around his own waist instead while Aden and Cadence laughed.

"I've got this. Hand over those burgers."

"You know, I think that pink might be your color, bro." Cadence giggled. Maddox ignored her, and accompanied by Trey, went out to the grill. Cadence helped Aden wipe up the kitchen counters before they went to sit at the table outside.

A slight breeze took the edge off the lingering humidity and the candles flickered around them as the evening drew down. They talked and laughed over dinner, then ice cream as a dessert. They were still lingering around the table a couple of hours later when Drew came in.

"Hey, guys." He said, stepping out onto the deck. They all greeted him. "Looks like I missed the party."

"Nope, just dinner." Aden smiled. "Drew, this is Trey—"

"Miller." Drew nodded. "I know your older brother, Kyle." They shook hands. "You look a lot like him."

"Yeah, we get that a lot." Trey shrugged.

"Maddox, how's it goin'?" he asked.

"All good." Maddox smiled back. "Actually, I need to talk to you for a bit before I leave later, when you get a minute."

"Okay." Drew looked mystified. "I'm gonna go get showered, but I'll come back after that." Maddox just nodded, and Drew went out to the garage.

"What was that about?" Aden asked.

"Nothing. Just want to ask him about Billy Ray." He shrugged. "Following up."

"Should we tell somebody about the way he was acting today?" Trey asked, frowning.

"Don't worry. Maddox probably already told his Mom," Cadence said.

"Good. That jerk should definitely be checked out."

"Agreed. He was *really* weird." Cadence nodded, shuddering. "Just the way he kept staring at Aden gave me goose bumps."

"It wasn't only Aden he was staring at," Trey growled, glancing across at Maddox and then to Cadence. "I don't think either of the girls should be around him, ever."

"Expand that to *any* girls, any time," Maddox agreed.

"You should warn your sisters, too." Trey nodded to Cadence.

"Yeah, they don't have you two strapping young men to take up for them." Cadence smiled at Trey. "I thought you were both gonna throw down there for a minute."

"I was ready. I was taking my cue from Maddox, since the jerk was talking mostly to Aden."

"He was just waiting for one of us to make a move," Maddox said quietly. "He had a gun holstered under his arm."

"Oh my God!" Cadence's eyes were huge as she looked from Maddox to Trey.

"You're not serious." Aden demanded. Maddox just looked at each of them. "He had a gun? You're sure?"

"Positive. You could see it plain as day when he leaned back with his arms on the table." He frowned. "When he was doing his best to see past me and Trey so he could leer at the two of you some more."

"I missed that." Trey shook his head. "How'd I miss that?"

"Leering. That's a great word." Cadence nodded. "The Leering Letch."

180

"I think he showed it only because he was outnumbered," Maddox muttered. "It was just a warning for us to back off."

Aden crossed her arms and briskly rubbed her goose-bumped skin. "I can't believe…. okay, I'm not going back to the lake anytime soon."

"Seriously," Cadence chimed in. "It's like the Chimney is a magnet for criminals."

"Billy Ray may not be a criminal," Maddox spoke up. "He's an ass, but I don't think there's a law against that."

"But he had a gun," Cadence pointed out.

"Again, not necessarily against the law. If he's got a license to carry and conceal." Maddox shrugged. "I just want to be sure we don't jump to conclusions that could have some serious consequences. For everyone involved."

"Sorry you guys. I don't think it's the Chimney that's the magnet for bad guys," Aden mumbled. "I think it's just me." The others all frowned and began refuting her statement all at the same time. She shook her head adamantly waving them all into silence. "No, really, I honestly do appreciate that you're all still willing to hang out with me."

"Aden," Maddox spoke up first, raising her chin with his finger until she was looking at him. "Everything that's happening—it's not your fault." He stopped her as she began to speak. "The kidnappings started months ago, with three other women. All strangers to you, I might add."

"And the break in here at my house? And the truck—" she began.

"Still not your fault, and we can't rule out simple coincidence."

"Maddox, you know you don't—"

"Hey," he interrupted softly, and his eyes melted her heart with their sincerity. "Doesn't matter, either way. I'm not going to let anything happen to you. Or my sisters." He glanced at Cadence.

Cadence tilted her head to the side and sighed loudly, with a grin.

"I second that," Trey said, clearing his throat, and took Cadence's hand in his. Then, he looked out into the darkness where the lightning bugs twinkled among the branches. Cadence beamed.

They were clearing the table, bringing everything back inside when Drew came through the kitchen door.

"Mom back yet?" he asked Aden. She shook her head. "Any ice cream left?"

"Yeah, I think so." In just a few more minutes, the table outside was cleared, the grill was re-covered, and the candles were all blown out and put away. The dishes were all in the dishwasher, and the counters wiped clean again. The group had reconvened on the sofas in the den with the TV on.

"Man, you guys are good." Drew surveyed the tidy kitchen as he added his now-empty ice cream bowl to the dishwasher. Then, he sat beside Aden in the den. "So, Maddox, what did you need to talk about?"

"Would you mind stepping outside for a bit?" Maddox asked.

"Hey man, it's time for me to get Cadence home, anyway," Trey said, rising. "Just stay where you are." He held out a hand to Cadence and she grinned broadly as she took it.

"I'll walk you out," Aden said. "I get the impression that Maddox doesn't want me in on this conversation, either." Maddox frowned at her. "It's okay." She leaned down and kissed his cheek.

"So stinkin' cute." Cadence beamed at them before following Trey outside.

"Come back inside before they leave," Maddox said. "Don't stay out there by yourself." She sighed, but nodded before going out.

"Hey, thanks so much for coming over here today you two," she called.

"Thanks for having us—and for dinner," Cadence said, coming over to hug her.

"Yeah, dinner was great." Trey smiled. "I had a great time."

"Me too. We should do it again sometime soon," Aden enthused.

"Yeah, we'll find somewhere to go that doesn't involve the lake, or watching weirdoes," Cadence added.

"Oh yeah, what was that you called Billy Ray earlier?" Aden laughed. "You had a name for him…"

"Oh, the Leering Lech?" She grinned. "Yeah, I liked that one, too."

"The Leering Lech. That was it. You know I'm going to think that every time I see him from now on." Aden grinned back.

"Well, I hope neither one of you has to see him again, ever." Trey frowned. "Seriously, can you both promise that if you ever see him, you'll run the other way?"

"I'd love to." Aden nodded, and Cadence agreed. "Be careful driving home."

"Will do." Trey smiled, nodding to Aden before turning to open the passenger door for Cadence.

"Oh my God, he's perfect," Cadence whispered in Aden's ear, making her giggle.

"You behave yourself, young lady," Aden whispered back, hugging her. Then aloud, "Good night, guys."

Trey smiled again, closing the car door behind Cadence and walking to the driver's side.

"Go on back inside before I drive off," he said, climbing in. Aden waved and backed into the kitchen door. He waited until she'd closed it to pull away, Cadence waving wildly.

When she turned, Maddox and Drew rose from their seats.

"You don't have to stop talking on my account." Aden frowned. "I can go into my room or something."

"We wouldn't make you do that. We're all done anyway." Maddox smiled her favorite smile. "And it's time for me to be going, too." That disappointed her, and he smiled again at her frown. "Can I see you tomorrow?"

"Of course! I have to work though. I get off at 5:00."

"Can I pick you up then?" She nodded.

"I'm sure you two will excuse me for a moment." Drew grinned. "I'm gonna go lock up. Good to see you, man." He nodded to Maddox before heading into their Mom's room to check that door first. Aden followed Maddox out into the courtyard. He stopped her before she'd gone three steps out the door.

"That's far enough." He smiled as she rolled her eyes at him. "You don't need to be out here at all, but I wanted just a little privacy so I could do this…" he pulled her in for a smoldering kiss. Her arguments were forgotten in a second, thanks to the electric warmth that was Maddox Dixon. She was light-headed when he pulled back slightly to look at her face. "I've been wanting to do that all night."

"So why didn't you?"

"Because watching you in the candlelight…I might not have been able to stop myself." He grinned crookedly. "And I don't think Cadence or Trey would have appreciated the display."

"Always the gentleman." She pouted up at him, hoping he'd kiss her again.

"Not always," he growled, catching her face between his hands and kissing her again, more insistently. Her emotions spiraled upwards as she held him tighter, and one of his hands relinquished her face to slowly slide down to her waist before pulling her in even more tightly. *Oh. My. God.* She was ecstatic to hear his breathing, as ragged as hers, when he pulled away and rested his forehead against her own. "I enjoyed spending the day with you," he breathed.

"Me too," was all she could manage. She grasped her wrists behind his neck to hold him in place. She might not ever let him go.

Drew cleared his throat from the kitchen. "All locked up tight." She could hear the grin in his voice.

"Great, Drew," Aden growled, not relinquishing her hold on Maddox. She held him in place against her forehead. "I'll be there in a minute."

"Um-hum," he muttered, turning back for the den.

"That was my cue." Maddox smiled, reaching back to take her hands in his. His eyes roamed her face slowly before he pulled her in for another quick kiss. It was over too soon, though, and Aden sighed. "I'll see you tomorrow," he promised.

"Okay." She sighed again.

"Get on in there before Drew comes and drags you inside." He grinned.

"He wouldn't do that," Aden declared.

"Yes, I would," Drew called over his shoulder from his seat in the den.

"Oh my God, Drew!"

"Shhh." Maddox chuckled. "He's right; I have to go. Lock that door behind you."

"I know. I know." She pouted again until one of his cheeks pulled up into the smile. She stood on tiptoe to kiss him again. "Drive carefully."

"I will. Sweet dreams." He gently pulled away and waited for her to go inside.

"Alright already," she grumbled, backing through the doorway. "Good night," she called and closed the door, only to open it as soon as he'd started the car's engine. His window instantly began sliding down.

"Lock it," he commanded, trying not to smile. She waved and closed the door again, locking it this time. She leaned against it, listening to the sound of the engine diminishing into the night.

"Sweet dreams," she muttered, still smiling.

"I'm gonna watch some TV in here until Mom comes home," Drew said over his shoulder again. "You goin' to bed?"

"No, I'll watch some TV for a while," Aden said, plopping down beside him.

S o," Drew said after a while. "Mom's on a date." Aden just stared at the TV, waiting. "Probably about time, huh?"

"Probably." Aden nodded weakly.

"She deserves to be happy," he said, watching the TV too.

"Yes, she does."

"So she didn't leave for dinner until after you guys had gotten here, right?"

"Yeah, they were here when we got here." She wasn't sure why they wouldn't look at each other during this conversation. It was easier somehow, she decided. "Mr. Case was dressed nicely…so was Mom." Drew nodded, mutely. "He seems like a nice man," she added.

"He'd better be."

"So what is it with all you guys? All this 'protect the little women' stuff all of a sudden."

"All of us guys?" Drew raised his eyebrows and looked at her for the first time. "You know why we're so much more protective lately." He frowned. "Maddox told me about Billy Ray at the lake today."

Aden nodded, "Yeah, he was…downright creepy."

"It won't happen again," Drew promised, still frowning.

"You're not going to say anything to him."

"Not yet. Maddox asked me to hold off for now."

"What does that mean?"

"It means I won't be saying anything to him…Yet," Drew vowed, "But he won't get anywhere near you again, or your friends."

"Drew, he had a gun today," Aden pleaded. "Just drop it. Nothing really happened."

"He's always got a gun." Drew waved her off. "But if he made you uncomfortable…and made all your friends uncomfortable—"

"So what? Leave it alone."

They both turned as a car pulled up in the courtyard to idle outside.

"Please don't say anything to Mom," Aden wheedled. "Not tonight. Let her have tonight."

Drew nodded, sighing. "But you know that Maddox's mom will tell her. They talk all the time."

"Really?"

"Almost every day."

Not sure how I feel about that. "Well, fine. But she doesn't need to know tonight."

Drew nodded as the kitchen door was unlocked from the outside. It didn't immediately open. Aden remembered standing just outside the door a little while ago with Maddox, and she blushed. *Was Mr. Case kissing her Mom goodnight? No, it's just a first date. Mom wouldn't do that.*

She and Drew sat rigidly on the couch, staring straight ahead at the TV again and straining to listen for any sound from behind them.

"You know, I don't see you going out there to hassle Mom like you do to me every time Maddox is here," Aden mumbled, whacking his arm.

"You're my little sister. She's my Mom," he said simply.

"You know, I'm not so little any—" she broke off as the door opened behind them, and they both turned to see their mother coming inside. She was smiling, happier than Aden could remember seeing her in ages.

"Hey, guys." She laughed. "Waiting up for me?"

"Just watching some TV." Aden shrugged.

"And waiting up for you," Drew confirmed. Aden elbowed him in the ribs.

"Did you have a good time?" she asked as her Mom kicked off her shoes.

"I did." Her Mom beamed. "And what about you two? How was your evening?"

"It was okay," Drew answered.

"Mine was good. We all had a good time," Aden said. "So where did you go?"

"We went to Aricelli's Attic." Her mom waited to see if they'd heard of it. "It's a really elegant restaurant in Spartanburg. The food was excellent."

"And the company?" Aden grinned.

"That was excellent, too." Janet smiled. "We practically closed the place down, talking and dancing."

"Dancing?" Drew frowned.

"Yes, dancing. Maybe you've heard of it." His Mom smiled back. "It's been ages and ages since I went dancing."

"I'm glad you had a good time, Mom." Aden grinned, really happy to see her Mom in such good spirits.

"Yeah, me too." Drew chimed in. "You look really nice."

"Well, thank you, both of you." She bent to pick up her shoes. "I'm going to bed now, so turn that TV down a bit, okay?"

"I'm turning in, too," Drew said, getting up and stretching. "Aden, come lock the door behind me."

Aden followed him to the door and insisted on watching him climb the stairs to his room. He ducked inside and turned on a light before waving her back inside. He stood watch as she closed and locked the door. She turned to find the den empty, and her mother's door was closed. She smiled fondly at the day's events and turned off the TV to go to bed.

The next afternoon, she rocked from side to side on aching feet as she stood behind the watch counter at the jewelry store. These heels always hurt after standing for hours at work. She should have worn the flats she'd debated on this morning. The heels made her legs look better with the short skirt she was wearing, but the flats would have been more comfortable. Maybe next time she'd bring both, wear the flats while standing behind the counter for hours, and then change into the heels for Maddox. She smiled, glancing at the clock for the thousandth time. *Fifteen more minutes.* It seemed like a lifetime since she'd seen him last night, and fifteen minutes was an eternity to wait.

The store had been relatively busy today with browsing customers. Mr. Keith had spent most of the day in the showroom instead of back in his office. He'd helped customers, strolled outside the front window to bring in new ones, reorganized the forms and receipts behind the sales counter, and even wiped down the glass cases on occasion. He'd made a little small talk with Aden earlier in the day before Mrs. McConnell came in for her shift, but between customers, it was mostly quiet as Aden daydreamed.

As soon as Mrs. McConnell clocked in and came out to the showroom, Mr. Keith vanished back into his office. She couldn't blame him; Mrs. McConnell was a bit much to take except in small doses. She was a very sweet, very curious older lady, who was always inquiring into everyone's business. Loudly. Her hearing wasn't what it used to be, and she didn't modulate her volume very well.

"Well, Aden, good afternoon." She smiled, watching Mr. Keith scurry away. "How are you, my dear? And your dear Mother, bless her soul?" She always did that, too: asked about her Mother and blessed her soul. But then, she blessed everybody's soul, or their heart, depending on what she thought of them.

"I'm just fine, and my Mother is wonderful, thank you for asking." Aden smiled, giving her usual answer. *It's like a dance, talking with Mrs. McConnell. Back and forth, the same steps every time.*

"You know, Mrs. Hewitt at the church told me that your house had been broken into." Mrs. McConnell looked utterly scandalized. "Is your family recovering alright?"

"Um, yes ma'am. We're all just fine," Aden assured her. "They were scared away before they could take anything, and none of us were hurt. We've changed the locks," she finished.

"I should hope so." Mrs. McConnell nodded. "Did you use those Locktite Locksmith people? From the TV? I've heard they're very good."

"I'm really not sure. My brother handled it all, and I was still in school."

"Well, it's just dreadful that you had to go through that at all. I cannot believe what this world is coming to. I remember when we never locked our doors. Our cars didn't even have locks, and the only time you'd lock your house is if you were going out of town for a while."

"Sounds nice." Aden smiled, her eyes sliding to the clock again. She saw Mr. Keith's shoulder, standing just inside his partly-open office door. He must have heard about the break in too but was too polite to ask her about it. Maybe that's why he hung around out front all day. He might have been waiting for a chance to bring it up.

"So I hear you're dating the Mayor's boy, Maddox," Mrs. McConnell said matter-of-factly. Aden just smiled again, caught off guard. She wasn't so much surprised that Mrs. McConnell had heard—the woman heard everything. "He's devilish handsome, that one. Got it mostly from his Mother, you know." She continued without waiting for Aden to comment. "You watch out. Those handsome devils can break your heart. Oh, the stories I could tell." She shook her head with a pained expression. Just then, Mr. Keith came out to the sales counter.

"Mrs. McConnell, do you know where last year's credit account application files might have gone?"

"Yes, Mr. Keith, I showed you just last week where I'd filed them." She walked briskly into the back, and Mr. Keith winked at Aden, smiling. She mouthed "thank you" back to him before he followed Mrs. McConnell to the back.

"You see? I moved all of last year's files into this cabinet. Everything from the last three years is in here. Older files are in the big cabinet by the back door." Mrs. McConnell's voice carried out to the showroom. Aden's eyes glanced at the clock. *Just a few more minutes.*

The bell above the front door announced a new customer. Aden turned to find Billy Ray Payne standing just inside the door grinning at her. *Crap.*

"Hello, Aden." He came to lean over the counter where she was standing, and she took an involuntary step backward. "Thought I'd come by and apologize for yesterday at the lake." Aden was speechless, caught completely off guard. "Your friends and me, well, I guess we just ruffled each other's feathers. That happens with fightin' cocks sometimes." He grinned. "I didn't mean to be rude to you girls. Actually, when I recognized you out there in the water, I was just watching out for you, like Drew and I had talked about. Brotherly-like."

"Um, uh—" Aden stuttered, trying to gather her thoughts.

"She has plenty of people watching out for her," came Maddox's voice from the doorway, "And I would appreciate it if you would back off."

Billy Ray scowled, but he stood up off the counter. "Oh look, it's the *boy*-friend."

"Is everything okay out here?" Mr. Keith had come from the back, hands on his hips, glaring from Billy Ray to Maddox and back.

"Just fine, Mr. Keith." Aden smiled stiffly, turning to Billy Ray. "Thank you for your apology." She glanced meaningfully at Maddox. "I'm at work right now, and this isn't the best place for this conversation."

"This conversation is over," Maddox declared, glaring at Billy Ray. "We were just leaving." He held the door open for Billy Ray, who grinned darkly back. *Oh crap.*

"Is there going to be a problem, gentlemen?" Mr. Keith stepped forward, flexing his meaty fists.

"No," Aden insisted, coming from behind the counter. "Billy Ray, really, thank you, but I think you should go now. Maddox, could you wait for just a moment while I clock out and get my things?"

Billy Ray sneered at Mr. Keith, and Maddox before nonchalantly strolling through the door. "See you around, Aden." He grinned over his shoulder. Aden grabbed Maddox's arm.

"Let him go," she sighed, then turned, "Mr. Keith, I'm so sorry."

"It's alright, Aden." Mr. Keith frowned at Maddox. "Is your brother coming? Would you like me to escort you out?"

"No, thank you. Maddox is my ride this afternoon." Mr. Keith looked from Aden to Maddox and back.

"I trust he'll see you home safely?" he asked dubiously. "I'd be happy to give you a ride—"

"Looked to me like Billy Ray Payne was the problem," Mrs. McConnell interjected from the hallway at the back of the store.

"Thank you both for your concern. I'm really sorry for all of this, and I promise I'm just fine." Aden smiled. "I'll go clock out and be out of your hair." She glanced at Maddox. "Will you wait here for me?"

He just nodded, frowning.

"That Payne boy's a wild one since his Mother left 'em." Mrs. McConnell announced as Aden passed her by. "You stay far away from that one. He's a devil without *any* of the handsome. Bad, bad news." She shook her head, frowning deeply.

"I'm doing my best to stay away from him," Aden said quietly, gathering her things.

"Would you like me to speak to his father? I've seen enough today to give him a piece of my mind."

"No, please, Mrs. McConnell. Thank you, but I'm afraid that might make it worse. He came here to apologize, and he's done that. Let's all just move on."

Mrs. McConnell stared at her disapprovingly. "Well, then, I'll keep my peace, for now, but you watch out for that devil. He worries me, and that's a fact."

Aden smiled and slipped out to the showroom. Mr. Keith stood, arms crossed, in the center of the showroom floor looking at nothing in particular, or so he'd like everyone to think. Maddox stood just inside the front door, surveying the street outside.

"This won't happen again," she promised one more time while she passed Mr. Keith.

"Has he harassed you before?" he asked suddenly, halting Aden. "Is that what he's apologizing for?" Aden sighed. *I just want to get out of here and kick off these heels.* "Have you told him to lay off?" he pressed.

"It's really nothing, I swear," Aden began.

"He was very rude and disrespectful to the ladies the last time we ran into him with some friends of ours," Maddox explained.

"And he apologized," Aden interjected.

"And it *won't* happen again," Maddox vowed, glaring out at the street.

"You take care of her, Mr. Dixon," Mrs. McConnell commanded, nodding.

"If you need anything—" Mr. Keith began.

"Thank you." She smiled back. "I really appreciate it, and I'm very sorry for...all this." She shrugged.

"Take care." He nodded, and Maddox escorted her outside.

They both looked up and down the street. There was no sign of Billy Ray, thankfully.

"Where's your car?" she asked.

"I had to park around back," he said. "The parking lot's full over there." He nodded toward the park in the square and led her around the corner. She'd never been in the alley behind the store before. Mom, Drew or Maddox had always dropped her off in front, or she'd walked to or from Drew's work at the garage down the main street.

Beyond Maddox's Audi parked near the alley's end nearest them, she saw an ancient, gleaming Cadillac that she imagined was Mrs. McConnell's. She wondered if the older woman still drove herself. Beyond that was a dumpster and a pickup truck on the other side. The hairs on the back of her neck and arms stood on end, but it wasn't the same truck Billy Ray had been in the day before. This one was a darker color. She shook it off. *There are hundreds of trucks around here; don't go freaking out every time you see one.*

Maddox opened the Audi's passenger door for her, and she sank gratefully into the seat, immediately kicking off her shoes. He chuckled as he closed the door and went around to the driver's side.

"You look like you might need a foot rub," he said, starting the car and taking another look around the alley.

"Sounds nice." She smiled. "Listen, thank you for coming to my defense with Billy Ray again. Your timing is impeccable."

"Not really." He frowned. "I should have seen him sooner and prevented him from going inside at all."

"He came to apologize."

"So he said."

"Okay," she sighed, ready to drop the subject, "Where are we going?"

"Anywhere you'd like." He smiled. "But we have been…invited to join our mothers and LeighAnn for a debrief."

"What?" She giggled. "Invited for a debrief?"

"Well, my Mom is at LeighAnn's, and your Mom is coming over, and the three of them would like to sit down with all of us to re-hash everything that's gone on this week."

"Sounds like fun." Aden frowned.

"We don't have to go if you don't want to." He shrugged, smiling at her tone. "But Cadence is supposed to be there, if that helps, and we'll keep it as brief as possible, skip out at the first opportunity."

"A brief debrief," she intoned. "Awesome."

"Should we just go get it over with?" he suggested. "Otherwise, they'll just reschedule it for another time."

"Sure, can't wait." She tried to smile. "Rehashing the past week for the fifteenth time sounds…great."

"Just remember that they mean well, the Moms, and they haven't heard it all directly from us as many times as we've discussed it amongst ourselves. They're just worried."

"Well, let's go ease their minds."

Two hours later, Cadence led Aden, Maddox, and Trey onto the front porch of her house.

"So what was that all about, anyway?" she whined, dropping into a rocking chair.

"My Mom wanted to walk through the timeline of all that's happened with all of us who were there," Maddox said, "And then your Moms wanted to hear it. Throw in that bottle of wine they're now sharing in there, and they've got themselves a party."

"Okay, so why was Patience here? I mean, Grace was at the lake that first day, but Patience…" Cadence grumbled.

"Your Mom's just worried about all three of you," Trey said quietly. "Although, Patience *was* really annoying, interrupting every two minutes."

"She can't stand not being the center of attention," Cadence sighed.

"Well, now, we've gone all through everything with everyone, forwards and backwards," Aden said, "Did your Mom learn anything new? Anything helpful to the kidnapping cases?" she asked Maddox.

He shrugged, "Dunno. She took a lot of notes we'll have to re-analyze."

"Well, I learned there was a lot more going on at that lake outing last week than I knew about." Trey frowned. "Add that to the gun holster I didn't even see right in front of me, and I'm thinking I need to pay more attention."

"Guess we all do. At least until we catch this guy." Maddox frowned.

"You know, you keep saying 'we' when you talk about catching the guy," Aden pointed out.

"You know what I mean. Them, the cops. I'm just feeling more closely involved lately." He pulled her closer to his side.

"You really believe the creep is after Aden, don't you?" Cadence asked quietly.

"Who knows? He could be after anyone," Maddox insisted.

"Yeah, but after our last conversation here on this porch, I know there's more to this story that you *and* your Mom aren't telling." Cadence was uncharacteristically serious. "You know something, and it's something to do with Aden."

Trey looked from face to face around their suddenly tense circle. "Is that why you two are suddenly inseparable?" he asked. "Are you protecting Aden because she really is a target?"

"Look, we don't *know* anything—" Maddox began, but Cadence interrupted, rolling her eyes to the ceiling fans above.

"Sure. Don't believe a word of it, Trey."

"Seriously, I'm just as concerned that *you* could be a target, or Grace or Patience," he huffed.

"I believe that." Cadence nodded shrewdly, "But you're not shadowing every move that *we* make and keeping tabs as close as you are on Aden."

"Well, she's a lot less aggravating." Maddox grinned.

"I'm still watching you." Cadence squinted and tilted her head.

"You know, if there is something else…going on, we could help," Trey said, frowning uncertainly.

"Just being here, all of us together. That's what we can do." Maddox shook his head. "Safety in numbers." He elbowed Cadence before she could respond and continued. "Help me keep an eye on this one, and her crazy sisters when you can."

"You know you sound like an old man talking to children." Cadence sniffed, "We're not stupid."

"Never said you were stupid. I said you were aggravating."

Cadence shook her head, still eyeing him suspiciously.

"Ugh! Can we *please* talk about something else?" Aden groaned. "Let's get outta here before the Moms come up with more questions."

"Agreed, but don't think I'm not watchin' you, too." Cadence answered. "You've always been a horrible liar, and I know that you know what's really going on. You're in cahoots with the old man over here."

"Fine, whatever. Can we discuss your conspiracy theories over dinner? Besides those pralines your Mom set out, I haven't eaten since 11:30 this morning." Aden looked wilted.

"Wow, it's almost 7:30 already." Trey exclaimed, looking at his phone.

"Exactly!" Aden stood with her hands on her hips.

They ended up going to the fast food joint on the highway to appease Aden's need for immediate and abundant sustenance. Actually, though she really *was* famished, her repeated dinner demands came mainly in response to Cadence or Trey's insistence to discuss the kidnappings or theories surrounding the case. Only Maddox had caught on to her tactics.

"Oh my God, get that girl the buffet!" Candace complained to Maddox as they pulled up to the restaurant. "When did you become so high maintenance, anyway?" she asked Aden.

"Sorry." Aden chuckled. "I get cranky when I'm hungry."

"And she doesn't want to talk about the kidnapping case stuff anymore," Maddox said drily. "Seriously, Cadence, you're her best friend. You didn't pick up on that yet?"

"Hold on. Are you telling me we've had to listen to her hunger pangs all this time just so we wouldn't talk about the case anymore?"

Aden shrugged guiltily, and Maddox just shook his head, exasperated.

"For the love of sacred possums, why didn't you just say that?" Cadence exclaimed. "You've been driving us all nuts."

"Sacred possums?" Aden burst out laughing.

"Oh, shut up, Ms. McStuffin." Cadence frowned.

"McStuffin?!!" Aden, Maddox, and Trey all burst into laughter. Cadence tried hard to look at them with disdain but very soon melted into laughter herself.

"Yes, McStuffin. It's not like you're the only one who's hungry." Cadence giggled.

"Must feed the women." Maddox nodded, still laughing. "Point taken."

"And hurry!" Trey begged, grinning.

"This really isn't all that funny, you know," Cadence said, sobering.

Trey laughed again, "Sacred McStuffin Possums is not funny?"

"Ok, now you're just being silly." She sniffed, stifling a smile.

"I'm pretty sure you're all delirious from lack of food." Maddox nodded with a serious expression.

"Oh like you didn't just snort a lugey!" Cadence poked the back of his head from the back seat.

"Eeew!" Aden pulled a sour face. "I'm outta here."

"I was going to suggest we go through the drive-thru!" Maddox called, leaning across the console to the open passenger door.

"Too late." Trey chuckled as Cadence jumped out, also.

"What the heck was in those pralines, anyway?" Maddox mumbled, setting Trey's laughter off again as they parked the car. "Maybe we should make our escape now."

"Nah." Trey chuckled, "What would they do without us?"

"You're right." Maddox nodded, grinning. "I mean, McStuffin Possums?? Really?" he emulated Cadence's high pitch.

"*SACRED* McStuffin Possums." Trey deadpanned, making them both laugh again.

"Hello? We're starving here?" Cadence called from the restaurant's entrance.

A while later, as they all nibbled at the remains on the table, the light mood lingered.

"So Maddox, will you take us all to your 'super-secret spot' in the mountains tonight?" Cadence asked, hitting Trey's knee under the table with her own.

"No!" It was Aden who spoke up, surprising them all. "It's not just 'his' place anymore, and it's still secret." Maddox just smiled, looking down at Aden ensconced at his side.

"Well, then," Trey said with raised eyebrows and a small grin. He glanced at Cadence. "Wonder what the 'secret password' was that granted her entrance?" Cadence giggled.

"Sorry, it's just…special," Aden said uncomfortably.

"And we don't rate." Cadence nodded, still smiling. "We get it."

"I didn't mean—" Aden frowned.

"She's just messing with us." Maddox stage-whispered in her ear.

"I know that, but–," she ended quickly, looking past Maddox with wide eyes, "Oh."

"Well look-y what we have here." Billy Ray grinned, elbowing his companion in the gut.

"Crap," Trey said stiffly under his breath, frowning at the three men standing over their table. Billy Ray was flanked by two good-ol'-boys in jeans and camo shirts.

"We just gotta stop meetin' like this." Billy Ray shook his head gleefully. "I'd swear you're stalkin' me, Aden. It's embarassin'."

"I just threw up a little in my mouth," Cadence mumbled, scowling.

"Oh, I'm sorry sugar, I didn't mean to leave you out." Billy Ray turned his predatory gaze to her. "Which one o' them Kendall girls are you, again?"

Trey stood up, and Maddox, blocked in the booth seat by Aden, nudged her thigh with his hand, trying to get by. Billy Ray and his friends sized up Trey as Aden rose slowly to face them.

"What do you want?" she asked him, toe to toe. His sudden, unwanted appearance and demeanor made her angrier than she could remember being.

Billy Ray chuckled, surprised. "Well, look at this, boys. I think I got me an admirer." His eyes slid slowly upward, and she felt Maddox right behind her. His hands were on her waist, trying to push her aside, but she resisted. She wasn't going to let Maddox fight this battle for her.

"Billy Ray, I'm trying to be patient since you apologized earlier and because my brother's your friend," she said quietly. "But I've had enough, and you need to *back off*." She enunciated the last two words slowly, glaring into his eyes. Billy Ray's boys exchanged a confused glance behind his back and took a few small steps backward. Billy Ray acknowledged their tacit retreat with a quick sideways glance and a leering grin directed toward Maddox and Trey at her shoulders. "No, you look at *me*," Aden snapped, "And you listen. I am not impressed by all your creepy…swagger." She heard Trey's faint chuckle at her left shoulder, and Maddox still gripped her waist on the right hand side. She rushed on before her anger drained. "You're obnoxious and offensive—"

"Well, don't hold back that passion, baby." Billy Ray grinned, but she could see the uncertainty in his eyes as he lost control of the situation.

"—And to be bluntly honest, the way you act towards females creeps me out," she continued as though he hadn't spoken.

"Ohhhh!" He shouted, "Kitty's got claws; I like it."

"I mean it. I'm over this. We're done," Aden warned.

"Oh, is that right?"

"Yes. It is." A deep, unamused voice made them all turn. Sheriff Richey stood in an adjacent aisle with his arms crossed beneath a deep scowl. "Billy Ray, you clear on outta here before I get my Breathalyzer out, and don't let me hear about you harassin' these kids again. You hear me?"

Billy Ray took a small step backward with his palms up, and the insolent grin even broader on his face. "I'm just talkin' with my friends here, Sheriff. Ain't no law against that."

"There are laws against harassment. I clearly heard your 'friends' tellin' you to leave 'em alone."

"Aww, now—" Billy Ray started, laughing.

"You better get one of your boys to drive you on outta here. I see your truck out there, and you don't want another DUI."

"Hey, man, I ain't drinkin' yet." He frowned.

"Come on, Billy Ray," one of his friends coaxed quietly, "I'll drive."

"Well ain't this a bitch?" Billy Ray asked loudly, looking around the restaurant. "Come in to eat, talk to some friends, and I'm the one gettin' kicked out."

"Start walkin'," Sheriff Richey commanded with a warning glare.

"A'ight boys, the good sheriff has spoken." Billy Ray chuckled, backing slowly toward the door. "Guess we'll go eat somewhere else." He bowed to the entire restaurant before shoving the door violently open and stalking to his truck. He tossed the keys to his friend and glared at Aden through the windshield as they drove off.

"Everything okay over here?" the Sheriff asked the still-standing group at the table.

"What would have to happen for Aden to file a restraining order against him?" Maddox asked, surprising Aden again.

The Sheriff sighed. "You'd have to prove the occurrence of actual, physical violence or a very credible, imminent threat." He looked at the group unhappily. "I heard this wasn't the first run-in you've had with him this week, but from what I gather, and what I've seen here tonight, he's all talk and bluster. Has he threatened you?"

"He has a gun. He had it with him when we ran into him yesterday at the lake." Trey spoke up.

The Sheriff didn't look surprised. "Did he pull it on you? Point it at you? Threaten you in any way?"

"It was in a shoulder holster. He just made sure we saw it," Maddox answered.

The Sheriff nodded, sighing again.

"I don't think a restraining order is necessary." Aden frowned at them. "It'll probably just make it all worse."

"Well, I don't think you'd get one right now, anyway," The Sheriff said, unhappily.

"So we'll just have to wait until he actually hurts her?" Maddox growled.

"Look, I've known Billy Ray a long time. He's always been a punk, all talk. Most folks around here own guns, and a lot of 'em are arming themselves since those women have gone missing." He held up a hand as Maddox started to speak. "Now, I'm not saying he's not an asshole, and I'm aware of his harassment towards y'all but the fact is, he hasn't broken any laws."

"Yet," Trey said quietly.

"You just need to steer clear of him," Sheriff Richey continued.

"We haven't been the ones seeking him out," Aden said.

"I spoke with Herman Keith at the jewelry store," the Sheriff said, "We'll be making patrols, making sure Billy Ray knows he's not welcome in there while you're workin'."

"Mr. Keith called you?" Aden asked, surprised again. He nodded. "This is getting out of hand."

"It doesn't have to. Y'all just avoid Billy Ray for a while. Shouldn't be that hard. He mostly hangs out at bars and places you shouldn't be, anyway, and if you do see him, you turn around and go the other way. If he seeks you out and starts something again, you call us. That's what we're here for."

"Thanks," Aden said lamely.

"Okay, why don't we get outta here," Maddox sighed.

"Good idea." The Sheriff nodded. "Y'all have a safe evenin'," he finished, and he walked back to the front counter, seeming oblivious to the stares of the restaurant staff and few patrons who'd witnessed the encounter.

"I really hate that guy," Trey said mildly as they settled back into the Audi. "Billy Ray, I mean."

"Ditto," Maddox ground out.

"Well, what about our girl, here?" Cadence grinned, "Gettin' all feisty. I thought you might whack him."

"I've just had enough drama for one week. I'm completely over all of it," Aden said drily. Maddox squeezed her hand before pulling out onto the road.

"Well, I'm proud of you, standing up to that creep like that," Cadence said.

"Yeah, that was pretty boss." Trey smiled. "I went from thinking somebody better hold me back to thinking we might have to grab hold of Aden."

"I did grab hold of her." Maddox smiled.

"Did not," she said, feeling embarrassed. "You had a hand on my waist…and I wasn't gonna fight the jerk."

"Well, anyway, everybody at the restaurant got dinner *and* a show tonight." Cadence giggled. "It'll be all over town by tomorrow."

"Awesome," Aden sighed, looking out the window. "I don't have to work tomorrow; I just might spend the day in bed with the covers pulled over my head. Maybe then nothing else crazy will happen."

The next day, Aden slept in until 11:00. Cadence was missing from the other side of the bed where she'd spent the night. Aden stretched and reached for her cell phone, charging on the nightstand. No messages. She flopped back over, sighing, and wondered where Maddox might be. She smiled just thinking about him. *His hypnotic eyes, perfect face, the sound of his voice…*Okay, maybe she'd call him.

She sighed again, remembering her plan to do some housework today. Maybe she'd get that done first. Groaning, she got up and stripped the bedclothes, dumping them in the laundry room at the end of the hall. Then, she went to add her mother's to the pile and found Cadence on the couch, huddled under a blanket watching TV. It was dark in the den; ominous grey clouds crouched over the forest outside. It looked like they were in for storms.

"I wondered where you'd gone." Aden yawned.

"Couldn't sleep anymore and didn't want to wake you." Cadence shrugged.

"I'm just taking care of a few chores. Sit tight," Aden said, continuing on through the room. She stripped her mother's bed and grabbed an empty water glass off her nightstand. Before she turned to go, she went to bump the nightstand drawer closed with her hip but stopped. It was only open an inch or so, but she could swear that looked like…a gun. In her mother's nightstand. Setting the glass down again, she pulled the drawer open a few more inches. It was a small silver handgun nestled on top of her mother's scarves and a couple of fashion magazines. She closed the drawer and went back to work.

When the laundry was started, she became a whirlwind, vacuuming and dusting. Cadence had pitched in, and they'd made quick work of most of the cleaning, but she bowed out when it came to the bathrooms.

"Sorry girl, you're on your own with that," Cadence huffed and went back to the TV.

Aden had just finished scrubbing the last bathroom when her phone rang. She'd left it on the kitchen counter in the center of the house, so she ran to get it, and she was a little out of breath when she answered.

"Good morning, are you okay?" Maddox sounded concerned.

"Afternoon," she corrected. "I'm fine. I'm just cleaning my house."

"Sounds vigorous."

"Ha," she said. "What are you up to?"

"Well, I've endured breakfast with the women in my family. I've helped my Mom organize paperwork for a new case she's been assigned—"

"Your Mom has a new case?"

"Yeah, she'll be working it from here for now though…So then, I took some lunch over to my Dad at his office, and I wondered if you'd had lunch yet? Maybe I could bring you something?"

"Um," She wondered if her mother would mind him coming over, but she really wanted to see him. "Sure. That'd be great."

"What would you like?"

"Oh." She frowned. She hadn't eaten breakfast, but she wasn't all that hungry. "Cadence, Maddox is bringing lunch, what would you like?" Cadence just shrugged.

"I kinda made a sandwich just a little while ago. I'm good."

"Okay, Cadence doesn't want anything. Maybe just a salad for me? Nothing big, and just whatever's easiest for you."

"Salad it is. I'll see you soon." Her heart melted at the smile in his voice.

"See you soon," she replied. When she ended the call, she texted her mom.

Staying home today with Cadence. Is it okay if Maddox keeps us company? She bit her lip and hit send. She didn't expect an immediate reply as her mother was at work, so she set the phone down and went to get the sheets out of the dryer. As she plopped the basket of warm sheets on her mattress, she heard her phone chime in the kitchen. Her mom must have texted back already. She quickly made her bed and straightened her room, on the off-chance that Maddox would see in here. Then, she took the basket with her Mom's bed sheets with her to the kitchen and checked the phone.

Okay I guess. She read.

She'd just finished making her Mom's bed when somebody knocked on the kitchen door. It startled her. Maddox must have been closer by than she thought. As she went to answer it, a gust of wind tossed the trees outside in a frenzy. As she entered the kitchen, she shouted, playfully. "Who is it?"

There was no answer as she rounded the counter and approached the door. Prickles of alarm tickled her neck and she tried again, louder and more serious. "Who is it?"

"It's me, Grace," came the reply. Aden relaxed and opened the door.

"Hey, I wasn't expecting you." She smiled, waving Grace inside.

"I know. You're expecting Maddox, but I was bored and thought I'd come join the party." She shrugged.

"Actually, my Mom will probably feel better about the both of you here to chaperone."

"Well, here I am." She grinned. "Look at us, bein' all responsible."

"Where are Trey and Greg today?" Aden asked, texting to let her Mom know Grace had joined them too.

"Trey's interviewing for a job," Cadence called from her corner of the couch.

"Really? Where?"

"With the phone company. His Dad works there."

Aden just nodded.

"Greg's home watching his younger brother. Hey, I brought a couple of movies." Grace held them up.

"Nice! Mayhem, blood and gore," Aden approved. "I do love a good slasher flick."

"I know; Cadence told me, several times." Grace smiled. "Though our dear brother was making fun of us for it when I was picking these out."

"Oh, well." Aden shrugged. "So he said he had breakfast with you?"

"Yeah, he's been a nuisance, counting the minutes until he thought you might be awake and he could call."

"That's kind of sweet though." Aden smiled.

"I know, right? I think he's in love." Cadence laughed happily behind them. "Even our Moms were talking about it."

"Talking about Maddox?" Aden bit her lip.

"About you both. About how you haven't gone more than a handful of waking hours without being together since you met. His Mom said she'd never seen him like this. I mean, he's had girlfriends before, but the way you two are together, it's just more... intense."

"Sounds kind of ominous." Aden frowned.

Cadence shrugged, smiling. "Well, keep it up, and maybe we'll become sisters." They both laughed at Aden's expression. "Come on, it could happen."

"I've known him for a week, and, as he keeps reminding me, he'll be leaving town at some point in the near future."

"Maybe. Maybe not," Grace said mysteriously. "I mean, his Dad lives here, right? And he's an adult after all. He can live wherever he wants."

"Well, he seems pretty set on going back to Virginia with his Mom." She frowned.

"Unless you change his mind."

"I would never manipulate him—" Aden started.

"Who said anything about manipulation? I just mean creating a desirable option for him to stay."

Aden needed to change the subject.

"So Maddox doesn't like slasher films?" the sisters were unamused, so she continued. "Hey, I haven't seen this one. Isn't this the one they filmed up in Charlotte a couple years ago?"

Cadence sighed and shook her head slowly, frowning. "Fine. We'll change the subject."

"How are things going with you and Trey?" Aden tried again. That did it. Cadence softened.

"It's going great. He's supposed to call when he's done with the interview."

"You should invite him over."

"It'd be a while. He's supposed to mow their yard and do some other chores this afternoon." Cadence got a mischievous look on her face. "Some of us aren't at that inseparable stage quite yet." She looked innocently out the big glass doors, trying not to laugh.

"Really?" Aden asked, drily. The doorbell rang, and Cadence giggled.

"He's heeeere," Grace sang. Aden tossed a pillow at her before going to open the door.

"Who is it?" she paused.

"Salad delivery," Maddox shouted. She grinned and opened the door. "Good afternoon," he said and smiled, bending to kiss her cheek before setting a plastic bag on the counter.

"Good afternoon to you, too," she answered happily.

"Ahhh, young love," Cadence said, leaning on the back of the couch with her chin on her hands.

"You know, for as much crap as you give us, this is all your doing," Aden pointed out.

"I know. I am so good, right? You can thank me after you kiss him. Go ahead." She fluttered her eyelashes and waited.

Aden turned, and Maddox was already there. She looked up at him as he gathered her in his arms and picked her up off her feet for a slow kiss. "I've been waiting for that all day," he said, lowering her back to the floor.

"Me too." She sighed, hugging him close.

"Well?" Cadence prompted.

"Thank-you-Cay-dence," they both said, almost in unison, and laughed.

"You're welcome. Now, let the girl eat her lunch," she said to Maddox.

"I brought you cookies," he said to Cadence and Grace.

"Chocolate chip?" Cadence perked up like a five year old.

"Of course." He smiled. "And I got one for you, too," he said to Aden, opening the bag and producing a salad from the deli in town. The cookies came next.

"You can be a really good guy when properly motivated," Grace observed, coming to claim a cookie. "That salad looks good."

"You want some?" Aden offered.

"Hello?? Chocolate chip?" Grace brandished the cookie. "Did you just get the one?"

"No, I bought a box. Full dozen." Maddox pointed. "Here, Cadence."

Cadence sighed loudly, "Don't you just love him?" Aden glanced at Maddox and tried to stop the blush. It didn't work.

"What? You haven't said the 'L' word yet?" Cadence asked between bites. Maddox looked unconcerned, and Aden ignored her. "Seriously? It's so obvious that you're both head over heels."

"Thanks, Cadence. This isn't awkward at all." Aden took her salad to sit on the couch, and they followed.

"So which of the gory movie selection are we watching first?" Maddox asked, settling in to the couch beside Aden.

"Oh yeah, Grace said you didn't appreciate a good bloody film. We can watch something else if you want," Aden offered between bites.

"Nope. I don't really mind watching blood and guts, it just surprised me that you'd like them."

Aden shrugged one shoulder. "They're just so fake, they make me laugh. And the dialogue in some of them are just classic." She grinned.

Cadence put the movie into the player, and she and Grace shared the blanket. Aden finished her lunch and curled comfortably into Maddox' chest to watch the movie. A couple of hours later, they stretched and laughed as the credits rolled.

"See?" Aden giggled. "These movies are awesome."

"I have to admit, with the running commentary from the three of you, it was entertaining." Maddox grinned.

"It's all about perspective." Cadence informed him. "Making fear and blood and gore into entertainment takes a very refined sense of sophisticated humor."

"Sure," Maddox said gravely. "Your 'oh my God the hot guy's intestines are even steaming' was a truly refined comment."

208

"It was funny!" she defended herself. "He was hot. The blond chick had just said how steaming hot he was and then the slasher dude cut him open, and his intestines were steaming." She raised her eyebrows and looked to her sister for corroboration.

"Yes, hilarious…very sophisticated," he agreed, nodding.

"Well I enjoyed it." Aden smiled. "They make me laugh and forget all the craziness that's going on in my real life."

"Like that pesky Maddox guy. He's just making your life hell, isn't he?" Cadence teased.

"You are so annoying," Maddox said drily as Cadence's phone began to ring.

"It's Trey!" Cadence beamed, walking to the kitchen before she answered.

"Should I put another movie in?" Grace offered.

"Not yet. Let's wait and see what Cadence's plans are with Trey." Aden said.

"Actually, that reminds me, I think I left my phone in the car. I'll be right back." Aden reluctantly rose so that Maddox could get up, and he kissed her on the forehead. She smiled and followed him into the kitchen with the mess from her lunch and the cookies they'd all shared. Out of the corner of her eye, she saw Maddox open the door to go outside, pause and then bend down. She turned to look as he stood back up with something in his hand.

"Um, this is addressed to you." He frowned.

"What?" she asked as he handed her an envelope with just her first name typed on the front.

"Trey is on his way." Cadence smiled, joining them. "What's that?"

Aden shook her head, turning it over to open the sealed envelope.

"It must have been stuck into the door jamb. It fell when I opened the door." Maddox was looking more uneasy by the second though he was trying to hide it.

Aden pulled out the single piece of folded white paper and scanned it briefly before her eyes widened, and she dropped it to the floor, covering her mouth with her hands.

Maddox grabbed it and began reading aloud:

PIERCING THE HEART OF PEGASUS
SO MANY THINGS I SEE.
YOU ARE THE WILD-WINGED HORSE,
AND THE SHOOTING STAR IS ME.

SO MANY ADMIRERS YOU HAVE SNARED,
PLYING YOUR NOT-SO-INNOCENT ART.
I TOO AM CAUGHT, AS THEY ARE,
BUT ONLY ONE SHALL PIERCE YOUR HEART.

WATCHING. WAITING. I WILL COME FOR YOU SOON.

Cadence stared at Aden with horror in her eyes as Maddox read. Then, he dropped the note on the counter, pulling Aden into his arms. Grace had joined them in the kitchen while he read.

"Oh my God. We have to call the police," Cadence said wringing her hands anxiously. She reached for the note, but Maddox stopped her.

"No! Don't touch it. It's evidence." He pulled Cadence over and pushed Aden into her arms. "Stay here. Don't move." He practically ran out the door.

"I don't understand." Grace practically danced with agitation.

"Um, he left his phone in his car. He's probably going out to call his Mom," Aden said quietly. She was much more subdued than Cadence or Grace, though inside she felt like screaming bloody murder. "Come with me."

"What? Where are we going?" Aden pulled Cadence by the hand through the den and to the sliding glass doors as Grace stayed behind to read the note on the counter. Aden checked the locks in the den and then the ones in her Mom's room.

"I'll check the front door." Cadence offered, jogging over. Aden went through the house re-checking all the window locks, too, while Cadence followed.

"Where's Maddox?" Grace asked. "He should be back by now." Aden had been wondering the same thing. She headed for the kitchen door just as someone began knocking on it.

"Aden, it's me," Maddox called through the door.

"Did you see anything else out there?" she asked, letting him inside and locking the door behind him. He shook his head, frowning.

"Nothing. I circled the house. Didn't find a thing out of place."

"He was right there," Cadence whispered, pointing to the door. "While we all sat around laughing at that movie, he came right up and—"

"Stop, please." Aden shivered.

"Did you call your Mom already? Or the police?" Grace asked Maddox.

"I left Mom a voice mail. She didn't answer." He frowned at the phone in his hand. "But I guess we should go ahead and call the police. Get somebody out—" his phone rang, stopping him mid-sentence. "Mom, I'm at Aden's, and somebody left a threatening message on her door. Can you come over? Bring a forensics kit for fingerprints or something?" he ran his free hand distractedly through his hair. "Yeah, Cadence and Grace are here, too. We watched a movie, and I remembered I'd left my phone in the car, so when I opened the door to go out, an envelope fell to the ground. I think it must have been wedged in the door jamb. Aden's name was typed on the front, printed from a computer I think, and the paper inside is a poem, I can read it to you...okay. Yeah, see you in a few." He ended the call. "We need to lock all the doors until they get here."

"We just checked them all," Aden said, hugging herself tightly.

"How 'bout that door upstairs?" he asked.

"We didn't go up there." Cadence shook her head, looking at Aden.

Maddox took the stairs two at a time. They could hear him walk to the door and then back.

"Okay, my Mom's on the way, and she was calling Sheriff Richey," he said, descending the stairs. He slowly walked to where the girls huddled together by the couch and put his arms around them. "Are you all okay?" They just nodded. "It's alright. He didn't try to get in; he just wanted to send a message."

"Message received," Aden mumbled. "I wish I knew what it was I supposedly did to this psychopath."

"You didn't do anything." Maddox tightened his arm around her.

"Piercing the heart of Pegasus." Aden glanced at Maddox. "You said that—that night— the meteor."

"I know," he sighed.

"What?" Cadence pulled away and looked from one to the other. "What meteor?" They all sat on one of the couches.

"On the mountain one night, Aden and I saw a shooting star. It burned out in the middle of the constellation Pegasus, and I said something about it 'piercing the heart of Pegasus'....I don't know." He looked away.

"He was there," Aden said quietly, "He had to be. He followed us, and he heard you say that."

"That's impossible." Maddox scowled at the view out the window. "There's no way somebody could have gotten that close on that trail without us hearing them."

"But it's word for word." Aden stared at his profile as he continued to scowl into space.

"Um, did you say any of the other stuff in that poem?" Grace asked hesitantly. They both shook their heads.

"Just the Pegasus thing," Aden confirmed. "I'm so confused. I don't know how anybody could have known. It's bizarre."

"Twilight Zone," Cadence agreed. They all jumped at the sound of car doors slamming outside and a knock at the door.

"Police, Miss Garrett." A man's voice called through the door. Maddox stepped around Aden to open it before she could. "Mr. Dixon." The uniformed officer clearly recognized Maddox. "Agent Dixon called in a disturbance at this address?"

"Yes, please come in." Maddox stood aside to let the officer and his partner inside the kitchen.

"You're Aden Garrett?" the first officer asked, looking at Aden. "I was here when you had the recent break-in as well. Sgt. Hughes," he introduced himself.

"Yes, I remember you." Aden smiled briefly.

"So please tell us what's happened today."

"Cadence spent the night with me, and then Grace and Maddox came over to watch a movie earlier today. When it was over, Maddox remembered he'd left his phone in his car and went to get it. When he opened the door, an envelope fell to the ground. It had my name on it, so he handed it to me, and I opened it and read the note inside."

She pointed at the single, printed sheet, still lying on the kitchen counter. Both officers stepped to the counter and read the note without touching it. "I actually dropped it before I finished reading, and Maddox picked it up and read it aloud before he put it there on the counter."

"It was left at this door?" the second officer asked, moving toward the door.

"Yes, it fell when I opened the door, so I guess it'd been wedged in the door jamb," Maddox answered. The officer opened the door and examined the door, knob, frame and door mat as the first officer took up the questioning again.

"What time did Mr. Dixon and Miss Kendall arrive?"

"Umm...Grace got here sometime...just past 12:30 I think?" She glanced at Grace, who nodded. "And Maddox got here just after 1:00."

"And you watched a movie? In here?" he pointed to the TV as they nodded. "And about what time was it that you opened the door to go out and get your phone?"

"Um...it was only 10 to 15 minutes ago. You guys got here quick."

"We've stepped up patrols in this area." Sgt. Hughes said, glancing at Aden.

"I'm gonna go check outside," the second officer called, stepping out.

"Did you hear anything? Or see anything else out of the ordinary?" Sgt. Hughes asked Aden.

"Just the letter." Aden looked at it as though it were a poisonous snake lying on her counter.

"There is something else," Maddox spoke up, frowning. "The phrase in the poem, the line about 'piercing the heart of Pegasus'...I used that phrase several days ago." The officer stared at him more intently. "Aden and I were up on the mountain sky-watching one night, and we saw a shooting star that burned out in the constellation Pegasus." The officer didn't move. "I said something about it piercing the heart of Pegasus, and we talked about the constellation a little bit."

"And you and Miss Garrett were there alone?"

"We thought so." Maddox shrugged. "I don't see how anyone could have followed us without us hearing them. The trail to where we were is really steep and rugged." The officer stared at him.

"And where and when did this take place?"

"It was Friday night around 9:30 or 10:00, and I can show you on a map where we were," Maddox said, glancing slyly at Cadence, who frowned back at him.

"And did you talk to anyone about the meteor sighting?"

"Not until we saw the poem today. We told Cadence and Grace while we waited for you guys to get here," Aden answered.

"And you, Mr. Dixon? You didn't discuss it with anyone that you remember?"

"No, I hadn't discussed it with anyone."

Sgt. Hughes made some notes on a small pad from his pocket and gave Maddox a hard look again before turning to Aden. "So Mr. Dixon picked up the envelope and handed it to you, correct?" Aden nodded. "And you took it and dropped it, then Mr. Dixon retrieved it and read it aloud." She nodded again. "And did either of the Miss Kendalls touch it?"

"No, just the two of us. We dropped it right there by the envelope on the counter and haven't touched it since."

Sgt. Hughes nodded, making more notes as his partner came back inside.

"Agent Dixon is here," the second officer announced, "And the Sheriff should be right behind her with forensics."

"I should probably call my mom." Aden realized, speaking the thought aloud. Maddox nodded to her, smiling as she began to search for her phone. She found it on a table in the den and placed the call.

"So...I think you may be a suspect," Cadence whispered to Maddox as the police officers quietly compared notes. Outside, a gust of wind whipped the trees into a slow dance.

"I think we may get a storm today, after all," Maddox mused, looking out into the gray forest. "The one that came through earlier must have gone around us. It never did rain."

"Maddox!" Cadence hissed, pulling him to a side of the den away from where Aden was talking on the phone. "Did you hear what I said?"

"I heard you."

214

"Well?"

"Well, it's not me, and I hope they don't waste a whole lot of time investigating that before they figure it out. I have a feeling we may not have much time left." He was looking wistfully at Aden.

"Hello, gentlemen, show me this letter." Agent Kim Phillips came into the kitchen followed by Sheriff Richey and yet another officer. She nodded at Maddox, Grace, and Cadence, and her eyes found Aden on the phone in the den, but she went straight to the kitchen counter. Sgt. Hughes spoke quietly, presumably filling her in on all that he'd learned. Thunder rumbled faintly in the distance.

"Yep, sounds like it's heading this way," Maddox said quietly.

"Maddox," Cadence barked. "Forget the weather! I think you're being framed."

"Don't be so dramatic." Maddox smiled at his sisters, but Cadence could tell he was more worried than he wanted her to know. "If I was being framed, they wouldn't choose to use a random phrase that nobody could possibly know about, except for Aden and me."

"But—"

"No, I think it was just intended to rattle us a bit more. Somebody's just playing with us."

"This is not a game."

"But to him it is, and if he really wanted to frame me, he'd use something a lot more concrete. This is just his way of saying that he can get to us. That he *has* gotten to us. Followed us. Watched us. Heard us."

"You're giving me goosebumps again." Cadence shivered. "This is all so creepy."

"Imagine how Aden must feel," he said quietly, watching her across the room. "It's all being directed at her."

"Maybe she should go somewhere. Get out of town," Grace joined in.

"I've thought about it, but she's safer here where we can all stick together and keep watch."

There was a commotion outside in the courtyard. The kitchen door still stood open, and they could hear raised voices. Sheriff Richey, closest to the door, went to investigate and came back shortly with Trey following close behind.

"Hey guys!" he called. "Sorry, they wouldn't let me in."

"It's a possible crime scene," Sheriff Richey growled. "But there isn't much here, and it's all been previously contaminated..." he mumbled to himself.

"So what happened?" Trey asked Maddox. "They wouldn't tell me anything."

Cadence filled him in, leading him to sit on one of the couches. Maddox went to sit near where Aden paced, still on the phone. She smiled at him as she ended the call and sat beside him.

"Tried to talk my mom out of coming home early. There really isn't anything she could do here." She shrugged. "Hi, Trey." She smiled at him.

"Hey, Aden, I can't believe your house is filled with cops again." He grinned. "You okay?"

"Yeah, just fine." She sighed. "So did they find anything?" she asked Maddox, nodding toward the kitchen full of uniforms. One of the officers was dusting the entire door for prints. It was going to be a mess to clean up later.

"I don't think so." He put an arm around her. "We'll see what my Mom has to tell us."

An hour later, Maddox and his mom sat on Aden's left, and her own mother sat on her right. Cadence, Grace and Trey were on the other couch. The police officers were gone, along with the letter they'd taken to examine more closely. Nobody had any real hope of finding anything significant.

"So when will we know if they found fingerprints or anything?" Janet asked Kim.

"I'll let you know as soon as I hear anything," Kim assured her.

"I'm thinking of putting up a twenty-foot electrified fence around the house," Janet joked weakly. "I can't believe this guy just keeps coming back, and in broad daylight, no less."

"He would have walked right past both our cars in the driveway," Maddox said, looking at Grace. "He knew Aden wasn't alone."

"I'm starving. Anybody wanna order a pizza?" Kim asked, obviously changing the subject. "I know it's a little early. If you guys wouldn't mind us staying, that is." She looked to Janet, smiling.

"Not at all. We'd love the company." Janet smiled at Aden and Maddox. "And pizza sounds great."

"We could eat out on the deck—" Aden was interrupted by a brilliant flash of light, followed by a loud tremor of low thunder. "Or not." She laughed. "Guess that storm is finally heading this way."

"Drew should be coming home from work soon. I'll call him and see if he can pick it up on his way." Janet grinned. She was enjoying herself despite the circumstances. "Should we be doing this? Having fun I mean? With everything—"

"This is *exactly* what we should be doing." Aden smiled at her.

"Wow, it's getting dark out there," Grace observed. "The sun shouldn't be setting yet. I'm supposed to meet Greg in a while, so I'm gonna scoot."

Cadence and Aden walked Grace to the door, and Maddox followed her to the car with instructions to be careful on her way home.

It wasn't long before Drew and Natalie came through the kitchen door, loaded down with hot pizzas that they set out on the counter.

The sky grew more threatening as the afternoon wore down into evening, and the wind was swallowed in an eerie green glow.

CHAPTER 12
blue showers

H ey guys, we're under a tornado warning!" Cadence called loudly, waving her phone in the air. "Somebody turn on the TV."

"A warning? Or a watch?" Janet asked.

"No, a warning," Cadence confirmed. "Turn it to a local channel," she directed Aden, who'd picked up the remote.

"—rotation indicated here on Doppler radar in Western Oconee County. This line of storms is still heading northeast since crossing the Georgia state line and regaining cohesion..." A local weatherman stood in front of a digitized weather map colored in angry shades of dark green, yellow, and lots of red, deepening to dark red and purple. "...this storm cell has produced several possible funnel clouds, downbursts, and tornadoes responsible for at least three confirmed deaths in Georgia. If you are in Oconee County, take shelter immediately in a basement or lower level interior room with no windows..."

"Um, that looks like it's heading right for us," Natalie said, looking worriedly at Drew.

"Yeah, looks like it'll get here in a few minutes." Drew nodded, looking at the still, dark forest outside. "The lowest room we have without windows is Aden's bathroom. Or the garage."

"We can't all fit in the bathroom, Drew," Janet said, to Aden's relief. Even though she'd just cleaned in there, she couldn't imagine this crowd all huddled in that space. "Just to be on the safe side, let's all go out to the garage for a little while. The walls are constructed of reinforced concrete, and there are no windows, as Drew said earlier. We can take some flashlights and candles."

"And the leftover pizza and some drinks." Kim smiled, rising to gather those items. "Come on, kids."

Drew ran upstairs to his rooms for an old weather radio, and they set out folding chairs, cushions, and blankets in the light of several candles and flashlights. The food and drinks were set on a folding table in the corner, and they settled in to listen to the storm's advance.

The wind began to gust harder, causing the pines to bend and crack like gunshots in the forest, and it howled loudly through the courtyard outside. The radio interrupted a weather reporter with the three unmistakable, obnoxious tones of an emergency broadcast, but it was a repeat of what they'd seen already on the news broadcast.

"You sure know how to throw a party," Cadence mused to Aden as they huddled, listening to thunder roll around them. "Listen to that pounding rain; this thing blew up faster than any storm I've ever seen."

"Actually, I think that might be hail," Drew said, opening the farthest garage door a few inches. "We should have pulled your cars in here."

"Still could," Maddox said, starting to stand.

"Don't bother." Kim shook her head. "You're not going out in that. I can replace the car, but I can't get a new son."

"Speaking of which," Janet nodded to Drew, "Close that door and get back over here away from it, please." Drew complied, settling in next to Natalie just as the overhead lights flickered and went out.

A moment later, the unmistakable crack of a tree was followed by a resounding thump that shook the ground.

"That didn't sound good," Drew mumbled. "At least it didn't sound too close." Several more cracks and thuds were heard as the wind kicked up another notch, unleashing its fury on the forest around them. White light erupted suddenly from around the edges of the three garage doors, followed almost immediately by a shocking blast of sound that ripped the air and rumbled through the ground, echoing even above the sound of the wind off the mountain. Several involuntary shrieks went up as they all jumped.

"Okay, *that* was close," Drew said, going toward the door again.

"Get back here, now!" Janet ordered. Another dull thud reverberated through the ground from farther away, and the loud cracks and groans of shrieking trees grew impossibly loud.

Anxiously huddled together, they peered into the flickering shadows of the candles and listened intently to the storm's inexorable progress.

"Sounds like it's shredding the forest out there" Drew mumbled after several tense minutes.

"Actually, it sounds like it may be passing over and starting to let up," Trey answered back. "The hail has stopped anyway, sounds like." They listened again for several long, tense minutes.

"I think you're right," Cadence said to Trey, "it does sound like it's quieting down."

It was still raining, but not pounding as hard, and the wind seemed to have passed on with the front of the storm; the howling and crackling between the trees was slowly progressing into the distance. The thunder and lightning continued, but it, too, was moving away. After several more minutes, the huddle began to unwind as first Drew, and then Maddox and Trey, went to open the furthest garage door for a look outside.

"Would you look at that?" Trey said as the door came up, revealing forest debris scattered across the courtyard and roof of the house beyond. Drew and Maddox stepped out in the rain.

A very large oak bough lay between the garage and the house, but it had somehow missed the cars in the driveway. After a quick inspection, Maddox reported that there seemed to be no damage to the cars.

"Holy cow." Trey whistled softly. Drew and Maddox joined him as the others looked on from the shelter of the garage. He was gazing at a clear path of destruction that ran on an angle through the forest a mere 50 yards beyond the house. Trees were snapped in half like twigs, their bright golden hearts wrenched open and twisted into grotesque forms. Their trunks and limbs were tossed in a chaotic pattern that followed the wind's direction toward the roiling black clouds in the distance, and the tangy scent of pine permeated the air.

"Oh my...was that a tornado? It passed right by us," Cadence said in an awed, quiet voice and turned to Aden, "It just missed your house."

"It might have been a funnel cloud or just strong-line winds instead of a tornado," Drew suggested. "The trees are snapped off about ten feet off the ground. A tornado on the ground would have uprooted everything and caused more widespread damage."

"Thank you, Mr. Weatherman." Cadence said drily.

"He's right, though." Maddox shrugged back at her. Suddenly frowning, he abruptly walked into the comparative darkness of the garage.

"We should call you Wolf-something," Cadence continued, "All weathermen have wolf in their name these days."

That sparked a lively discussion of suggested names as everyone ventured out into the lessening rain to survey storm damage. All except Aden, who followed Maddox into the garage.

Wet. Wind is dying down. Running. Plastic flapping. Heart thumping wildly. Have to get away. Blue plastic rippling behind...slipping on wet ground, tripping over scattered limbs...strong smell of pine in the air, over the smell of rain. Have to keep going. Blue flowers, stretching and ripping...caught. Keep going...have to get away. Stupid! Stayed too long. Stupid! Stupid!

Maddox shuddered and blinked rapidly to focus in the gloom.

"Are you okay?" Aden asked quietly. She held his hand tentatively in one of hers and reached up with the other to smooth his wet hair out of his eyes. He sighed, beginning to relax. "What did you see?"

"Blue flowers, running through the forest," he mumbled, frowning.

"The flowers were running?" Aden smiled hesitantly.

"No, plastic. Like a sheet of plastic draped over someone running through the forest, through the rain."

Aden frowned. "Like right now? Through this storm?"

Maddox shrugged and blinked again, shaking his head from side to side. "I don't know. It was just..."

"Flashes," she supplied, searching his face. "You okay?"

"Yes." He nodded distractedly as Kim joined them.

"We're going back inside the house, if you—" Kim stopped suddenly, taking in Maddox's expression.

"He saw something," Aden told her, concern for him written all over her face.

"Come sit down." Kim led him to one of the folding chairs in the corner.

"I'll go keep the others busy for a minute outside," Aden said and slipped away, still frowning. She met Cadence just outside the open door. "Hey!" she jumped guiltily. "What, um, what's it look like out here?"

222

"It's surreal," Cadence answered. "Everybody's on the phone checking in with other family and friends." She pointed to the scattered group, all on cell phones talking excitedly. Aden led her away from the garage as she continued. "I talked to Mom; they're all fine. The worst of it seemed to be here, closer to the mountain and outside of town."

Aden followed Cadence's gaze to the ravaged forest. "Wow, that was a close call."

"Yeah, tornado or not, that's just crazy." Cadence nodded. "Hey, the rain's starting to get heavier again. Let's go take everything back inside before another storm cell moves in." She moved toward the garage again.

"Wait," Aden started, but at that moment, Maddox came through the garage door with an armload of cushions and blankets. She lifted her brows in question, and he smiled in response.

"Wait for what?" Cadence asked.

"Never mind. Let's go help."

As they brought the food and candles back into the darkened kitchen, the radio was still blaring emergency signals, and Drew turned the volume down. "The worst of it's passed us now. There's some storms coming behind it, but they're not as dangerous as the front that just went through."

"We should all probably take advantage of the lull and get ourselves home as soon as we've cleaned up the mess we made here," Kim suggested.

"Hope the power's not out for long; it's getting really dark in here," Cadence observed.

"It's still lighter than it was earlier when the storm came through." Trey smiled at her.

"Yeah, but not for long."

"Aden," Janet called from the hallway off the kitchen, silencing the chatter. "What have you done with the shower curtain in your bathroom?" Aden turned toward her, confused. Before she could answer, a loud thump from above drew their attention.

"Was that another branch falling on the roof?" Trey suggested, as Maddox and Drew moved toward the staircase.

"It sounded like the door up there." Drew frowned, taking the lead as Trey followed Maddox, taking the stairs two at a time to catch up.

Aden rushed toward the stairs until Kim stopped her. "Let them check it out. There's no need for all of us to be up there." Aden just nodded and strained to hear what they were saying upstairs. Cadence and Natalie went to huddle on the couch, turning the news channel on again to check the weather. Janet and Kim joined Aden at the foot of the stairs just as Maddox appeared at the second floor doorway, frowning furiously.

"What is it?" Janet asked as he rushed toward them, followed closely by the other two guys.

"We need to check the house. Door's been kicked in," he said quietly to his mother. Over the gasps from Aden and her mom, Kim took control. Quickly and quietly, she pulled a gun from an ankle holster and threw open the closet door in the adjacent foyer. Finding it empty, she turned back to the stunned group.

"Trey, will you please stay with the ladies here, in the foyer? Keep everyone calm for me?" She smiled at him briefly before turning away. "Drew, take my phone, I've already speed-dialed the police, please tell them what's going on." She shoved the phone at Drew while surveying the rest of the house beyond the staircase. Turning to Maddox, she asked quietly, "Are you sure it was kicked in? And not just knocked open in the storm?"

"There are muddy footprints on the door and the floor up there—" he was shaking his head while his eyes scanned for signs of the intruder beyond her.

"Okay, listen to me. You all stay put here in the foyer and keep quiet for a minute."

"Mom, I can—"

"No, Maddox. Stay right here," she commanded, then, in a suddenly loud voice, she called past him. "F.B.I. If there is anyone in this house, surrender now." She listened intently. "I am armed. Come out slowly with your hands up where I can see them." Silently kicking off her high-heeled shoes, she hugged the walls and disappeared into the master bedroom suite. The group in the foyer held its breath, waiting and listening. There was nothing but the patter of the rain on the roof for several minutes. Maddox began inching toward the den when Aden caught his hand and shook her head. He frowned, beginning to shake her off, when Kim appeared at the bedroom door again.

Sweeping the den in a practiced pattern, she made her careful way across the large, open space and into the kitchen, out of sight around the corner. They could hear doors opening and closing quietly, and then she emerged again, hugging the wall, only to disappear down the hallway toward the bedrooms on Aden's side of the house. Trey and Drew slowly crept up to join Maddox. Drew's brows went up in silent question to Maddox. Maddox took a deep breath, listening intently, and seemed to come to a decision just before Kim re-appeared.

"It's all clear. There's nobody here now," she announced, jogging up the stairs. "No, stay there for another minute." She instructed as the guys started to follow. Maddox hesitated a couple of seconds and then went up anyway, followed by Drew. Trey stood at the foot of the stairs with a guarded stance as the group in the foyer slowly edged forward to peer up the stairs.

"I don't believe this," Aden muttered to no one in particular. She felt shell-shocked and tired. "All of this just cannot really be happening…"

"Afraid it is," Trey said grimly.

"What a day." Cadence nodded. "What a week, actually."

"We'd just checked that door, though," Aden continued as if she hadn't heard them, in a daze. "Earlier today, we checked that door, and everything was just fine."

"The police went up there, too." Cadence nodded, sympathetic.

"Had to have happened during the storm, while we were out of the house, or we'd have heard it," Trey said, scowling. "Those muddy footprints were certainly made *after* the rain started."

"Okay everyone, police are on their way," Kim announced, descending the stairs.

"Again." Aden droned. Maddox drew her to a couch and made her sit.

"Cadence, will you please bring Aden a glass of water?" he asked as the rest of the group were finding seats.

"Anyone else need anything?" Cadence asked.

"I'll help you," Natalie said, following her into the kitchen with a flashlight as everyone else congregated in the den. Janet and Maddox flanked Aden on one end of the longest couch.

"Are you okay?" Kim asked her kindly, re-lighting candles they'd placed haphazardly on the coffee table.

"It's just so bizarre. It's like we're all caught in a nightmare, and things just keep getting crazier and crazier. Every time I turn around—" her voice broke on a sob.

"Shhh." Maddox pulled her into a hug. "It's okay. We're all okay." He looked around at the group.

"That's right," Kim said. "Everything is going to be just fine. We're going to catch whoever is responsible for all this." She smiled reassuringly. "Aden, honey, I know it's been a horrible day, and you're upset, but I have to ask you a question." Aden sniffed and nodded. "Your mother asked you earlier about the shower curtain in the bathroom?" Aden looked back blankly so she continued. "I noticed it was missing when I searched the house earlier. It appears to have been ripped off the rod. There is a fragment left, and two of the curtain rings are lying on the floor."

"What?" Aden looked even more dazed. "Last I was in there, the shower curtain was, you know, fine." She frowned. "It was there."

"Can you describe it for me?" Kim asked, glancing at Maddox and quickly away again.

"Um, I don't—" she took a deep breath. "It's blue, light blue, I guess. At the bottom is a row of blue flowers..." she trailed off, raising her eyes to meet Maddox's suddenly intense gaze.

"Right," Kim spoke abruptly, drawing everyone's attention. "It seems we may have a shower curtain thief on our hands." She chuckled lamely. "Girls? Can I help you with those drinks?" she stood to join Cadence and Natalie in the kitchen. Her ruse worked, drawing everyone's attention away from Maddox and Aden's dawning realization. Everyone except for Trey. As the chatter rose once again and drinks were handed out, he sat by quietly, watching Maddox and Aden thoughtfully.

Lightning lit the darker corners of the large room where the candles' glow couldn't reach. They all turned toward the window wall and waited a moment for the answering thunder.

"Looks like the rain has stopped," Drew said. "Wonder what's taking the cops so long?"

"The storm," Trey said. "Probably a lot of debris in the road, or other calls about damage. I hope it didn't hit any houses."

"With everything going on here, I hadn't even thought..." Drew frowned. "What are they saying on the radio? About any damage, I mean?"

"Not a lot about Blackwater Falls yet. Most of the reports are from towns west of us that got hit before we did, but there are three confirmed deaths in Georgia, and a fire station and courthouse were hit over near Lake Cherokee," Cadence answered from the kitchen. "Mom said all they got in town was rain, thunder and lightning. No hail, and the wind wasn't bad."

Kim's phone rang, and she went to the kitchen to answer it.

"I guess we should go see if anything is missing," Janet said, tiredly, rising. Drew stood to join her. "Do you want me to go with you to check your room and bathroom?" she asked Aden.

"No, I got it," she sighed.

"I'll go with you if you want," Maddox said, and Aden nodded.

"The police are here," Kim announced, coming back in the den. "Apparently, there are a couple of trees down across your driveway, and they're walking up. They'll be here any minute."

"We're just going to go check to see if anything is missing," Janet said, pointing to her bedroom door.

"Do you mind waiting for the officers to get here? I want to be sure we don't touch anything else before they've surveyed the scene." She nodded, sympathetic. "Especially in that bathroom where the shower curtain is missing."

"Sure." Janet sank bank down to the couch.

"I'm gonna go see if we have any gas for the chain saw," Drew said, "or you guys aren't goin' anywhere."

"I'll go with you to hold the flashlight," Trey suggested. "It's gettin' pretty dark out there, and you might need more hands to move those trees."

"True. I'll help too," Maddox said.

"Nah, you stay here with Aden," Drew said quietly. "I think she needs you. We'll call if we need more help." Natalie followed them out the door.

"I'm totally fine if you want to go with them," Aden scowled.

"Honestly, I'd like to stay and get a look at that bathroom."

A moment later, the same two officers from earlier entered the kitchen door, wielding large flashlights. They were followed by Mayor Max Dixon.

"Stay here. I've got it." Maddox smiled at Aden and went to speak with them. She sighed and closed her eyes. It had been a long and dramatic day. She kept her eyes closed as she heard first her mother, and then Cadence and Kim, join the officers and Mayor Max in the kitchen. The discussion grew lively as everyone added in the details they recalled about the storm and the latest break-in.

It still felt so dream-like, all that had happened in just a week's time. If she wasn't so tired and angry, it would be almost funny. But she *was* angry, she realized, more than any other emotion, even more than the fear of the unknown and what might happen next. She was angry at the faceless man who so brazenly intruded in her life…but that was selfish. There were three other women whose lives he'd altered more severely than hers, and she felt ashamed for her petty thoughts. *Thank God I'm here, in my own home surrounded by friends and family. Where are they? Are they alive?* She couldn't bring herself to think how they might have suffered and she shivered involuntarily as another flash of lightning revealed the dark forest outside.

"Are you alright?" Maddox's question startled her. He was standing behind her, and she hadn't heard him return from the kitchen.

"I'm fine," she mumbled, still thinking about the real victims. "How is it this guy has kidnapped three women, broken into my house twice, followed us around on at least one occasion that we can verify, and the cops still have no clue?" Maddox sighed, coming to sit with her.

"I know. We're all frustrated," Maddox said quietly, his jaw tensed. "But we're getting closer."

"Closer?" she scowled. "How do you figure? There are zero leads, zero suspects, the first victim disappeared *four* months ago, and they've found nothing! And this guy just keeps coming back, running around doing whatever he wants to whoever he wants—" Her voice was rising, and all other conversation stopped as everyone turned toward her. She took a deep breath. "Sorry. It just makes me so angry."

"Me too," Maddox said quietly. "But I think they do have something. They're just not telling us." Aden's eyes widened.

"What makes you say that?"

"Something the Sheriff said when he got here." Maddox glanced into the kitchen where more law enforcement officers had arrived and conversation was resuming. "I'll tell you later." He smiled at her suddenly hopeful, questioning posture. "Right now, they'd like to know if you would tour your rooms with one of the officers."

Aden nodded as a female officer she hadn't seen before walked toward them. Short and stocky, she frowned as she took in the room, the windows beyond, and finally turned to Aden, all business.

"Aden, you can call me Sherry," she announced without fanfare or smile. "I'm here to escort you through your room and bathroom looking for anything out of place."

Aden's eyebrows rose, and she shot a look at Maddox as she shrugged. "Okay." As she and Maddox stood, Kim joined them.

"I'd like to tag along, if you don't mind." Kim smiled at Aden. "Maddox, why don't you have a seat? We'll be right back." Maddox looked surprised, but resigned and fell back on the couch.

Kim led the way, going straight to Aden's bathroom, stopping just outside the door. We'll be looking for prints and photographing this room as soon as the techs get here, so we're not going in or touching anything, but from the doorway, can you tell me if anything is out of place? Anything that we should pay particular attention to?" She stepped back and gestured Aden forward, the female officer hanging back in the hallway. Aden would have sworn she was sulking.

"Um, well the shower curtain is missing, of course. I just cleaned earlier today and scrubbed the tub, and well, everything else in here." Aden shrugged, peering intently at the shower curtain rings still lying on the floor. She saw that there was a small corner of the blue plastic curtain still attached to three rings on the rod. "The curtain rod has obviously been wrenched loose on that side." She pointed. "Sorry, guess that's not really ground-breaking information." Kim just smiled.

"Anything and everything that you can tell us will help."

"Well, that drawer is slightly open, and I know that I had closed both of them while I straightened up in here, but this is the bathroom that everybody would have been using all day, so it could have been anybody, I guess." Kim nodded and glanced meaningfully at Officer Sherry as Aden continued. "I don't really see much. Hold on…my shampoo. I keep it on that shelf in the tub." Aden raised her eyebrows. "The bottle of conditioner is still there, but the shampoo is missing." Kim nodded again. "Why would anybody take shampoo?"

"Do you see anything else out of the ordinary in here?" Kim avoided her question with one of her own.

"Don't think so."

"Then let's take a look at the bedroom." Once again, she stopped just outside the doorway but gestured Aden inside. "Don't touch anything but take a look around for signs that could indicate someone has been in here."

"Somebody's definitely been in here." Aden's eyes were wide as she surveyed her room. "I'd washed my sheets and remade my bed neater than I normally do just this morning. It looks like somebody sat on it, here…" she pointed, stepping toward the bed. "And the dust ruffle is pulled out like they looked under the bed—wait, did you look under the beds when you searched the house earlier?" she asked Kim.

"I did, but I didn't touch the bedding. I used your mirror to check under the bed." She pointed to the crowded vanity top where an ornately carved silver mirror and comb lay, part of a set that had been Aden's grandmother's.

"There's a brush," Aden said, walking to the vanity, "The silver brush is missing." She looked around the room and then back to the vanity. "And somebody's been in my jewelry box." She pointed to a small, oblong silver box, its lid propped open to reveal a blue velvet interior. "I know I didn't leave it open like that." She leaned over, careful not to touch anything and peered into the box. "Doesn't look like anything's missing. I don't have anything in there worth stealing, mostly sentimental stuff." Suddenly, something on the floor caught her attention and she walked around the corner of the bed. "There's something here." Kim joined her quickly, leaning over her shoulder. "Is that a leaf?"

"It does look like a leaf, but I think…" Kim knelt down to get a closer look, "That looks like a hair or a fiber caught in the stem." She tried to hide the excitement building in her eyes. "Your mother and Maddox both said that nobody had come into this room since the storm that they know about."

"That's right. Nobody's been in here all day that I know of."

"Not even before the storm? Cadence? Or Grace?" Aden shook her head, staring at the leaf. "And when you were cleaning this morning, did you vacuum this room?"

"I did." Aden said, searching the carpet for telltale footprints. She couldn't see anything that stood out, and of course, Kim had been in here searching for the intruder, and now Aden and the officer, Sherry, were in here, too. "That leaf was definitely not here."

"Okay." Kim nodded, glancing at Sherry. "Anything else stand out?"

Aden searched the room, stepping tentatively to the closet door that was open about an inch. "Should I open the door?"

"Hold on." Kim stepped around her and nudged the door open with her foot. Aden peered in and shrugged.

"Looks okay, I guess."

"Alright, if you don't see anything else?" Aden shook her head. Kim smiled and gestured toward the door.

Coming back into the den, Aden's eyes immediately went to Maddox. He was seated stiffly on the couch where she'd left him, surrounded by Sheriff Richey and two uniformed officers. They were standing over him with grave faces carrying on a quiet, but intense, conversation. Mayor Max was just coming back through the kitchen door and headed for Maddox and the officers.

"Sheriff, can I have a word? Outside?" Kim called. Frowning at the officers surrounding her son, she turned and stalked out the kitchen door. The Sheriff sighed and followed, gesturing his officers away as well. As they left, Maddox looked up to see Aden and smiled at her across the room. At least, he tried to smile, anyway.

"So?" he asked, rising.

"Well, in addition to the shower curtain, my shampoo and a hairbrush seem to be missing, and there's a leaf on the floor of my room." Maddox frowned grimly at the news. "So what was up with the Sheriff just now?"

"They just had some more questions," he answered, as his Dad and Cadence joined them in the den.

"They really do suspect you, don't they?" Cadence looked worriedly toward the kitchen door where Kim had just led the Sheriff outside and then at Mayor Max.

"What?" Aden grabbed her arm. "What are you talking about?"

"The police think Maddox might have something to do with…everything that's been happening," Cadence explained quietly.

"That's ridiculous!" Aden burst out, smiling. Her smile fell rapidly as she took in their worried faces, Maddox's Dad's face last of all. "Why in the world—"

"I've been there. Every time something has happened to you. I'm always there," Maddox said quietly.

"Listen, it's just police procedure. They're gonna ask all kinds of questions to everybody who might possibly have any little piece of information." Mayor Max smiled kindly, "Don't you worry."

"But, you're there *with* me. You were there with all of us in the garage the whole time, too. You couldn't have done this. Any of it." Aden gushed.

"I know. Somebody already pointed that out to them." Maddox smiled at his sister. "But that doesn't change the fact that every time something bad has happened to you, I'm around. They *have* to investigate every lead. There are three women still missing, on top of…everything else."

"You mean the Twilight Zone that my house has become." Aden frowned.

"Seriously." Cadence nodded. "What? It *is* a Twilight Zone around here. Break-ins and threatening letters and storms and—"

"We get it," Maddox interrupted. Mayor Max sighed heavily and rose from the couch.

"I better be gettin' home. Your Mama's gonna be waitin' to hear how you're all doin' out here."

"So maybe we should get outta here, too," Cadence suggested.

"And go where?" Aden asked tiredly. "It's still stormy outside, and everywhere I go, this crap seems to follow me anyway." She shrugged, defeated. Maddox drew her in and kissed her temple.

"Maddox, can you come out here for a moment, please?" Kim called from the doorway in the kitchen. They could see Sheriff Richey, his arms crossed, waiting behind her. Mayor Max hurried to join them.

Maddox gave Aden a reassuring squeeze. "I'll be right back."

"I'm coming with you," Aden stated.

"Me too," Cadence asserted, hands on her hips.

"No, you stay right here," Maddox said, "Please."

"But—"

"I'll be back." He smiled and abruptly left before they could argue further.

"They can't seriously suspect Maddox," Aden huffed. "He was in Virginia when this whole thing started."

"They're mostly asking him about all the incidents involving you and your house," Cadence answered.

"Well, they need to be focusing their suspicions somewhere else and find the *real* psychopath behind all this."

"Agreed."

"So did I hear you say that some of your stuff is missing? Besides the shower curtain?"

Cadence asked.

"Yeah, my shampoo and a hairbrush."

"Okay that's just weird." She shivered. "Think it's some kind of hair fetish?"

"Don't know. Don't care." Aden sighed. "But there's a leaf on the floor by my bed they think might have a fiber or hair or something on it, so maybe they'll finally have something to go on and find this guy."

She nodded as Cadence's phone began to vibrate with an incoming text message.

"It's Trey. He says they were able to drag two of the trees off the driveway, and they're cutting the last one into pieces. They should be done soon."

"That was pretty quick." Cadence smiled. "I figured they'd be out there for a lot longer."

"Guess it helps having most of the police department out here to lend a hand, too." Cadence shrugged, frowning at the still-open door where Maddox had gone out. "You'd think they could close the door. It's still raining out."

"I'll get it," Aden said. "Where'd everybody go, anyway?"

The kitchen had emptied out, and the house was quiet. Outside was a different story. Uniforms swarmed the driveway and the empty bay of the garage where one of the folding tables had been commandeered for a make-shift desk. The Sheriff was bent over what looked like maps on the table, pointing and shouting orders at both the people nearby and into a walkie-talkie clamped in one hand.

"They're searching the woods." Cadence pointed. "The way they're all running, they must have found something."

Aden spotted her mother standing in the garage with Kim and Maddox and went to join them.

"Did they find something?" she asked, dodging a man in plain clothes with latex gloves on.

"Not yet," Kim answered. "But we can't be very far behind him. He's got to be close."

Aden glanced at Maddox, who stood with his hands jammed into the pockets of his jeans, staring intently toward the woods.

"Can you tell which way he went?" Cadence asked, pointedly watching where most of the activity was centered, on one side of the house.

"We're fanning out in all directions, but it looks like he might have gone into the river," Kim said.

"Do you have like, hunting dogs or kayaks or something to go after him?" Cadence asked excitedly.

"I think the Sheriff has called in every asset he can get his hands on. Apparently, the river can't be navigated by kayak on this stretch. Too shallow with too many rocks and falls. We're walking the banks, both sides, upriver and down."

"Can we do something to help?" Cadence asked.

"Yes, you can stay right here with Aden."

"But," Cadence blinked, "there's like a hundred police running around here. We could help search."

"And what would you do if you found the guy?" Maddox asked quietly.

"We'd get the police to arrest him. I'm not saying we'd be out there alone," she scoffed.

"I was thinking actually about asking your Mom if Aden, at least, could stay at your house tonight," Janet spoke up for the first time. "If you left now, while the guy is busy running from all this," she waved a vague hand, "He wouldn't be able to follow or know where to find her. If he even gets away." She sighed.

"He's messed up this time. Left evidence behind, at least a partial trail," Kim began. "We're gonna get him."

"I hope so." Janet shuddered.

CHAPTER 13
board up the door

Hours later, the search had wound down in the darkness. Most of the people who had swarmed around the house and surrounding woods were gone. There was still a very young officer stationed on the back deck and another sat in a folding chair with a cooler under the eaves of the front door, where he could keep an eye on the kitchen door and driveway as well. A third officer was camped out upstairs to watch the door the intruder had used both times before.

"Why don't we just rip out that stairway outside leading up to that door?" Janet suggested. "We don't ever use it, anyway."

Drew, sitting beside her on one of the couches, rubbed his eyes. "We could do that tomorrow. Or later today, I guess," He amended, looking at his watch. "For that matter, we could board up the door from the inside, too, barricade it totally."

"Nobody ever uses that door." Aden nodded. "Except the intruder."

"Maybe we should brick it up permanently." Janet yawned. "And we could look into steel shutters for all the other doors and windows." She smiled half-heartedly.

"We're going to get this guy soon. Leave your lovely house alone," Kim muttered.

"I still can't believe he got away." Maddox slumped on the couch beside Aden, his arm hung tiredly around her shoulders, and his head thrown back, eyes closed. "Where could he have gone?"

"I heard a couple of the cops saying he might have been here the whole time. If he was one of them, a cop, or one of the volunteers who showed up," Drew offered. "There were cops from other jurisdictions who came to help, too." Aden glanced at the officer barely visible on the back deck and shuddered.

"I don't think it's a cop," Kim sighed. They'd had this same conversation earlier in the evening, but their thoughts kept circling around. "Are you sure you don't want us to leave? Let you go to bed?"

Janet immediately began shaking her head. "No, please. The guest bedroom is all made up. I thought you could sleep in there, and Maddox could sleep on the couch, or there's an air mattress in Drew's rooms over the garage." She smiled. "I know it's silly, but I just feel better with you here."

"I don't think I could sleep in my room. Maybe ever again." Aden frowned. "He was in there. Sitting on my bed. Going through my things." She shook her head slowly. "I'm not moving from this spot."

"Honey, you're exhausted," Janet began.

"We all are," Aden answered her. "But I'm not sleeping in that room again until I can scrub every inch of it. *With bleach*." Maddox smiled wanly. "Besides, I couldn't possibly get to sleep with everything running through my head the way it is."

"True that." Drew nodded, sighing. "I can't stop thinking about it. He was here, again, walking through here while we all huddled in the garage during the storm, right after the police had been here. He's probably been here all day, maybe since he left the note on the door. He probably watched the police come through and leave. He had to know we'd all gone into the garage before he kicked in the door upstairs. I mean, the balls on this guy—"

"Drew," His mother admonished.

"Sorry, but seriously, Mom. The sheer arrogance and dogged persistence. I mean, he just keeps coming back…" his voice trailed off as he glanced at Aden. Her fists were clenched in her lap.

Just a few hours later, the rising sun began to brighten the eastern sky. Janet and Kim sat at the kitchen counter clutching mugs of coffee. Drew had finally gone to his own room to sleep for a bit. Aden and Maddox were curled together on the couch, fast asleep.

"Young love," Kim sighed quietly, looking at her son. Janet just smiled. "I've never seen Maddox fall this hard before."

"And so fast." Janet was nodding with a slight frown. "Aden's dated a few other boys, but it was nothing like…this."

Kim's brows lowered into her own frown. "I'm worried, honestly." Janet turned to her. "What's going to happen when we do catch this guy and go back home to Virginia?"

"You don't think he'd decide to stay? Live with Max and LeighAnn?" Janet asked hesitantly.

Kim sighed, "Well, I would think that, except he has other plans waiting for him, back in Virginia. I had to beg him to come with me to help on this case. He wasn't going to come."

"Other plans?" Janet asked.

Just then, Maddox slowly extricated himself from Aden's embrace. She roused a bit, but he whispered he'd be right back and kissed her forehead before she slumped back into sleep. He came into the dark kitchen yawning and stretching.

"Morning." He smiled. "I thought I'd run back to the hotel for a shower and get back here before Aden wakes up. Want a ride?" he directed the last at his mother.

"You just don't want us talking about you," she answered.

"I'd rather you didn't." He smiled apologetically at Janet. "At least while I'm not here to defend myself."

"But you do understand our concern?" Janet asked, placing a tentative hand on his arm. "I don't mean to pry into your personal business."

"But Aden is *your* personal business." He smiled back at her. "I get it. I do." He hesitated, looking at them both and then glancing back at Aden, still asleep. "Believe me when I tell you, I had zero intention of getting involved with anyone on this trip, but from the minute I met your daughter…" he hesitated awkwardly, "Well, I would never, ever do anything to intentionally cause her harm."

"I do believe that your intentions are good." Janet glanced at Aden, still worried. Maddox followed her gaze and sighed.

"I don't know what to say. Maybe I shouldn't come back from the hotel."

"No, Maddox." Janet tightened her grip on his arm. "That's not what I meant. You've been incredible, doing so much to protect her—"

"I actually tried, you know, to keep more distance between us." He shrugged. "I mean, we've talked about it—when I have to leave." He looked pained. "I don't want to hurt her."

He met Janet's gaze, and she seemed to search his eyes, uncertain, before she released his arm.

"Well, you'd better shake a leg if you plan to get back here before Aden wakes up," she said with a small smile. "I guess your relationship is between you and Aden. I can't protect her from everything." Her smile faltered, "Try as I might."

Maddox started to say something, but he stopped and just nodded instead before letting himself quietly out the kitchen door. Kim rose, placing her mug in the sink and grabbing her purse.

"He's a very impressive young man." Janet smiled at her.

"I know." Kim smiled back, pulling the door closed behind her.

Aden slowly became aware of a hushed conversation somewhere nearby. She stretched, realizing she was still on the couch. Her eyes popped open. Maddox was gone.

"I'll be here all day," Drew was saying to someone through the open kitchen door. "Whenever you guys need to come inside or whatever."

The answering voice was muffled, and Aden couldn't make it out. She listened as Drew thanked someone and quietly closed the door. Must have been one of the officers outside. She sat up, still stretching.

"Morning, sunshine." Drew stage-whispered from the kitchen. "Mom's asleep in her room."

"Maddox?"

"He went to the hotel with his Mom. He'll be back."

Aden just nodded, noting her own disappointment to find him gone. "I'm gonna go shower." She announced.

"Looks like a good idea," he teased.

She hesitated in the hallway when she first headed for her bedroom, shadowy visions of hulking intruders invading the corners, but looking into her room, she grew angry again. *It's my room, damnit. I'm not going to let some sick psychopath keep me from my own home.* She stalked purposefully to her closet, the door still open from the search the day before and took her time selecting her outfit for the day.

She took her clothes to her bathroom and stopped mid-stride. The empty shower curtain rings seemed to mock her. "Freaking pervert!" she muttered quietly. Apparently, not as quiet as she'd thought. Drew stuck his head around the door jamb a moment later.

"You can use my bathroom," he offered.

"Thanks, but I'll just take a bath." She grabbed a bottle of bath cleaner from under her sink and dumped a large amount into the tub. Drew raised his eyebrows before he left, shaking his head. Aden scrubbed the entire tub, inside and out, and the tile surrounding it before rinsing it all off. Then, she scrubbed inside the tub again, for good measure. As she waited for the tub to fill, she slipped into her mother's bathroom and borrowed her shampoo, scowling at this necessity.

She took her time bathing, dressing, and drying her hair. She hoped that Maddox would be back by the time she emerged.

When she walked out into the great room, she was rewarded with the sound of Maddox's voice. He sat on the couch with Drew discussing music. He smiled when he saw her, making her almost stumble as her knees literally went weak. *Weirdo*, she smiled at herself.

"Guess I wasn't quick enough." He retrieved a bag from the coffee table and held it out toward her. She took the bag and sat beside him before peeking inside. She had to pull the plastic-wrapped rectangle out of the bag to see it was a new shower curtain. "I found a blue one, but it doesn't have flowers on it." He grinned.

"You are just spoiling her for all other men." Drew rolled his eyes. "Making the rest of us look like schmucks."

Maddox just chuckled. "I would have gotten you shampoo, too, if I'd thought to ask what kind you like."

"What? No hairbrush?" Aden tried not to laugh.

"Oh, I forgot about the brush." Maddox frowned, glancing at her perfectly smoothed hair.

"Oh my God, I'm kidding!" she squealed. "Thank you so much for the shower curtain. You're so sweet, but you shouldn't have."

Drew grunted in mock disgust.

"The missing brush was mostly decorative. It's not the one I use every day." Aden shrugged, ignoring her brother.

"Because he cares." Drew said sarcastically and rolled his eyes.

"Oh, but I do care." Maddox grinned at him, teasing.

"Man—I'm outta here," Drew said, rising. "Maybe I'll go see what kind of hair products Natalie uses."

"You're not working today?" Aden asked, looking towards the nearest clock.

"Called in. Mr. Payne said to tell you to be careful. Oh, and I called in for you, too, by the way. The very loud old lady I talked to said that you were not to worry and to take all the time you need. Well, after she asked me a million questions. I got the impression she was writing it all down."

"That'd be Mrs. McConnell. She was taking notes so she'd get all the details right when she told everybody in town every word you said." Aden shook her head. "Well, thanks for calling in for me. I hadn't even thought about work." She frowned. "I was supposed to be there at 1:00 today."

"You're welcome." He patted her on the head as he went to the kitchen in search of his cell phone.

"Have you eaten?" Maddox asked.

"Actually, no. I wonder what we have." She started to get up. "Are you hungry?"

"I brought some sub-sandwiches and chips from the deli. There's enough for everyone."

"You are the most thoughtful human being I've ever known." Aden smiled.

"Actually, it was Mom's suggestion." He smiled back. "I was going to wait until she got back, but I'm starving. Let's eat."

Aden, Maddox and Drew were eating while standing at the kitchen counter and talking quietly when Janet emerged from her bedroom.

"Did we wake you?" Aden winced apologetically.

"No, but look at the time. I can't believe I slept so hard."

"You needed it." Aden shrugged. "Are you hungry? Maddox brought subs from the deli."

"You are a darling boy." Janet smiled at him. "I'm starving. Guess I should go to the store today, too."

"Just make a list. I'll take care of it," Drew mumbled through a mouthful of food. When Janet raised a surprised eyebrow, he continued, "Can't have Maddox keep showing me up. Brown-nosing schmuck." He grinned.

There was a knock on the door, and Drew reached back to unlock and open it. It was Kim, with Cadence and Trey in tow.

"Hi, all. Hope you don't mind—I stopped by Max and LeighAnn's for a minute, and Cadence and Trey were there, asking about you all. Oh, are those the sandwiches you got Maddox? I'm famished!" she gushed, grabbing an unopened sandwich before she finished speaking.

"Hey, guys!" Cadence laughed. "We came in Trey's car, so if you were busy or whatever, we can take off."

"Make yourself at home." Janet smiled. "Looks like we're all taking the day off."

"Help yourself to a sandwich," Maddox waved to the counter, "There's plenty."

"Thanks, but we've already eaten," Cadence answered. "I'm surprised that you're all up and around already."

"Yeah, that was some night," Trey chimed in.

"We throw all the best parties." Aden shrugged dramatically. "Actually, I'm shocked that any of you would want to spend one more minute out here. I think our house is jinxed."

"You have had more than your fair share of excitement this past week. Makes our house seem deathly boring by comparison." Cadence nodded. "And that's with Grace and Patience screaming at each other like banshees all morning and Mama catching the neighbor's dog digging up her garden again."

"Not sure what to say to that." Aden stared at her with a quizzical eyebrow. Cadence just laughed and changed the subject.

"So what are you guys up to today?"

"Besides being on lock-down from some crazy criminal while we clean up storm damage?" Aden half-chuckled. "Actually, if we were serious about tearing down that staircase outside, I definitely want to get in a few good whacks. Sounds therapeutic, somehow."

"I think it should come down." Janet nodded hesitantly. "Maybe I should call somebody—"

"Mom, please. We're talking about tearing down a 'temporary' staircase." Drew rolled his eyes. "I think we can handle it."

A couple of hours later, the sweaty group cheered as the last couple of boards crashed to the ground. It had been built sturdier and taken longer to dismantle than they'd thought. Miscellaneous tools lay strewn across the yard where they'd tried different methods, but the lumber now lay in a haphazard heap on the ground. Drew began shifting some of the boards, pulling out a select few.

"We can take these upstairs and nail them across that damn door, just to be sure," he huffed.

"Let's drag all this into the garage first," Maddox suggested. Everyone pitched in, and with just a couple of trips back and forth, the dismantled lumber was stacked in the garage, and the tools were put away. After that, the girls went inside to make drinks for everyone while the guys went upstairs and boarded up the door to nowhere.

"Nobody's getting in that way again," Drew announced as they convened on the couches in the den.

"That was kind of fun," Cadence mused, and Aden smiled, nodding. "There's enough broken trees and limbs and stuff from the storm; we could build something cool."

"Build something?" Aden laughed. "Like what?"

"I dunno. A treehouse? A fort? Maybe build some booby-traps all around your house."

They all laughed. "What? I was serious."

"We know." Maddox chuckled. "That's what was so funny."

She stuck her tongue out at him, undaunted.

"So what kind of trap were you planning?" Maddox wanted to know.

"Oh forget it." She sniffed. "Just go back to making googly-eyes at Aden."

"Googly eyes?" Trey laughed. "I haven't heard that since elementary school."

"You've just been hanging out with all the wrong people," she informed him with mock seriousness.

There was a knock on the kitchen door, and Drew went to answer it. It was the officer keeping watch on the day shift. He spoke in low tones, gesturing behind him out into the courtyard. Drew glanced quickly back to the group in the den. "Be right back." He pulled the door closed behind him.

"That was weird." Aden frowned. "Wonder what that's all about?"

"Want me to go check?" Maddox offered.

"No, I'm just gonna peek out the window." Aden walked over to the window above the kitchen sink and almost immediately ducked back out of sight. "Crap."

"What?" Maddox was already on his feet, followed closely by Trey and Cadence.

"It's Billy Ray. He's in the driveway talking to the police officer and Drew."

Maddox went to the window as Aden tried to stop him. "Don't let him see you!"

"Why?" Maddox shrugged. "Too late anyway. He's waving." Maddox saluted tersely. Trey joined him in the window, and Aden sighed loudly.

"What do you two think you're doing?" she demanded.

"Looking outside." Trey shrugged innocently.

"What's he doing?" Cadence wanted to know.

"Looks like Drew is trying to walk him to his truck," Maddox answered.

"That cop doesn't look too happy," Trey commented.

"He's probably familiar with Billy Ray." Maddox frowned. "Drew doesn't look very hospitable himself."

"Should we go out there?" Trey asked.

"No," Aden answered firmly. "No one is going out there."

"Dude—" Trey looked uneasy, cracking his knuckles as he made tight fists.

"What?" Aden and Cadence asked at the same time.

"Nothing," Maddox answered quickly. He side-stepped Aden and was at the door in a flash with Trey on his heels. They both stopped just outside the door and stood silent, blocking the view Cadence was desperately seeking from behind them.

"Sir, you have exactly three seconds to get in your truck and get off this property," the officer's voice boomed.

"Holy crap! He's got his gun pulled," Cadence whispered from her new vantage point at the window.

"The cop?" Aden whispered back, still crouching on the floor. "Get out of that window!"

"What's going on?" Janet and Kim came in from the back deck. "Who's shouting out front?"

Aden stood to go meet them, dragging Cadence by the wrist. "It's Billy Ray Payne. Drew went out to ask him to leave, and I guess he doesn't want to."

"That cop has his gun out," Cadence added. Both women started for the door just as an engine revved loudly outside, followed by squealing tires. Maddox and Trey stepped further out into the driveway, followed by Kim and Janet.

"Come on." Cadence pulled the wrist Aden was still gripping. Aden followed reluctantly but stopped in the doorway.

"It's alright. Let's go back inside." Drew was waving everyone back through the door as the officer spoke briskly into a radio on his shoulder. There was another squeal of tires through the trees as the truck pulled out of the driveway onto the highway and sped into the distance. A siren soon came from the other direction and passed by on the highway, in pursuit. The sound receded again before the door was closed behind them.

"What did he want?" Aden asked.

"Just came by to check on us," Drew said tersely. At the looks he received from the entire group, he held up his hands in surrender and elaborated. "He told the officer outside that he works with me at the garage and came by to check on us, since I'd called out of work today. When I went outside, I started leading him to my room upstairs. I guess it offended him that I didn't invite him in the main house. He got belligerent, saying how I thought he wasn't good enough to invite inside the house. It just sort of went downhill from there. The officer advised him to leave, and it took a bit of persuasion to make Billy Ray understand we were serious." He shrugged. "The guy's always had a wicked temper. Guess he had a liquid lunch and was just spoiling for a fight."

"And the officer let him drive knowing he was probably intoxicated?" Janet wondered aloud.

"Billy Ray has been known to carry firearms. Knowing his history, and with so many bystanders, the officer opted to stand down from a possible shoot out in your driveway. There was a patrol car nearby, and he called them in to apprehend Billy Ray before he could get too far." Kim answered, distracted.

"He showed the cop the gun he was carrying," Trey commented. Kim looked stunned. "He didn't pull it, but he made sure the cop knew he had it."

"You're *supposed* to disclose a concealed weapon immediately," Kim said, frowning.

"Seriously, you guys aren't interested in booby-trapping this place?" Cadence asked with half a smile.

"So are they going to hold him?" Janet asked Kim a while later as they all gathered on the back deck.

"The preliminary blood tests indicate he wasn't intoxicated. They're keeping him now on resisting arrest, but he'll be out later today, tomorrow if his Dad is in a cooperative mood or angry with him." Kim shrugged. "That's what the Sherriff says."

"Have they searched his house and his Dad's garage?" Trey asked. "He's Kidnapping Suspect #1 in my book." Several others nodded agreement.

"Old Mr. Payne has consented to searches both at their house and at the garage. We'll see if anything turns up." Kim frowned.

"But you don't think anything will turn up." Janet sighed.

"No, I don't think Billy Ray is the kidnapper." Kim shrugged.

"Why not?" Aden asked.

"Just doesn't…feel right." Kim smiled. "He doesn't fit the profile."

"So, do you have any suspects who *do* fit the profile?" Cadence asked.

"I couldn't tell you that right now, even if I did." Kim laughed. "Suffice it to say, if I thought I knew who could be doing all this, I wouldn't be sitting here." Noting the disappointment around the room at her statement, she continued, "Don't get me wrong, it's not like we have *nothing* to go on. We've made some huge progress. He screwed up for the first time and left actual evidence behind."

"The leaf," Aden said quietly.

Kim smiled, turning to her. "Yes, the leaf, and we should hear soon what kind of fiber that was caught on the stem. If it was hair…" she paused.

"There could be DNA." Maddox took up the narrative. "Of course, that would only tell us the sex of the suspect outright, unless the individual was already in a database somewhere."

"*If* it was hair, and *if* it was human." Kim frowned at him.

"When will we find out?" Janet asked. "What it was, I mean. When will their tests be done?"

"I'll let you know as soon as I know," Kim assured her, which, Aden noted, wasn't really an answer. "And of course there were all the muddy partial footprints upstairs, on the door…and we're still processing all the other trace evidence."

"Okay, anybody else feel like getting out of here for a while?" Aden asked hopefully.

"I don't know that you should be going out," Janet said, surprised.

"Mom, come on. You're telling me that you don't feel like getting away from the target's center for a bit?"

"We could go to my house," Cadence offered.

"Well, I wouldn't mind you going to Cadence's. Tried to get you to go last night," Janet said.

"So?" Aden questioned the guys.

A few minutes later, the four of them were in Trey's car heading down the winding drive toward the highway.

"Would you all mind if we went somewhere else?" Maddox asked, squeezing Aden's hand as they sat in the back seat. "We could go to Dad's house afterward?"

Cadence turned around in the front seat to look suspiciously at him. "Sure. We can go wherever Trey says his car can go, I guess." She glanced at Trey for confirmation and he nodded. "Where do you wanna go?"

"Trey, take a right on the highway," Maddox directed. Cadence waited, looking back at him expectantly.

"So where are we headed?" she prompted when he said nothing. Maddox sighed and turned to Aden, still holding her hand between them on the seat.

"I thought we could go check out the trails on the mountain, where we saw the meteor."

"You mean your Super-Secret Spot?!" Cadence asked, looking shocked. "Seriously?"

Trey chuckled, and Aden looked just as surprised as Cadence.

"I want to look at it from the perspective of somebody trying to follow us on those trails." He shrugged.

"You're sure?" Aden grinned mischievously. "I mean, you've kept Cadence away from there for years."

"I know, but we're grown-ups now, or, some of us are, anyway." Maddox smiled. "I guess I'm learning to appreciate the company of my sisters a bit more lately."

"We're going to Maddox's secret spot!" Cadence announced excitedly to Trey, bouncing in her seat.

"Um, yeah, I heard." Trey grinned, shaking his head.

Maddox directed the occasional turn as they headed deeper into the mountainous terrain, finally directing Trey to park in a scenic pull-off.

"Wow, I've been by here before, but I never stopped." Cadence bounced out of the car. "So what's so special about this place?"

"Jeez, let the rest of us get out of the car," Maddox groaned. Cadence didn't hear him; she'd already stepped up to the low stone wall guarding the steep drop off and was surveying the horizon.

"Sweet view." Trey nodded, joining her.

"It gets better." Aden smiled at Maddox; they joined hands and turned toward one of the trails on one side.

"C'mon, you two," Maddox called over his shoulder. They led the way slowly, taking more notice of the surrounding trees, rocks, and low, wind-swept vegetation as they climbed.

"What are you looking for, anyway?" Cadence asked after several minutes. "Didn't the police already search here?"

"I don't know if they did or not. I gave them the location." Maddox shrugged. "And the truth is, there's probably nothing to find. I mean, this is public property, and there's no telling how many people have been here since then. I was mainly trying to listen – to the sounds we're making, and imagining that it's dark out because you hear more in the dark."

"Yeah, there were just the two of us that night, too." Aden grinned back as Cadence let out a short yelp as she slipped on a loose rock. "But the wind was blowing a bit more that night."

"Yes, there would have been more wind noise and rustling in all these leaves and branches." Maddox frowned, stopping abruptly. "I still think we could have heard somebody following us, though."

"All these rocks sliding around?" Trey nodded. "It'd be really hard to be in stealth mode climbing up here."

"Wait, are we stopping?" Cadence asked, looking around dubiously.

"No, we're listening." Maddox glared at her. "Or trying to."

"Oh, okay then." She shrugged, leaning against a large rock outcrop. "Is it much farther?" Maddox sighed and closed his eyes, turning in a slow, complete circle. Cadence turned questioning eyes to Aden, who put her finger to her lips in mute answer. "Oh my God, seriously?" Cadence whined as Maddox opened his eyes.

"Hold your horses, Miss Impatience; it's not that far." He answered, and he stalked up the path once more.

"My horses are fine, thank you very much." Cadence informed his back. "I just wondered how much farther we had to climb; my calves are going to be sore tomorrow."

"So it's not the horses, it's the calves?" Trey grinned quietly behind Cadence, and she chuckled with him.

"And you two make fun of *us*?" Aden rolled her eyes, bringing up the rear.

Their friendly sparring continued up the trail, right up until Maddox hoisted Cadence onto the flat rock column at the top, then turned to offer Trey a hand. Cadence stood, speechless, much like Aden had been the first time.

"Wow." Trey whistled, looking around after he'd offered a hand to Aden, coming up behind him.

"Okay, this was worth it," Cadence admitted. "I really didn't think it could possibly live up to all those years of hype and mystery." She shrugged. "Wait, this *is* it, right? The trail ends here?"

"Well, technically, the trail keeps going along the spine of that ridge for a bit before it heads down that side of the mountain." He met Cadence's glare and laughed. "But this is the spot."

"Wow, you've gone down that side? And over that?" Trey whistled again, leaning over the far side to see where the trail continued. "You're braver than I am."

"I did once." Maddox chuckled. "It's not as bad as it looks…if you're really bored with hours stretching ahead of you."

"Anything interesting on that side of the trail?" Cadence asked.

"Not really. This is the best view I've found within miles and miles. There's an old house back up there above the ridge. Dunno if anybody lives there."

"There's a house over there?" Trey leaned further out.

"Get back here." Cadence grabbed his arm. "We're not going any further and you're making me nervous leaning over the edge that far." Trey just grinned at her.

"Yeah, it's back up in the trees. Looks like it's been there a long time." Maddox shrugged. "There's an old, overgrown trail that branches off the ridge and leads to the back of the house. That's how I saw it, just the once. I turned back around to the main trail when I saw the house."

"You didn't check it out while you were there?" Cadence asked.

"Check what out? It was a house…and there are some crazy people who live up in these mountains. I didn't want to get shot for trespassing."

Trey just chuckled, and Maddox sank down between the tree roots and leaned back against the rock wall. He was joined by Aden, who sat smiling absently at Cadence's constant chatter.

S o, are we boring you two?" Cadence asked after several minutes of chattering about the view. "I mean, you're just sitting there."

"Just not used to such a crowd on this little rock." Maddox smiled. "It's usually quieter up here."

Trey chuckled again, and Cadence just stuck out her tongue, then said, "Whatever. Anybody else getting thirsty?"

"Seriously? You want to leave already?" Aden couldn't hold back her laugh. "This is the place your brother kept secret from you for years."

"And it's really cool. And I'll love coming back sometime," she raised her eyebrows at Maddox's frown, "when I know he won't be here. And that's *if* I can find it again. There were a lot of criss-crossing trails, and it's so steep getting here."

"You know you memorized every foot." Maddox smiled. "I know a place where we can get some milkshakes on the way back."

"So we're leaving?" Aden sat up.

"Cadence is thirsty," Maddox said, helping her stand the rest of the way.

"Well, I could use a little something cold, myself," Trey said, smiling at Cadence.

"See? It's not just me. It's hot out here," Cadence fake-pouted until Trey grabbed her hand and helped her down the side of the rock to the path.

Aden hesitated, looking out into the blue void, then closed her eyes to listen. She couldn't hear the voice of the rock over Cadence and Trey, talking as they started down the path.

"I can't hear him either right now," Maddox whispered in her ear, wrapping his arms around her. "We'll have to come back again soon."

"It's a date." Aden grinned, eyes still closed.

"Come on," Maddox said, releasing her except for one hand, which he wrapped with his own. Aden reluctantly let him lead her back down to the car. They caught up with Trey and Cadence quickly, and Maddox led the way down to the car.

They were finishing their milkshakes as Trey pulled into Cadence's driveway.

"Can you stay a while?" Cadence asked Trey.

"I promised Bunkie I'd help him move some of his band's equipment after he gets off work." He glanced at the clock in the dashboard, "but I've got a couple of hours 'til I'll have to leave. You don't mind me staying?"

"Are you kidding?" Maddox teased from the back seat as he climbed out of the car.

"You guys up for an old-fashioned board game?" Cadence asked, climbing the stairs to the porch. "I found our old Monopoly game the other day when I was helping Mom. Come on, it'll be fun."

A little over two hours later, the game was winding down. Trey was winning, owning most of the real estate on the board and raking in cash with every throw of the dice. Aden had been holding her own until she'd landed on Boardwalk and had to pay Trey for her hotel stay. Maddox had cashed in twenty minutes before, admitting defeat.

"You know you lost on purpose," Cadence had huffed when he'd sold off his last property. "You always win this game. You're just too preoccupied with Aden." Maddox had just shrugged.

"And that, my friends, is all she wrote." Trey chuckled, gathering the last of the property deeds and ending the game.

"Good game, man." Maddox smiled.

"I think you cheated." Cadence grinned mischievously. "We'll have to play again."

"Next time." Trey stretched and yawned. "I've gotta get to Bunkie's barn."

"But it's supper time," Cadence whined. "Can't you stay a bit longer? I mean, you have to eat, right?"

252

"Sorry, I'm already late. He got off work a half hour ago, and I'd promised to be there." Cadence's shoulders drooped. "But if you're free tomorrow, I could—wait, I have a second interview at 11:00."

"You got a second interview?" Cadence perked up. "That's awesome."

"Yeah, they emailed me earlier today. Kinda forgot with everything that's been going on."

"Can you call me afterwards?" Cadence smiled hopefully, and Trey nodded, returning the smile. She and Trey got up from the kitchen table where'd they'd been playing just as Mayor Max walked in the kitchen door.

"Well, looks like there was a show-down in here." He observed the remains of the game. "Who's winning?"

"Trey won," Cadence informed him.

"Good to see you again, son." Mayor Max shook Trey's hand and looked to Maddox and Aden.

"I'm just walking Trey out; be back shortly." Cadence said as Trey waved a final good bye.

"Hey there, Aden, how are you holding up?" Max asked kindly, pulling out a chair to sit opposite her and Maddox.

"I'm okay." She smiled. "I should probably be getting home, too. I didn't realize it'd gotten so late."

"Oh, it's not even time for supper yet." Max waved her off.

"Not in *this* house, anyway," Maddox muttered, making Aden laugh. "Actually, Dad, could I borrow your car to take Aden home? Mom's got the Audi."

"Yes, that'll be fine." Max nodded, head tilted. "But I'm not finished with the two of you just yet." Aden's eyebrows went up, and Maddox sighed heavily. "I've been hearin' about the two of you from just about everybody in town this past week. Seems you've been makin' quite the impression."

Maddox squeezed Aden's hand under the table and leaned forward. "What kind of impression is that?"

"Well," his Dad drawled, "I've had to listen to complaints from Dave - uh, Sheriff Richey

253

about you interfering in crime scenes? And you two suddenly seem sewn together at the hip. If Aden is involved, there you are." Max frowned at his son. "Do you know how many officers in our fine department think you might be involved in some sort of copycat hoax? That *you're* the intruder at the Garrett's property?"

"Mr. Dixon—" Aden began, but Maddox interrupted.

"So what else are 'they' saying?"

"I've heard that Billy Ray Payne may have an interest in Aden," Max paused, "And that you've asked about protective orders? Son, are you—"

"Dad, Billy Ray is an asshole. A concealed-weapon-carrying asshole. He's insulted not only Aden, but Cadence and Grace and, well, who knows how many other women?"

"So steer clear of him." Max frowned.

"We're trying," Aden interjected, and Max sighed deeply.

"I've been keeping up with things – through the Sheriff, and your Mother of course," Max nodded to Maddox, then turned back to Aden. "I'm worried, and I won't hide it. I personally think this is a great time for you to go someplace far away on vacation." He gestured Maddox into silence. "Now I know that the F.B.I. presence disagrees with me—"

"Just say Mom." Maddox rolled his eyes.

"All the 'profiling' stuff…" He glanced at Maddox again, "Well, they seem to think this perpetrator might follow you, come for you when you're vulnerable, with your guard down. They're convinced that you're safer here, as long as you're with other people." Maddox nodded involuntarily, and Mayor Max took a deep breath. Then, he leaned forward, getting on the same level with Aden's eyes. "You be careful, Aden. Take this seriously and listen to them, okay?"

Aden smiled, reaching out to put her hand over his on the table. "I am, Mr. Dixon. I promise."

"You call me Max; you've been family for years." He smiled and turned his hand to give hers a brief squeeze before abruptly standing. "You be suspicious of *everybody*, you hear? I mean it. Every single person you come into contact with until they nail this guy." Aden nodded. "And I guess you two spendin' so much time together isn't such a horrible thing in light of…well, just try and keep the town gossip to a minimum, will ya?" He grinned. "Elections are comin' up again before you know it, and I don't need any family scandals."

"Dad," Maddox groaned.

Just then, LeighAnn Dixon came into the kitchen and, lifting the lid on a huge stockpot on the stove, began stirring dinner.

"Max, you're home early." She smiled and tilted her head so he could kiss her cheek.

"I heard you were makin' my favorite chili." He chuckled. "I'm gonna run and go make a quick phone call in my study. I'll be back shortly to help you with the cornbread."

"Hi, Aden." Leigh Ann smiled, turning from the stove. "Will you stay for some chili? It'll be ready in another half hour or so."

"Well, I should probably—" she began

"There's gonna be plenty. Why don't I call your Mom and see if she and Drew would like to join us, too?"

"Oh, well, I guess so." Aden grinned. "I do like your chili."

"I'll call her now, then, as soon as I figure out where I left my cell phone." She left the kitchen in search of it.

"See? That wasn't so hard." Maddox squeezed her hand.

"What?"

"Just saying 'yes, I can stay' instead of all that 'I should be doing something else' nonsense."

"Nonsense?"

"You know you want to stay." His eyes smoldered as he leaned closer.

"I do?" She lost her train of thought as she stared into the depths of his eyes, so close to hers. Then, their lips met, and the room around them receded for a moment.

"Get a room, you two." Cadence grinned, noisily pulling out a chair and sitting with them at the table. Aden sighed as Maddox pulled away to glare at his sister. "Want to play another game?"

"No, it's almost dinner time. We should put this mess away," Maddox answered.

"Well, we can put this away and play a different game until supper's ready," Cadence offered.

"It's dinner," Maddox corrected, "Not supper."

"Actually, it's supper. Get over it." Cadence smiled sweetly. "Right, Aden?"

"Oh I don't care what you call it. I just eat it." Aden began to gather Monopoly money and cards from the table. Cadence just made a sour face.

"So you and Trey seem to be getting along nicely," Maddox said smoothly.

"Nice segue," Cadence acknowledged, "And yes, we are," she beamed. "Even Daddy Max approves of him, I think, and that's sayin' something considering the third-degree any guy gets when he comes to take one of us out."

"Yeah, Dad asked me about him the other day." Maddox nodded.

"And?" Cadence froze, waiting for him to continue.

"And I told him Trey seems to be a stand-up guy." Maddox shrugged, raising his eyebrows.

"Seems to be?" Cadence seemed affronted.

"Well, I mean, I've only known him for a few days—"

"You've only known Aden for a few days," Cadence pointed out. "Is she a 'stand-up gal?'"

"Stop it. It's what Dad needed to hear. Trey seems like a decent guy from my limited acquaintance with him."

"You couldn't have said he's sweet and generous and funny and gorgeous?" Cadence fumed.

"No," Maddox declared decisively. "I couldn't have said that."

Aden laughed, and the siblings followed suit as they cleared the table.

"Okay, Aden, your Mom is on her way. Drew had other plans, so we'll eat when she gets here." LeighAnn announced, coming back in to stir her chili on the stove. "Maddox, Kim is coming too. Oh, I need to hurry and make the cornbread." She threw up her hands and turned from them to the pantry.

"Can we help?" Aden asked.

"No," she called from inside the pantry, "I can do it quicker myself, but, with everyone who's coming, we'll have to eat in the dining room. We won't all fit at the kitchen table. Would you three mind setting the table in there?"

With the three of them pitching in, it was done pretty quickly.

"Okay, people, cornbread takes over half an hour to mix and bake, even for Mom. Can I interest anyone in a hand or two of Five Card Draw?" Cadence waved an inlaid mahogany box.

"Did you have that in your pocket?" Aden laughed as Cadence opened the lid to display two decks of cards and nestled stacks of poker chips.

"No, Daddy Max keeps it in the china cabinet. He used to host his poker games here."

"Used to?"

"Before he ran for mayor. Now, the job takes up all his free time." Cadence frowned.

"Weird for such a small town, don't you think?"

"Wow. It *is* a small town." A new voice grated from the doorway.

"Hello Patience." Maddox greeted her with a tight smile.

"Brother dear. And Aden, flavor of the week? You're looking droopier than usual," Patience simpered. "I hear it's been an exciting week for you."

Maddox put his arm around Aden's waist as she bristled. "I've heard some interesting things about you, too." Maddox countered, eyes narrowing a tiny fraction. "Kit Pierce?"

Patience's smile widened as she took a breath. "So, is the happy couple joining us for dinner?" Patience turned to Cadence, dismissing Maddox and Aden.

"Yes! Happily, they are." Cadence grinned.

"Fantastic." Patience's smile was almost a grimace as she stalked out of the room and up the stairs.

"Why does she hate me so much?" Aden asked, glaring at the empty doorway.

"Don't know. Don't care." Cadence waved her dismissal. "We love you. Right, Maddox?"

Maddox just smiled an enigmatic smile and squeezed Aden's waist. Aden tried not to be bothered by his silence.

"So are you going to tell us about Kit Pierce?" Cadence asked, one eyebrow arched.

"Nope, just like I won't tell Patience about Trey Miller." He smiled.

"Kit Pierce is like a sophomore in college isn't he?" Aden asked.

"Rising junior, I think." Cadence nodded. "He's the same age as you, right?" she asked Maddox. His smile fell a bit.

"Are we playing cards? We'll have to go back to the kitchen table so we have room." He released Aden's waist but grabbed her hand and gently tugged her back to the kitchen. Cadence followed silently, scowling.

They played a few half-hearted hands of poker, and then Cadence played a couple of hands of Solitaire while Aden and Maddox watched. Aden wasn't sure why Maddox became so subdued so suddenly, and she wasn't sure now was the time to bring it up, with all the families convening. Kim and Janet arrived within minutes of each other, and everyone was seated in the dining room.

The chili was a hit, and everyone lingered over their empty bowls and plates. Grace had come in mid-way through the meal and joined them, sitting beside Patience at one end of the long table. Cadence sat at the end, and Aden and Maddox on the other side, so Aden had an unobstructed view of the Kendall triplets. It was rare these days that they were all together.

"Well, he should have kept his wrinkly old nose out of my business," Patience was saying more quietly than usual. The adults at the other end of the table were engaged in their own conversation.

"Well what exactly were you and Cade up to in the back row of the theater that a stranger would feel compelled—" Grace started.

"Oh, forget it," Patience huffed. "I was talking about the nosy old guy. Not my date."

Grace and Cadence exchanged a grinning glance.

"What did he say to you, anyway?" Cadence asked, swallowing a smile.

"He said 'Miss,' —called me Miss— 'Your Daddy might not approve of your conduct,' or something like that," she scowled. "Like he'd know."

"Well, your Father is very well known around town," Maddox pointed out with a small smile. She cut him with a look and abruptly left the table.

"That supper was amazin'," Max announced, patting his slightly protruding middle. "But I ate too much."

"Me too," Maddox mock-groaned.

"Thank you, LeighAnn. It really was delicious," Janet said. LeighAnn smiled and nodded modestly.

"I've got homemade lime sherbet for dessert. We can have it out back," she said, rising. At the sighs and groans, she laughed. "Later. We'll do that in a while."

Aden began gathering dishes, along with Cadence and Maddox.

"No kids, leave it. The kitchen's not big enough for all of us, and Janet and I can help Leigh Ann while we all visit," Kim directed.

Aden, Maddox, Cadence, and Grace went outside. It was almost fully dark. Stars were beginning to twinkle in the broad space between the two ancient oaks on either side of the large yard. In the center, where the sun reached down between the canopies, LeighAnn had created an outdoor room delineated by carefully-tended plants. Light strings of warm, bare bulbs were suspended above, between the boughs of the trees. There were rustic chandeliers hung in the branches of each tree and soft spotlights up-lighting some of the larger plants, and there was a large running fountain in the rear of the yard. A generous flagstone path meandered through the plantings—various areas of herbs and vegetables interspersed with many decorative shrubs and flowers. At the very center was a large, round patio of flagstone where a table and chairs were ringed by benches following the outside border of the flagstone circle.

Cadence and Grace produced colorful seat cushions and pillows for all the benches and chairs and brought out several large pillar candles in hurricane glass globes, which were placed on the table and lit. Aden sighed as she settled on a bench with Maddox. The whole garden glowed with a warmth she felt flowing from Maddox's warm hand around hers.

"You know, I always used to make fun of your Mom puttering around out here all the time," Maddox said to his siblings as the two of them lounged on adjacent benches, "But this really is nice."

"It smells so good out here." Aden breathed deeply, eyes closed.

"Mom can tell you exactly what you're smelling. What's in bloom, what'll be coming out next this season. There's always something blooming out here," Grace said.

"We used to have plans to landscape the paths behind our house," Aden said quietly.

"Still could," Cadence said. Aden just shrugged.

"We could help," Cadence offered. "It would be fun."

"I heard you guys had a blast taking down a staircase the other day." Grace smiled. "Sounded like fun. I could do some planting and pruning and path-laying and stuff. For a while."

"You're both so sweet, but we're probably not going to be doing anything like that anytime soon." Aden sighed.

"Why not?" Cadence persisted. "Is this about your Dad, too?"

"What do you mean, 'too'?" Aden sat up to look at her.

"I mean," she intoned, "ever since the accident, you won't learn to drive, you won't make any changes in your house, including a temporary staircase to an unfinished part of the house—"

"We tore that down!" Aden's voice was rising, and Maddox sat up, too.

"It's been two years," Cadence said quietly.

"Two and a half," Aden corrected harshly. "My Dad *died* two and a half years ago. And no, we haven't had the heart or the money, or the, the…" her voice was beginning to crack.

"Cadence, what the hell?" Maddox stood, dragging Aden with him.

"I just meant, maybe it's time—"

"Drop it," Maddox commanded, leading Aden around the side of the house. She used the covering darkness to swipe at the tears and take several deep breaths. He led her to the porch swing, and he sat, bringing her with him and silently holding her until she spoke.

"Sorry. I overreacted." She sighed, sniffing.

"*You* have nothing to be sorry for." He shook his head. "I can't believe Cadence."

"No, she's right. It's been two and a half years." Aden swallowed hard.

"Doesn't matter. He was your Dad. Could be ten years; she didn't have any right."

"Just doesn't seem that long." A tear rolled unbidden down her cheek, and Maddox wiped it away with his thumb, replacing it with a kiss. She tried a smile for his benefit. "I can still hear the sounds from that night." She stopped.

"Do you want to talk about it?" he asked quietly.

She thought about that. She'd never wanted to talk about it before, had gone to great lengths to avoid voicing any string of words that might bring back the memories of that night. The sheer weight and final reality of those memories could crush her.

"I don't know. Maybe I should." She took a deep breath. "But tonight's not the time or place." He just nodded. "Don't be mad at Cadence."

"She's your best friend," he growled.

"Yes, she is, and this isn't the first time she's pointed out that maybe I'm avoiding… things…And she's right." She smiled again, weakly. "It takes a best friend to be able to say those things, you know, when you're just unable to face reality. It's a true friend who knows when it's time to stop coddling, take off the kid gloves, and start…living again." She met his eyes as he searched her face in the dim light from the dining room windows.

"So you're okay?" he was hesitant. She nodded slowly.

"I'm sorry."

"Will you stop apologizing?" he sighed. He closed his eyes and inhaled deeply. "I just wish I could help."

"You have." Her smile was genuine this time. "More than you know." His eyes still searched her face, and she tilted her head up to kiss him softly. His warmth spread through her from the brief contact, and she squared her shoulders. "Come on, let's go back."

"Aden—" he stopped, and she could see the indecision in his silhouette as she thrilled to hear him speak her name.

"It's okay, Maddox. Come on." She stood and held out her hand, waiting for his.

"If you're sure that's what you really want." He frowned, hesitating on the swing.

"Well, what I really want is to be on top of the world, alone with you." She grinned.

"Then, let's go." He stood, still frowning.

"But that would be rude." She shook her head emphatically. "We can't just leave—"

"Sure we can."

"But my Mom."

"Text her. Call her. Tell her you'll be home by curfew."

"Seriously, Maddox. Let's just go back for a while—"

"Seriously, Aden, you don't owe anyone anything." She stared, incredulous at his intensity. She couldn't read his mood; she'd never seen him like this. "Do you really *want* to go back and hang out with all of them right now?"

She searched his face, half hidden in shadows, and she had to admit to the reluctance she felt to go and pretend everything was okay. She bit her lip. Maddox's eyes didn't miss her gesture of indecision.

"I really don't think they'll miss us," he said, more gently. "The moms have probably opened the first bottle of wine by now, and something tells me that Cadence and Grace have better things to do than worry about us tonight."

The sound of laughter drifted on a sultry breeze from the back garden. The moms had joined Cadence and Grace. Aden could pick out Janet's trilling giggle among the rest.

"Okay, but can we at least go tell them goodbye? In person?"

"You sure?"

"I'd feel so guilty if we just left. I wouldn't be able to enjoy myself the rest of the night."

He shook his head, smiling. "Come on, then." He led her back around the house to the garden, where the laughter continued to bubble into the humid night, above the gurgling of the fountain. "Mrs. Garrett, would you mind if Aden and I went for a drive? I'll have her home by curfew."

Janet looked surprised, but nodded. "Sure. Aden, what time do you have to work tomorrow?"

"I have to be there at 1:00 tomorrow afternoon."

"Okay, so be home by 12:30. No later, okay?" she mock-scowled at her now-surprised daughter who just nodded, blinking.

"Take the Audi." Kim said, re-filling three wine glasses. "Drew has agreed to come by and drive me and Janet home this evening."

"We'll be home by 12:30, too," Janet added. "So we'll be there when you get there. You two be careful."

"Um, okay," Aden said, frowning. Then, she turned to where Cadence and Grace sat on a bench together now. "I'll see you guys. Call you in the morning?"

"Not too early." Cadence smiled, rising. "Hug?" She hesitated a few feet away with her arms outstretched. Aden shook her head, opening her own arms. They met halfway in a big bear hug. Grace jumped up and put her arms around both of them.

"Okay, then." Maddox smiled, crossing his arms and shaking his head.

CHAPTER 15

she's a wreck

Aden was quiet on the ride back through the mountains, and Maddox let her be. He knew stress had taken its toll on him, and he could only image how much worse it was for Aden. Sometimes, you just needed some peace and quiet, some space to breathe, and that was what he was going to give her.

She was silent as he parked the car and led her up the familiar trail. It was much cooler now that the sun had gone down, and there was a hint of a breeze again. He pulled her up onto the stone shelf, and the world fell away once more. Aden took a deep breath and smiled at him.

"Thank you," she said just above a whisper.

"For what?"

"Not...expecting anything." She frowned. "Not trying to make me talk, or answer questions, or...trying to fix it and make it all better."

"If I could fix it, believe me, I would." He wasn't sure if they were talking about her father's death or the stalking psychopath.

"But you can't."

"No, I can't," he agreed unhappily. "But I can be here for you. Whatever you need."

She smiled at him and then turned toward the view, pulling his arms around her from behind as they'd stood before. She closed her eyes and listened. There it was, just below her normal perception; she could hear the voice of the stone on the wind. It was faint and fading in and out with the breeze. She found herself tensed up, trying to catch it, and sighed. *Idiot. You wanted to come up here to relax.*

"Why don't we sit for a while?" His close, quiet voice soothed her nerves.

Maddox was still, listening intently to discern any sound that would be out of place, any

265

shadow that stood out in the darkness around them. He couldn't see how they would have been followed.

"Do you know anything about the accident?" Aden asked after several long minutes.

"Your Dad's accident?" Maddox asked, making sure he was on the same page. She nodded. "Not much, actually."

"I wasn't sure if Cadence or anybody else had talked to you about it."

"I wasn't here when it happened, and by the time I came back for a visit, it was several months to a year afterwards. I heard about it, of course. Cadence did bring it up, but I don't remember us talking about any of the details." Aden just nodded again. When she didn't speak after another minute, Maddox went back to analyzing their surroundings.

"Dad had just gotten back from a business trip to Atlanta. He'd been gone three days, and I knew he was tired, having just gotten off the road from a three-hour drive. He'd been teaching me to drive. We'd go out every weekend to the big cemetery in town—he said I couldn't possibly hurt anybody there." She smiled at the memory. "Anyway, I begged and begged for him to take me out for another lesson, and he finally agreed. We'd go for just a little while after dinner. I hadn't ever driven in the dark, and he thought it'd be good experience." She paused and glanced up at Maddox. He was looking out into the darkness but turned to smile encouragingly. She took a deep breath.

"So on the way home, he decided to take the back way; Anderson Road on the back side of the cemetery runs straight out to the highway about seven miles up the mountain above my house. We were driving down the mountain, about five miles from home, when Dad suddenly swore. He never swore around me. Never." She took another deep breath.

"He was looking in the rear view mirror, so I turned around to see what was going on. There was an eighteen-wheeler with its headlights flashing, obviously out of control and careening all over the highway, and it was coming up on us fast. The truck's horn started blowing, and my Dad swore again. We were rounding a curve where there was no shoulder to speak of, just a steep drop-off on our right, and we could see light from an oncoming car approaching the curve from the other side. We had no place to go... and that truck was zig-zagging right on our bumper, the horn blaring, the lights—" she blinked back tears.

"I remember seeing the headlights of the oncoming car round the bend. It was like I was watching everything in slow motion. I started to turn around to see how close the truck was when there was big, loud thump, and I banged my head on the window." Aden was crying now, but oblivious to the fact as she relived that night. "I guess that's when the truck hit us. It knocked me out. When I came to again, I was being strapped into a stretcher by paramedics. It was surreal. There were so many huge, bright lights, all moving around. They were big, heavy flashlights and spotlights that were bouncing around as the police, firemen, and paramedics slid their way down the hill to where our car had come to rest against a tree.

"I was so confused; I couldn't figure out what was happening. I didn't remember where I was, and everyone was shouting. It was just loud and glaringly bright. Then, one of the spotlights lit up the big hulking shadow to one side…It was the underside of our car. We'd been pushed through the guard rail and down the embankment. Somehow, the car had turned around facing the opposite direction and came to rest on its side, against a tree. I asked where my Dad was, but nobody would answer. I got louder and louder, screaming for my father. I remember one of the paramedics squeezed my hand, and he looked at me with such a sad face, just before the stretcher lurched, and they began hauling me up the hill.

"I knew then. I didn't want to know that I knew, so I pushed it back, just swallowed that thought. I stopped screaming and squeezed my eyes shut. I was terrified that they were going to drop me, and I'd go rolling down the hill again. I felt so helpless lying there. I could hear the heavy breathing of the men who carried me. I could smell fresh pine sap, burnt rubber, and hot oil. I opened my eyes and could see swarms of people making their slow way either down or back up the embankment and even more people looking over the mangled guard rail from the road above…I didn't know how all those people had gotten there so fast. I didn't know until later that we'd lain in that crumpled car for close to twenty minutes before anybody could get to us. Twenty minutes. Dad could have been alive, and I might have…" she took a breath to stifle a sob.

"Aden—"

She shook her head violently, determined to continue.

"I found out later that the truck had lost its brakes coming down the mountain. Happens a lot, apparently. We were just in the wrong place at the wrong time. We reached the big curve, with no shoulder on the right side, at the exact moment another car was coming around the bend in the other direction. The other car locked up their brakes and slid into our lane just as the truck hit us from behind. While we were pushed over the guard rail and down the embankment, the truck had begun to jackknife, hit the other car, and came to rest in the opposite lane, against the mountainside.

The truck driver and the couple in the other car walked away with just bruises, and I just had a sprained wrist and a sore neck. But Dad…" She inhaled. "He had internal injuries, probably from the steering wheel, they think. Or the seatbelt—that's what's supposed to keep you safe, right? But he died from internal bleeding. They're not exactly sure when that happened, but he was dead when the paramedics arrived."

She glanced at Maddox and saw a tear slide down his cheek as he stared into the darkness. "So the next time I saw Dad was at the funeral. He could have been asleep. He was so very pale, looked a little older somehow, but he could have just been sleeping." She shook her head. "And I told him then, at the church, how sorry I was..." her voice broke completely as she sobbed.

"Aden, it wasn't—"

"No, it *was* my fault," she interrupted him. "I made him take me out driving. We wouldn't even have been there if it hadn't been for me, and I just laid there, or hung there, or whatever, while my Dad was...dying." She turned to him with the most vulnerable face he'd ever seen on any human.

He was shaking his head slowly, tears streaming silently down his face. "It wasn't your fault," he said slowly, confidently. "You are not responsible for your father's death."

She was shaking her head in adamant denial, so he gently took her face in his hands and made her look into his eyes. "It's not your fault." He kissed her forehead. "It is not your fault." He kissed her cheek. "It. Is. Not. Your. Fault." His lips brushed hers, and he wrapped her in a tight embrace, rocking slowly, and he held her that way while the grief of the memories ran its course. After a while, the sobs wound down, and he wiped her cheeks with his thumbs.

Her eyes had been downcast, and she looked up at him hesitantly.

"I'm sor—"

"Don't you dare say you're sorry," he ordered. "I'm sorry for you, for what you've been through. And Aden, as God is my witness, not one thing in that story was your fault. You asked your Dad to take you out driving. Kids do that all the time. How many other times had you asked your Dad to take you places? And everything was fine. Hundreds of times, I'm sure. Accidents happen, and there's not always a reason. Nobody planned for those three vehicles to meet at the exact spot where there was no shoulder on the outside of a big curve, and Aden, nobody but you would think you could have saved your father."

He suddenly realized that the expression on Aden's shadowed face looked a lot like amusement.

"Um, did you just quote Scarlett O'Hara?" He could hear the suppressed laughter in her voice and sat back in utter confusion.

"What?"

"As God is my witness?" She raised her eyebrows, still sniffing, but definitely amused.

"That's a fairly widely-used expression, maybe a little old-fashioned." He frowned. "It was just the most incorruptible vow I could come up with on short notice." She was giggling, very quietly, but definitely giggling. "Aden, are you okay?" her giggles grew louder as she shook her head slowly.

"No, I'm not okay." She smiled. "But I'm a whole lot better." Maddox just glared at her, confounded. She sighed and shrugged. "I didn't mean to make you mad."

"I'm not mad. I'm—" he huffed, "I don't know what I am."

"I warned you; I'm not normal. More than once, as I recall." As she reached for him, they both jumped at the sound of shifting rocks and soil suddenly bouncing down the side of the mountain close by. Maddox was instantly on his feet, pulling Aden with him.

"Where did that come from? I was listening to you." He looked around wildly from side to side.

"I'm not sure, either; I wasn't paying attention." She answered in a whisper, examining the shadows.

"We should go," Maddox ground out quietly and immediately began the trek back to the car at a faster than normal clip.

"Maddox, hold on," Aden huffed. She was having a hard time keeping up.

"Sorry, but we need to keep moving." His eyes never stopped their surveillance, but he did slow his pace a little. When they reached the car, Maddox asked her to stand back while he walked all around the vehicle, checking underneath it and inside before he opened her door and motioned her in.

"Do you think he was there?" Aden asked as he peeled out onto the road.

"Not sure, but I'm not taking any more chances." He seemed angrier than ever.

"Maddox?"

He sighed, "I shouldn't have taken you there. That was stupid. I don't know what I was thinking."

She wasn't sure that was all of it, but she let it drop and let him concentrate on the winding road. After several minutes with no headlights behind them, Maddox began to relax.

"You only took me there because I asked you to," she said quietly.

"No, you asked to stay at Cadence's. I talked you into leaving." He was still angry. "And then I took you back to the place where we know for certain that psychopath has followed us at least once."

"We know for certain he's been in my house more than once." She shrugged. "Most likely knows where I work—" He let out a frustrated sigh. "So where *is* safe?"

He stared at the road for a long moment before replying. "With me," he said quietly. Then, he shook his head, and she could see him working his jaw as he glared at the road once again.

They drove in silence the rest of the way to her house. Janet and Drew were in the driveway, talking with the officer on duty when they pulled in.

"Sleep well. I'll call you tomorrow," Maddox said, making no move to turn off the car or walk her to the door. It's not that he had to or anything; it was just unusual.

"Are you—" Aden huffed, not knowing which question to ask. *Was he okay? Was he angry? Was he ready to run back to Virginia as fast as he could leave this place?*

"I'm fine." He tried to smile. It didn't work. Aden stared at him until he turned, reluctantly, to meet her gaze. "Really. You should go on in. They're going to wonder what's taking you so long."

She waited, thinking he would kiss her goodnight, but he turned back to watch the cop in the driveway.

"Okay, then." She frowned and opened the door to get out. "Good night." She hesitated, hoping.

"Good night." He didn't even look at her. He began backing into a turn as soon as she'd closed the door and drove away without even a wave. There was a cold, dark stone in the pit of her stomach that grew as she watched the Audi's brake lights disappear in the trees. She heard him punch the accelerator hard when he hit the highway.

She turned, unseeing, and walked slowly toward the house, bypassing her mother and brother.

"Hey, did you have fun?" her mother called.

"Yep." She waved and went inside.

It was a long, miserable night. The pit of fear in Aden's gut spread as the hours inched by. By the time she finally fell asleep around 4:00a.m., she was convinced that Maddox would be gone by morning. It was inevitable, really, with everything that had happened. He'd only come here to help his mother on a case. Then, he was saddled with a clingy, neurotic, teenaged girl who was constantly whining about one thing or other. She was surprised that he'd stuck around as long as he had. Her pillow was soaked as she mourned his loss even into her dreams.

At some point during the night, she recognized that she would probably be sleeping late, so she set her alarm for 11:00. She had to be to work at 1:00 and wasn't sure how she was getting there. She groaned when the alarm went off and dutifully rolled over to grab her phone. No waiting texts or calls. From anyone. She texted Cadence to ask for a ride to work. The reply said that her mother was home and was driving her to work. Aden read the message twice. *My mother is home? And Cadence knew this how?*

Aden got up and peeked into the kitchen where her mother sat with a cup of coffee and her laptop.

"Hi, Mom." She yawned involuntarily. "What are you doing here?"

"I'm taking you to work." Her mother shrugged. "Go get dressed."

"But, aren't *you* supposed to be at work?"

"I've arranged a more flexible schedule until the kidnapper psycho is caught."

Aden sighed and went to dress, missing Maddox more with each passing second. She checked her phone again, twice, before she got into the shower. Then, she checked it again as soon as she stepped out. Nothing. Disgusted with herself, she dropped her phone on her bed, determined not to look at it again, but she left the bathroom three times while she was applying makeup and drying her hair, just to check.

"Hey, what would you like for breakfast?" Her mother stuck her head around the door jamb when the hair dryer stopped for the third time.

"Not hungry."

"Banana?" Janet suggested. "Apple? Yogurt?"

"Still not hungry," Aden scowled.

"How 'bout some juice then? I'll pack you a lunch for later."

Aden bit back the reply she really wanted to make. "Fabulous," she ground out, instead.

"You're welcome."

Aden rolled her eyes and went into her bedroom. Still no texts. No calls. Radio silence. She slumped onto the bed. *I will not cry; I will not cry; I will not cry.*

"All we have is turkey and swiss; is that okay?" her mother called from the kitchen. Aden sighed loudly.

"Fine." She couldn't believe her mother was making her lunch. Not that she hadn't done it before, but she was little then. She couldn't remember the last time…yes, she could. It was after the accident that the lunches had stopped, one of the many things that had stopped and just never resumed. Not that she needed it, she was perfectly capable of making her own lunch and perfectly capable of getting through this day without weeping over Maddox Dixon every two minutes. Taking a deep breath, she mentally pulled on her Big Girl Panties and went out to the kitchen.

"I can finish that, Mom. Thanks."

"Almost done, anyway. Why don't you grab an apple or banana to put in the bag for later?"

Aden grabbed an apple and a bottle of water from the fridge. Her mother was watching her when she turned back to the counter.

"Everything okay, honey?" her mother's face exuded worry.

"No, everything's not okay." Aden smiled wanly, "But I'll be just fine."

Janet searched her face, obviously biting back more questions.

"I love you, Mom." Aden hugged her fiercely.

"I love you, too, Aden." She sounded surprised. "You know, we don't have to—"

"Yes," Aden interrupted, "We do."

"You know I'm here when you're ready to talk."

"Yes, I do know that, and thank you."

"Okay, then." Sighing, her mother turned to gather her purse and keys from the counter. Aden ducked back into her room and grabbed her bag, then followed her mother out the door to leave.

"James told me this morning that there weren't any new leads in the case, but that he suspected the results would be back any day from the forensics on the leaf and fiber."

"James?"

"Officer Pollack." Her mother answered, as though Aden should have known who James was. "He's worked three shifts at our house since…this thing started." Aden just stared. "And there's Jeff, who's worked a couple of shifts, and Sam…what?"

"You know all their names? Their first names?" Aden asked. Janet shrugged, mystified. "So you chat with them often?

"Aden, what are you getting at?

"Mom, for all we know, one of them could be the psycho. No, wait." She cut off her mother's protest. "Everybody's been telling me to be suspicious of every single person I come into contact with, and you're outside our house chatting up strangers."

Her mother looked angry for a few minutes, then sighed. "You know what? You're right, and I'm sorry. This is just all so…bizarre. To have to look at everybody as a potential suspect."

"I know. They even suspect Maddox." Janet didn't answer. "But you obviously already knew that."

"I don't believe Maddox would be capable of such a thing."

"Well, we agree on one thing, then."

"You know Sheriff Richey is just waiting for any excuse."

"I know. Maddox knows." *May not be a problem if he's gone back to Virginia like I think he has.*

"Well, just…be careful," Janet finished. Aden knew it wasn't what she really wanted to say. *What was that about?*

"Okay, Drew is picking you up. Nine o'clock, right?" her mother had pulled to the curb outside the jewelry store. Aden nodded, thinking how much she wished it were Maddox picking her up. Then, something hit her. Like a train.

"Mom, why are you and Drew driving me around today?"

"Well, Maddox texted your brother, saying he was busy helping his Mom today and asked if he could take you to work and get you home." Her mother frowned, questioning. Her mother assumed she already knew.

"Right." She swallowed hard. Maddox had texted Drew, but not her. She thanked her Mom again and climbed out of the car. She walked into the store with her head held high and her jaw slightly clenched. *I will not cry; I will not cry; I will not cry.*

"Good afternoon, Aden." Mrs. McConnell greeted her before the door had closed behind her.

"Good afternoon, Mrs. McConnell." Aden tried to smile.

"How are you, my dear? And your dear Mother, bless her soul?"

"We're all fine, thank you for asking." She barely glanced at the older lady as she walked toward the back to clock in.

"I've heard rumors about all the unpleasant circumstances you've had to deal with," the old lady clucked. Aden was sure the woman had started most of those rumors.

"Well, you can't believe everything you hear." Her mind was still on Maddox, and she didn't notice the look of surprised indignation as she continued on her way. "I should get clocked in before it looks like I was late."

She could hear Mr. Keith's desk chair squeaking as she went past his office door. She stowed her bag, clocked in, and reluctantly went back out front. Mrs. McConnell was busily nudging trays of jewelry in minute degrees inside of one of the display cases and didn't look up at Aden's return. She was obviously offended by Aden's previous remark. Aden felt slightly ashamed, but not enough to try and strike up another conversation. She busied herself behind the sales desk, dusting filing cabinets and counter tops, even wiping down the clunky old computer they used to record sales and print receipts. When she felt she'd straightened and re-straightened stacks of mailers, brochures on gemstones, brochures on diamond ratings, layaway and credit applications, and other piles of paper she didn't register through her brooding thoughts, she grabbed a clean rag and joined Mrs. McConnell on the showroom floor. She had just begun polishing the already-pristine glass countertops on the opposite side of the store from Mrs. McConnell when a figure outside caught her eye. It was Maddox, walking so fast he was almost jogging. He passed the store without slowing and without glancing inside. Aden stared at the empty sidewalk where he'd been for several seconds before she resumed her pointless busy-work. Mrs. McConnell watched her with a knowing look.

"Boy trouble?" she finally asked, unable to help herself.

"Sorry?" Aden feigned ignorance.

"I just saw young Mr. Dixon go past without a wink. Last I'd heard, you two were cozier than hens in winter."

Aden blinked. *Hens in winter, seriously?*

"He's helping his mother today, and I'm obviously at work." She shrugged innocently. Mrs. McConnell pursed her lips.

"Never stopped him before." She remarked archly.

"Mrs. McConnell, I don't mean to be rude, but I don't want to discuss my personal life with anyone right now. It's been a very difficult time; I'm sure you can understand, since you've 'heard all the rumors.'" Aden thought she'd maintained an air of perfect innocence, but then she noted Mrs. McConnell's lowering brow.

"I don't mean to pry. I thought we were friends, and I thought I could offer you the benefit of my extra decades of wisdom."

Aden bit her tongue, and then said, "I appreciate that, Mrs. McConnell. We are friends. I'm just extremely tired and cranky today. I've had enough of all this kidnapping, stalking, psychopath business to last me…well, forever. I was looking forward to escaping everything for a few hours here at work."

"Alright, then." Mrs. McConnell nodded. "But I wasn't talking about kidnappers or stalkers, was I?" She went back to her own busy work, and Aden let her mind drift back to Maddox, but it didn't last very long.

"Do you know Mrs. Vintner? Katherine – well everyone calls her Kate? She's Abby Garner's sister." Aden just shook her head, dreading the long string of gossip to come. "Well, it seems she's missing." Mrs. McConnell paused for effect.

"You mean like kidnapped?" Aden's head had snapped up.

"Well, not like the others." The old lady clucked again. "Her sister, Mrs. Garner, hasn't been able to get in touch with her for a while. Now, they'd had a falling out several years ago because Mrs. Garner's husband—well, that's another story. But Mrs. Garner told me—wait, you do know Mrs. Garner, don't you? She practically runs the church." When Aden shook her head, the old woman huffed, hands on her hips. "Well, do you know anybody in this town? I just told you Mrs. Garner is the lady who secretaries down at the church."

"Which church?" Aden bit back a smile. "There are five churches inside the town limits and three more just outside it."

"Are you sassin' me, Miss?"

"No, ma'am, just asking which church you're referring to. I'm not familiar with a Mrs. Garner." Mrs. McConnell shook her head so long that Aden knew she'd done it now—there was a storm of lecture coming. On important people, churches, denominations, religion in general, she wasn't sure, but she knew it was coming.

Almost an hour and a half later, Beverly walked in and interrupted the running stream of words that Aden had long since tuned out. Mrs. McConnell had begun with a history of the Methodist church that somehow transitioned into a story about some shocking adulterous priest in the catholic church, that was only interrupted by a couple of browsing customers. But she'd started back in again as soon as customers would leave. Though Aden hadn't been listening, just nodding at any pauses, she was pretty sure Mrs. McConnell hadn't ever made it back to a Mrs. Garner or her original story.

"Good afternoon, Beverly," Mrs. McConnell greeted her when she walked in. "I didn't realize it was 3:00 already. Time does run on, doesn't it?"

"Guess so," was Beverly's only reply as she continued into the back.

"Well, Aden, it seems I'm 'off the clock' now. I do hope you'll think about what I've said to you today."

Aden was surprised. *What had she said today that I'm supposed to think about?*

"Of course, Mrs. McConnell."

"I'm always here if you need to talk or are looking for some friendly advice."

Aden just smiled and nodded. Beverly came back out front as Mrs. McConnell was leaving.

"Have a good afternoon, ladies."

"Back 'atcha." Beverly smirked.

Mrs. McConnell's bosom heaved with indignation, and Aden caught the word "impertinence" as she swept grandly out the door.

Aden didn't look at Beverly, returning to the imaginary smudges on the glass on her side of the store. Beverly did the same. There were no caustic remarks, no sneering stares. It seemed as though they were avoiding each other.

Thank God. Aden relaxed. She was mentally exhausted after fending off Mrs.

McConnell's running diatribe for hours. As the clock ticked, it became harder and harder to keep the empty pit of despair from her thoughts. Over the next couple of hours, Aden caught Beverly glaring at her with obvious malice, but she would drop her gaze as soon as she realized Aden was looking. She never spoke though, which suited Aden just fine.

A few customers came and went, browsers and small sales. Beverly had jumped to help them when they came in, which also suited Aden just fine. She spent her time with a notebook, planning new layouts for the store's merchandise. She was contemplating the front window when Mayor Max walked in, followed by Maddox.

"Aden! Good to see you again." Max greeted her with a warm smile. Maddox hung back a couple of feet. He smiled briefly at Aden before turning his attention to the front window.

"Mr. Dixon, good to see you, too." She worked up a smile.

"I thought I told you to call me Max." He smiled amiably.

"You're right, Max. Sorry, old habits and all." She was trying very hard to focus on Max and not Maddox. "What can I do for you today?"

"Well, you probably know that the girls' birthday is coming up, and I'm looking for some help to find the right gifts. Thought you might have some insight." He beamed at her. Aden felt a little guilty; she hadn't even thought about Cadence's birthday coming up, and she never imagined she'd be helping to pick out gifts for Grace and Patience too.

"Well, did you have something in mind?"

"Not really," He said sheepishly. "It's always so hard to find the right gift for each of them *and* keep everything completely equal and balanced. I was kind of hoping you might know something that all three of them might like?"

Aden sneaked a peek at Maddox by the front window. He was off to one side, watching outside intently.

"Um, I'm sure all three of them would love jewelry." She sneaked another peek to find he was looking at her, too. She quickly turned her attention back to his father. "What kind of budget are we talking about?"

"Mr. Mayor, welcome!" Mr. Keith boomed as he came out onto the sales floor for the first time since Aden had been there. "What brings you in today?"

"Oh, I was browsing for ideas for my girls' birthday presents," Max said absently, shaking Mr. Keith's hand. "And since Aden is Cadence's best friend, I thought she was uniquely qualified to help me out."

"Well, then, I'll leave you to it. Please let me know if I can help." Mr. Keith smiled. Max thanked him and turned back to Aden. Mr. Keith retreated, but only to the sales counter at the back of the showroom, where he could keep a close eye on things.

Twenty minutes later, Mr. Keith was ringing up the purchase of three identical gold bracelets with diamond-chip studded heart charms that Aden had helped Max pick out. As he and Max stood across the sales counter making small talk, Aden walked to where Maddox still stood, staring through the front window of the store.

"You know, I've seen every angle of the view out that window, over several seasons and times of day and night, but I've never found it nearly as compelling as you have today."

Maddox sighed and turned to her for the first time. "Sorry, this wasn't exactly my idea."

"Obviously," Aden said icily. Maddox froze, examining her face in a slow gaze.

"You're upset." He frowned. Aden's eyebrows went up in disbelief as she searched for something caustic enough to say to him. "I know I didn't call you like I promised—"

"Didn't call me? You inexplicably dumped me in my driveway, and I haven't heard from you. Then, I find out you've been in contact with my brother and my best friend, but you can't be bothered to make eye contact, let alone say hello."

Maddox was looking over her shoulder, and she turned to see Beverly smugly taking in every word of their conversation. *Perfect.* She also saw that Mr. Keith was leading Max toward them, bag in hand, and speaking in low voices. She turned back to find Maddox gazing at her with a pained look.

"I'm so sorry; I didn't realize—" He spoke so low she could barely hear him.

"...and I haven't seen him since then. I don't think he'll be coming back in here." Mr. Keith was saying as they drew near.

"Well, we all appreciate your efforts." Max shook his hand. "Dave Richey has spoken with his father, too. I think the message is out that we're all watching closely." Aden was suddenly aware that they were all looking at her. "Well, thank you again, Aden. My girls are gonna be very happy I think."

"You're welcome," she answered a beat late.

"Aden, do you have a break coming up?" Maddox asked.

"Why don't you go ahead and take your break now?" Mr. Keith smiled at her. "Take your time; it's been a little slow today."

"Um, thank you." Aden tried another smile and went to get her bag out of the back room. Max and Maddox were waiting for her by the door when she returned. Beverly was still standing as close to them as she could without being overtly obvious and clearly eavesdropping on their conversation.

"Can I get you anything while I'm out, Beverly?" Aden asked, smiling sweetly. Beverly's answering gaze would have curdled milk. Max's eyebrows went up in surprise, but he didn't comment as he held the door for Aden. On the sidewalk outside, he paused.

"Everything okay back there Aden?"

"Just fine." Aden shrugged. "Well, not great, but it's normal. Nothing to worry about."

Max hesitated, sighing. "Alright, then, but you let me know if I can do anything to help you." Aden nodded, smiling. "Well, I've gotta get back to the office. Thank you again, Aden." With a fatherly nod to Maddox, he crossed the street toward the courthouse.

"Would you like to go to the deli?" Maddox asked.

"No, I brought a sandwich from home."

"The park, then? There's a table in the shade over there." He pointed, then led the way, frowning, with his hand protectively on the small of her back.

"Have you eaten?" she asked.

"Yeah, dad and I grabbed lunch a while back. Listen, Aden, I didn't realize; I just didn't think—" he rolled his eyes in frustration. "Okay, let me start from the beginning. Last night was, well, you surprised me by telling me about the accident." Aden closed her eyes. She couldn't look at him. "It's just…I know that you don't like to talk about it. I know how hard that was for you."

"You don't have to say anything else," Aden ground out, eyes still closed. *I will not cry.* "I get it."

"No, I don't think you –"

"It's okay. I know this has all been way too much to deal with."

"Aden, stop. Please listen to me." He held her face between his hands, and she opened her eyes to meet his. "I screwed up, clearly. I should have called you this morning, and

I'm so sorry, but I don't understand why you suddenly think, well, whatever it is you're thinking." Aden blinked, feeling as confused as he looked. "What I was trying to say is that I was humbled, honored that you would want to share something so important with me. Something that hurt you so much I could feel it myself. Hold on." He gently moved one of his thumbs over her lips when she started to say something. "I'm not quite finished. So when we heard whatever it was we heard that startled us, it just sort of hit me how incredibly stupid I'd been, taking you back there. There I sat, with you so emotionally raw and vulnerable in the exact spot that we *knew* we'd been followed to, listened to, watched before. I couldn't believe how completely thoughtless…how irresponsible I was. And there's just no excuse; I'm an idiot. I put you in danger. The very last thing I would ever want to do, and there I sat, practically offering you up. I was so angry and so…scared, genuinely frightened that I'd let myself get so caught up in… us that I—" he searched her eyes. "Aden, I'm so sorry."

"But why didn't you just tell me all that last night?"

"I know. I should have. I was so pissed at myself; all I could think about was getting you home, where it was safe. Getting you away from me." Aden frowned as he dropped his hands to his lap. "I can't trust myself. You shouldn't trust me."

"Wait, is that why you haven't called me?"

"I wasn't avoiding you. I thought you'd sleep late after last night, and I was helping my Mom with stacks of paperwork for her other case, then I realized how late it had gotten and that you'd be getting ready for work, so I thought I'd just come by the store to see you. Then Dad wanted to have lunch, and he decided to tag along." He shrugged.

"You could have texted." She bit her lip.

"What?"

"I get why you didn't call, but you could have sent me a text. I mean, all day I thought—"

"What *were* you thinking?" He smiled tentatively. "Do you really think that I'm so shallow I would just walk away like that? With no explanation?"

"Kind of how it looked from my perspective." She frowned.

"Please accept my formal, heartfelt apology. It was never my intention to hurt you. My actions were selfish and thoughtless, and I promise I will never let it happen again."

"Oh my God, stop." Aden was fighting a smile. "Keep going, and you'll be quoting Scarlett again."

280

"Frankly my dear," he grinned at Aden's surprise. "I prefer to quote Gable."

"You mean Rhett." She couldn't stop the giggle.

"Nope, I meant Gable." His smile fell, and he searched her face. "Am I forgiven?"

"Dunno, am I forgiven? For doubting you?"

"This whole conversation is…"

"Stupid." She nodded. "We're both nuts."

"So we're good then?"

Aden nodded. "Can I ask just one more thing?" After he nodded, she continued, "Why wouldn't you look at me back at the store? You kept staring out the window."

"Oh, it was probably nothing." He frowned. "As Dad and I walked over, I noticed a guy in a black hoodie sitting at one of the tables outside the coffee shop. It was just odd."

"Odd how?"

"Well, it's like a hundred degrees out here, and this guy is sitting in the sun with a jacket on and the hood up."

"I pointed him out to Dad because he seemed to be watching the jewelry store, but before we got close, the guy walked away."

"What'd he look like?"

"Dunno. Between the black hood and the dark sunglasses, all I know is he was male, blue jeans, black loafers…and the jacket."

Aden frowned, "Loafers? Who wears loafers?"

Maddox shrugged, frowning back at her. "Anyway, I was watching to see if he was still in the area."

"Huh."

"What?"

"So I just totally made it all about me, and it wasn't."

"Actually, it was all about you." He smiled. "So when do you have to be back? You haven't eaten a thing."

"Oh, we have a few minutes." She took a bite of the sandwich she'd been holding. "So do you think it's any safer out here?" She looked around the square for a dark figure. "Than last night, I mean."

"Well, it's broad daylight, lots of people out, and I've been paying attention today." His scanning eyes met hers. "We're going to keep you safe."

They walked hand-in-hand back to the store when she finished her lunch. Beverly's expression screwed into a sneer as Maddox opened the door for Aden and pecked her on the cheek.

"Can I pick you up later?" he asked.

"Didn't you ask Drew to give me a ride?"

"I did, but now, I think spending some time with you is more important."

"Well what were you planning to do?"

"Just helping Mom."

"Go help her then. We can hang out tomorrow." He was shaking his head.

"Nope, I'll be here. I'll let Drew know." He smiled. "See you later."

His easy smile touched her soul. "See you then." He squeezed her hand before turning away and letting the door close behind him. She inhaled deeply and watched him walk away.

"So all is good in Camelot." Beverly sighed.

"Yes, sorry to disappoint you." Aden went to stow her bag.

"Because I care."

"Apparently, you do. You brought it up." Aden smiled as she stepped into the back.

It was a quiet evening as Beverly and Aden avoided each other until closing. Beverly stayed on her side of the store, and Aden did the same on the opposite side. At one point, Aden caught sight of Maddox sitting at one of the tables across the street while she retrieved a ring from the front window for a browsing customer. She smiled, and he winked back before looking down at the paperwork in front of him.

music and doughnuts

At 8:58, the Audi pulled up outside the front door. Aden rushed to finish transferring things to the safe.

"Good job today, ladies." Mr. Keith said, looking over receipts. "By the way, Aden, could you come in tomorrow morning instead of the afternoon? Mrs. McConnell needs to switch shifts if she can."

"Sure, I guess." Aden shrugged. That would mean she'd have Friday night free, and she was off on Saturday.

"Great, thank you. I'll see you at 9:00 then."

"See you then." Aden smiled and grabbed her bag. She ignored Beverly's mumbled commentary as she practically sprinted through the front door. Maddox saw her coming and stepped out of the car.

"Hi there." He smiled.

"Hello." She grinned, wrapping her arms around his neck.

"Wow, I'm definitely picking you up every day from now on." He held her tight.

"Sounds good. So what would you like to do this evening Mr. Dixon?"

"Well, Miss Garrett, we've been invited to an after dinner show. If you'd care to accompany me, that is." He'd walked her around the car and opened her door.

"A show?" She was mystified. Maddox climbed behind the wheel before answering.

"Drew invited me over to play some music tonight, and I guess he asked Natalie to come over, too, but we're to eat first because apparently, he has no food in his place."

"You're gonna play?"

"I'm gonna try. It's been a little while since I had time for my guitar." He shrugged. "You don't have to go if you don't want to. I'd be happy to drop you off at Cadence's if you'd rather."

"Are you kidding? I want to hear you play."

"You're sure? I dunno; it sounds like it could get pretty boring for you."

"Just drive." She shook her head.

"Are you hungry?"

"Yeah, we could grab a sandwich at my house. I do have some food in the house."

"You've had a lot of sandwiches lately." He pursed his lips. "You like Italian, right?"

"Sure."

He took her to Provino's, the restaurant where she'd gone with her Mom and Drew the same night Maddox and his Mom were there. It was busy, but a small table for two had just opened up, so they were seated immediately.

"You know, I was totally stalking you the last time I was here," Aden admitted.

"I know." He shrugged, grinning. She playfully punched his shoulder across the table. "I was watching you, too. I just know how to hide it better than you do."

"I thought I was going to fall through the cracks of the floor when I found you standing in my living room with Cadence the next day."

"I know," He said again, reaching across the table to hold her hand. "It was adorable." Aden shook her head slowly, unable to be irritated when his eyes were melting her resolve. Several times throughout their meal, she'd realize that people at nearby tables were watching them. She wondered if Mrs. McConnell was working overtime on the rumor mill. *It's probably Maddox they're looking at; he's so gorgeous.* She smiled at him and thanked God again for bringing them together. *For however long this lasts, I'll be forever grateful for the time I've had with him.*

"Are you ready?" he asked, noting the napkin she'd placed over her plate. She nodded. Maddox looked around to find the waitress to ask for the check.

"I'll be right back." Aden smiled, standing and nodding toward the hallway where the restrooms were located. Many of the faces she passed were slightly familiar, even if she couldn't put names to them. She wondered if any of them knew who she was or that she was being stalked by the local resident kidnapper. A couple of heads turned to smile as she passed, and she'd smile back politely. She'd almost reached the dim hallway leading to the restrooms when something made her stumble. A dark figure sat alone at the head of the large table at the back where Maddox and his Mom had spread out their papers and files the last time she was here. There was no plate or glass in front of him. She thought it was a him, anyway. The hood of his black jacket was pulled low over his forehead. Shivers instantly raced up her spine, and she turned to where Maddox was conversing with the waitress as he paid the bill. When she glanced back, the big table was empty. She looked wildly around the restaurant but didn't see the dark figure anywhere.

"I'm losing my mind," she mumbled, shaking her head. She cautiously continued toward the restroom. A middle-aged lady holding hands with a little girl came out of the women's restroom, and Aden paused to let them by. Then, she decided she could wait until she got home, and made her way back to the table.

"Everything alright?" Maddox stood when she approached. She nodded, smiling. "Let's go then."

Aden was quiet as they drove to her house. She wasn't sure she'd actually seen anything. She'd probably just imagined it. There was no reason to tell Maddox about her hallucination.

When they reached her house, Aden ducked inside to use her own bathroom before they went up to Drew's rooms. Maddox insisted on going in first and looking around; then, he waited in the kitchen speaking with the officer on guard duty that night.

Drew heard them coming up the stairs and opened the door before they reached it.

"Hey guys, come on in." Natalie sat at one end of the sagging couch in the small room Drew used as a den. There was a scratched coffee table, a decent-looking arm chair, a TV that sat on a dresser, a refrigerator, a microwave, and a drum set in the corner that made up the rest of his living space. Two doors led to the bathroom and bedroom beyond.

"You cleaned," Aden noted, impressed as she sat beside Natalie. Drew ignored her.

"I couldn't cook you dinner, so I made dessert." He pointed grandly to a box of Krispy Kreme doughnuts on the coffee table with a stack of napkins.

"Oooh, Krispy Kremes." Aden flipped open the box. "And you got some chocolate iced ones, too." She rolled her eyes in pleasure as she bit into the still-warm confection.

"Yeah, forget flowers, man." Drew laughed toward Maddox. "If you ever screw up, just bring her doughnuts."

"Noted." Maddox nodded.

"Not doughnuts. Krispy Kremes." Aden mumbled around a mouthful.

"You guys better dig in if you want one," Drew cautioned them, grabbing one for himself.

"How are you Natalie?" Maddox sat back with his doughnut.

"Great. How are you two?"

"Much better now." Aden grinned at her, making her laugh.

"Alright, enough small talk. Maddox, you didn't bring your guitar?" Drew frowned.

"It's in the car," Maddox answered. "I'll go get it in a second." He finished his doughnut and wiped his sticky fingers on a napkin.

"What have you been up to?" Aden asked Natalie between bites of a second doughnut.

"Same old stuff. Working. Hanging out with your brother." She smiled at Drew. "I got a promotion at work, so I'm a little busier."

"That's great! Where do you work again?" Aden couldn't remember if she'd asked her that before.

"I work at the hospital pharmacy. I'm the new operations manager. I'm not a pharmacist or anything."

"Wow, that sounds pretty cool." Aden had no idea what an operations manager might do, but it sounded a lot more impressive than jewelry salesperson.

"Not really. It's just about keeping track of everything coming in, going out, working with our phone, security, and computer vendors to keep the systems running...but you don't really want to hear all that."

"She's being modest," Drew spoke up. "It's a really important position, and she got a great raise in pay with that promotion."

"Well, congrats." Aden smiled.

"Thanks."

Maddox came back in with his guitar. "I only have the acoustic with me. The others are at home in Virginia."

"Others? Plural?" Aden wanted to know.

"Well, I have an electric guitar and a bass guitar at home. If you're playing with a band, they mostly want electric guitars."

"Are you in a band?"

"Not anymore." He turned away, and Aden knew he had closed the subject.

"What kind of music do you play?" Natalie asked. She didn't know they'd strayed onto a subject Maddox wanted to avoid.

"A little bit of everything. Rock mostly, a lot of jazz, some folk tunes, and a tiny bit of classical."

"No country?" Natalie asked good-naturedly.

"Not my thing." Maddox shrugged.

"Alright, then." Drew announced with a few beats on the snare. "What's your poison?"

"Dunno…why don't you just gimme a beat, and let's see what happens?"

Drew nodded, grinning his approval.

It was like magic. Aden was sure they'd never played together before, but the simple beat Drew created grew in complexity with each repeating phrase, and Maddox began weaving a melody around it that grew along with the complex rhythms and complemented them, creating a story of sound. She didn't recognize the song, but it was beautiful, captivating. She watched in awe as the music poured out of these two men she'd thought she knew. She hadn't heard Drew play his drums in a long time. Apparently, he'd been practicing, and watching Maddox making music was a heady thing. He obviously loved playing, and his face glowed. Aden didn't know how long they played, one song melting into the next seamlessly. Her soul was full with Maddox, and she'd forgotten Drew and Natalie were in the room. When the last note rested, Natalie began to applaud, startling Aden at first, but she joined in, with a standing ovation.

"Wow." She couldn't think of any words big enough. "That was incredible."

"You looked bored to death." Maddox laughed, setting aside the guitar.

"No I did not!"

"You guys were pretty good together," Natalie said, taking a drum stick from Drew and trying it out on a cymbal.

"You guys were great," Aden corrected her.

"I don't know about that, but it was fun." Maddox saluted Drew.

"Yeah, it was. We should do that again sometime. Maybe after I've practiced some more."

"I hear that. I lost count of how many wonky notes I found in there." Maddox shook his head.

"It was jazz, right?" Natalie asked, and they both shrugged. "There are no wrong notes in Jazz."

"I don't know what it was, technically. For my part, I was just playing whatever came to mind."

"You mean you were making all that up as you went along?" Aden asked him, awed again.

"Well, not all of it, but yeah, most of the time, we were just jamming." He looked to Drew, who was nodding.

"I think you've got a groupie." Drew laughed.

"She's not a groupie. She's my girl." Maddox hugged her and kissed her forehead. Aden's head swam. *Had he just called her His Girl?*

"Aw, that's so sweet." Natalie smiled at them.

"Well, I hate to be a buzzkill, but I have to kick you two out now so that I can spend a little time with *my* girl." Drew grinned at Natalie.

"Wait, you're kicking us out?" Aden blinked.

"Well, it is a little late." Maddox pointed out the digital clock on the microwave. It was 12:40. How did that happen?

"Crap! I didn't know it was that late! I have to work tomorrow morning."

"Time flies when you're having fun." Natalie smiled at her. "Actually, I need to be going, too." At Drew's pout, she laughed. "We both have to work in the morning, you know."

"It's only 12:30! How old are you people??" Drew lamented.

"Some of us can't get away with dragging into work in the same clothes we left in the day before and then hiding under a car all day." Natalie play-pouted back.

Drew sighed. "Fine. Want me to drive you home?"

"I drove here, remember? I can drive myself."

"Alright, we're going. Thanks for dessert and everything." Maddox nodded to Drew and led Aden down the stairs to the courtyard. "Oops. Left my guitar." He turned and ran back up to retrieve it. Aden looked toward the house and was distracted by a movement in the shadows. It was the officer on duty, but it still sent a shiver down her spine. Maddox was back in a moment. "Okay, I'm just gonna put this in the car." He squeezed her arm as he passed. When he came back, he gathered her into his own arms.

"You know, we're being watched," Aden reminded him with a nod toward the policeman.

"I don't care. I'm going to kiss my girl good night." And he did. Aden almost swooned before he raised his head to smolder at her in the darkness.

"So I'm your girl?"

"Who else would be my girl?" he laughed.

"I just didn't think you were looking for a girl."

"I wasn't looking. You found me."

"We found each other."

"Always a compromise." He sighed good-naturedly before kissing her again. "Now, I will have to make myself let you go inside—" he stopped, an odd expression slicing across his smile.

"Maddox?" he didn't answer, staring off into space. "Maddox, come sit in the car." With a desperate glance around, she tried to pull him toward the Audi. He was just so solid…he groaned. "Maddox?" she whispered. He shook his head, and she could see him coming back to the present.

"Inside," he croaked. "Get inside. Lock the door."

"What is it? What did you see?" Aden hissed, searching his face.

"Hood in the trees." He was still shaking his head. "Wait. I don't know…I think it's from earlier…" Aden waited. "It's much darker out here now."

"A hood?"

"Look, it's probably nothing. I'm not exactly foolproof, you know? But you do need to get inside please." He smiled. "Your house is guarded, now. We've torn down that staircase and sealed that door shut upstairs. This is the safest place. You asked earlier. Your house is safe."

She could tell he wasn't telling her everything. "Maddox—"

"It's really late. You should get some sleep, and I should get home, too."

Aden sighed. "It was almost a perfect night."

"It was still a perfect night." He kissed her forehead. "Nothing happened. It's just my crazy brain acting up, probably from all those doughnuts." He was trying to make her smile as he walked her to the door. "Drew is taking you to work in the morning, and I'll be there to pick you up. What time do you get off, by the way?"

"I'm off at 3:00, but Maddox—"

"Shhh, my girl needs her rest. We can talk more tomorrow, okay?" Aden searched his face, unhappy. "Okay?"

"Fine," she huffed. "Just don't think all the 'my girl' stuff means I'm going to blindly follow your every whim."

"Wouldn't dream of it." He chuckled. "Will you please consider going inside and locking that door behind you?"

"Yes, yes, I'm going to lock the damn door."

"After you kiss me one more time?"

"Is that you asking? Or order—" he cut her off with a kiss.

"It's not an order, just a suggestion I couldn't wait for you to consider."

"Bully."

"You've stalled long enough."

Sighing, she pushed him away and reluctantly went inside, locking the door behind her.

The next morning, a full ten minutes before she needed to leave for work, she peeked out to find the Audi waiting in her driveway. She opened the kitchen door to wave him in, but he was on his phone. She went back inside and hurriedly finished packing for the day. Cadence had texted first thing this morning asking if she'd go shopping and said Maddox would be taking her to work this morning after all. Cadence needed a new outfit for a date with Trey that evening and wanted to go to the big mall in Greenville. They planned to leave right after Aden got off work. Cadence said she'd invited Maddox to go along, and Aden hoped he was really okay with the plan. She ran through the first floor double-checking all the locks before going outside and locking the kitchen door.

Maddox was just hanging up his call and got out to open her door for her. She thought she caught a laugh or a grunt from the officer on duty, but when she glanced that way, he was staring off into the woods.

"Did you sleep well?" Maddox asked as he started the car.

"Okay, I guess. What are you doing here?" She examined his face, gorgeous as always. "I thought you said Drew was driving this morning."

"The garage is opening late today. I texted him to let him know that he could sleep in a couple hours."

"Why is it opening late? And how would you know that?"

"Billy Ray was arrested last night in Spartanburg. Bar brawl or something like that. His Dad is over there bailing him out this morning. Sheriff Richey told my Mom this morning."

"Oh." Before she could ask more questions, he asked his own.

"So Cadence tells me we're going to Greenville this afternoon?"

"Is that okay with you?"

"Well, shopping's not my first choice, but I'll be with you." He smiled, taking her hand.

"The good news is that there's a deadline. She'll have to be back in time to get dressed for the date." Maddox nodded. "And we'll be out of Blackwater Falls. Maybe we can finally relax for a few hours."

He frowned at the road. "I don't want to take any chances—"

"Will you relax? I didn't say I was going to go skipping off into crowds of strange men asking for candy or anything." He almost smiled. "I'll be with you and Cadence the whole time. We won't leave each other's sight. I just meant…" she paused, and he squeezed her hand.

"I know what you meant. I'm sorry." He was quiet for a moment. "So, um, is Beverly supposed to work this morning?"

"No, why?"

"Apparently, she was with Billy Ray last night. She was arrested too."

"You're joking!"

He just raised his eyebrows.

"Beverly and Billy Ray?"

"Well, there were close to twenty arrests. Sounds like quite the party. I don't have any details. I just know those two from Blackwater Falls were on the list. I don't know if they were together."

"It'd be quite the coincidence if they were both in Spartanburg, at the same bar, no less."

"Probably. Listen, keep that to yourself. It wouldn't do any good for your working relationship if Mr. Keith found out from you."

"Please give me a little credit," she huffed.

"I do. I know. I'm just…" he frowned.

"What?"

"Well, Billy Ray would have been in Spartanburg last night when I saw…"

"The hood in the woods? Is that what you mean?"

"I don't know what I mean. None of it makes one bit of sense right now."

They were both lost in their own thoughts for the rest of the drive.

"Sorry to drop all that on you right before work." He looked unhappy as he pulled up to the curb outside the front door.

"I'm glad you told me." She smiled, looking at the store. "Looks like Mr. Keith is late again. The lights aren't on in there yet."

"We can wait right here."

"You don't have to do that." She rolled her eyes.

"Like I'm going to leave you standing on the sidewalk?" he huffed. "Please, give me some credit."

"Are you mocking me?"

"Nope, the lights just came on in there." He grinned. "Have a good day."

"I'll try. See you later."

"Bye."

She reluctantly stepped out of the car just as Mr. Keith came to unlock the front door. She waved to Maddox before going inside, and he winked before driving slowly away.

It was an uneventful shift at the store, with enough customers coming in to make the time go by faster. It was just Mr. Keith and Aden working, and he seemed preoccupied, so she left him to his own devices. She couldn't stop thinking about Beverly with Billy Ray in between customers. She caught sight of Maddox walking by the front window a couple of times during the day, and that kept her going. Before she knew it, the Audi was pulling up out front. She looked at the clock in disbelief.

"Do you have someone else coming in?" Aden asked Mr. Keith. She wondered if it was Beverly who was late for her shift.

"Yes, Mrs. McConnell will be here shortly. She's been helping a friend whose sister is missing."

"Oh, she mentioned that." Aden frowned. "Should I stay until she gets here?"

Mr. Keith looked at the clock on the back wall. "No, you go ahead. She'll be here soon. I think I can hold the fort until then."

"You're sure?"

"Go." He smiled. "I see your boyfriend waiting out there."

She opened her mouth to refute the boyfriend title, and then just smiled, dismissing his odd manner, and went to grab her bag. Maddox was waiting just outside the door when she came outside.

"Hi, there. How was work?"

"Not so bad. It went by quickly today." She smiled.

"Well, Cadence is going to fly apart with impatience if I don't get you to the house in the next thirty seconds."

Aden dug her phone out of her bag. There were fifteen texts waiting, and all of them looked to be from Cadence. "So I see."

"Come on." He opened her door for her once again, and they were off. Cadence was waiting in the yard when they pulled up.

"I thought you'd never get here!"

"I didn't get off work until 3:00," Aden pointed out. "And it's only…" she checked her phone, "3:07 for heaven's sake."

"I don't know about heaven, but for *my* sake, we've got to *go*. Get in that house and change your clothes. Maddox, leave that car running," she ordered.

"Cadence," Aden began, then just shook her head. "I'll be right back." She ran inside and changed her blouse and skirt for a t shirt and jeans. When she came back outside, Cadence and Maddox were in an apparent stand-off.

"I don't have to do this, you know," Maddox was saying, "I could be spending time with Aden."

"You will be spending time with Aden," Cadence snapped. "But I get to spend some time with her every now and then, too."

"Okay, I'm ready," Aden called to break the tension. Maddox and Cadence climbed into the car without another word. "Oh, this is going to be so much fun." Aden mumbled to herself.

It wasn't as bad as she'd feared, once they got going. The siblings apologized to each other. Maddox quietly followed the girls from store to store, carrying the shopping bags. Cadence bought him a shirt and then offered to buy his lunch for accompanying them.

"That's not necessary," Maddox started.

"Oh, shut it." Cadence waved him off. "Aden wouldn't have been able to come along if it weren't for you coming with us as bodyguard, and I need her. Without her, I'd have bought that green dress that you both said looked like a corn husk on me. I'm buying your lunch, both of you." She led them to the food court at the center of the mall. "Whatever you want, it's on me."

With their lunches purchased, they navigated the crowds and found a table. Maddox dumped his load of shopping bags in the fourth chair at the table and slumped down beside Aden.

"This is exhausting," he complained.

"This is nothing." Cadence laughed. "Usually, our shopping trips last all day long. This has been incredibly short and sweet."

Maddox looked to Aden for confirmation, and she reluctantly had to just nod in agreement with Cadence.

"Anyway, I'm in love with the outfit we found for me to wear tonight, and I can't believe how lucky we were to run across those shoes! They just pull it all together."

"They really do." Aden smiled at Maddox sheepishly. "I'll have to borrow them sometime."

"Done, and I can't believe that blue top you bought. It looks a-ma-zing on you," Cadence cooed. "Don't you think so, Maddox?"

"It's very nice," he mumbled through a bite. "Seriously, I love that color on you," he responded to Aden.

"Okay, so last thing—I need to find a pair of silver, dangly earrings." Maddox groaned. "Well, the neckline I bought just screams for upswept hair, and you can't have an up-do without dangling earrings. It simply isn't done." She rolled her eyes at his ignorance.

"It simply isn't done." Aden grinned when he looked to her for help. "There's a store right over there that should have exactly what you're looking for." She pointed. "But after that, we *have* to get you home if you stand a chance of getting a shower in *and* your hair put up."

"You're right. We've got to hop to it." She started to stand.

"Hold on! I haven't even finished my lunch," Maddox declared.

"Well, what have you been doing?"

Maddox shot her a withering look. "We haven't been sitting here for five minutes yet. Sit down."

"Oh, fine." Cadence sat back down impatiently.

When everyone had eaten, they completed the search for the perfect earrings and then practically sprinted back to the car. Cadence urged her brother to speed up with every mile they drove back to Blackwater Falls.

CHAPTER 17
more pause for prose

When they arrived at the house, he helped them carry all the bags up to Cadence's room and sighed in pleasure when he was summarily ordered out. He went downstairs and sank onto the big couch in the den, turning on the TV. He was asleep in minutes.

The doorbell ringing for the second time pulled him back to consciousness. He got up slowly and went to the door, surprised at the long shadows stretching through the house. He'd slept for a while, apparently. He pulled the door open to find Trey, frowning, on the doorstep.

"Hey, man." Trey greeted him.

"Come on in." Maddox stretched. "Looks like I fell asleep. Cadence should be ready though—"

"Hold on a minute." Trey grabbed his arm. "As I was walking past your car in the driveway, I saw this on your windshield. Thought I should bring it in." He held out a white envelope, and Maddox took it in confusion. Turning it over, he found it was the same typed message he'd seen before.

ADEN.

"No," he croaked, ripping open the envelope and tearing out the single sheet inside.

MY HEART IS RED. YOUR NEW BLOUSE IS BLUE.
TIME'S ALMOST HERE. I'M COMING FOR YOU.
I LIKE THE EARRINGS CADENCE CHOSE, TOO,
PERHAPS WE'LL BORROW THEM, WHEN I COME FOR YOU.
ON TOP OF THE MOUNTAIN, ECLIPSING THE VIEW,
YOUR STORY SO SAD, MY HEART BREAKS FOR YOU.

FOR SO LONG, I'VE WATCHED, AND YOU'VE HAD NO CLUE,
FINALLY TO TOUCH, I CAN'T WAIT FOR YOU.
SO MANY PLANS FOR ALL THAT WE'LL DO...
DEAREST ADEN, I COME FOR YOU.

Maddox roared in frustration, dropping the letter. He took the stairs two at time, with Trey on his heels.

"Aden! Cadence!" He screamed. "Answer me!"

He reached the second floor landing and turned toward Cadence's room when a door opened in the hallway.

"What? Good grief, you scared us half to death yellin' like that," Cadence scowled.

"Is Aden in there with you?"

The door opened wider, and Aden came into view.

"What's going on?" She looked frightened. Maddox couldn't speak; he grabbed her in his arms like he'd never let go.

"What in the world is going on up there?" LeighAnn called from the bottom of the stairs. "I could hear y'all yellin' from the backyard."

"Call the police!" Maddox shouted to her. Trey quickly went back to the top of the stairs.

"It's okay, Mrs. Dixon. Everybody's fine. We just found a letter on Maddox's car that the police should see."

"Oh my God!" She ran to find her cell phone, leaving the letter still lying in the foyer where Maddox had dropped it.

"Oh my God, I thought..." Maddox was murmuring into Aden's hair, still holding her tightly to him. "I can't believe I fell asleep. You're safe. You're safe."

"I'm okay," Aden assured him. "What's going on?"

"He was here. There was a letter on my car."

"What?" Cadence screeched. "You mean...?"

300

Trey nodded, still scowling. "You look really nice, by the way."

"Crap. I'm not even ready yet. Get out of here." She kissed his cheek hurriedly and then pushed him toward the door. "You too." She pointed at Maddox, still holding Aden.

Maddox scowled blackly. "Did you hear what I just said?"

"I did, but I've spent all day working on my grand entrance, and by God, none of you are going to spoil it."

"You don't need an entrance," Trey said quietly, coming back into the room. He pulled her into an embrace and held her there, meeting Maddox's gaze across the room. "You look absolutely beautiful."

"But my hair's not done," she complained. He shushed her and held her closer.

"You're safe." Maddox whispered again.

"I am safe," Aden answered. "Where's the letter?"

"Downstairs. Don't worry, you don't even have to see it."

"But I *want* to see it." She pushed him gently away. "There could be clues in it."

"The police are on their way." He frowned.

"How was it addressed?" She had assumed the position, hands on hips.

"What?"

"The letter. Was it addressed to someone specific?"

"It had your name on the envelope," Maddox mumbled.

"And you opened it?" He nodded. "Even though it was addressed to me?"

"It looked just like the first one—" he started.

"He was afraid for you." Trey broke in.

Aden sighed loudly, "I want to see it."

She stalked out the door and down the stairs, and they all followed. She picked up the single sheet of white paper still lying in the foyer and read it through.

"The police will be here shortly," LeighAnn announced from the adjacent dining room. "Put that thing down."

"The bastard followed us," Aden was fuming. "He was there, again. Right there."

"Honey, put that thing over here on the table," LeighAnn begged Aden, who was waving the letter indignantly as she spoke.

"Have you seen it? The cowardly little bastard followed us to the mall," she shouted, waving the letter in LeighAnn's direction.

"Aden, honey, I don't think your mother would approve of that language." LeighAnn looked shell-shocked.

"Seriously? What exactly *is* the etiquette for being stalked by sociopathic criminals?"

"Aden," Maddox spoke quietly. She turned on him, but immediately lost steam looking into his pained face.

"I'm sorry," she said to LeighAnn. "I'm just so…pissed off."

LeighAnn smiled wanly just before the doorbell rang. Maddox opened it to four uniformed officers, hands on their guns. More officers were surrounding the house.

"Thank you for coming," Maddox said, gesturing toward the letter that Aden still held.

Sherriff Richey stormed the porch seconds before Max arrived in the driveway.

"Maddox Dixon!" he called loudly. "Charles Maddox Dixon, III," he corrected himself, formally, in the doorway. "You are under arrest for suspicion of—"

"What the hell?" Aden shouted.

"Is that the letter?" the Sherriff asked, nodding to one of his officers. "Miss Garrett, you'll need to go with Officer Halstead—"

"I'm not going anywhere with anyone," Aden declared just as Mayor Max arrived in the doorway.

"Dave, what the hell do you think you're doing?" he growled.

"You know what I'm doing, and you know why," he answered, fitting handcuffs to Maddox's wrists. "Maddox Dixon, you have the right to remain silent," he began.

"Max!" LeighAnn shrieked. "What's going on?"

"Dave! Look at me," Max shouted. "You don't have any evidence. You cannot arrest him on suspicion alone. Where's your evidence?"

"He is coming to the station to answer some questions," Sheriff Richey growled. "Every time, Max. Every scene. The one common denominator since he came to town—"

"Summoning him for questioning is entirely different than arresting him. I ask again to see the evidence that would be grounds for arrest."

Maddox's cell phone began ringing in his pocket. "Aden, can you get that? It's my Mom's ringtone." He turned a hip toward her.

"Don't move!" Sheriff Richey barked at her.

"I'll get it." Max glared at the Sheriff. Quickly slipping the phone from Maddox's pocket, it took him a moment to figure out how to answer. "Kim. Yes, everyone is safe. The police are here. No, I haven't seen it...I'll ask LeighAnn if she can pick you up." After a pause, he glanced at his son, still in handcuffs. "Yes, but I'm handling it. I'll see you soon."

"If you need somebody to pick up...Maddox's Mom, I can do it," Trey offered. "Mrs. Dixon will probably want to be here."

LeighAnn hugged him and Max nodded. "Thank you, Trey. That would be most appreciated. She's at the Embassy Suites hotel just off the interstate. She'll be in the lobby." Trey squeezed Cadence's hand and slipped out the door.

"Evidence?" Max glowered at the Sheriff. "Or get those cuffs off my son."

"Max, you know you're too close to—"

"What I *know* is that he's innocent, and what I further know is that you can't arrest him without evidence tying him to a crime, so where is it?"

Dave Richey glared and inhaled deeply. "He has hindered this investigation at every turn—"

"Hindered how? What has he done?"

"He doesn't belong at crime scenes."

"He lives here, and the other crime scenes have been at his girlfriend's house."

"He's staying at the hotel, and he doesn't live at the convenience store at Devil's Fork. Or Payne Automotive, or the salon—"

"He is assisting his mother, who is here at my request," Max interrupted. "His mere presence does not constitute evidence of a crime in any court of law. No matter how suspicious you find it, you can't arrest him on suspicion."

Sheriff Richey's face had gone a deep red, and he worked his jaw furiously. "I have lots of questions for this suspect...person of interest," he corrected. "I insist, within the bounds of my purview as Sheriff, that he accompany me to the station for questioning. Every letter of protocol will be followed, I assure you." He held up a hand to stop Max's next interruption. "I will release him to your custody at this time, but you will be responsible for him."

"I've been responsible for him since the day he was born," Max growled, indignant, as the Sheriff reluctantly removed the handcuffs.

"You are all wasting time!" Aden shouted. "The real criminal is out there, probably listening to all of this and laughing his ass off." She still held the letter and was waving it wildly as she gestured.

"Aden, will you please hand the letter to Officer Halstead?" the Sheriff frowned furiously. "We'll need to question everyone who was in this house, including...Trey, is it? When he returns. So nobody leaves."

"I'm going with Maddox," Max said to LeighAnn. "Stay here. Have you spoken to Grace and Patience?"

LeighAnn nodded. "I asked them to come home. I need them all here."

"Maddox is an adult, Max," the Sheriff said quietly. "You won't be allowed in the interro...in the room."

"I am going with my son," Max ground out slowly, then turned back to his wife, sighing. "I think the girls should all stay home tonight. I'm going to ask Kim to stay here, too, is that okay?" LeighAnn nodded. "I'll be back with Maddox as soon as I can." He hugged her and then turned to Aden. "Have you spoken with your Mom?"

"No, I haven't had a chance."

"I called her." LeighAnn smiled at Aden. "She's on her way here."

"Thank you." Aden hugged her.

"My officers will be here to question each of you and to keep an eye on things," the Sheriff said stiffly. Then, he turned to Aden and Maddox, holding each other in a death grip. His eyes narrowed. "Aden, one of the officers will escort you and your mother to your house after you've been questioned. I'll be doubling the security there as well… just in case." He glared at Maddox.

"Why don't you all just stay here tonight?" LeighAnn suggested. "If there's safety in numbers…and it would mean fewer officers would be spread out across both locations." Aden was shaking her head slowly.

"Thank you so much. You are so kind to offer, but I'm the target." She looked up at Maddox for a second and then back to LeighAnn. "Every one of you is in danger because I'm here."

"Aden honey—" LeighAnn began.

"Sincerely, it means so much to me that you want me to stay, but the psychopath knows that my house is already guarded 24/7. He might think your house would be more vulnerable, and if any of you were hurt because of me—"

"But that's…there'll be police here too," LeighAnn insisted.

"Okay, Maddox, time to go," the Sheriff interrupted. "Aden, wherever you wish to spend tonight, we'll deploy an officer for your protection."

Maddox smiled at Aden. "Stay safe. Be suspicious of everybody. I'll be back soon." Then, he and Max left with the Sheriff.

"This is just crazy." Cadence spoke up for the first time, watching them leave. Looking down at her new outfit, she sighed. "Guess my date is cancelled."

"I'm so sorry, Cadence." Aden reached to hug her.

"What are you sorry about? You didn't do anything." Cadence pushed her back. "Seriously, stop it. It's annoying. We're all in this together."

LeighAnn nodded, putting her arms around both girls. "Yes, we are. I'm going to talk to Janet when she gets here about staying tonight. Aden can sleep with you, and Grace and Patience can double up. That leaves three more bedrooms upstairs—"

"Mom, I think Aden is right." Cadence broke in, stepping out of the embrace. "Our house has a million windows, that old cellar door…There are a thousand ways to get in here. Her house is safer." Aden was nodding reluctantly. "I would say we should all stay over there instead, except their house doesn't have as many bedrooms for all of us. But

Aden has a point—the psycho isn't after any of us. If she's at her house, then everyone here should be safe."

"Cadence!" LeighAnn admonished. "I can't believe you'd say that."

"But it's true, which is why I'm going to go spend the night with Aden at her house."

"No," Aden and LeighAnn said at the same time.

"Hold on!" Cadence crossed her arms. "I think Aden is safer at her house, and she's safer if she's not alone—hence, my staying with her. And her Mom will be there, and we'll ask Drew to stay too, and I'll know that you're all safe, together, here. And they're doubling the guard at her house—"

"Okay," LeighAnn stopped her, frowning. "If Aden would rather stay at home, but you have to promise me that the two of you will stick to each other like glue, the whole time."

"Super glue," Cadence promised. "We'll barricade ourselves inside the house." LeighAnn didn't look happy, but she let it drop for now.

The two officers who'd hung back in the foyer since the sheriff had taken Maddox stepped forward, clearing their throats. "We're going to need for you to sit in the living room for a while." One of them gestured. "We'll interview each of you in the dining room, if that's okay?"

LeighAnn nodded, still frowning.

They questioned Aden first, then Cadence. When they asked LeighAnn into the dining room, Cadence turned to Aden, feeling as though she might burst with curiosity.

"What did the letter say? I never got to read it."

"Oh, same crap as last time." Aden shrugged. "He knew I'd bought a blue top, and he complimented your new earrings," Cadence gasped. "There was something that suggested he was on the mountain again listening to us when I told Maddox about the accident—"

"You told Maddox about the accident?" Cadence's eyebrows went up, but Aden just nodded. "You've barely ever talked to *me* about the accident." Aden frowned.

"And basically it just said he was coming for me, over and over. That it was finally time or something like that."

Cadence digested that for a moment. "Did it rhyme again?"

"What? Yeah, I guess, why?"

"It's just creepier that he keeps taking the time to write poetry about stalking you and kidnapping you."

Aden shivered and changed the subject. "I wonder where everybody is."

"What?"

"Why isn't Trey back yet with Kim? And where's my Mom? And I wonder how long they'll keep Maddox at the station?" She fired the questions in rapid succession.

Cadence got up to look out the window. "I can only see part of the front yard from here, but there's a lot of people out there." She sounded surprised. Aden came to look, too.

"Guess everybody's trying to find out what's going on—all the police cars that came screeching in. Is that crime scene tape stretched across the yard?"

"Wow," was all Cadence said. She recognized neighbors among the small crowd of people lined up at the taped-off edge of her yard. "Should we go talk to them?"

"Are you insane?"

Cadence shrugged. "Well, we could tell them what's going on, so no weird rumors – wow."

"What now?"

"The news. A news van just pulled up. My house is going to be on the news." Aden wasn't sure from the tone of her voice how Cadence felt about that.

"I'm so sor—"

"Stop it."

Aden sighed and sank back into the couch just as raised voices on the front porch caught her attention.

"My daughter is in there, and you aren't going to stop me!"

Aden and Cadence flew toward the door, but LeighAnn beat them to it. Throwing open the door, she pulled herself to her greatest height (all of 5 feet) and glared at the scene

307

in general.

"This is my home, and I will decide who's welcome and who's not." She stopped one of the officer's protests with a look Aden wouldn't have believed possible from the diminutive woman. "Janet, Drew, please come in." She smiled at them and stepped aside for a moment. Then, she stepped out onto the porch and surveyed the growing crowd. "Excuse me! Hello? We appreciate your concern and your support," she shouted as the clamor died down to listen. "But I ask for your cooperation as the authorities work to identify the person responsible for…all the atrocities affecting so many of us over the past few months." Silence had descended as even the officers stopped to listen, and the news camera rolled. "Please, everybody, go home. Keep your families safe. Report anything suspicious, but let's keep out of their way—these people who are working around the clock to secure our community." She stopped, uncertainly, as if she'd just realized where she was. "Thank you," she called and slipped back inside.

"Go, Mom!" Cadence smiled at her. "I never would have believed you'd do such a thing if I hadn't seen it myself."

"I think they heard you." Drew smiled, turning from a window. "Most of the crowd is starting to disperse, except the news guy, of course."

"I just felt like my house was turning into a fish bowl." She sighed. "I'm glad you were able to come." She smiled at Janet and Drew.

"Well, I wanted Drew here, too." She looked apologetically to Aden. "I wanted us all together. I didn't know it would take so long to convince Mr. Payne to let him leave work early. Apparently, he'd just gotten there, and Billy Ray wasn't working today—"

"Billy Ray was arrested in Spartanburg last night." Aden nodded.

"News travels fast." Drew nodded. "How'd you find out? Wait, never mind." He chuckled as Kim came in the door, followed by Trey.

"Sorry, we stopped by the station." Kim explained, dropping an overstuffed bag by the door. "Maddox is fine. They should be home soon." She smiled at LeighAnn and Aden.

Trey went to stand beside Cadence. "You're standing right where I left you." He grinned.

"How was Maddox?" she asked.

"I didn't see him, but his Mom said he's holding up. They're still questioning him, I guess, but he hasn't been charged with anything."

"I didn't get a chance to thank you before you left." She smiled. "That was so gallant of you to offer to pick Kim up."

"Gallant is my middle name." He grinned back.

"And you two make fun of us." Aden rolled her eyes. "But seriously, Trey, that was really nice of you."

"Mrs. Dixon?" One of the officers in the dining room cleared his throat. "We weren't quite finished. And you…Trey -?"

"Miller," Trey provided.

"We'll need to speak with you next. Please don't go anywhere."

"It's ever so much fun," Cadence assured him. "They ask for your story and then ask the same questions fifteen different ways."

"If y'all could wait back in the living room?" the officer sighed at them.

"I wonder if Mom had anything planned for dinner," Cadence mumbled on their way to the living room. "Not that she's had time to start anything."

"Probably not," Aden agreed. "Should we go get something started?"

"Are you kidding? After the day we've had? Let's just order something delivered." Cadence headed to the kitchen and produced a handful of menus from a drawer. Janet, Kim and Drew joined them in the kitchen a few moments later.

"We're ordering pizza delivery," Cadence informed them. "I really wanted Chinese, but we don't know what everybody would want. Pizza seemed safer."

"I'll let the officers outside know it's coming." Kim nodded.

"Aden, honey, how are you holding up?" Janet drew her into a hug.

"I'm fine, Mom." She hugged her back. "Maddox and Cadence have been right beside me all day." Janet sighed, not letting her go. "Actually, can I talk to you for just a sec?"

"Of course." Janet nodded as Aden pulled her away from the others.

"LeighAnn wants us all to stay here tonight. Their house is going to be under guard now, too, but I'd really rather go home if you're okay with that. I mean, you can stay if you'd like – but like I told them, *I'm* the target, and they'll all be safer if I'm not here, and I do think our house is safer than theirs. As Cadence pointed out, there's a thousand ways into this big old place. And—"

"Sweetie, that's fine if you'd rather be home." Janet smiled, and they hugged again.

"Thanks, Mom."

The evening wore on very slowly. Grace and Patience came home. The pizzas were delivered and devoured. The latest poetic stylings of the stalker were reviewed and discussed at length. The police finally finished all their questioning and left. Two other officers remained outside the house, and still, Maddox and Max were at the station.

"We should probably get going soon," Janet said to Aden. "I know you wanted to wait for Maddox to get back, but—"

"It's okay Mom. It's getting late."

"I still wish you'd reconsider staying here." LeighAnn looked hopeful.

"Another time," Janet promised. "We can have a big slumber party when this whole thing is over."

"Sounds like fun," LeighAnn acquiesced.

"I'll just go get my stuff real quick." Cadence jumped up. Janet looked confused.

"Cadence wants to spend the night. Is that okay?" Aden asked.

"Of course, if LeighAnn is okay with it?" LeighAnn was already nodding.

"Safety in numbers. There's plenty of us here, and I think Cadence might feel safer at your house tonight." She shrugged. "I just hope they catch this guy soon."

"Hear, hear!" Kim chimed in.

"Would it be silly if I wanted to follow you guys to your house?" Trey asked sheepishly. "I wouldn't come in or anything. Just if...anything happened on the road or when we pull in, I could help Drew..."

"It's not silly at all." Janet smiled. "Unnecessary though."

"Still, if he doesn't mind," Kim spoke up, "it wouldn't hurt anything. We don't know what this guy's got planned, where he is, who he's watching, or how he plans to come at us next."

Janet just frowned and started thanking everyone and saying goodbyes. They went as a group to the foyer, all talking at once, when Cadence came down the stairs with her bag.

"Okay Mom, I don't want you worrying all night. We'll be just fine. I'll text you before I go to sleep, okay?" she said to LeighAnn.

"Text me when you get there, too."

"Okay." Cadence hugged her.

"We'll take care of her," Drew promised.

They were met on the porch by one of the officers who explained he'd be escorting them home.

"I forgot about that," Janet said, looking for Trey. "You really don't have to come all the way out—"

Trey interrupted her, "I know I don't have to, but if you don't mind, it's not too far for me to be sure everybody's home safe."

"Why don't you ride with Trey?" Aden suggested to Cadence. Cadence flashed her a grin.

"My car's just over here." Trey pointed toward the street. "They wouldn't let anyone in the driveway."

"Ours is over that way, too," Drew said. The officer who'd be their escort checked their car before he let them get in it. A second officer pulled up in a police cruiser beside them, and the first officer jumped in.

"Taxes are going to have to go up to pay for all this police overtime," Janet mumbled. They pulled out, the police escort following behind, and Trey and Cadence bringing up the rear. Aden thought the whole procession would have been funnier if she wasn't so worried about Maddox.

The convoy home was uneventful. The guard on duty at the house reported no unusual activity. One of the escorting officers from the cruiser went through the house with Drew before leaving while Cadence said good night to Trey. Janet thanked the officers graciously before locking the door and leaning her head against it.

"You okay, Mom?" Drew asked.

"Just another long day." She smiled, standing upright.

"I'm gonna grab a few things from upstairs and sleep in my old room tonight," Drew said.

"You don't have to do that."

"I'll sleep better, I think, if I can keep an eye and ear out closer to you all." He slipped out the door.

"Girls, I think I'm going to make a hot chocolate before I go to bed. Would you like one?" Janet asked.

Cadence and Aden curled up on one sofa with their steaming mugs, and Drew and Janet were on the other. They all looked tired.

"I can't believe Maddox isn't home yet," Aden sighed.

"I think Sheriff Richey is just making a point." Drew frowned. "We'd have heard if they'd charged him."

"I think he's just incredibly frustrated. Three women are missing; they believe the same person is stalking Aden, and they have nothing to go on." Janet sighed. "Maddox has gotten in his way a couple of times, and the Sheriff is taking it all out on him."

"Those taunting letters must haunt his dreams." Cadence nodded.

"I know they haunt mine," Aden mumbled.

"Actually, they seem to just make you really angry," Cadence observed.

"I'm just tired of being scared." Aden shrugged, yawning. "At first, I was mostly terrified all the time. Now, I think I might just kick this guy's ass for all the trouble he's caused."

"Aden," Her mother admonished.

"Again, what's the etiquette for being stalked by a psychopath?" Aden sighed. Her mother pursed her lips but let it go. "I'm just over all of it. Being indirectly manipulated, watched, taunted..." She frowned at Cadence. "That's exactly what those letters are about: taunting us all. He's tweaking our noses at the fact that he can come and go as he pleases, while we all huddle in fear."

"Why don't we watch a movie while we huddle?" Cadence suggested. "I don't think I could get to sleep just yet."

"Sure." Aden nodded, agreeing with the sentiment. All she could think about was Maddox. She got up and opened the cabinet that held their DVD collection. "What are you in the mood for?"

Cadence joined her, and they were considering titles when both their phones buzzed on the coffee table at the same time. Drew reached into the pocket of his jeans to pull his out, too, as the girls lunged for theirs.

"It's Maddox!" Aden beamed, relieved. She read the text aloud. "They've let him go. He's on his way home." Drew and Cadence had gotten the same message.

"Oh thank goodness!" Janet sighed. "I'm so glad."

Aden's phone rang. "Oh, we're so glad to hear from you!" she gushed when she answered. "How are you? Wait, let me put you on speaker...Cadence, Mom, and Drew are here."

"Hi everyone," Maddox sounded tired. "Are you still at Dad's house?"

"No, we're at my house. Everybody else is still at yours. Cadence is spending the night here," Aden explained.

"Oh." She could hear his disappointment.

"So what happened?"

He let out a long sigh before answering. "Probably just what you'd expect. They had me sit in a tiny room all day, answering questions. Over. And Over. And Over." They heard Max mumble something in the background. "They let Mom and Dad in a couple of times, for short periods, but mostly, they left me on my own in there. When they'd come in, they were trying to get me to confess."

"Confess to what?" Drew asked.

"Everything. All of it." Maddox chuckled. "Apparently, they believe I masterminded all the disappearances from Virginia and manipulated Dad into getting Mom to bring me here. That's supposed to be my alibi, by the way."

"Seriously?" Cadence was incredulous.

"I don't know how serious they were about all of that. I guess they thought they'd wear me down until I confessed to something, anything."

"Well, are they satisfied? Have they let you go for good?" Aden asked.

"I don't know, but at least I'm out of there for now." He paused. "My Dad says to tell you all to stay safe tonight."

"Tell him thanks." Aden smiled. "We will."

"Can I see you tomorrow?"

"You'd better." Aden smiled, picking up the phone and turning off the speaker. "Call me in the morning?...You too. Good night."

"Aw, did he tell you he loves you?" Cadence teased.

"No," Aden said, irritated, "he told me to sleep well."

"Okay then, I'm going to bed," Janet said, getting up with a small smile.

"Are you guys still gonna watch that movie?" Drew asked. The girls looked at each other and shrugged. "Mind if I stay up with you for a while?"

They chose a movie and settled in on the couches. Drew fell asleep halfway through. When he started snoring, Aden woke him up and made him go to bed. She and Cadence decided to watch the sequel to the first movie, and Aden brought out pillows and blankets so they could snuggle in for the second feature.

CHAPTER 18

grey day

adence woke up early the next morning. The sun wasn't quite up yet, and the room was grey with pools of receding night. She had to go to the bathroom, but she didn't want to get up yet. She stretched slowly, not wanting to make any noise in the otherwise silent room. She couldn't even hear Aden breathing on the other couch. Sighing, she kicked off the blanket. She wasn't going to get back to sleep without that trip to the bathroom.

She sat up slowly and stood, closing her eyes as her knees popped in the stillness. Aden didn't move. She tiptoed to the bathroom without hearing anything that would suggest she'd woken anyone up. On her way back to the couch, she was still listening intently. She wasn't quite sure why, but everyone seemed to be sleeping deeply. Then, she noticed several things at once: a bent page on a magazine on the coffee table was slowly waving as if there was a draft, and looking out to the back deck, she saw there was absolutely no breeze in the pre-dawn stillness. But there seemed to be a lighter section of glass beside the door's handle. She squinted at it for a second and then glanced to where Aden… wasn't on the couch. The pillow and blanket were there, discarded. Weird. She must have gone to bed at some point.

Cadence turned around and went to peek into Aden's bedroom. It was darker in here than in the den with the huge glass doors, but she could tell that Aden's bed was still made, minus the pillows, but Aden wasn't in there. Frowning, she turned to make sure she wasn't in the bathroom behind her before she tiptoed to Drew's door. It was ajar, so she peeked in slowly. Drew was spread-eagled, face down, across the whole bed, snoring lightly. She looked around the rest of the room, and Aden wasn't there.

Becoming really concerned, she walked much faster back to the den. She made a quick detour into the kitchen. Nothing. Her eyes swept the room, and the brighter spot in the glass door caught her attention again. She walked slowly closer, blinking. There was something on the floor just underneath…she squinted. Glass. She glanced back up—it had fallen out of the door. There was a hole in the glass of the door.

"Oh, God." Cadence said, feeling suddenly nauseous. She sprinted to Janet's bedroom door on the other side of the room. She only knocked once before opening it. "Mrs.

315

Garrett, um…" She wasn't sure what to say, "Is Aden in there with you?"

"Cadence? What?" Janet sat up blinking.

"Is Aden in there with you?" Cadence repeated, knowing she wouldn't be, but still hoping, praying.

"Aden? She was with you." Janet got out of bed and threw on a robe. Cadence immediately ran to the kitchen door and opened it.

"Officer!" she yelled, "Officer!" A uniformed man jogged around the corner. "Aden is missing!" He followed her inside just as Drew came running out of the bedroom. "There's glass broken out of the door." Cadence pointed, now in tears. She couldn't deny it any more. He'd taken Aden.

"Aden!" Janet screamed, looking toward Aden's bedroom. "Aden, answer me!"

"She's not in her room," Drew said. "I just looked in there."

"We fell asleep out here last night. I woke up, went to the bathroom. When I came back, I saw she wasn't on the couch. I looked everywhere…" Cadence was crying too hard to continue.

The officer was frantically barking into his radio. Drew stepped toward the glass door, reaching for the handle, but the cop stopped him.

"Please, stand back, all of you."

"I'm going to look out front," Drew declared.

"Mr. Garrett, if you go out, you could contaminate the scene, even destroy evidence that might help us—"

"Alright!" Drew shouted. "What *can* I do? My sister is missing!"

"Drew, come sit down," Janet said shakily. She had an arm around Cadence, and it looked like they were holding each other up. "You can come call Kim for me."

Drew ran to retrieve his phone from the bedroom. "What's her number?"

"It's in my phone, in my bedroom."

"Nevermind, I have Maddox's," he said impatiently, already dialing.

"Maddox, it's Drew." He paused, and Cadence knew what was going through his head. How do you tell someone… "Aden is missing." Cadence closed her eyes. "Yes, they're… yes. No. Okay." He sighed, setting his phone down. "They're on the way."

Janet just nodded, still clinging to Cadence.

The police officer stood between the couches and began firing questions at them.

"We fell asleep watching a movie. I slept right here, and Aden was on that couch."

"Do you know what time that was?"

"Um, I don't. 2:00? 2:30 maybe?"

"And you?" he asked Janet and Drew.

"I slept in my bedroom," Janet pointed. "And Drew was in his old room, down that hall next to Aden's."

"So Aden was here when you fell asleep?" he turned back to Cadence. She nodded. "Did you see anything, hear anything during the night?"

"No, I didn't hear a thing. I woke up this morning and used the bathroom. I saw that Aden wasn't there when I was coming to lay back down."

"And who found the glass?"

"I noticed it when I was looking for Aden. It was brighter there where the glass is broken out, and it caught my attention."

"That glass was cut, not broken," he told them solemnly. Janet closed her eyes, her hands in tight fists.

"Is anything else out of place?"

They all looked at each other and then around the room, shaking their heads. Everything was just as they' left it. Except Aden.

The officer asked more questions and minutely examined the couch where Aden had last been seen, and then the surrounding room, in an outward spiral.

Drew paced furiously around the house while Janet and Cadence clung to each other on the couch. Other officers began to arrive outside, and a few came in with more questions. Others fanned out around the property in an organized chaos the Garretts had seen before.

Before they would have thought possible, Maddox pushed his way through the kitchen door, followed closely by Kim. Both their faces betrayed the panic just below the surface.

"Have you heard anything?" he asked Cadence loudly as soon as he spotted her. She shook her head, still crying.

"I was going to ask you the same thing."

"Tell me what happened," he demanded. She'd never seen him so disheveled, or so… empty. His eyes searched the room frantically, over and over. His hands were fisted so tight she thought she might see tendons begin to pop through the stretched, angry, red and white skin, and the veins on his temple and neck stood out and pulsed with his heart, which she could almost see breaking in his heaving chest.

He looked like she felt. Instead of answering, she hugged him hard, sobbing loudly again.

"Cadence." It was Daddy Max. "Are you okay?" Maddox transferred her to Max's arms, and LeighAnn joined the embrace, crying softly.

"Why don't you all come sit down?" Drew offered, gesturing them toward the couches, still strewn with bedding. Janet still sat in a corner of one couch, looking shell-shocked. She tried to greet Max and LeighAnn, but could only smile and nod through never-ending tears. Max and LeighAnn sat down next to her. Cadence stood, looking stricken at the couch where Aden had been.

"You can't sit over here," a female officer said as kindly as possible. She held a camera and had plastic evidence bags tucked into her belt. "I can't believe they let you all into this room." She shook her head and sighed.

"That's where Aden was sleeping," Cadence informed Maddox. He inhaled raggedly, closing his eyes briefly before examining the couch as well as he could from where they stood. "Tell me what happened please," he croaked unevenly.

"Not in here," Kim said softly from behind her son. "Forensics needs the room for now. Let's go outside for a bit."

"We're not even dressed." Janet spoke up, looking confused. She, Cadence, and Drew were still in pajamas.

"I don't think anybody cares," LeighAnn said, helping Janet stand. "That's a beautiful robe."

"What? Oh, thank you. My husband gave it to me…"

Cadence wiped the tears from her face for the hundredth time and followed them.

"I'll be right there," Maddox said, ducking into the bathroom. He joined them as they sat on the stairs beside the garage. He handed Janet a roll of bathroom tissue. "Sorry, I couldn't find any Kleenex on short notice." He shrugged.

Janet actually laughed, and after tearing off a few sheets to wipe her wet face, she passed the roll to Cadence. "Always classy at the Garrett house." She sniffed. "Thank you so very much, Maddox. You're so thoughtful."

Maddox just nodded. He was tapping his foot incessantly, and Cadence asked him to stop.

"I need to *do* something," he said, shaking out his hands. "What can I do?" he asked his mother. Kim opened her mouth, then closed it, sighing.

"Pray," LeighAnn answered. "We can all pray."

"Believe me, I've been sending up every kind of prayer I can come up with since I got Drew's call." Maddox's shoulders slumped.

"You can relax," Cadence said quietly, "and try to 'see' something."

"What?" Maddox, Max and Kim all stared at her. Cadence rolled her eyes, looking around at the uniformed officers running past. No one was paying the families any attention at present.

"You know exactly what I mean." She arched her brow at Maddox and then at Kim.

"Cadence—" Maddox started.

"Shut it, Maddox. I know you want to keep it some big secret, but I've known about it for years."

"I don't know what you're—" Kim started.

"Oh, you shut it, too. We don't have time for this."

"Cadence!" LeighAnn shrieked. "What are you—"

"I know that you know, too. We all know. Well, except for probably Janet and Drew, but I know that Aden is in on it."

319

"What are you talking about?" Drew barked at Cadence. "We should be doing something—"

"Exactly!" Maddox nodded.

"Oh my God! I don't know why this has to be such a big deal!" Cadence threw her hands up and stood to face the staircase. Lowering her voice to a hiss, she glared at them all. "Kim and Maddox both get 'visions' of the bad guys they're chasing. Kim is an excellent profiler, but her ability to actually see into the bad guy's heads is what makes her the best in her field, and because Maddox gets the same kind of visions as his mother, he helps her on some of her cases. Everybody with me so far?"

Everybody just looked back, stunned.

"I know you didn't want me to know—didn't want anybody to know, but guess what? That psychopath came into this house last night, and with me sleeping right beside her, took Aden. He has her right now, and we are going to do everything, and I mean *everything* to find her. Are we clear?" She glared at Maddox and Kim especially.

"Will you lower your voice, please?" Maddox ground out, coming to stand beside Cadence.

"Is that true?" Janet asked, searching Maddox's face before turning to Kim. "Please, tell me." Drew stared Maddox down.

Maddox looked at his Mom, then his Dad, then back at Janet before slowly closing his eyes and nodding.

"Can you—" She stopped and leaned forward to whisper desperately, "Can you see her?"

"It doesn't work on command, most of the time." Kim frowned furiously. She shot Cadence an anxious glance. "It's not something either of us has learned to control."

"It kind of just happens," Maddox said, looking even more miserable.

"But you can try," Cadence begged. "Just try." She was crying again.

"Cadence—" Max let out a huge sigh.

"She's right." LeighAnn stood up. "What will it hurt to try?" She looked at Kim and then at Maddox. "Have you? Have either of you tried to…see anything this morning?"

Kim looked pained, and Maddox had closed his eyes again.

"I *have* tried," Maddox said, "Repeatedly, but—"

"We've both tried. But it's harder—" She looked around at them, tears streaming. "Sometimes it's very hard to see…what we can see."

"So, you're afraid." Drew frowned. "Of what you might see?"

"You don't want to know…the things I've been made to see over the years," Kim whispered.

"Have you seen Aden?" Janet asked quietly, grasping Drew's arm beside her.

"No." Kim shook her head. "I don't know if we're just not seeing, or if we're too close, involved, or if we just subconsciously don't want to see…" She let her voice trail off.

"Well, man-up," Cadence bit out furiously. "What can we do to help you?"

"Cadence!" Max began again.

"No, Max, please. If there's anything we can do…" Janet begged with her eyes.

"If anybody has a connection with Aden," Cadence sniffed, "It's Maddox. He's in love with her."

Maddox was standing, fists tightly clenched and eyes closed, facing them all. Tears streamed down his face as he opened his eyes.

"I promised her," he croaked unevenly, "That I would keep her safe. That *we* would keep her safe."

Cadence stepped up to him, taking him by the shoulders gently. "And that's what we're going to do. We're going to find her." She spoke with absolute certainty. His wounded eyes searched her face and seemed to find resolve. He began nodding, minutely at first, but gaining momentum as he inhaled deeply and looked up to the assembled families before him.

"I need to get back inside, to that couch," he announced, looking at his mother. She hesitated for a moment with a questioning look before nodding herself and standing up.

"We haven't finished processing the scene in here," an officer explained, holding out his arms to bar their entry into the house.

"I'm F.B.I.," Kim growled, flashing her badge—even though they all knew who she was. "I'm officially taking charge of this investigation."

"You don't have the authority," Sheriff Richey practically shouted from the kitchen.

Kim had pulled out her phone and hit just one button. "Oh, don't I?" she put the phone to her ear.

"Mom?" Maddox whispered. She waved him off.

"Garcia? Dixon," she said into the phone. "Yes, I'm still in South Carolina, and I need you to confirm for the local yokels that we still have jurisdiction over Federal matters," she paused. "Yes, there's a fourth victim as of this morning. I sent you images of the latest letter the perpetrator had left…yes, Sir. Thank you, Sir." She held the phone out to Sheriff Richey.

Dave Richey took the phone she held with an unyielding glare. "This is Sheriff Dave Richey," he said in a clipped voice and waited. He sighed deeply, narrowing his constant glare at Kim before speaking again. "I understand." He handed the phone back to Kim.

She put it to her ear. "Sir?...Yes, Sir, I will, Sir. Thank you." She ended the call and slipped the phone into her pocket with a smile to the officer in the doorway.

"Let 'em in," the Sheriff growled, turning away.

The officer reluctantly stepped back, after glancing between the Sheriff and Kim more than once.

"Mom," Maddox hissed under his breath. "Are you trying to get fired?"

"No worries," Kim whispered back. "As long as we find her before…it'll all work out." At Maddox's deepening frown, she smiled at him. "We're going to find her."

Maddox just nodded.

"Okay," Kim sighed, turning to the group behind her. "I'm really not trying to be dramatic, but would you all mind waiting out here for a bit? We're going to need a little space to give this…everything we've got."

"Of course." Janet nodded; Drew scowled. Max and LeighAnn just stepped back.

"Thank you, we'll call you in shortly." She entered the kitchen. "Sheriff?" Dave turned to her reluctantly. "Where are we on processing the scene in here?"

"*We*," he enunciated carefully, "have completed a visual sweep, collected fibrous samples, dusted the entire door inside and out for prints, dusted most of the room in fact, and are just finishing photo documentation of the scene."

"Perfect," Kim chirped. "I'd like to be notified the second the results of those samples come in." Dave just nodded, curtly. "Now, I think we've kept the family waiting in the yard long enough. Can we give them their house back?"

"Smith! Reed! Grab everybody, we're moving outside." He barked, sweeping through the kitchen door without another word.

Several people filed through the kitchen door, leaving the house silent and empty except for her and Maddox.

"We'll be right back." Kim promised the families outside, closing the door. She faced Maddox. "Alright, we can do this."

"Can we?"

"We have no choice." She straightened her back. "You love this girl?"

He frowned and nodded.

"Then reach out to her."

"I've only ever seen the criminals' point of view," he huffed.

"I know." She examined his face. "But that doesn't mean it's all that you can see."

Maddox walked to the couch where Cadence said Aden had been sleeping. The blankets, pillows, and cushions from both couches were missing now, and he sank down on the floor, lying his head on the bare frame with his eyes screwed shut.

"You're trying too hard," Kim said from her perch on the other couch. Her eyes were closed, too. "Reach out with your mind, as if you were calling her."

Maddox took a deep breath and tried to clear his mind, pushing away the images of all the panicked faces waiting outside. He tried to picture Aden's face in his mind, but it was dark and blurred. He opened his eyes as his Mom sat beside him on the floor, taking his hand.

"Let's try together," she suggested. He raised his eyebrows dubiously but closed his eyes again; gripping his mother's hand, he inhaled slowly. "Call to her."

Maddox sighed inwardly, but tried calling out to her again. *Aden! Where are you?* An indistinct light shimmered in the dark distance, grey against the black void. *Aden! Please!* He begged. *Can you hear me?* The grey shapes shifted with movement, but it was still dark. *It's me. It's Maddox. Please Aden. Where are you? Open your eyes. Show me where you are.* The shadows pulled back suddenly, revealing shapes. Indistinct, but they were something. Round vertical…metal…a pole. And smooth, horizontal…a metal table. Leather straps bound a slender wrist.

"No!" Maddox moaned.

"Shh. Concentrate." His mother's voice coaxed.

Aden! Look around! We need more. Where are you? Do you know your location? Can you tell me? He was begging. The darkness shifted, and there were more shadowy figures he could barely make out. One filthy, tiny window let in a strangled light…concrete walls and floor. Wood beams holding up the ceiling. A basement. He'd seen this basement before.

Mattresses. There were mattresses lined up on the floor. Something…piles of something on them. Wait. It moved. People. Bound people on the mattresses.

"At least one of the other women is alive," Maddox whispered, eyes still closed. *Aden! You're doing great. Can you give us anything? Tell us where the house is. Who is holding you?*

Maddox screwed his eyes even more tightly shut, going deeper into the space within his mind than he would have believed before. *Aden! All I see is darkness. Come on! Try harder! Who is it? Where are you?* The grey shapes had shrunk to pinpricks of indistinct light in the vast darkness. *Aden!* Then he noticed a faint sound, growing louder. A low moan, just below the range of hearing, arching up to a high-pitched keening. Floating in the darkness was a triangular image…circles stacked in diminishing rows….he huffed in frustration as the image quickly faded, along with the breathy sounds back into empty darkness.

"Wait!" he begged, hunched over with his free hand gripping his forehead viciously. *Aden! I need more! Please! Please, come on! We can do this. We have to do this.*

"Kim?" It was Max, who'd come unnoticed into the house. "They found a trail, looks like she was dragged to a vehicle parked on the highway. Dave's outside trying to figure out what you're doing in here—"

"He dragged her through the woods?" Kim frowned.

"That would mean she was unconscious or—" Maddox was instantly on his feet. "We should go take a look."

"Wait, before we go, were you able to see anything?" Max asked quietly, keeping an eye on the kitchen door.

"I saw the basement again. Mattresses on the floor—one of the other women is alive; I saw movement…and um, there was a shape. A triangle? Rows of circles in a triangular shape. And there were sounds. I don't know. I don't know what any of that means! We need more." Maddox was rapidly opening and closing his fists again, his foot tapping on the floor.

"Agent Dixon?" Sheriff Richey called from the kitchen doorway, still scowling.

"We're going to find her." Kim smiled, squeezing Maddox's arm on her way to the kitchen door.

"So this triangle," Max frowned at his son. "You don't have any idea what that could be?" Maddox was shaking his head in frustration. "Look, you know you need to stay as far away from Dave Richey as you can. Don't go out there getting in his way."

"Dad, I have to—"

"No, listen to me. There's something you *can* do that the rest of us can't. Find a quiet place where you can…concentrate. Focus all that energy on seeing Aden. Your Mom and I will handle everything else here, all the physical evidence and the police and Aden's family. We can do that. Take the Audi, but please be careful, your faculties are a little compromised right now." Maddox nodded, sighing. "And if you do see anything, you call us. You hear me? Don't go off trying to play hero or anything. Let the police do their jobs."

Max led Maddox through the kitchen and outside where the others stood in a huddle watching the police activity around them. Janet and Drew came to meet them with a desperate, questioning look on their faces. Maddox sighed, shoulders slumped.

"I didn't see much yet, but I'm not giving up."

"Maddox is going to go somewhere quiet," Max began quietly explaining.

"You need to stay away from the Sheriff." Drew nodded, frowning. "I didn't catch it all, but I heard your name when he was talking with some of the other cops while you and your Mom were inside."

"Yeah, you're distracting them from finding the real kidnapper," Cadence spoke up.

"I'm going to go do…everything I can do to find her." Maddox spoke directly to Janet and Drew.

"I'll go with you, I can help—" Cadence began.

"No," Maddox barked, then rolled his head on his neck. "Sorry. I need some space, and some silence." He looked at her with a ghost of a grin. "You have many strengths, but silence is not one of them." As Cadence pouted, he looked around to where his Mother stood with the Sheriff just visible between the trees to one side of the driveway. "I'll stay in touch; I promise."

"Can I help? Do something?" Drew practically begged. Maddox frowned, shaking his head slowly.

"There's not much any of us can do until we get some more information." Pulling the car keys from his pocket, he stepped toward the Audi, parked behind two police cruisers in the courtyard. "I'll be back soon."

He felt all the eyes watching him as he navigated the car between police vehicles to get down the driveway. When he reached the highway, he realized he had no destination in mind. There were more police vehicles pulled off to the side of the highway just up the road, about where they'd seen the truck pulled off to the side that night. He turned that way and drove by slowly, trying to see…anything. He couldn't. He drove on slowly for a moment until he suddenly knew where he'd been headed all along.

Aden's nose wrinkled, and she coughed, almost retching at the putrid smell…What the hell is that? She tried to open her eyes, but she was so sleepy. She couldn't keep them open. And she was so uncomfortable, she realized. *The couch. Right. I should have gone to bed. So tired. Too tired.* She sank back into the depths.

At some later point, the smell was back, and she frowned, still unable to drag her eyelids up. She tried to reach up and physically pull up her eyelids with one hand, but her arm was too heavy. She couldn't move it. Then she felt something…heard something? Almost a prickle in her mind. It was warm, it was safe, love, Maddox. She was dreaming about Maddox. He was looking for her, and she wanted to be found. I'm here. She called to the dream Maddox. *I'm just so tired. Why am I so tired? Maddox?* She pried her eyes open once again and looked around in confusion. *What is this place?* Her eyes closed involuntarily again as something clicked in her slow thoughts. Danger. *Maddox! Help me…it's…fruit…*the dream dispersed as she was pulled back into darkness.

The sun baked the still air around him as he trudged purposefully up the steep trail. Pulling himself up onto the rock shelf, Maddox squinted and searched the horizon for a moment before turning around to stare at the spot in the roots of the tree where he'd held Aden. She was out there, somewhere, in danger. After everything he'd done, that they'd all done, to try to protect her, the bastard waltzed in and took her, just like he said he would. Maddox clenched his fists at his sides and let out the roar of frustration he'd been holding back since he'd gotten Drew's call. It echoed in the distance, sounding like laughter bouncing back, slowly dying into utter silence as the birds, squirrels and other nearby creatures froze into watchfulness. The very air was silent, with not a hint of a breeze to stir the heavy atmosphere. Maddox sank down and ran both hands through his hair, breathing deeply. He laid back on the hot stone, shielding his eyes with one hand from the merciless sun.

"You can't have her," he vowed, closing his eyes.

Thirsty. Aden's first thought as she swam back to consciousness again. Her throat felt cracked and dry; she was faintly nauseous, and the couch must be bouncing where she lay with the pounding in her head. She opened her eyes only to shut them quickly with a groan.

"Hey, you," a voice hissed nearby. Aden's eyes flew open again, and she winced at the meager beam of light struggling into the shadowy space. "Hey!" The whisperer insisted.

Aden tried to sit up, but couldn't. Aside from the skull-splitting pain, she found that her arms and legs were buckled into leather straps that held her on a metal table. She bucked in panic, gasping for air in her desiccated throat, to scream.

"Shhh!!!!!" the voice implored. "Shut up! If he hears you, he'll come down." Aden gulped in terror, strangling the scream, she glanced wildly around the dark room.

"Who is that? Where are we?"

"Introductions can wait. I think you know where you are, or close enough. What are they saying out there? Are they still looking for us?" a different voice urged, just above a whisper. "Do they have any clues? Any leads?"

"Oh, God." Aden shivered as full realization sank in with icy-sharp claws. She raised her pounding head to see a row of filthy mattresses on the floor, each with a wretched-looking human being bound in various ways to either a wall or the floor. She stared at the three women trying to make sense of...anything.

All of them seemed to be in costume, or something. Shonda, the first girl who disappeared, wore an old-fashioned evening gown. Too small to be zipped up in back, it hung precariously on one shoulder, and her dirt-blackened, bare feet showed under the hem as she sat on a mattress, chained around the waist to a metal ring in the concrete wall. The second victim, the older lady, looked to be draped in an old sheet, but her dark hair was piled elaborately on top of her head, and her makeup, though badly smeared, had been meticulously applied with a heavy hand. Her wrists were bound in leather straps like the ones on Aden's, but with a length of chain running between them and through another metal ring embedded in the concrete floor above her head. Her legs were similarly bound at the bottom of the mattress with a pair of high heeled shoes lying cast off nearby. The last, the blond who'd been taken from the convenience store, wore a flouncy, ruffled child's party dress, complete with a large bow in her hair that had been recently curled into ringlets. She held a broken, naked doll with an empty eye socket in the crook of one arm. The other arm seemed bound underneath her body as she lay haphazardly with ropes binding her to the mattress.

"Can you tell us anything?" the blond scowled quietly.

Aden stared at her for only a moment before turning to look around the rest of the room. A wooden staircase ascended in one corner, with some kind of work bench underneath. She shuddered at the sharp implements she could make out hanging on the wall among the chains and ropes and looked quickly away. Turning her aching head to the other side, she was assaulted with a horror she couldn't fathom was real. The screams came in earnest, clawing their way from her wounded soul up her dry throat. She bucked and kicked, trying to get away.

Sitting in an old wicker chair right beside her head was a rotting corpse, grinning at her useless screams. The empty eye sockets stared from under wispy, gray hair, and dangling precariously from thin, shrunken earlobes were a pair of pearl and diamond earrings that Aden immediately recognized.

The smell hit her again as she gasped for air between ragged screams, and she gagged, becoming aware of the women's voices on her other side, begging desperately for her to stop screaming. Then a long, jagged squeak stretched out from the hidden top of the stairs, and the women immediately went silent. Still gasping with horror, Aden's head swam, and her vision began to close in. She was sure she was going to pass out and then strangle on her own vomit...her eyes were closing involuntarily again. *Oh God!* She heard a smug chuckle from the staircase and the unmistakable sound of a bold tread beginning to descend.

CHAPTER 19
welcome party

*A*nswer me! Aden, where are you? Please! Please! Hear me. Maddox lay motionless under the glaring sky, oblivious to the rivulets of sweat dripping onto the thirsty rock underneath him. He took a deep, but ragged breath as he lay with one arm across his face. *Nothing.* He hadn't seen or heard a thing since he'd been here. Counting slowly down from ten, he attempted to clear his mind. The gnawing pit in his gut was growing with every passing minute. Frustration. Fear. He swallowed it down and continued counting. He had to find her. Taking another deep breath, he forced his bunched muscles to relax and let the stillness settle in. *Aden? It's Maddox. I'm going to find you; I just need a little help, a sign, anything. Can you give me something to go on?*

"Ah, my lovelies!" the voice was getting closer as Aden squeezed her eyes tightly shut. She recognized that voice. Confusing blips, somewhere between a dream and an almost-memory, played in her mind: breath on her neck, a painful prick, opening her eyes to a face looming in the darkness. A smiling face. Familiar, but out of place. Wrong. Very wrong. Then darkness, and pinpricks of light in the darkness, wind in the vast, dark void… "She is awake? Yes?" a drawn out sigh, a sibilance of evil, her skin prickled with his approach, and she had to see. Opening her eyes, she could only see the dark silhouette gliding purposefully toward her. Every cell of her being wanted to shrink away from him, but even if she could move, the bejeweled, grinning corpse was on her other side. *Oh God, please no!* He stood over her, and in one long inhaled breath, took in every inch of her body with a leer she could almost feel, starting at her feet and, in interminably slow motion, finally reaching her face. His face bore a sickly possessive smile as his eyes met hers.

"Welcome home, my dear." He gently wiped the tears from her cheeks and then ran his hand through her hair. "We've been waiting for you." He leaned down and kissed her forehead as Aden swallowed bile with the scream that desperately clawed up her throat.

"You." She shuddered in revulsion and disbelief. "How can it be -"

"Little old me?" he chuckled. "Well, for starters, I'm not as old or frail as you might think. Eh, my lovelies?" he turned to the motionless women behind him before turning back to Aden. "And, well, I had a little help. For a while." His eyes strayed fondly to the corpse. "Oh that reminds me, I've left the water on the stove for the tea. I'll just go and freshen up a bit before we set it out. Please excuse me, ladies."

As he retreated, Aden felt...or heard...something. She looked around, confused. Inexplicably, she felt...as though someone else was near. Someone she knew and trusted. Someone she loved. *Maddox.* She closed her eyes and desperately hoped that he was seeing...her and that he would find her, find them all. She imagined that he could see her, hear her, right now. Desperate hopes, she knew. But it was all she had to hold on to. *Maddox! Maddox, can you hear me? It's Mr. Vinings! Julian Vinings!* She shouted in her mind, praying that she could somehow be heard. She pictured his face, the sane, normal face he'd presented in the jewelry store when she first met him. *Vinings! Like... vine...grape vine! Grapes!* She sighed as she was interrupted by the hissing whispers of the other women. She ignored them and, closing her eyes tightly, concentrated on Maddox and envisioning Julian's face, vines, grapes...anything she could think of that might get a message across.

Maddox sat up suddenly. *Grapes!* He felt energized. The triangular rows of circles were grapes. He'd clearly seen a bunch of grapes hanging from the vine. Then the vine, and a face. He fumbled frantically for the phone in his pocket and almost dropped it trying to dial the single number that would connect him to his mother.

"Did you get something?" he almost dropped the phone again at the unexpected voice. Cadence and Trey peeked over the edge of the stone from the trail below.

"Cadence! How did you get here?"

"Trey came over right after you left, and I figured that this is where you'd come."

"And how long have you been skulking over there?"

"Does it matter? What happened? You saw something, didn't you?" He didn't answer, just put the phone to his ear.

"Mom? Yeah, Julian Vinings. Old man approached me at the deli in town, and then went to the jewelry store while Aden was there. She helped him buy an anniversary gift for his wife. I think it might be him. Or he's involved somehow....yes. Vinings." He paused, frowning as Drew climbed up onto the rock behind Cadence and Trey. "I can be there in...but..." he sighed, rolling his eyes. "Yes, call me as soon as you hear," He ended the call abruptly.

"Is that him? Julian Vinings?" Cadence looked hopeful.

"How many more of you are there, following me up this mountain?" he asked. Drew frowned furiously.

"She's my sister, man."

Maddox closed his eyes, "You're right. I'm sorry."

"Do you know who it is??" Cadence asked impatiently. Maddox sighed.

"I'm not sure. I did get something…an older man, a customer at the jewelry store, but I don't know if it's The Guy." He looked to Drew. "My Mom has the cops looking into it right now, and we'll know more soon."

Trey had his phone out, scrolling intently. "I don't see any Vinings in the local phone listings."

"V-I-N-I-N-G-S?" Maddox was furiously tapping on his own phone's screen now, too.

"No." Trey shook his head.

"Nothing in the real estate records, either," Maddox growled several moments later, "At least, not online that I can see."

"There are a few in Spartanburg." Trey raised his eyebrows, still looking at his phone. "Several in Anderson. But not so much here…there's a Viening? Wolfgang Viening, and a Vintner…" He frowned. "Maybe this guy's not local?"

"He's local," Maddox scowled. "I feel it. Been here a long time."

"You seemed to know this Julian guy?" Drew asked.

"Not really. I met him in town, but I don't know anything about him, let alone where he lives."

"So how'd you meet?" Cadence piped up. "Seems too much for mere coincidence."

Maddox frowned furiously. Of course Cadence would pick up on the one thread of the story that was drowning him in guilt.

"I was at the café on the square last week. Aden was at work, and I was just…hanging out in the area. It was crowded, and an older gentleman asked if he could share the table. I said sure, not really intending to strike up any conversation. I had my iPad with me, and I was reading news headlines on it while I kept an eye on the jewelry store—"

"Older gentleman?" Drew interrupted. "How old? What'd he look like?"

Maddox shrugged. "I couldn't really tell you his age. He's got one of those faces, you know? But his mannerisms, his impeccable suit tailoring, the way he sat, the phrases he used when he spoke," Maddox was shaking his head. "He was just an old guy." He could tell Drew wanted to say more, but he continued. "So he sat down at my table, remarked on my "gadget" and launched into a story about how it was his anniversary, and his wife was pissed at him because he'd bought her some appliance the year before that he thought she would have liked. Apparently, she wasn't impressed, and he was in town that day searching for inspiration so he wouldn't repeat the experience. I sent him to the jewelry store." Maddox sighed dramatically, "Gave him Aden's name." At Drew's look he rushed on, "I thought he was just a clueless old geezer, and I was doing him a favor. What female doesn't like jewelry? And Aden would get a sale out of it, too." He abruptly closed his mouth.

"You sent him to her?" Drew bit out. Maddox stared back, wordlessly.

"Yes, Maddox sent him straight over," Cadence rushed, "Even though he clearly recognized that the old man was a crazed kidnapper, and he just *knew* the creepy geezer had been stalking your sister and writing creepy poetry, following her around—"

"Okay," Drew conceded. "Sorry." Maddox just scowled at the infinite view. "But seriously, how did some old guy overpower four women?" Maddox turned to look at him, along with Cadence and Trey. "I mean, he might have surprised one of them, gotten the upper hand, but all four? It doesn't make any sense."

"A 99 year-old with a gun could get control of just about anybody." Trey shrugged. "As long as he could hold it steady enough to look menacing."

"I guess." Drew nodded, feeling defeated.

"But Aden has been pissed off enough to kick a gun out of a senior citizen's hand, lately." Cadence said. "And I was *right there*; don't forget. There wasn't any struggle." She was on the verge of tears again. "I would have heard it; I know I would. Somehow, he came in and got her without making any noise." Drew was nodding, slowly.

Maddox's phone rang. He fumbled to get it to his ear again and waited. "Yeah…Yes, I'm sure…I don't know, V-I-N-I-N-G-S…I know. We've Googled it, too. I saw his face, though…I know that he said Vinings, that's what he told both of us…No. Yeah, they're here. But…okay, I said okay." He ended the call with a growl. They were all looking expectantly at him, waiting. He took a deep breath, shoulders slumped.

"My Mom says there's no record of a Julian Vinings. It's a dead end."

"But you *saw* him." Cadence blinked, confused. "You met him. You sent him to the jewelry store, and something made you think of him today."

"I told you." Maddox was furiously shaking his head, "*We* told you we can't control what we…see. It's not like watching a documentary with everything all laid out neatly for you."

"So what *did* you see?" Drew asked. Maddox hesitated a moment.

"Grapes." He winced. "I saw a bunch of grapes. Well, to be honest, at first I saw a bunch of circles in rows, in a triangular shape—"

"Like grapes." Cadence frowned.

"Yeah," Maddox sighed. "And I saw the guy's face. Julian Vinings. At least, that's what he told me his name was. I *know* he has something to do with all this."

"Grapes…" Trey stared at his phone with a rapt expression. "There are wineries over in North Georgia. Maybe this guy is connected somehow?"

Maddox was shaking his head slowly. "It feels like…I know it sounds crazy, and I can't really explain, but it *feels* like the name itself…Vinings is the key. Or maybe Julian." He huffed loudly. "Oh my God, I don't know."

"Okay, back up." Drew was pacing back and forth. "Grapes, right?" he asked Maddox, who nodded. "Didn't you say there was a Vintner in town?" he directed to Trey.

Trey swiped his screen a couple of times and nodded. "Yes, there's a K. Vintner listed, but no Julian…no J."

"So what can we find out about K. Vintner?" Drew asked him. "I mean, Vintner? 'Maker of wine?' It's sort of close to Vinings, isn't it?"

Maddox and Cadence looked skeptical, but Trey was researching furiously on his phone.

"Looks like K. Vintner owns more than one property in the county, but cell service is spotty this high up, and I lost it. It'll take a minute to try and get it back," Trey ground out, frustrated.

"Maybe we should head back toward town," Cadence suggested.

Maddox hesitated. He wasn't sure why, but he felt they were where they needed to be.

Aden sighed loudly as the whispers interrupted her daydreams again.

"Hey! Hey! Golden Girl!" Shonda hissed. "Who are you? He's been talking about you for months."

"I'm nobody," Aden sighed. "I just met him a few days ago."

"You're joking!" the blond girl rolled her eyes.

"She looks like Kate," the older woman interceded. "Younger Kate. I saw the pictures upstairs."

"I sold him those earrings." Aden shuddered, "For his wife."

"That ain't his wife," the blond chuckled.

"It's his mother." Shonda nodded at Aden's confused look. "She's the one who convinced me to get in the car with them the night I broke down."

"The night she disappeared," the older brunette provided. "It was Kate, the sweet old lady, who fooled us."

"Not all of us," the blond mumbled. "Julian is pretty convincing too."

"It was Kate who came in my shop, late that afternoon without an appointment." The brunette frowned. "I'd been doing her weekly wash and set for...years, I guess. She was always quiet, unassuming. She told me there was a special occasion that made her come in before her regular appointment, and asked if I could make an exception. I told my husband and son there was a frozen pizza in the freezer, and I'd be a while. Kate never said much at her appointments, but this time, she started talking about her son. I didn't even know she had a son. It got awkward fast. Before I knew it, he was standing in the doorway, like he'd been listening, and he was angry that she'd told me about him. She acted all surprised...at first. But then the old bitch smiled at me in the car. Turned around in her seat and smiled back at me, while I was gagged and handcuffed in the back seat. She smiled at me and then...caressed...yes, caressed his neck as he drove us here." She closed her eyes, shivering.

"Do you know where we are?" Aden asked. The older woman shook her head.

"Up the mountains." She shrugged, looking at the other two women with a hopeless expression. "I know we climbed up, but I don't know where to. They had me layin' down in the back seat of the car, and I was so scared—"

"We're high up." Shonda nodded. "They kept me somewhere else at first, then brought me here one day, right before Raylene was abducted. Must've been over half an hour, at least, outside town. I was blindfolded, but the car was climbing, and there were lots of big curves, and my blindfold slipped getting out of the car. We're way up on a mountain somewhere. The wind whips around the rocks up here sometimes…sounds like somebody cryin' or something."

"It was dark when he brought me here," the blond spoke up again, "but the way I was chained when I first got here, I could see out that window. There's a path that looks pretty worn, that goes down the slope toward a big drop off. I saw him walk down it a couple times."

"Do you know where it goes? Anything down there?" Aden asked, but the girl just shook her head. High up a mountain, vast view, wind in the rocks…couldn't be. They could be anywhere, on any mountain. But she still felt inexplicably close to Maddox.

"Okay, got a couple bars now," Trey said, holding up his phone.

"Yeah, I'm searching too." Maddox frowned. Drew and Cadence huddled close to both of them, looking over their shoulders.

"Okay, here's a Vintner. Louis? Owns a house on Church Street."

"Louis Vintner…" Maddox mumbled, searching frantically.

"There's another property. Wait, this is the same one. Church Street, but it says K. Vintner."

"Louis Vintner, he's dead. Here's an obit," Maddox scowled. "Another dead end."

"Wait, lemme see that." Cadence reached for the phone and began reading out loud, "Mr. Vintner is survived by his wife Katherine and a son."

"Katherine." Trey nodded. "K. Vintner. She inherited the properties when her husband died, maybe?"

"So a house on Church Street? That's over past where the Payne's Garage is," Drew said.

"So could the son be Julian, maybe?" Cadence mused.

Maddox dialed a number and put the phone to his ear again. "Mom, try looking up Vintner, instead of Vinings. Yeah, V-I-N-T-N-E-R. There's a Katherine Vintner in town we think...No, the internet. There's a house we think, on Church Street, and an obituary mentions a son, but doesn't name him. I know, but it's something...Thanks." He ended the call and turned to his waiting friends, "They're running it down now."

"Hold on! Here it is!" Trey whooped. "Julian Vintner. He was interviewed by the newspaper over 20 years ago during a big flu season...says he's a pharmacist." They all crowded around the phone, reading the article.

"Reed's Pharmacy? Where's that?" Cadence frowned. They all looked at each other while Maddox searched on his phone. Cadence continued scrolling through the article on Trey's phone.

"It closed, eight years ago," Maddox read, frowning. "It used to be on Highway 81."

"He was a Professor at Duke," Cadence spoke up. "Julian Vintner...he taught biochemistry."

"On it," Maddox said, searching furiously. Several minutes later, he was growling in frustration. "Nothing. I can't find a thing. You?" He looked to Trey, who was also shaking his head.

"How can there be so little about this guy?" Trey huffed.

"There doesn't seem to be a whole lot about the whole Vintner clan." Maddox nodded.

"I vote we take a drive to Church Street," Drew proposed.

"Hold on." Maddox dialed again. "Mom? We found a Julian Vintner online. Pharmacist and maybe taught biochemistry at Duke...I know. No, we're not in town—" He looked at the anxious faces staring back at him, "I'm on hold. Apparently, there's a car en route to the Vintner residence on Church—Yeah, I'm here...no, we thought about it though." He frowned. "Okay...yes. Got it...Mom, I said okay." He sighed as he ended the call.

"What was all that about?" Cadence asked.

"Ordering us to stay put." He frowned. "But there was something going on. She wasn't telling me everything."

"Something going on?" Drew wanted to know. Maddox shrugged.

"Just seemed like she was distracted, and there was a lot of commotion in the background, but she had to go before I could ask."

"Do you think they got another lead?" Trey wanted to know.

"Or maybe they just aren't taking our suggestions seriously." Cadence frowned.

"But we found Julian!" Drew said to her.

"We might have found a Julian…but we have no idea if it's the same guy I met, or even if *that* guy actually has anything whatsoever to do with any of this," Maddox ground out.

"But you saw him, right?" Cadence asked.

"Yeah, but I don't know—"

"How many times have you seen things before that turned out to be…false or misleading?" Cadence interrupted.

"Well, never, but I've never tried so hard before to…make the connection with someone. It's always just happened."

"So why would you think that would matter?"

"I'm saying maybe I'm trying so hard to…make something happen, that I'm not sure I can trust what I saw."

"You think you're just making it up?" Trey asked, dubiously.

"No." Maddox shook his head. "Not consciously. I'm just saying we can't be sure."

"You seemed pretty sure," Cadence pointed out. "And it was kind of random, right?"

"Yeah, some guy you met one time at the deli??" Trey nodded. "Why would your subconscious go there when you'd be more likely to suspect somebody like Billy Ray?"

"Agreed." Drew nodded.

"Okay, look, I really do appreciate the vote of confidence, I'm just saying we can't know for sure that it's even the same guy, or if it is, that he's involved. We just need to be careful."

"Careful with what?" Cadence asked. "We're just standing here on a rock, talking amongst ourselves."

"Actually, there's a squad car on the way to the guy's house right now, or his mother's."

"It's a lead, though, right?" Drew asked. "I mean, we're just following up on leads. There are four people missing, and one of them is Aden, so cut yourself some slack."

"Okay, have they had time to get there, you think?" Cadence asked.

"Probably not," Trey answered. "I think most of the department was out at Drew's house."

"Kim will call us though, right? Let us know something?" Cadence asked.

"Yeah." Maddox nodded. "She'll call when they have something."

"What if they don't have anything?" Cadence countered, causing Maddox to roll his eyes in frustration again. "No, seriously…What if nobody's home? They can't just go in, right? If nobody answers the door, they'll probably take a quick look around and leave." They all frowned at her. "I'm just thinking that maybe we keep going—look for more leads."

"Okay," Maddox prompted. "Where would you suggest we start?"

"Don't be like that." She frowned.

"Like what? I'm totally open to suggestions here. I *know* what a long shot it is that the cops might find something on Church Street. I know they're probably chasing their tails trying to find evidence that will link me to Aden's disappearance, and wasting time and resources that be looking for the real culprit, and I know that all the time I stand here, spinning my freaking wheels, Aden is…in danger." His voice broke with his frustration level. "And I don't know what to do."

They were silent for several moments before Cadence tried again.

"The second property." Cadence turned to Trey. "You said at first there were two properties owned by Vintners."

"It was just two different listings of the same property." He shrugged.

"But did you finish looking? I mean, we jumped off on drug store names and Duke University and trying to find anything on Julian Vintner. We could have missed something." Trey shrugged and started searching.

"We can't find anything on Julian Vintner online," Maddox huffed.

"But did you search Katherine? She's the one listed on the Church Street property."

Sighing, Maddox looked at Trey, who was scrolling slowly, and then he picked up his own phone and started looking.

Several minutes later, Trey growled. "There's just nothing." Maddox was reading intently on his phone.

"Maiden name?" he mumbled to himself.

"What?" Cadence skipped to his side. "What'd you find?"

"Nothing yet." He glanced at Trey. "Did you run across Katherine Vintner's maiden name anywhere?"

Trey immediately delved back into the Internet. "I saw something earlier on a church website; hold on. It was a list of deacons and marriages and births and deaths, and I don't even know what else, but Katherine Vintner was listed, here it is." He scrolled slowly. "Katherine Liddell Vintner."

"That's on there?" Maddox asked, excitedly scrolling on his phone. "Okay, so I found something for a Julian Liddell...but it's old. Really old. Like I think Julian Liddell might be Katherine's father...The Julian I met may be named for his grandfather, and look at this! There's a property listed in this old census document for a 'Family Liddell' home. The records list Julian Liddell, Owner, in 1920. Then, in a different search, it's listed as Katherine and Abigail Liddell, Owners in 1950. Then, in 1983 or 84, it's listed as K. L. Vintner. And now, if you look up that address in current records...it shows Julian V. Liddell, Owner since sometime around 1980."

"Julian Liddell?" Trey squinted at the phone in Maddox's hand, then searched again on his own.

"Julian *V.* Liddell," Cadence said excitedly. "Do you think he's changed his name?" She didn't wait for an answer. "You should call your Mom. We found him, I'm sure of it. We're so on top of this!"

"Um...we're more on top of this than you know." Trey said, holding out his phone showing a picture of a pin on a map. He looked at Maddox with an awed expression, and Maddox was nodding slowly at him with the same expression.

"What?" Cadence stamped her foot. "What are you talking about?"

"You've got to be kidding." Drew frowned, grabbing the phone from Trey's hand for a closer look. He looked around them suddenly, back to the phone, and then up at Maddox.

"So you say you just met Kray-Jay?" Shonda whispered suspiciously. "'Cuz he's been talkin' about you from the first day he took me." Aden didn't answer. She was trying to concentrate on Maddox again. "Hey! Red! I'm talkin' to you."

"Shhhh!!" Raylene cautioned. "Good God, do you want to bring him back down here? Is it really that important?"

"It is if she knows somethin'." Shonda sniffed. "She's the reason we're all here."

"What?" Aden opened her eyes. "What did you say?"

"I said, all of us are just like window dressing for your arrival." Shonda frowned. "He talked about you all the time. 'Aden this' and 'Aden that.'"

"You're serious." Aden stared at her, confused. "I swear, I met him last week for the very first time."

"Well, when did your Daddy die?" Shonda asked.

"Excuse me?!"

"Your Daddy, how long ago was that wreck?"

"What does—what the hell are you talking about?"

"That's when you met him. Kray-Jay told me about it one night. He was explaining why I had to stay with him and Kate. We're some kind of set, the four of us." She indicated the other women. "But you're the star attraction."

Aden looked wildly to Raylene and Cindy, but they weren't looking at her.

"Kray-Jay?" Aden started. *Cadence would love that.*

"Crazy Julian. 'Kray-Jay.'" Shonda explained.

"He was at the accident?" Aden's head was swimming again. She was sure she was going to vomit this time.

"He was in the accident," Shonda said.

"Oh my God." Aden began sobbing uncontrollably. "Too much. That's just...it's not true." She was shaking her head in denial.

"He told me your car went off the highway and down a steep hill. That your Daddy was killed but they brought you back up, and he said you looked like an angel." Aden was still shaking her head, staring in horror. "He said he was rounding a curve, and there was your car and your Daddy; he over-corrected, and that's what caused it."

"The truck," Aden mumbled. "There was an eighteen-wheeler that pushed us over."

"He didn't say anything about a truck. He said your Daddy was over the line, into his lane when he came around the curve—" Aden's head shook harder.

"No, the semi hit us from behind…"

"I remember reading about that accident," Raylene chimed in. "There was a truck involved. The driver went to your Father's funeral, didn't he? He and his wife?" Aden nodded.

"That's not what Kray-Jay said."

"He wasn't there," Aden whispered. "He couldn't have been there."

"He says he was driving the other car." Shonda sniffed. "There was another car involved, wasn't there?"

Aden desperately tried to remember anything about the occupants of that other car.

"Was there? Another car?" Cindy asked.

"Yes." Aden nodded once. "But I don't remember…the driver."

"Well, he remembers you." Shonda stated.

"This is ridiculous," Raylene interrupted. "Who cares? It's not like she *wanted* to be abducted, no matter when he first saw her or what the hell happened. It doesn't make a whole lot of difference right now, does it? How is this helping?"

"She might know something that can help us, or…well, he likes her so much, maybe she can get us out of here," Shonda said.

"You mean, you think he'd just let us go now that he has her?" Cindy asked. "You're insane."

Aden's mind was reeling. Was he really at the accident? In that other car? Had this all started two years ago on the day her father died? She closed her eyes and tried to think back to that night, but it was all such a blur. There was so much she didn't remember, and what she did remember was chaotic, disjointed. She tried to remember the faces she saw that night and in the days following, but there were just so many. They sort of ran together.

"All I know is, she was the one he saved for last." Shonda was saying. "And now she's here. So what happens now? To all of us?"

"We're getting out of here," Aden answered, opening her eyes. "All of us." Then she closed her eyes again, inhaling slowly and ignoring the questions hissing in her ears.

Maddox! Maddox Dixon! If you can hear me, we're on a mountain. A house on a mountain. In the basement. Julian Vinings is the guy. Old Mr. Vinings. Jules. His mother's corpse is here too. I don't know if he killed her... not important. Maddox! Can you hear me? Can you give me a sign or something? I know how stupid and desperate this is...but I thought I felt...you, earlier. She sighed and tried harder to project her thoughts into the darkness. *Maddox!! House on the mountain! Julian Vinings! Basement! Can you even hear me? Oh, God, I hope you can hear me. Maddox? Are you there?*

"Yeah, that address is right around here." Trey nodded to Drew. "Could be that old house you said you saw over there above the ridge?" he directed to Maddox.

"Maybe." Maddox tried to temper the adrenaline running through him.

"Holy hog muffins! You're saying Aden could be right down that path?" Cadence nearly shouted.

They all shushed her.

"What are the odds?" she spoke more quietly. "Seriously, that's just...unbelievable."

"Calm down; we don't know anything yet." Maddox tried to take his own admonition to heart.

"Call your Mom," Cadence urged. "Call it in. Come on."

Maddox walked to the edge of the stone shelf and looked down to where the trail led on to the rocky ridge and beyond as he waited for the call to be picked up.

"Mom, Julian Liddell. Katherine's maiden name...what? But wait, we found...what? No, listen...Mom? Mom!" He exhaled loudly, and it turned into a growl. "Damn it!" he shouted.

He turned to find identically questioning faces staring at him.

"They're issuing a warrant for my arrest. They found my guitar at the Vintner's Church Street house. Place is empty except for a mattress on the floor in one room and my guitar." He looked at Drew. "It was in the backseat of the car. I never got it back out after that night."

"*What?*" Cadence grabbed his arm. "Your guitar?"

"You didn't tell her about the house over there." Drew looked devastated.

"She hung up. Didn't want me to let her know where I am. They're looking for me." His voice trailed off to just above a whisper. "Meanwhile, maybe just right over there..."

"Aden could be right over there." Cadence nodded. "What should we do?"

"We should check it out," Drew answered, immediately. "The cops won't be coming up here any time soon, except to arrest Maddox." He shrugged apologetically. "They could be gone by the time we can get any cops over there."

"So it's up to us. Let's go." Cadence stepped toward the far edge of the stone.

"Hold it. We can't just go waltzing over there." Maddox scowled. "We have no idea who is there, if they're armed, what we're walking into."

"There's a rifle in my trunk," Trey announced excitedly. "And some rounds of ammo, not much, but it's better than nothing." At Cadence's raised brows, he continued. "It's been in there since deer season. I just haven't taken it out."

"Let's go." Drew nodded to him, and he and Trey leapt down the path toward the cars before anything more could be said. Maddox stood looking in the opposite direction, toward the trail's continuation along the rocky ridge.

"They're going to bring back a gun," Cadence said quietly. "I don't know how I feel about that."

"I do." Maddox sighed, "And it's all bad."

"Well, we need to do something. Soon." Cadence followed his gaze along the side of the mountain to where they both hoped Aden was still safe. "You told the cops about this place the other day, and it's only a matter of time before they show up here looking for you."

"I know. I don't guess there's any way I could convince you to stay right here? Wait for Trey and Drew to get back."

"Not if you think you're going somewhere." She narrowed her eyes. "You're not going over there alone."

"There might not be a damn thing to find over there," Maddox pointed out.

"But you don't believe that." Cadence glared at him. "I'm not going to let you—" she stopped as his face suddenly went slack, and she caught him as he swayed. "Maddox? Maddox!"

CHAPTER 20
off the map

*H*umming. Somebody was humming while their hands were busy…dishes on a tray. Cups and saucers. There are so many; this isn't going to fit. I'll have to bring the sandwiches down afterward, a second trip. But that's no bother, there are so many because she's finally home. My darling angel. A complete set. Kate would be so proud. Well, she is proud, isn't she? She looked so happy to see our angel, finally home. But I was going to change this shirt before we have tea. I can't go down like this. I wish I had time to shower, properly, but if I just change my shirt, maybe splash a little water, some cologne. Kate always liked that cologne. I hope my angel likes it…

Maddox! Maddox Dixon!

Aden! I hear you!

If you can hear me, we're on a mountain. A house on a mountain. In the basement. Julian Vinings is the guy.

Oh my God, Aden! I'm coming! We're coming. Hold on!

"Maddox!" Cadence was shaking him, and he stepped back abruptly.

"She's there! It's him. It's got to be that house. It all makes sense," Maddox gushed. "That's how he heard us. He didn't follow us; he came from the other direction. His house is right over there."

"You saw her?"

"Heard her. Saw him," Maddox growled, shaking his head. "No time to explain. Wait here for Trey and Drew. Tell them I've gone on ahead to scout things out. Call my Mom, or the police, or both. Call everybody. Tell them where the house is and that I've gone over there to check it out. But you *stay here*. Swear to me."

"You must be out of your—"

"Cadence! I have to go find Aden. I can't do that if I'm worried about where you are, now can I?"

"Well—"

"Well, nothing. The best way for you to help Aden right now is to wait right here for Drew and Trey. You have your phone?" she nodded. "Call my Mom. Hurry. Tell her everything. When those guys get back, tell them I'll be right back, and we'll go in together. You understand?"

Cadence looked at him, wild-eyed, phone in hand.

"Cadence! Tell them to wait here for me to come back. You got that, right?" She nodded, hesitantly. "Call my Mom. Tell her to hurry."

With that, he dropped the long way down onto the path beyond the rock shelf, springing upright instantly and disappearing among the rocks.

"Crap." Cadence dialed her phone, looking over the side to where he'd landed, dubiously.

"Hold on, Cadence?" Kim waved off an officer who was coming toward her and put a hand over her other ear so she might hear better. "Wait, what? Slow down! Liddell, yes. Maddox said that earlier. Where? He saw it? What's the address…no. Wait, Cadence! You tell them…Cadence? Where are you?"

"Was that Cadence?" Max asked from behind her, as she took the phone from her ear to try re-connecting the call. Kim nodded, dialing.

"The connection was awful, and I couldn't make it all out. But I think they think they know where Aden is, and we've got to convince this whole department somehow to—"

"DAVE!" Max roared, not waiting for her to finish. "Get over here!" He watched as Kim groaned, taking the phone from her ear.

"I don't know where they are, but the reception—"

"I have an idea where they've gone," Max growled as a very intense Dave Richey stalked toward them. Max didn't wait for him to reach them.

"We need a map! Maddox showed you where he took Aden, right? When they were followed? Up on one of the mountains?"

Sheriff Richey's scowl deepened. "When they were allegedly followed –"

"He showed you where they went," Max ground out, and Dave nodded, turning back toward a police cruiser with a map spread on its hood.

Kim was on the phone again. "L-I-D-D-E-L-L, yes, or try with one D, or just one L... try it all. Hurry." She hung up.

"Liddell?" Sheriff Richey turned narrowed eyes to her.

"There's a possibility that Julian Vinings, a.k.a. Vintner, may be using his mother's maiden name, Liddell."

"Where'd you get that?" he asked, halting abruptly.

"Not important right now. I think the kids are three steps ahead of us, and we've got to catch up—"

"What kids?"

"Dave, the map," Max urged.

"Hold on." Dave turned to Kim. "Are you talking about Kate Liddell?"

"Katherine." She nodded. "Could be Kate, sure."

Dave turned without a word and strode to the map. Kim and Max hurried to follow.

"This is the old Liddell place." Dave stabbed a finger on the map. "My Dad was a lawyer, and he handled the Liddell property. Kate Liddell Vintner—her married name—is well known at my church. She owns the house at Church Street where we found Maddox's guitar." Kim and Max both growled with annoyed impatience, but the Sheriff continued. "I rode along on a couple of welfare checks up to that house, years ago. But it's been vacant for...a long time."

"Perfect place to hide victims, then," Kim said.

"Could be." He stared at them both before continuing. "This," he moved his finger a minute distance on the map, "is the overlook where Maddox told us they followed a path up toward the peak of the mountain. Said he's gone there previously, knows the area well."

"I think that's where they are," Kim said to Max.

"Greer!" the Sheriff bellowed at a passing officer. "New location. Bring several cars." His finger was still pointing at the spot on the map. "Have either of you been in touch with Maddox in the last hour?"

"Sheriff, I know where you're going with this—" Kim began.

"Are you going to keep protecting him, then?"

"Dave!" Max shouted. "Maddox isn't alone up there. There are a bunch of other kids, and maybe Aden and the other women. If you don't go up there with an open mind, somebody's going to get hurt. Somebody that shouldn't."

"Max—"

"No, you listen to me. Suspicion aside, I need to know that you're going to lead your department up there with an open mind to all the possibilities for suspects. Innocent until proven guilty, Dave."

"With all due respect, Mayor, we're going up there to do a job: find those women and arrest the sicko who took them, no matter who it is. That's the job."

"So who were you checking on at the Liddell place?" Kim interrupted. "Those welfare checks?"

"What?" the Sheriff turned reluctantly.

"Who lived there that you were checking on? Katherine?"

"No, Kate lives in town. We were checking on her son."

"Julian." Kim stated, brows raised. He nodded.

"He would be…out of touch, for periods. Mrs. Vintner would ask us to look in on him from time to time."

"And why didn't you mention any of that when I brought up Katherine Vintner? And checking on the Church Street house?" The Sheriff just stared at her. "I mentioned Julian Vintner by name. It never occurred to you that you knew exactly where he lived?"

"I'm not sure it's relevant."

"Are you kidding me?" Kim snapped. "Those kids figured it out. They're up there at that house right now."

"Speaking of which, we should get going," Max huffed.

"Julian Vintner is dead," Dave growled loudly. "He's buried next to his father in the Oak Hill cemetery." Kim and Max stared. "D.U.I. back in the early 90's."

"But you're aware that someone using the name Julian Vinings introduced himself to Maddox and purchased jewelry from Aden at the store where she works. Why have you never mentioned—"

"I had my people check it out just like every other lead we've gotten, but it was a dead end. Kate Vintner's in her 80's; she lives alone. The only family she has left is a sister who's married and lives two blocks over from the Vintner house in town."

"But that house was empty, so where is Kate Vintner?"

"The house wasn't empty a week ago when my deputies stopped by." The sheriff sighed in frustration. "No one answered the door, but they could see furniture inside. Everything looked normal."

"And when were you going to fill us in on all this information?" Kim ground out furiously. The sheriff shrugged, unconcerned.

"As soon as we figured out where your son has gone."

Kim was livid. "Greer!" she shouted to the officer Dave had spoken to earlier. "We're pulling out."

Maddox winced as he sprinted along the trail; the leap from the rock shelf was much longer than he'd remembered. He should have climbed down slowly, the way he had before. Now, with every step, it felt as though there was a red-hot ice pick stabbing his ankle, and his calf burned with every movement. No time for that. Aden could be just over the ridge.

He ran bent over at the waist. He couldn't remember exactly where the house was along this trail, and he didn't want to chance being seen. The element of surprise was all that they had. Trying to run as fast as possible and do it quietly wasn't helping his ankle, but he was focused on frantically searching the quiet vacuum in his head where he was certain he'd heard Aden.

Aden! Can you hear me? I'm coming! I'm on my way! Aden?

He couldn't concentrate too deeply because he was trying to stay aware of his surroundings at the same time. This guy had followed them on more than one occasion without being detected; Maddox had no intention of either being caught off guard or tipping the creep off that he may be found.

Oh please, please, please let them be here, Maddox thought desperately. He wasn't sure how he would go on if he reached the house only to find it long abandoned. Exactly what he was going to do if he found them inside the house, he wasn't entirely sure, either. He'd worry about that when he found them. *Hold on Aden!*

The wind-twisted vegetation gave way suddenly, and a rock-strewn trail meandered through stunted growth up to the old house perched near the top of the slope. Maddox skidded to a stop and tried to catch his breath behind the scant cover of a slender, leaning pine; he leaned slowly around it to peek at the house above him. There was no movement. It was just as dilapidated and quiet as the last time he'd peered up at it from this path. The small windows from another century lined up along its façade facing the endless vista beyond the ridge's drop off. The windows that weren't boarded over were grimy, darkened by time and neglect, as was the old wooden siding, curling away from the frame in spots and grey with age and the unrelenting elements on this unsheltered peak.

There were three entry points that Maddox could see from his vantage point; a door led out from the upper story onto a small deck; there was another door on the lower story underneath the deck, and there looked to be a third entry stoop on one side of the house, but the stairs to that tiny porch had collapsed. He could climb up to it, but he'd try the other two entrances first, and there would be at least one entrance at the front of the house, too.

Unfortunately, the scant vegetation died out before the trail reached the back of the house, leaving a large and exposed, rocky yard with nowhere to hide. Maddox inched upward until he was at the edge of the yard, systematically examining every window and door for signs of recent habitation. Nothing moved. He took a deep breath and took a step into the open.

Maddox! Julian Vinings! On a mountain! I...don't know where. Please, please Maddox let me know if you can hear this. Or am I just a lunatic? Oh my God, I'm shouting in my own head...to myself. This is crazy. I've got to get out of here. Aden opened her eyes to find the other three captives subdued for the moment on their mattresses. They each lay listlessly either with eyes closed or staring off, away from her.

"We've got to get out of here," Aden repeated aloud.

"No shit," Shonda grimaced. "None of us had thought of that before. Please, go on. Tell us how you plan to get away."

"Can any of you reach your shackles? Or locks or whatever? Or maybe reach someone else's?"

"Yeah, we hadn't thought of that before you got here," Shonda sneered.

"There's a reason my arms have been bound behind my back for days, now." The blond, Cindy, sniffed. "They're completely numb now—I won't be able to use them for anything for…a long time."

Aden raised her head, hesitantly; her skull was still reverberating to its own rhythm, but she tried to ignore it. She looked around the dark space and could see several things: there was a door that looked like it led outside over by the stairs; the opposite wall was covered by a huge old, painted pegboard on which hung an evil collection of tools and sharp implements that looked as though they'd been oiled and polished many times since anything else in the room had seen attention, and lastly, on the workbench tucked underneath the stairs lay an open case that contained syringes neatly held in leather straps, and though most of the syringes looked clean and empty, there were two that appeared to have something, she wasn't sure what, in them.

"Alright, well, if nothing else, we've got the numbers to take this guy out, right? There's four of us. Is there anyone else helping him?"

"Not since the old bitch died." Raylene nodded toward the corpse. "Problem is, he never lets us loose from the chains."

"But you'd have to be free enough to change clothes, right?" Aden asked. "I mean, you can't exactly shimmy into evening gowns and party dresses while you're chained to a wall. He had to let you free for a minute?"

"Yeah, well these fancy get-ups are for your arrival, apparently. We've either been in the clothes we had on when he grabbed us, or—" Shonda started.

"Or we've been naked," Raylene finished. "There's no fancy clothes under this old sheet." Aden couldn't meet her eyes.

"Okay, well, he mentioned tea before he left. That's a fancy affair, right? Or it used to be? Didn't you 'dress' for tea?" Aden asked, desperate for one of them to agree with her. Raylene shrugged. The other two ignored her outright.

"Okay, so when he comes back down, we tell him we want to dress for tea. But he has to let us loose…"

"Seriously?" Cindy mocked, "You think we haven't tried that kind of thing already?"

"Well, has he ever freed more than one of you at a time?"

"No," Raylene sighed, and the other two looked more dejected.

They were interrupted by a long, high-pitched squeal from the top of the staircase. The door had opened again. Four pairs of eyes immediately snapped wide to focus on the first stair tread they could see descending from the unknown floor above.

"Hello, my Lovelies!" the sing-song voice floated down. "I have a treat for you all. It's a special day, you know." They watched anxiously as his feet appeared, descending carefully, tread by tread. As he descended, they could see that he was carrying a large tray crowded with items of various size. He reached the bottom of the stairs safely with his precarious load and turned toward them with a broad smile. "It's time for tea in all the civilized societies on the planet."

He set the tray on the workbench and pulled a large, round table from the corner toward the center of the room where the four women watched. Then, he brought over five mismatched chairs to set around it and produced a white eyelet lace tablecloth from a shelf over the workbench before transferring the tray to the table and began setting out the items he'd brought down.

There were four teacups on saucers, with delicate silver tea spoons laid on heavy, linen napkins, a large, beautiful china tea pot steaming from its delicate spout, a matching china plate heaped with a carefully arranged pyramid of Oreo cookies, and one, unopened plastic bottle of orange soda.

"So Oreos and orange soda are all the rage in all those civilized societies you spoke of?" Aden squinted.

"Well," he seemed put out for a moment, "Mother's biscuits were always better than any scones I ever tried, but I never learned how to make them, and she certainly can't. Her biscuit making days are over, aren't they?" To Aden's surprise, he let out a loud guffaw before continuing, "I really did mean to make a trip to the bakery for this occasion, but I just let time get away from me again." He grinned impishly. "We'll just have to make do." He smiled sublimely at them all.

"Mother always used to set out orange soda for me. I can't stand that insipid plant water you all drink, and the cookies are the best I could do, given my timeline." As he spoke, he dragged heavy cinder blocks to sit beneath each chair and then wound a heavy chain through the cinder blocks and the cross bars of the chairs. One by one, he chained each of his captives to a chair. Nobody was going to go anywhere fast.

He saved Aden for last and seemed genuinely awkward and embarrassed when he finally came to free her from the metal gurney to which she was bound.

"Aden, darling, are you well?" His smile was full of concern as he unbuckled the leather bands around her wrists.

"I'd be a hell of a lot better if you'd let us all go home," Aden spat. Julian chuckled politely, if a little forced.

"Of course, darling. I know you all miss the lives you had…before, but you'll see. You'll learn how much happier you'll be here with me. We're going to have…such a life!" he spread his arms as if to encompass them all, and his face beamed his certainty.

As he freed her legs and then her arms, Aden got a closer look at his face. It looked as though sections of his skin were starting to peel away, and then it hit her – make up. He was wearing prosthetic pieces on his face just where the wrinkles were deepest. He definitely wasn't as old as she'd first thought…as old as he'd wanted everyone to think.

"Come, my love," he helped her sit up. "We're going to have a little party in your honor." Aden surreptitiously examined him as he freed her and led her to the largest, most ornate chair at the table. "Sit here, my darling." He motioned toward the chair.

"I don't want to sit there," Aden stated. "I don't want to be here. I want to go home, to my family."

"Sweetheart," he almost growled, "*I'm* your family now. *We* are family." He indicated the other women around the table. "Now, sit. Please." His smile was a bit more strained. Aden could clearly see sparks of black insanity in his gaze, giving her goose bumps, and so she acquiesced and sat, staring at the steam curling out of the teapot's spout. She glanced meaningfully from the teapot to the other women as he chained her to the chair and the cinder block underneath, but there was no sign of response or recognition from them.

He finished Aden's bonds with another pair of leather cuff shackles. Aden noted they were all shackled the same way except Cindy, with one arm still bound behind her. He'd loosed one arm, apparently so she could drink her tea, but it was on a short "leash" from the chair back. Aden's heart sank as she felt the weight of the chains and leather. She closed her eyes.

Maddox! Oh God, I hope you can hear me. Julian Vinings. House on a mountain. Basement. Oh please God, let him hear me. Please God. Help us!

"Now." Julian beamed again, taking his seat and reaching to stroke the back of Aden's hand. "The gang's all here." She jerked it away, but he just continued. "Let's start by welcoming Aden, officially, to the family." He began pouring tea and placing cookies on the saucers as he spoke, setting each cup just out of their reach in the center of the table. "We are so happy that you're finally able to join us. We've all been waiting so long. None longer than I, of course." He chuckled. "There are so very many things we're going to do, but let's not get ahead of ourselves. Today is for resting from our busy night and making final preparations for the big day tomorrow."

"What's tomorrow?" Aden asked sullenly. She wasn't sure she wanted to know.

"Oh, it's a surprise!" he teased in his sing-song voice. "I can't wait for you to see…but I won't ruin it for you. I've worked too hard and too long to spoil it now. Everything is going to be just perfect; you'll see."

"Nothing you do will be perfect until you let us all go," Aden challenged.

"Shut. Up." He whispered, barely constrained evil emanating instantly from every pore. "You will not speak to me like that. Do you understand? Ever." Aden froze in terror at the sudden change, as did the others. She watched every movement as he closed his eyes, breathing deeply, and his tightly clenched fists slowly relaxed. After several moments, he spoke again, "There are rules. Everywhere has rules." He opened his eyes to stare blankly at Aden. "In this house, we do not speak to each other in that manner. We do not criticize." He inhaled deeply again. "But there will be plenty of time for that. The other girls can help to explain some of the rules. There is still so much for all of you to learn." He forced a smile again. "But I am here. I will teach you."

Aden moved only her eyes as she surveyed the others. They sat perfectly still, hunched over and staring at their laps. He suddenly reached for her hand again, and she flinched away, making him struggle harder with his smile.

"Don't be frightened, my angel. This is all for you." He gave a broad motion with his hand, and Aden wasn't sure if he meant the tea and cookies or her fellow captives. Not that it mattered. She closed her eyes again.

Please God! Help us. Help Maddox find us…Maddox! Julian Vinings! House on a mountain! Please…hurry. She sighed quietly, opening her eyes.

"Now, where were we?" he smiled more broadly, though it still looked forced. "I believe as Aden is our guest of honor today; she should go first." He reached for one of the cups and saucers and pulled it closer to Aden, then picked up the cup and brought it to her lips. "I'd thought to allow some of you to hold your own tea, but perhaps it's safer for everyone if I do the honors, for now, until you all learn the rules." He glanced at Cindy and then back to Aden who simply stared, mouth closed, at the cup he held to her lips. "Drink up, my darling." He tipped the cup slightly, and hot tea dribbled down her chin, startling her lips open, and she tasted the weak, overly-sweetened tea. "Good girl." He picked up her napkin and dabbed at the tea on her chin before standing. He walked to Shonda, who meekly drank in a large gulp, as did Raylene in her turn. He paused before inviting Cindy to drink.

"Have you been thinking about your earlier misconduct?" he asked sternly. Cindy just nodded without looking up. "And?" he prompted.

"It won't happen again," she said quietly.

"The rules are very important. They keep us all safe, and happy, and alive." His tone had grown ominous. "Do you understand?" Cindy nodded. "I asked you a question," he ground out between clenched teeth, roughly grabbing the arm bound behind her back and making her head snap up in pain as she gasped.

"Yes, yes I understand." He released her as her silent tears fell in her lap.

"Good. Now, drink some tea." He shoved the cup to her face, sloshing tea over the side, and breathed deeply as she sipped. "I don't tolerate unpleasantness." He said, looking at Aden. "We are a family, and we will treat each other with respect." Cindy shot him a brief, grimacing sneer, as he was behind her and wouldn't be able to see. The others kept their eyes downcast and didn't move. "We will speak and act with the utmost civility, and you will all learn to love each other as I love each of you. This will be a happy house, a happy life...there is no harm in love..." His voice slowly trailed off, and his eyes were vacant for a moment as if he were distracted, staring at a spot above Aden's head. They waited in stillness until he blinked and became animated once again.

"Alright, my lovelies. How about some cookies?" Setting their cups back out of reach, he set a saucer with cookies in front of each of them. "Go on. You must be hungry." He encouraged when no one moved. "I know I missed breakfast this morning. I have some sandwiches for you upstairs...I just thought we could have our special celebration first."

Aden still felt nauseous and didn't even want to think about food. The others suddenly moved in the same moment, grabbing their cookies as though he might change his mind.

"See? I knew you'd like them." He smiled a more genuine smile. "Aden? You're not eating."

"I don't feel very well."

"Of course, darling. The sedative...but some food will help you feel better, I promise." He watched as she slowly took a cookie and looked at it with a sick grimace, swallowing heavily. "Maybe a sandwich, then." He moved the teapot to the workbench, surveying the remaining items on the table before jogging up the stairs.

Aden immediately began testing her bonds, straining against the leather straps and searching frantically for a sharp edge that might cut through the thick leather.

"Don't waste your strength," Raylene whispered. "The only way those are coming off is when he takes them off." Aden ignored her. "Seriously, save it for when he does take 'em off you. Maybe you can get in a good swing or two…if we can just find a way to knock him out."

Aden's head came up, and she remembered the syringes lying on the workbench. Maybe if she could drag the chair over there…she tried to stand, but the chain around her waist was too tight. Her feet were shackled together like her hands and chained to the chair's cross brace. She tried jumping in her seat, attempted to pull with her legs, squirmed and swayed, and at last found that she could lift her body off the chair a fraction of an inch and drag it a tiny distance at a time, but she'd only moved a couple of inches when his tread could be heard on the stairs again. Her arms and legs were shaking with the effort she'd expended, and she knew she hadn't reached the end of the chain length when she would have had to try dragging the concrete block. Raylene was right; the only way out would be to convince him to release the chains.

"Alright, my beauties, lunchtime!" he called, setting a plate with sandwiches on the table. "Bologna and cheese today, with a little mayo and mustard." Smiling proudly, he placed a sandwich on each saucer and pushed it within reach of their hands. The others immediately began eating greedily and faced with Julian's perplexed gaze, Aden clumsily picked up her sandwich as well and nibbled daintily. She thought he might be right, and the food would help her headache if she could keep it down, and if it wasn't poisoned…then, she thought of the corpse in the room with them and almost spit out the bite in her mouth. She forced herself to swallow and laid the rest of the sandwich on her saucer. She noticed the other three women all looking at it intently.

"Still not feeling well?" He asked, concerned. "Maybe you should lie down." Before she could answer, he was kneeling behind her chair to release the chains. She glanced wildly toward the syringes again. Maybe if she pushed back hard enough, the chair would tip over on him—too late, he stood, chain in hand where he'd released it from the chair and concrete block. She couldn't think fast enough to try to come up with a plan of escape, and then her thoughts were scattered again as he put his hands on her shoulders in an overly-familiar caress. "You'll be staying down here tonight, but after tomorrow…well, it will be so much better after tomorrow. For all of us." He grinned excitedly at the others. "I can't wait to see your faces when you find out what I have planned for you." Aden shivered. "Oh, but you need to lie down, dearest, come." He helped her stand. "You'll be all better tomorrow; you'll see. It's going to be perfect." He led Aden back toward the metal gurney.

Aden stopped in her tracks, gagging as the full stench of the corpse hit her again. At the thought of lying all night on the hard metal with that thing right beside her again, the meager contents of her stomach came up, and she spent several more minutes dry heaving.

"Now, look at this mess you've made," He was growing angry.

"It's the smell." She pointed at the corpse.

"What? Mother?" He looked annoyed. "You get used to it. Besides, it's just one night. After tomorrow, you'll sleep with me, and we'll both be in a new skin—but look, there I go giving away secrets." She shuddered again, not knowing which sounded worse.

"Can we move…her? Or the table? I can't stand it."

"But Mother couldn't wait to meet you! She watched over you all last night."

"But it's her, the smell, that's making me sick," Aden spoke meekly, knowing how volatile his anger could be. "And if tomorrow is such a big day…"

"Oh, alright," he huffed, dragging Aden after him as he walked toward the corpse. He didn't seem at all affected by the putrid stench that made tears stream down Aden's face. "Mother, our angel has requested some privacy for this evening." He went behind the wicker chair and began dragging it backwards, tugging Aden along on her chain. "You'll have to go back in the closet for now. I know you didn't misbehave or break any rules, but, well, that's what Aden wants."

"Aden wants to go home," she said quietly, fighting the nausea. He rounded on her, violently backhanding her so hard she crumpled in a heap to the floor with her shackled hands held above her head by the chain in his hand.

"What did I tell you?" he raged. "What did I *just* tell you?" he yanked viciously on the chain, dragging her across the floor toward the closet. "Now, you'll be all bruised and battered tomorrow…damn it all! You've ruined it! You've ruined everything." He stopped dragging her long enough to send a sharp, swift kick to her midsection, knocking the breath out of her. "Now, we'll have to postpone…damn it! All my preparations…"

CHAPTER 21
breaking out

Maddox crept quickly across the yard, bent at the waist, and put his back to the wall of the house. The lower door was to his right; he'd have to bend down under what looked like two boarded up windows, just in case anyone may be able to see through a crack. He took a deep breath to calm the loud beating of his heart so he could listen for any sounds from inside the house, but there was nothing that he could hear above the soft, sighing breeze.

Creeping slowly toward the door, he kept his back to the wall, staying under the windows. He stopped just to the right of the door, listening intently. He was leaning to peek in the door's grimy, glass window when he heard a voice from inside and jumped back again.

"Alright, my beauties, lunchtime!" he could clearly hear the voice. Instant chills ran down the length of his body. This had to be it; he'd found them. Pulling out his phone, he hammered out a text to his Mom.

Found 'em. N on Parris Falls, last overlook w/parking before NC border. House on peak just S of overlook. Hurry.

He desperately wanted to get a look inside, but he didn't want to risk being seen or heard. As he deliberated, he was startled by sudden movement to his left. Trey, Drew, and Cadence were creeping, one-by-one from the tree line at the side of the house and were headed to join him. Of course. He motioned wildly for them to stay put, but they ignored him, again, of course.

Trey led the way, holding a hunting rifle; Drew came next armed with a tire iron, and Cadence joined them carrying what looked like a nail file in one hand and a large stick in the other.

"Shhh, they're inside." Maddox hissed under his breath.

"You saw them?" Cadence hissed back. Maddox just shook his head.

"Heard them. We can't let him know we're here, or he might run or do something to the girls." Trey and Drew nodded. "Let's go back before he hears us." Maddox nodded back the way they'd come.

"Did you see Aden?" Drew asked, frowning. Maddox shook his head. "Are you sure they're in there?"

Maddox sighed. He thought so, but he wasn't sure. Before he could answer, Drew was creeping up toward the door. Maddox put a hand out to stop him, but Drew waved him off. Bending underneath the window in the door, he went to the other side, and they all froze, listening.

"Now look at this mess you've made!" they heard Julian growl.

Drew carefully leaned toward the window and frowned furiously at what he saw. Maddox immediately peeked from the other side and inhaled sharply. Cadence took a step toward them, but Trey stopped her. Maddox and Drew both leaned back from the window, staring at each other intently.

"What?" Cadence hissed. Trey put a finger to her lips and shook his head.

"Aden." Maddox's face was hard as he answered her, and Cadence's eyes grew even wider than they'd been. They froze as they heard movement from inside, something being dragged. "We should get back over there—" Maddox began quietly, pointing to the brush at the side of the house.

"What did I tell you?" an enraged scream broke the silence, and they all jumped. "What did I just tell you?"

Maddox and Drew were immediately back at the window. Maddox used the noise to try the doorknob, which was locked, of course. He glanced down inside to see a padlock bolting the door to the frame, and he grimaced. There was more screaming, and he looked up just in time to see the bastard kick Aden viciously as she lay on the floor. His eyes met Drew's, equally enraged, and they nodded once to each other. The plan had never been to confront this piece of filth, but that had just changed. Maddox nodded toward the side of the house, and they began a fast retreat to find an entrance they could breach.

Trey was leading the way and stopped them with a gesture as he reached the corner and peered carefully around. He slid around the corner, waving them to follow and crouched just beneath the overhanging porch stoop to the side entry.

"I need you guys to get back to the road and direct the cavalry up here. There's got to be a driveway—" Maddox began, pointing toward the front of the house.

"Screw that. I'm going with you," Drew hissed angrily, surveying the door above them.

"Does anyone have reception up here?" Maddox asked, digging his phone out of his pocket. "Mine is spotty at best— Damn. I tried to send a text to my Mom, but looks like it didn't get out."

"I've got one bar," Cadence announced.

"Okay, yours was working better than mine earlier, too." Maddox nodded. "I need you to go back through those trees and make your way around front, but stay out of sight! Look for the driveway; there's got to be a way in from the highway. Stay off it, but follow it down to the road. Maybe the reception will be better there. Call my Mom or Dad and get them here now." Cadence was furiously shaking her head. "Listen to me," he hissed back, "I need you to do this. We don't have time to waste arguing. Please, Cadence," he begged.

"What if he's not alone? What if there's somebody out front?" Trey asked.

"That's why she needs to stay in the trees and keep out of sight," Maddox answered, frowning heavily. "I don't like that she's here, either. I told you all to wait by the cars, you know, but she can do this."

Trey looked at Cadence, and she gave a determined nod. "Going. I'll bring the cavalry as fast as I can." Maddox sighed and nodded.

"Be careful." He and Trey said at the same time. She smiled at them both and darted into the brush.

"We tried to make her stay back." Trey shrugged.

"I know. It's Cadence." Maddox shrugged back.

"Hey, it looks like one of the panes of glass is broken out on the door up there and is only covered with cardboard." Drew hissed, drawing their attention back to the house. "I can't hear him anymore, but I'll bet he's still downstairs." His eyes were dark with rage.

Maddox nodded, and the three of them climbed as quietly as they could up onto the rickety stoop. It swayed wildly, but it held. Drew pushed on the cardboard covering the missing pane, and it fell silently inward. Reaching in, he tried the doorknob. It was locked, and it would take a key to open. His probing hand also found another padlock

361

that was bolted to the door and the frame beside it.

"Crap. Padlock," he growled.

Maddox was beside him, carefully pushing on the other panes to see if any were loose. He found that the wood frame and the slim pieces holding the glass in place was badly rotted. He jiggled the wooden slat above the missing pane and it didn't take much for it to crack away. He caught the falling pane of glass at the last second. Placing it quietly on the floor, he stood back up to find that Drew and Trey were already dismantling other sections. After a few moments, they had four panes in the bottom corner out, large enough for them to be able to see in more easily and survey the room. Drew stuck his head through the opening to look around while Trey and Maddox impatiently waited.

"I think we can get more of this glass out, and we'd be able to climb through." Trey whispered to Maddox.

"Hold on," Drew hissed, pulling his head out of the opening. "That hinge holding the padlock looks pretty loose." Putting the tire iron through the opening in the window, he began trying to use it to lever the hinge away from the doorframe. "If I can get this thing behind it…" he gritted quietly.

"Shhh. Don't let that thing fall." Maddox warned. Drew rolled his eyes at him and continued with both hands stuck through the door. Maddox opened and closed his fists in desperation as he waited, wondering what was transpiring downstairs and praying that Aden was going to be okay when they got there. There was a wrenching noise and a loud crack as the hinge gave way, and they all froze for half a second before Drew reached in with his hand and began pulling it the rest of the way out of the wood.

"Almost there," he whispered, straining. He repositioned himself and reached in again. His arms shook as he pulled with all his strength. When the last screw holding the padlock hinge to the doorframe came suddenly loose, Drew's arm hit the last pane of glass on the bottom row, and it cracked, a large piece falling out on the porch at their feet. "Crap."

"Let's go." Maddox reached in and turned the doorknob. It was still locked. "Damn it!"

Cadence held her phone at arms' length, slowly turning in place. A breeze whipped through the surrounding wind-bent pines and shorter brush and bushes as she stopped and began tapping out a text to Kim and Daddy Max that began with the address they'd found for this place, then:

911! Aden, others, bad guy all here. Hurry!

362

She waited to be sure the message was sent and then shut off her phone, shoving it back in her pocket. Glancing momentarily at the overgrown gravel drive just visible through the trees, Cadence turned and started back toward the front of the house.

This side of the structure was dominated by a deep, covered porch, with a wide set of aged wooden stairs leading up from the bare yard. Cadence hesitated a second behind the last tree before lightly sprinting to the corner of the house's stone foundation and the stairs. She froze, panting quietly, trying to hear anything above her own thumping heartbeat. All she could hear was the ever-present breeze rushing up the mountainside and around the house. She looked toward the side of the house where the guys were trying to play hero. *Well, what am I doing?* She thought, frowning. *I don't even know; but I refuse to just go sit on the side of the road.* She inched herself upward from her crouched position just enough to peer over the rough edge of the porch. The porch roof sheltered a solid-wood front door, centered mid-structure and flanked by two windows on each side. This side of the house looked to be in better shape than the back. Though what little paint that was left was peeling away, the window panes were all in place, and the whole façade looked much sturdier than she'd hoped to find it. *How are we ever going to get in there without him hearing us?* She scowled at the door as her thoughts raced her heartbeats. *Unless…A* mischievous smile slowly replaced the scowl. *We don't necessarily have to get inside. We just need to stall the bastard.* The smile turned predatory as she turned and surveyed the yard.

"I *told* you that *I'm* your family now. *This* is your home." Grabbing a fistful of her hair, the demented deviant wrenched Aden up to a standing position and screamed directly into her face, spittle flying. "So impatient! You don't even know what I have waiting for you, all that I've done! For you. This is all for you, you ungrateful—" he stopped himself, throwing her back to the floor and heaving with rage. Lying on her side, Aden pulled her knees up and sobbed as quietly as she could in a fetal position, eyes screwed shut. "I *saved* you! I saved you all. You have no idea what I've sacrificed, the betrayals, I went against them…to build this family. We're a perfect set. *Look* at us!" He kicked her. "This is a *happy* day!" He pulled her head up by her hair again, making her shriek in pain, and bent down until they were eye-to-eye, his heaving breath hot against her tear-traced cheeks. "You. Will. Be. *Happy*!" he screamed. "*You* are the angel, *my* angel." A deep, guttural groan erupted from his throat and spiraled up into a soul-splitting wail of torment as he dropped her and stepped back, wiping spit from his lip with the back of his hand. "There is no harm in love." He grunted quietly. "No harm in love." He rocked slowly on his feet, staring at the back wall. "No harm in love."

Aden watched him surreptitiously from under one lowered eyelid. The other eye was swelling closed fast. She desperately tried to subdue the trembling sobs wracking her between the waves of pain; she needed to be absolutely still, absolutely silent; not draw any attention.

He was still rocking slowly above her, mumbling his evil mantra under his breath. The prosthetic makeup pieces had come loose in several places, flapping listlessly with his slow motion. The skin underneath was smooth and tan, and there were tracks of the darker skin tone running down from his sweating forehead, washing away the pale powder. It had also begun to wash away whatever he'd used on his hair, revealing jet black under the temporary gray. His eyes stared, blank and black, directly ahead. His mumbling slowly wound down into a taut silence, making Aden shiver.

She couldn't see the others from where she lay, but there was absolutely no sound. They must be as motionless as she was trying to be. Her breath was ragged as she sucked in trembling gulps of air between suppressed sobs. Every part of her ached and throbbed from the force of abuse or the knotted tension of crouching and clenching to present the smallest target possible.

He stood motionless and silent above her with his eyes now closed. Somewhere toward the back corner of the dim and muggy room, a monotonously slow drip grew ominous in the heavy quiet. The sound was magnified and warped, like seeing yourself in a crazy carnival mirror, making the drops sound heavier, more viscous, evil.

Slowly, he opened his eyes and his black gaze sank to coldly caress Aden with a glare of pure malevolent intent.

Dear God, he's going to kill me. Shuddering involuntarily, she watched his calculating eyes follow the small movement.

"Are you testing me?" he hissed. "Have I not proven that I am worthy of your love?" Aden remained frozen, watching. "You don't even know!" he roared suddenly, making her jump. "You don't even know what *he* planned to do to you! What I saved you from! *Do you?*" He crumpled suddenly to straddle her folded form with his knees on either side. Grabbing her head between his hands, he turned her battered face to look directly at him. Bending slowly, as if to kiss her, he stopped a fraction of an inch away from touching her lips with his own. "Dolls," he breathed. "Playthings." His frenzied glare bore into the eye she could still open. "Objects that he can torture at whim. That's what you are to him. All of you." He sat up, but remained atop her. "*He* wants to hurt you. To slash and maim and burn. He wants to revel in your suffering, in your screams. He will rip your flesh to shreds and roll with exquisite, naked abandon in your hot blood. *That* is his plan…and I saved you. Saved you from him. Because I love you." He paused, wiping at a trickle of blood below her swollen eye with a callously heavy hand, eliciting a whimper from her. "Because I saw it with my own eyes. The angel rising from the depths. Rising from certain death. You came to me…in the form of my own Mother, when she was young. When she was innocent. Before he had changed her. You showed yourself to me. *Me!* Not to him." He blinked rapidly and looked around. "I took you for my own. To love. To cherish…" his gravelly voice faded out, and his face went blank again.

Dear God in Heaven, please, please help me. Help us all. Please Lord, give me strength. She began to unwind one leg in minute increments; if she could just move it a bit and kick him in the crotch as he straddled her…but he caught the small movement and became animated once more, looking down at her with his head tilted to the side.

"There is no harm in love." He shook his head. "There is punishment for breaking rules. Lessons must sometimes be taught in blood. But no *real* harm. I will never do you real harm because it is done in love. What he would create in death, I will deny with love. With us. This family."

Aden stared up at him, bewildered. His mood, his whole demeanor, was constantly shifting, and his words made no sense. They would never be able to rationalize their way to freedom; Julian was completely insane. He was going to kill them.

This should do it. Cadence grinned to herself, standing with one foot on a head-sized chunk of granite lying just inside the tree line at the front of the house. She whipped out her cell phone, turned it back on and ignoring the notifications that popped up of incoming texts—she knew they would be from Kim and Daddy Max, she furiously typed out a message. Tapping her foot impatiently on the rock, she waited for the notification that her text had been sent and then turned the phone off again. Pocketing it, she began levering the large rock on its side with her foot and waited, listening intently for sounds of the guys' approach.

After several minutes of silence, she started to worry. *What were they doing? It shouldn't be taking this long.* She'd just decided to make her own way toward them, back to the house, when she was startled by the shuffling snap of a branch behind her.

Whipping around, nail file in hand, she didn't see anyone, but the hair at the nape of her neck stood on end.

"Maddox? Trey?" she called, hesitantly quiet and ready to spring, just in case.

"What are you doing here?" Maddox stepped out from behind a tree, and Trey and Drew came forward from a different direction. "Is everything ok?" Cadence just frowned, confused. "We thought this could be a trap."

"Um, no. Just me."

"Why are you here? Did you get hold of my Mom?" he demanded.

"I sent her the address, told her we'd found them, and asked for her to bring the cavalry," Cadence related.

"And what are you doing back *here*? So close to the house?" he snapped back.

"Are they on their way? How long?" Drew interjected, before she could answer.

"And what is this plan you texted us about?" Trey added.

"Shut it. All of you. They have the address, and I'm assuming, given the situation, that they'll be here just as fast as they can get here. In the meantime though, I thought we could create a diversion."

"Diversion?" Maddox repeated.

"Distraction." Cadence nodded, grinning.

"I know what it means," Maddox growled.

"While we're stumbling around out here, trying so hard to sneak into that house, well, I don't even want to think about what could be going on inside. Hold on!" She held up a hand to halt Drew's interruption. "We don't necessarily have to go inside. If we create a diversion out here, he'll have to come out, or at least come upstairs and investigate."

"And we could jump him when he comes out," Trey concurred.

"Or go in while he's distracted." Drew narrowed his eyes.

"I was thinking more about just stalling, keeping his attention until the police get here." Cadence scowled, rolling her eyes.

"What kind of distraction are you talking about?" Maddox asked, eyeing the rock she continued to roll side-to-side with her foot.

"The world was so much gentler in Kate's time." The lunatic looked sadly down at Aden, still underneath him. "When I found her, she told me...how the world was different in her generation. I so wanted to go back and live in that time, back when society was civilized, when the nightmares humanity perpetrates upon each other, were still dark dreams. Before *our* time, when the evil began to seep out into the light of day, into reality. Perhaps when I tell you my story, you will understand...and you will love me. For I have triumphed." He smiled as a tear escaped to leave another dark track down his powdered face.

"We will live as they did, genteel, in our very own dream." He softly caressed her bruised cheek. "You'll see, my angel. When we leave the evils behind, we will be so happy. All of us. Together." Aden remained locked in immobility.

Oh God, I think we're running out of time! Maddox! Can you hear me? God, please hurry! Hurry! Julian Vinings! Mountain house! Please! Somebody find us! Please, please.

Julian's deteriorating face went slack again as he stared at nothing, retreating into his own world.

What if nobody's coming? Nobody knows where we are. Nobody's going to save us. Aden's horror and black dread were permeating any lingering hope. The harsh reality burned intense and bright: they were going to die. She closed her eyes and relaxed her tensed muscles. *I don't want to die today.* She tried to breathe slowly and deeply, but it hurt; her heart most of all. *Maddox, if you're there, if I don't make it out of this...I want you to know that I loved you. Love you. And these have been the best weeks of my life, knowing you. None of this is your fault. You couldn't have saved me. We're just out of time...*She took a shuddering breath and opened her eyes.

He was still 'out,' sitting slack, his full weight on her with his dark eyes deeply hooded. He could have been asleep, sitting up. Her side throbbed where he'd kicked her, and she thought a rib or three might be broken. Her left eye was swollen shut, both legs would have hellacious bruises from his vicious kicks, her scalp burned where it felt like he'd ripped out half her hair, and yet the bastard proclaimed this as love. *He doesn't know love. Not like I do. I'd almost feel sorry for him...if I didn't want to kill him myself.* She looked up at him again, unmoved. *Was he really there during the accident? Has he really followed me all this time? And the big one...Why am I here? Why are we all here? What do the other three have to do with any of this craziness?* She bleakly looked around again; the ominous drip continued in the corner, the only sound. None of this made sense. It would never make sense, he was just crazy. She would never understand the answers, even if she knew them. *And it doesn't matter. It's all so pointless. So random and irrational. I refuse to allow this waste of humanity to hurt me. To hurt any of us. We're getting out of here. Now.*

With her single eye, she frantically searched for anything within reach that she might use as a weapon. Nothing. *Damn it!* She glanced up to find him watching her. She must have moved.

"Do you understand?" he asked quietly. *NO! I don't understand, you crazy asshole,* Aden thought as she tried to nod, but it hurt too much.

"Yes," she spoke instead. He carefully examined her face.

"No. You don't. Not yet. You will learn. I will teach you." He turned to look behind, toward the others and rose up on his knees again before he continued to speak. "You will—"

Without warning, Aden thrust her knee upward, into his groin, with all the strength she could muster. He let out a small, gurgling "oomph" and rolled to his side, off of her, drawing his legs up just as Aden had lain. In the same second, Aden rolled away from him and staggered to her feet; a task made more difficult by her shackled hands and dragging the heavy length of chain. She whipped the end of the chain out of his reach and turned to her suddenly animated co-captives.

"The keys! Get the keys! On his belt!" Shonda was screaming at the same time Raylene shouted.

"Knock him out! Knock him out!"

Cindy was crying hysterically and moaning something that sounded like "Don't leave us!" over and over.

Ignoring them, Aden stumbled with laser focus toward the workbench under the stairs. Julian was still down, moaning, but she knew she only had seconds. Grabbing the two syringes she'd spied earlier with liquid still evident inside, she pulled the cap off one as she turned back to where he'd lain. He wasn't there.

An inhuman grunt was all the warning she had before she was hit by his flying tackle, landing hard on the unforgiving concrete floor. All the air in her lungs whooshed out and he climbed on top of her, further preventing any intake of breath.

"Where do you think you're going?" he snarled. "I'm not finished with this lesson just yet." He back-handed her again, hard, and she heard the bones in her neck crack loudly as her head was whipped to the side.

Oh God, did he just break my neck? The horror of that thought startled her lungs to suck in air. She was breathing, not getting full or deep breaths, but she was breathing. She kicked her feet and bucked wildly. *I can still move! My neck's not broken. Maybe. Still hurts like hell.* He was still on top her, but he hadn't gotten hold of her wrists yet. She surprised him by going completely still for a half-second, except for her arms that whipped up and plunged the uncapped syringe's needle deep into his neck. He screamed with an even deeper rage and, ignoring the syringe in his neck, grabbed Aden's throat in both hands.

"Go to hell!" She screamed with her last breath, depressing the plunger with her thumb. *Oh God, this is it. I can't breathe!* She fought wildly, kicking and bucking, but he just squeezed harder. The pressure in her head rose rapidly. *The sedative's not working!* She fumbled with the cap on the second syringe, trying to keep it hidden between her shackled hands, and finally got it off. There were black spots forming in her vision as she savagely plunged it into his side.

"No! Damn you!" he screamed, wild-eyed, plucking the syringe from his side and throwing it to shatter across the room. The first syringe still hung from his neck, but he didn't seem to notice. "I saved...you." It was like someone was turning his volume down, his voice shrinking as his eyes rolled back in his skull and he crumpled, limp and heavy, on top of her once more.

Gagging and coughing, Aden tried to open her crushed airway. After a moment, she felt the relief of a thin stream of air and sucked it in greedily. *Have to get up.* She thought, fighting for oxygen. Slowly, she was able to build up the volume of air she could take in with each breath, and the darkness that clouded her vision started to recede. Dragging in a large breath that hurt her throat, she pushed and rolled herself and her captor to the side just enough that she could begin to drag herself from underneath his weight.

She realized the other women were still screaming; all she'd heard for the last several minutes was her own pulse pounding out what she believed would be her last few seconds. *Keys. Have to get the keys off his belt.* She strained to free herself again. *Almost there. One more big push.* Kicking with the meager strength she had left, she pushed him off and paused, gasping on the floor. *Just a second. Need just a second.* The volume of the women's screams swelled into her consciousness. *Gotta breathe.* She envisioned everyone in the room with a big volume dial embedded in their abdomen and it almost made her smile. *Moron. Get up!* With another painfully deep breath, she rolled to her side and sat up - tentatively, as the room wasn't quite steady. *Oh, that's me that's not steady. Breathe. Okay.*

She wasn't sure if she could stand up without passing out, so she crawled to where Julian lay in a rumpled heap. His keychain was clipped to one of his front belt loops, which was now underneath him. *Great.* Taking another deep breath, she finally managed to roll him over just enough that she could get her shackled hands underneath while propping him with her shoulder. The large, full key ring came loose more quickly than she'd expected, and she let him drop back to the floor. *Okay.* She breathed.

"Hurry! He could wake up again!" Shonda's screams were the loudest, penetrating the beating in her head.

"Shut up," she finally managed to croak. "Coming." Slowly, she crawled toward the line of mattresses and the other captives, dragging the keys.

"My hands are more loose than yours, bring me the keys so I can help you," Raylene directed. Aden crawled over and collapsed on her back on the grimy mattress as Raylene took up the keys and freed Aden's hands first, then started on the shackles on her own feet.

"Let me do that," Aden said, sitting up slowly, and she freed Raylene after taking the keys.

369

"I'll get the others." Raylene jumped up. "Should we tie him up or something?"

"After we kick him in the head a few hundred times." Shonda glared at his inert form.

"Second that." Cindy sniffed.

Aden was blinking her eyes and tentatively turning her head on her battered neck. "You okay?" Cindy asked.

"Will be. Soon as we're outta here." Aden started to smile, but it hurt. Raylene had freed Shonda and went to kneel by Cindy when Aden realized she was still naked. She'd seen what looked like a pile of clothes between the mattress and the bare concrete wall and she went, slowly, to retrieve them.

By the time Raylene had Cindy free of her bonds and the first three captives were hugging each other, Aden reached the clothes and began to drag them, crawling back toward the others.

"Thank you, sweetie." Raylene was sobbing as she took the clothes and began to dress. "Do you think you can stand?"

"Yes, getting out of here," Aden rasped. She saw that Cindy and Shonda had taken the ring of keys to the door by the stairs and were trying them in both the padlock and the doorknob, one by one. She dragged herself to one of the chairs and pulled herself up to sit on it. *Progress.* She felt nauseous, and her head might explode, but she was sitting up.

"I think we should chain him, just in case," Raylene said, pulling her grungy shirt over her head. "Can you girls come help?"

"Let's just *go*," Shonda glowered. "We gotta get *out*."

"But if he wakes up—" Raylene started.

"Go, Shonda," Cindy directed. "It only takes one of us to find the key. Help chain him up so we can get away without looking over our shoulders."

With a long look out the door's uncovered glass panes, Shonda reluctantly walked toward Julian. Raylene had dragged the nearest chair as close to where he lay as the chained cinder block would allow and was pulling on the chains to move the block closer.

"How are we going to lift him into the chair?" Shonda asked.

"Don't have to. Just get the chain around him," Aden rasped out. "Use the shackles.

Or chain through his belt loops and then through the chair and the cinder block." She realized a pair of the thick leather shackles still lay on the table beside her. She thought they were the ones he'd used on her ankles. She tossed them to Raylene and slowly stood, holding to the table and chair back for support.

The room swayed a bit, and her knees felt weak, but she could do this. She went to help the two women bind their captor.

"Crazy bastard," Raylene said under her breath as she rolled him over with her foot. Shonda fit the leather cuffs to his wrists as tight as she could pull the straps, and then yanked some more for good measure. Roughly wrapping the chain around his neck, through his shackled hands, and then around his feet before threading it through the chair rungs and the cement block, they were silent.

"Let's go!" Cindy called, throwing the door open at last. "Thank you God—" She was interrupted by what sounded like an explosion upstairs. It sounded as though all the windows had been blown in, glass shattering amid several heavy thumps that shook the ceiling above them. They all instinctively froze for just a second.

"Go!" Raylene hissed, pushing them all toward the door.

"What if it's the police? Our rescue?" Cindy asked.

"What if it's the *he* that Kray-Jay was going on about—the one he supposedly saved us from?" Shonda asked.

"Let's just go," Aden urged, stepping unsteadily toward the door. Shonda put an arm around her waist and helped her outside. They all took an instinctive deep breath of fresh air as they cleared the doorway.

"Which way?" Shonda asked.

"There's a path right here." Cindy pointed. "Dunno where it goes."

"I think I do," Aden said, blinking to confirm the familiarity of the vast view. The arc of unrelenting blue was broken only by white wisps of cloud and the green, blue, and purple uneven peaks marched into the horizon. The valley below was obscured by a milky flow of low clouds that crept up the mountainside toward them on the sluggish breeze. "But they'd expect us to go that way. Let's go over there, into the trees and make our way around front, toward the highway."

"Stay hidden." Raylene nodded. "And quiet."

"But if it's the police?" Cindy whispered.

"Then we'll just surprise them. But we need to see who's up there before they see us."

As quickly and quietly as they could manage, they darted into the trees on the opposite side of the house from the stoop where the guys had tried to break in. Aden directed them in a wide arc, away from the house, to come around the front side.

"Are we really going along with this?" Drew grunted, shifting the weight of the large rock he carried.

"We're going to run up on the porch, throw our rocks through the front windows, and get back behind those trees over there as quickly as we can," Cadence stated for the third, or was it fourth, time.

Drew ignored her and looked to Maddox and Trey, eyebrows raised.

"Well, it should buy Aden and the others some time at least. We'll draw him away from them and hopefully keep him away until the cops arrive." Maddox shrugged uncertainly.

"As long as we don't get ourselves shot." Drew shook his head.

"Come on! Let's go." Cadence turned and led the way toward the house. They all paused at the shadowy edge of the tree line, looking and listening for any sign that the psycho had come back upstairs already. She looked questioningly to Maddox, who shifted his rock and looked back with worry. "Okay then." She took off running toward the porch stairs at full speed, followed and quickly overtaken by the others. They pounded up onto the porch, each hurling their large rocks through a different window. Cadence and Trey jumped back down the front stairs while Maddox and Drew both hurdled the porch railings and ran back to the trees. They hid behind tree trunks or bushes at the farthest distance where they could still see the house and waited, panting.

Cadence could see Trey and Drew from where she hid, listening for any sound from the house. They tensely stared back as long minutes dragged by.

"Do you think he heard it?" Cadence hissed. Trey put a finger to his lips and turned his head, straining to listen all around them.

"Could be going out the back," Drew whispered toward a neighboring tree. Maddox's scowling face peeked around it. "Why else wouldn't he—"

"Nah, I would have come up quietly, hide until I figured out what was going on." Trey frowned. "You'd want to know what was going on out here before you made your move,"

Cadence sighed. "Well, should we—"

"Stay where you are and don't move," Maddox instructed. "He could be sighting us with his own rifle from inside there, right now."

"Crap." She stood with her back to the tree trunk between her and the house and watched the three guys as they continued to survey the surroundings. "So we just wait?" They stared back without answering.

"Do you hear anything?" Raylene whispered as they picked their way carefully through the dense brush on the opposite side of the yard from where Aden's friends kept tense watch. They were all barefoot and tried to avoid the pinecones, sharp sticks, twigs, and sharp rocks lying on or buried by the thin carpet of dried, copper-colored pine needles.

"If it was police, there'd be more noise," Cindy said, eyes huge with terror.

"And we'd see them, vehicles or something, at least. I can see the house every now and then through the trees, and there's nothing. It's just all quiet." Aden frowned, coming to a stop. They all stopped with her to listen.

"Well, if it wasn't the police breaking into the house, should we re-think going to the highway?" Raylene hissed.

"We can stay hidden, stay in the trees, but I think the highway's our best bet to get help," Aden answered her.

"You seemed to know where we are, right?" Cindy looked at Aden with barely concealed suspicion. "Is there anything close by? A house or store or something?"

"I'm not positive that I know where we are. I just thought I recognized the view back there from a scenic overlook I've been to."

"So how do you know the highway's this way?" Shonda joined in.

"Well, there's got to be a road leading to the house, right? And that road will lead to another road." They stared back, unmoved.

"So if we *are* where you think we might be…" Cindy paused.

"There's nothing around for miles that I know about." Aden sighed. "But if we are on the same mountain, the highway would be this way." *I think.* She turned and trudged ahead, and they followed after a beat. *Maddox! Where are you? All I want is to lie in your arms. With a big glass of water. Water would be good.* She looked back to the others, following warily behind. "We're free, ladies, and we're going home."

CHAPTER 22
breaking back in...seriously

Where's the damn cops?" Drew hissed, staring at the house. "How long ago did you send that text?"

Cadence dug the phone out of her pocket and turned it on.

"Are you sure the text got out?" Maddox asked.

"Yes, brother dear. I made sure." Cadence glared back. "It went out..." she frowned at the screen, "about 8 minutes ago."

"That's all?" Drew hissed.

"They're cops. With sirens. They'll be here soon," Maddox said with an equally worried frown.

"Shh!" Trey held up a hand as he intently searched the trees toward the gravel drive. "Thought I heard somethin'." The others froze and stared in the same direction. "Twice now, I thought I heard voices, whispers, in that direction." They all strained to listen, then turned their attention to the softly rustling shadows surrounding them.

"Wind maybe?" Maddox offered after several moments. They continued to listen, dividing their attention between the house in front of them and off to the side where Trey had heard something. After a few more moments, Trey looked to the others and shrugged.

"Dunno. Maybe it was nothing."

"So what now?" Cadence prodded. "We just sit here?"

"We don't know who's in that house, how many, if they're armed, if they're still even in there..." Maddox muttered.

"I'm going to go take a closer look," Drew announced, his attitude daring a challenge. He retrieved the tire iron, leaning against a tree trunk from before their mad rush of the front porch, and purposefully edged through the trees toward the house.

Maddox sighed heavily, uncertainly watching Drew's advance toward the side door where they'd broken out the glass panes. He glanced at Cadence and then to Trey. "Stay here with her. Text us if you see anything." Trey just nodded, holding out the rifle he carried.

"Take this." When Maddox shook his head, "You'll probably need it in there before we would out here."

Reluctantly, Maddox gave in and took the gun before following Drew's route. He caught up with him at the tree line on the side of the house, directly across from the disintegrating side porch.

"Anything?" he breathed. Drew shook his head, turning to note the rifle Maddox carried, barrel down.

"Nothing's moved in there that I can see." He paused, listening. "I'm gonna climb up and take a peek through that door." Maddox started to protest, but the eerie quiet was breaking down his uneasy patience. He nodded and followed Drew to stand with backs against the rough wooden siding just beside the small side-porch. With barely a beat, Maddox set the gun on the porch floor that was at eye-level where they stood and pulled himself up. Drew watched anxiously as he crouched below the door's broken out window panes, grabbed the rifle, and slowly raised up to peek inside. Seconds later, he sank back into his crouch to shrug and shake his head to Drew. Nothing.

Glaring sternly at each other as they plotted their next move, Drew sighed quietly and wiped sweat from his forehead before motioning Maddox to come down. With a last hasty look inside, Maddox dropped to his side.

"Nothing. Glass is everywhere from the rocks we threw in, but it doesn't look like anybody's walked through it. Not in that room, anyway. Everything looks the same as before," he whispered, watching Drew's hazel eyes harden into a decision.

"They could all be dead by now," Drew breathed apprehensively. Maddox's jaw clenched as a shudder went through him.

"They're not dead," he insisted, whether to himself or Drew, neither was sure. "The window on this corner of the front porch is smashed to hell. We could climb through." They locked eyes for a tense second before they moved simultaneously toward the front corner of the house.

376

Maddox stopped at the corner, peering carefully around to the front. Seeing nothing, he squinted and surveyed the yard and surrounding woods, before looking for signs of Cadence and Trey where they'd left them in the trees. He couldn't see them, which was good on the one hand, if they were staying hidden, but not so good if they had moved, or been forced to move.

"I don't see 'em either," Drew hissed.

"Aden is more definitely in imminent danger," Maddox huffed, dragging his focus back to the porch. Handing the rifle to Drew, he pulled himself slowly over the porch railing to stand, back to the wall, beside the window. Swallowing the acrid steel anxiety coursing through him, he quickly surveyed inside before motioning for Drew to come up onto the porch. Drew handed him the gun first and quietly hoisted himself up to mirror Maddox' stance on the other side of the window.

"Alright, then," Maddox breathed with a determined smile that Drew reciprocated. Maddox climbed inside as quickly and quietly as he could, immediately crouching behind the arm of a large, overstuffed settee. The crunching grind of glass on wood was the only sound in the musty dimness. Motioning Drew to wait, he surveyed the room and the entry hall beyond, listening for the slightest breath of movement. Detecting nothing, he stepped lightly away from the window and crouched behind a wingback chair where he had a better vantage point and shot angle on the room's only exit into the foyer.

From outside, Drew watched his movements with trepidation. He was just waiting for the dark wood floorboards to creak and groan, or for one of the many fragile knick-knacks scattered about to be knocked or jarred to shatter on the floor, or for Maddox to stumble into any of the heavy, over-stuffed and carved-to-death mahogany furniture pieces choking the dark space, but Maddox glided through the shadows unhindered with just the slightest scraping of shattered glass underfoot. He realized Maddox was motioning him inside before turning to cover the room's wide arched entry with the rifle.

Drew stepped carefully through the window and crouched where Maddox had beside the settee to listen. Maddox didn't flinch a muscle as he sighted down the rifle's barrel into the hallway beyond. Drew's eyes slowly adjusted to the dim interior as Maddox breathed slowly, carefully, straining to detect the slightest sound.

A rank smell insinuated the shadows, mixing with the musk of furniture that appeared to have been rotting in place for several decades, and above it all, the smell of old garlic floated through layers of dust. Maddox rose slowly, keeping the gun trained on the entry and quietly went to one side of the arch, grabbing a needlepoint-covered pillow from the long, curved sofa on his way past. With a warning glance at Drew, he tossed the pillow across the entry hall and into the dining room they could see beyond. It

377

skidded across the dining table's top, knocking over a candle in its small, porcelain holder. They both winced at the sound as the candle thumped and rolled off the table to hit the floor. Comparative to the silence of the last several minutes, they were sure it couldn't have gone unnoticed. Maddox peered around the corner into the hallway.

The wide corridor ran from the front door to a door that would open on the deck at the back of the house. A flight of stairs hugged the other side of the wall where Maddox leaned. Following its ascent with his gaze, he saw that the upstairs landing was narrow and turned quickly out of sight. Seeing and hearing nothing from above, he stepped out to the stair's foot and carefully peered beyond it to see two doors on his left and a larger, arched opening on the right that looked like it led to the kitchen. Taking a deep breath, he stepped out into the open hallway and motioned Drew to follow him, keeping his back to the closest wall. He passed the first door, tucked under the stairwell, probably a closet, and hesitated, listening to the utter silence. In his head though, his thoughts were screaming. *Aden? Where are you? Are you okay?*

Search procedures would have called for him to check out the two closed doors, 'clearing' those rooms of potential danger before moving on, but he had to get to Aden *now*. The kitchen was ancient, grimy and reeked of old grease and garlic. There were clearer signs of recent habitation in this room: dirty dishes, paper plates, Styrofoam takeout containers, and old food stacked on every surface. There was a narrow passage between the kitchen and dining room. A door stood, slightly open, nestled between floor-to-ceiling cabinetry on one wall. A gleaming, new metal hinge with an open padlock hanging from it contrasted with the old faded green plank door, red-brown showing through the worn scratches and scrapes from underneath. The ancient linoleum was sticky, yellowed, and brittle, crackling underfoot. Maddox shuddered again, staring at this door he'd seen before, through someone else's eyes.

"Wait. That door creaks," Maddox hissed as Drew reached for the knob. Drew raised his eyebrows quizzically. "Never mind, just go slow."

Listening intently, Drew took a deep breath and slowly pushed the door open, pausing as it squealed, slicing the silence. They froze, waiting, but nothing moved. Letting out a pent-up breath, Drew swung the door all the way open into a dank, putrid stairwell. The stench that pervaded the house seemed to emanate from below. Maddox stopped Drew as he started toward the first stair and whispered in his ear.

"I should go first. I've got the gun." Drew looked like he would argue, but then nodded with a tormented look. Maddox understood. *Who knew what they'd find down there?* Drew stepped aside, and Maddox closed his eyes, summoning the memory of Aden's face in the lantern-light, her hair reflecting the flame in a red, satin shimmer that framed her awe-struck eyes gazing back at him with wonder, with love.

Inhaling deeply, he opened his eyes and started down the stairs. Though he went slowly, straining eyes and ears, he wasn't overly concerned with the sound of their descent. If anyone was down there, they already knew someone was coming.

Reaching the point where his feet and legs would be revealed to the room below, Maddox suddenly rushed, pounding to the floor below, sweeping the wide, dark space with the gun. Drew followed him down and slipped behind Maddox to the now-open door at the bottom of the stairs, carefully peeking outside.

"Damn it! They're gone!" Drew shouted. "Aden! Can you hear me?"

"No, no, NO!" Maddox roared at the wooden ceiling. "They were right here!" Maddox rushed heedless into the dark room, past a large table set for a meal, and he stumbled on the corner of a scummy-looking mattress on the floor. There were a line of mattresses, and chains snaking everywhere...cast-off leather cuffs. Where were they? "Aden!"

"Over here," Drew's voice brought Maddox's attention away from the open door leading outside to where he stood on the opposite side of the room. From Drew's hesitant posture and tone of voice, Maddox wasn't sure he wanted to know what he'd found. He couldn't breathe, a sudden weight crushed his chest. He didn't want to know. Didn't want to see. "Maddox." Drew turned to look at him.

Slowly, Maddox dragged his unwilling feet toward Drew, refusing to look down where Drew's attention was focused. He stared intently at Drew's face, trying to read the emotion there.

"Isn't that him?" Drew looked utterly...baffled. Maddox looked down to see that the inert figure on the slimy concrete floor was a man. Confusion, elation, tempered by a cautious hope all flooded him in a split second.

The man's head was turned away, a long, heavy chain coiled his neck more than once, to wind around and through his leather-cuffed hands, and then on to bind his feet before snaking through the rungs of a nearby chair and concrete block. Drew knelt down and felt for a pulse on the man's neck before turning the slack face toward the light coming in the open door.

"He's alive. It's him, right?"

Maddox nodded tightly, suppressing the longing to kick and punch the bastard as viciously as he'd attacked Aden. "It's him."

"So where's Aden? And the others?" Drew's face mirrored the anguished confusion Maddox felt. His eyes had better adjusted to the darkness down here, and he walked toward the back of the room. The smell became more unbearable with every step, but there was something back there. On a chair?

"Holy—" Maddox turned back, gagging as he leaned on the upended rifle's stock.

"What is it?" Drew rushed over. "Oh my God!" They both retreated to the open doorway. "A corpse! There's a rotting corpse in there!" Maddox just breathed deeply in and out, in and out. "Do you think it's one of them? The kidnapped women?"

Maddox peered back into the rank darkness. "I don't know, but we know it's not Aden, and there are at least two others that may still be alive somewhere." Drew nodded.

"Okay, so somebody took that psychopath out." He looked to Maddox with a hopeful air. "Do you think they escaped? Got the drop on him somehow?"

"Maybe. Did you see the syringe lying beside him?"

"Oh God, what if he had an accomplice?" Drew looked sick again. "A partner, who double-crossed him and took the girls?"

"We're wasting time. They're not here." The waning adrenaline was fueling a tired rage. "There was another door back there, behind the...corpse." He swallowed hard. "I'll check it out."

"Should we look upstairs?" Maddox was shaking his head, but Drew continued. "Just to be sure."

"Okay, I'll meet you back here, see if there's any sign of which way they went." Maddox pushed the gun into Drew's hands and took a deep breath to hold as he rushed inside, past the corpse. The only other door in the oblong, sweeping concrete room was another wood-plank door like the one at the top of the stairs. This one looked as though it had never been painted, though it, too, had a gleaming, new padlock hanging open from the aged wooden frame. Maddox flung the door open to find a black closet, out of which two insects flew and another landed drunkenly on the door's frame. Flies. He could only see that the closet wasn't deep and didn't harbor any humans, captive or not, before he slammed the door closed and got back outside to suck in another breath. Even out in the open air, he could still feel, still taste, the smell of death as if it coated his body, the inside of his nose and throat.

He breathed deeply as he walked in a slow circle just outside the door looking for signs of passage. The bare rock of the mountain was covered only sporadically with thin moss or pockets of soil where vegetation could take root. Their only hope would be to spot a patch of vegetation that was obviously trampled or disturbed. Spiraling outward and searching frantically, he kept finding himself staring down the worn trail that led down to the ridge, below his "secret" lookout. Could they have gone that way?

"Nobody's upstairs," Drew announced, jogging through the basement door. "But two of the bedrooms have wedding dresses lying on the beds. Four wedding dresses total. And rings, and bouquets." He looked nauseated. "What do you think –"

"I don't want to think," Maddox said harshly. "I want to find her." Drew stared him down, and they glared at each other for several seconds before Maddox dropped his head in frustration. "Drew, man, just ignore me." He offered a conciliatory hand. "Let's go find your sister."

Drew sighed and shook the offered hand. "Let's look on this side of the house." He led the way around the side they hadn't seen yet, scanning the ground and the woods to their left. Maddox almost called him back, with a swift glance to the trail behind but thought better of it. They could circle the house first, meet up with Cadence and Trey, and split up. One group could search the drive up from the highway, and the other could check out the trails in the back.

Pointing the gun toward the woods and sticking close to the wall, he caught up to where Drew had paused close to the side of the house.

"I think we should go through the woods," Drew pointed to the trees much closer to the house on this side. "Circle around the yard, cross the drive, and meet up with Trey and Cadence over there."

"We're on the same page." Maddox nodded. "Lead on." They darted into the trees, slowing when they were several feet in to proceed with more caution. There were more trees on this side of the house, still mostly pines, wind-warped into shapes reaching toward the mountain's peak, and the summer-dried brush was more abundant and tangled, slowing their progress and raising their anxiety.

"Well, we're good and hidden from view over here," Drew remarked in a whisper after several minutes. "But all these brittle branches...we sound like a herd of elephants coming through." Maddox had been silently stewing over their loud passage, coupled with the slow progress. He'd thought they would have come across the driveway up to the house by now.

"Have you seen the driveway? Any clearing through the trees?" Drew just shook his head and trudged on.

Maddox wasn't sure how many more agonizingly slow minutes passed before Drew stopped abruptly.

"Gravel crunching. Hear it?" he whispered, pointing to their right. Maddox nodded. Definitely movement of some kind. "Could be Cadence and Trey?" Maddox considered the suggestion. "Heard us coming and came to investigate?"

"Let's go find out." Maddox turned toward the sound and could see the gravel drive within a few steps. They were above it, on a small rise looking down on the rutted, overgrown trail that cut through the dense trees. A thin veneer of old gravel gathered in the deeply-worn tire ruts and water-carved gullies with the baked red clay rising up, visible in the high spots. There were patches of thigh-high grasses, weeds and even small trees that had taken root on the sparsely-used path.

"There." Drew pointed to the opposite bank where one section of bushy growth still swayed softly, like something had just brushed past it.

"Aden!" Maddox's sudden shout made Drew jump. "Can you hear me?" They froze, listening and searching the shadows across the way.

"Maddox?"

An electric chill slithered down Maddox's spine as he recognized Aden's voice.

"Maddox! Drew!" With blatant relief in her tremulous voice, she limped into view. Maddox and Drew hurdled down the embankment and up the other side where Aden and the others emerged from the shadowy brush. They both embraced her in a long hug. She grunted in pain, but held them both tightly when they tried to pull away. "But, how? What are you doing here?" Aden mumbled from the center of their embrace.

"What do you mean, 'what are we doing here?'" Drew chuckled.

"How did you find us?" Raylene asked. "Are the police here?"

"They're on their way." Maddox reluctantly released one arm from around Aden to acknowledge the other women. "Are you all okay?" They nodded.

"I can't believe you found us!" Shonda gushed.

"Yes, how?" Cindy began, but Maddox interrupted.

"How did you get away?"

"Aden." Raylene beamed at her. "She's one tough…" her voice trailed off as they all turned toward the sounds of approach from behind them.

"Aden!!" Cadence crashed through the underbrush almost knocking several people down in her rush to embrace her friend. Trey, grinning from ear to ear, followed on her heels.

"Cadence? Trey?" Aden was enclosed in another multi-armed embrace as they both hugged her awkwardly, as Maddox wouldn't remove his arm from around her waist.

"What happened? How'd you get them out?" Cadence asked Maddox.

"We didn't." Maddox shrugged, gazing at Aden. "They were already gone when we got there."

"We just found them right before you got here," Drew added.

"Yeah, we heard Maddox shouting." Cadence nodded. "Is everybody okay? Where's Julian?"

"He's chained and unconscious in the basement," Maddox answered, scrutinizing Aden's battered face.

"What? How?" Cadence began.

"We should get them to a hospital," Trey interrupted. "Cadence and I can go get the cars and pick you all up here."

"Right." Cadence frowned, surveying the disheveled women. "Maddox, I need your car keys."

"Wait, listen!" Cindy shushed the group, and in the sudden silence, they could hear gravel crunching and the hum of more than one engine as a car slid around the sharp curve and into view, coming to a grinding stop below them. The police car's doors flew open and uniformed officers vaulted out, guns drawn.

"Nobody move!" one of them bellowed. "Stay where you are!"

"Holy crap!" Cadence raised her hands above her head while everyone else just froze. Maddox was glad he'd dropped the rifle to the ground in his rush to pull Aden into his arms. Aden and the other women just looked too tired and previously traumatized to react to this latest confrontation.

More vehicles, marked and unmarked, had followed the first car in, and people began to swarm the scene.

"Get those paramedics in here!" A female voice shouted, and Maddox turned to see his mom and dad running toward them, the Sheriff following just behind. "Lower those weapons! Stand down!" she glowered.

"Aden!" Mayor Max Dixon barreled through the still-tense ring of officers to hug her gently. "Oh my, are you okay?" She nodded, grimacing at the pain of trying to smile again, and he turned to the others. "You're all here?"

"Where's Julian?" Kim asked abruptly.

"He's in the house. Chained in the basement," Maddox answered. At the questioning looks from Kim, Max, and the Sheriff who'd joined them, Raylene began to speak but was interrupted.

"One male suspect was last seen in the house. He may be restrained in the basement, but use caution." Dave Richey relayed to several officers nearby. They followed lines of other police who'd already passed by on their way toward the house at the end of the road. "Sorry, ma'am, are you well enough to give us a brief version of events?"

Raylene nodded as the Sheriff glared at Maddox, still holding Aden at his side. "Was this man involved?" he indicated Maddox. Raylene, Cindy, and Shonda looked confused, and Aden sighed deeply.

"Yes, he found us, well, he and Aden's other friends here." Raylene pointed uncertainly at Drew, Cadence, and Trey. "After we got out of the house, we went through the woods following the road hoping we'd find the highway. They were out here looking for us."

"Had you seen this man before today?"

"No." Raylene looked at Maddox, bewildered. "I don't understand."

"Can you identify the person or persons responsible for your kidnapping?"

"Yes. Julian Vinings and his mother, Kate." Cindy and Shonda nodded confirmation.

"His mother?" Kim asked before the Sheriff.

"Yes, she helped him. Sweet-looking old lady, she was the distraction."

"Where is she?" the Sheriff asked, flagging down a passing uniform.

"Dead. In the basement. He killed her." Raylene grimaced.

"Were there others?"

"Not that we saw." Raylene shook her head slowly. "But Julian spoke about somebody else. A man he claimed to have 'saved' us from."

"Was there a name?"

"No." Raylene glanced to the other women for confirmation, but they all shook their heads. Just then, paramedics arrived.

"Let's get you all taken care of, ladies. We'll talk more later," Sheriff Richey said gruffly, and then he turned to Maddox. "I have more questions for you and your friends," He added. "But let's just get a brief understanding of how you all came to be here." He looked pointedly at Maddox.

"We saw Aden when we first got here, through the window, but when we got inside… we came in the front, upstairs, and they went out the back basement door." Maddox added.

"You entered the house?" the Sheriff glowered.

"Start at the beginning, *quickly*," Kim overrode him.

"You know that we found this address online and sent it to you. We knew it would take you a while to get here, so we thought we'd try and verify if this was really where he was, where he was holding them, before you got all the way up here. We were just going to take a look, but we saw him viciously assaulting Aden, and we had to do *something*." Maddox spoke directly to Kim. "We broke out the front windows as a diversion, to get him away from the victims while we stalled, waiting for help to arrive." He glared at Sheriff Richey. "We hid and watched, but there was no response to our diversion. It was absolutely still, so we went inside and found Julian in the basement. Somebody had knocked him out and chained him up, and it looked like they left through the basement door, in the back of the house."

"And the gun my officers found on the ground right over there? Is that part of this 'diversion?'" the Sheriff practically sneered.

"It's Trey's hunting rifle. It was in the trunk of his car. We had it along as a precaution," Drew broke in.

"We can sort that out later, Sheriff," Kim bit out. "Have the families been notified yet that we've found them all safe?"

"Burnett! Get all these kids in squad cars." He turned to Kim. "And yes, the families are being notified and will be escorted to the hospital where they'll meet the victims. Now, let's get up to that house."

"Just go with them for now." Kim nodded to Maddox, Drew, Cadence, and Trey. "Stay with them?" She asked Max, and he nodded.

Kim and the Sheriff practically raced up the drive to the house's front porch. Officers were already inside, climbing through the windows to gain entry, as the front door was padlocked. Kim followed the Sheriff through a window as he barked orders for the padlock to be cut off the door and for someone to call up the paramedics. They stepped into a dingy sitting room, shattered glass covering large areas. Kim bit back a smile when she saw the large rock that had shattered the marble top of the sofa table. As diversionary tactics went, she was sure this would have made an impression. They followed another officer through a dining room and to a door in what Kim would call a butler's pantry. The foul stench of death that she'd detected outside had grown and enveloped them in earnest. Heavy-hearted dread settled in as they descended the stairs. The open door at the bottom of the stairwell wasn't enough to dissipate the reek, nor did it dispel the inky dankness of the concrete room.

Stepping around the sheriff, she went directly to where three officers stood above a male body on the floor.

"He's out cold," one of the officers informed her. "There's a syringe lying over here." He pointed to his feet. "We've called for a saw to get these chains off."

"No keys?" she looked around the horror-laden room.

"No ma'am, not yet," he answered.

There was another group of officers further back in the corner of the large room. Taking another long look at the face of the monster whose mind she'd touched, she looked up at the men surrounding him.

"Take your time with that saw."

"So the body over there does look like it's Kate Vintner," the Sheriff said quietly from behind her. Turning, she glanced over his shoulder to the corpse slumped in a wicker chair. He grimly inspected the line of soiled mattresses and the chains and shackles lying about. "The bedrooms upstairs are apparently laid out for a mass wedding." At Kim's expression, he continued. "Wedding dresses, four of 'em, are laid out on the beds. There's wedding bands and flowers and—" he stopped, shaking his head tiredly.

"So what do you think happened here?" she asked. He looked surprised that she'd ask his opinion, and he sighed, surveying the room.

"I don't know. None of this is rational, Agent Dixon."

"It never is, Sheriff Richey."

Holy hog muffins! I can't believe we really found them!" Cadence beamed, straining to see where Aden and the other three women were being carried on stretchers toward ambulances waiting down on the highway. "We should follow them to the hospital."

"The police aren't done questioning all of you yet." Max frowned, watching personnel scurry all around them. They'd all been herded into squad cars for a while, but as Aden was being loaded on the stretcher, Maddox and Drew had jumped out and followed. Then, they'd all gotten out to greet each of the women as they were carried past.

"They're not paying us any attention anymore, and they can ask questions in the hospital just as easily as here," Cadence said.

"They're not gonna let you see Aden, you know," Max pointed out. "Not for a while."

"Hey, has anybody talked to Aden's Mom?" Cadence asked, whipping out her phone.

"Dave said the families had been notified," Max said. "Do you have her number?"

Cadence didn't answer him as she was already dialing. She put the phone to her ear and danced agitatedly as she waited. "Mrs. Garrett! It's Cadence..." she was obviously interrupted by Janet on the other end. "Yes, we saw her. She's pretty beat up, but she seemed okay."

"Cadence—" Max began, scowling.

"Yes, they all seemed okay, you know, under the circumstances." She waved off Max's objection. "Well, she was walking and talking, lots of bruises but...yes. So you're on your way to the hospital?"

"Are they taking them to Oconee Medical or Spartanburg Regional?" Max asked her.

"Which hospital – oh, okay. Bye!" re-pocketing the phone, she explained. "Kim was calling through, and she probably knows a lot more than we do right now." Max and Trey nodded. "So what do *we* do now?"

"Let's find out which hospital they're going to—" Max grabbed Cadence's arm as she started to skitter away.

"Okay, let's go." She bounced impatiently. Trey flashed a sympathetic smile to Max before taking her hand in his.

"Take a breath, breathe. We found 'em, and we'll go see Aden as soon as we're able; she's in good hands, getting the help she needs." Max squeezed his shoulder in appreciation.

"As I was saying," Max intoned, "Let's find out which hospital they're going to and then find Kim. Maybe we can get an official okay for us to leave."

"Sorry." She still held Trey's hand and reached with the other to take Max's and squeezed them both. "Kim can probably tell us which hospital they're going to, also."

"They're not going to let Maddox ride in the ambulance with her, I'll bet," Trey said, looking toward the bend in the road the medical procession had already rounded. "Maybe Drew, he's her brother. But we should go get Maddox."

Max nodded. "I'll go down there. No need for all of us to hike back and forth in this heat."

"I'll go. I can't stand just hanging around. It's so anti-climactic," Cadence said.

"Anti-climactic?" Trey laughed outright.

"Yes, after all that we've done today, here we sit just kickin' up dust in the driveway."

"That's a good thing. It means we've done all that we can do for right now." Trey said, hugging her briefly. "Hey, Maddox has his phone, right? We can just call him instead of walking down there."

"If we want to just keep standing here," Cadence pouted and lifting her damp, blond hair off the back of her neck, fanned briskly with her hand.

"Calm down. I'll give Kim a few minutes to finish her call with Janet, and I'll call her phone. Maybe then, we can leave." Max said. "While we wait, why don't you two tell me about your escapades this afternoon?"

Cadence immediately launched into an animated play-by-play of the day's events and was still rapidly speaking a little while later, when Maddox walked around the bend toward them.

"Drew went with Aden in the ambulance. They wouldn't let me leave until it was cleared by the Sheriff," Maddox explained as he joined them.

"I'll see if I can get hold of Kim now." Max pulled out his phone.

"Trey said they probably wouldn't let you in the ambulance." Cadence kicked restlessly at the gravel as Maddox shrugged.

"It was worth a shot. I just wanted to be with her every second I could."

"Well, hopefully, we can get to the hospital soon," Cadence sighed.

"Did they tell you anything about her condition?" Trey asked. "She looked pretty rough."

"No, not really." He smiled, "but she was feisty enough to correct several people who referred to them as 'the victims.'"

"Correct them?" Cadence asked.

"She said they aren't victims, They're survivors."

Cadence nodded, smiling.

"Okay, well, we're out here by the cars, or as close as they'll let us get. See you in a minute." Max hung up and turned to them. "Kim is speaking with Sheriff Richey now. She's coming out here soon, but she says the two of you might as well leave," he said to Cadence and Trey. "It's going to be a while before they wrap up things at the scene here. They're asking if you'd both go to the station tomorrow to answer more questions."

"You mean answer the *same* questions, over and over again." Cadence grumped.

"Maddox, they want you to stay," he hesitated, "Apparently, the questions they have for you are more pressing." Maddox groaned loudly in frustration.

"Because I'm still a suspect. After I found her. Led them to her. Broke their case for them."

"More so *because* you found her. How would you know where to look if you weren't involved in the abductions? And then there's your guitar at the other Vintner residence. And—"

"You *know* how we found them," Maddox ground out.

"Yes, but are you going to tell the Sheriff about your visions? Think he'll buy it, if you did?" Max asked softly.

"But we found him on the Internet, the address," Trey broke in.

"But what led you to look for that name in the first place?"

"Well, Maddox and Aden had both met him before, right?" Cadence offered.

"And there's the fact that they *know* you've been here before," Max continued quietly. "You told them yourself."

"Well, not about this place, exactly," Maddox glowered. Max started to speak again, but Maddox held up a hand to stop him. "I know. I'm in trouble."

"But you didn't *do* anything!" Cadence pleaded.

"Except save all four of those women." Trey nodded grimly.

"We *all* saved them." Maddox smiled wanly. "Team effort."

"Go team." Cadence waved listlessly.

"Yes, go team." Max forced a smile. "You should all be recognized publicly for what you've done here today. I'll have to look into that."

"Yeah, we just need a contact inside the Mayor's office." Cadence rolled her eyes.

"Seriously, you should all be very proud. I know I'm proud of all of you."

"Will you still be proud if your son goes to jail?" Maddox mumbled.

"You're not going to jail."

"They'd have to *prove* that you're guilty, and they can't. Because you're *not*," Cadence said loudly.

"Shh!" Max said quickly. "We shouldn't be talking about this here."

"We *should* be on our way to the hospital," Maddox said.

"Yes, yes, let's walk toward the house and meet Kim and the Sheriff. I'll see if they can't get a policeman to drive you and Cadence to your car," Max said to Trey.

They walked as far as they were allowed to go, within sight of the house now bustling with people, and waited for Kim to come out. When she finally did, the Sheriff and another officer was with her, and neither looked happy. Kim approached Maddox with a worried look.

"The Sheriff would like to ask you a few questions. I've asked to be here, but if you don't want me to—"

"Why wouldn't I want you to?" Maddox looked from his Mom to his Dad and then to the Sheriff, who stepped forward.

"This is Lieutenant Barnes. He's going to take Cadence and Trey home."

"My car is here. Well, parked at the overlook just up the road. He can just drop us there," Trey said, and the Sheriff nodded.

"We'll catch you later, man," Trey said to Maddox.

"See you soon." Cadence nodded, hugging him before they left with the officer. The Sheriff watched them walk away several paces before turning abruptly to Maddox.

"How many times have you been to this house before?"

"I've never been 'to' it before. I've seen it from the trail down on the ridge behind the house."

"So you've never been inside it, prior to today?"

"No, I never got close to it. It was just an old house." He shrugged.

"What about 273 Church Street? Ever been there?" Sheriff Richey watched his face closely.

Maddox shook his head. "No, not that I'm aware of. I'm not familiar with the address. Well, before we found it online today, looking up anything we could find about Julian Vinings."

"Did you know Katherine Vintner?"

"No."

"Do you own a guitar?"

"Several, but I only brought one with me on this trip, and I'm assuming that's the one you're interested in."

"Could you describe it for me?"

"Black Fender Dreadnought with a cutaway. Strap is pretty basic, black."

"And the case?"

"Oh, um basic beat-up hard-sided case. Inside is lined in red, and I'm sure you found the card I keep in there with my name, address, and phone number."

"Can you tell me how your guitar came to be inside the Vintner house at 273 Church Street?"

"No Sir, I cannot."

"When did you last see the guitar?"

"I played it at Drew's the other night and laid it on the back seat of my car for the drive back to the hotel."

"What night was that, exactly?"

"Ummm, Thursday night."

"This past Thursday?" Maddox nodded. "Did you take it out at the hotel?"

"No, I forgot to. Normally, I'd never leave it in the car, but I completely forgot it was back there."

"And when did you realize it was missing?"

"I didn't know it was missing until my Mom said it'd been found at the house on Church Street."

"So you just didn't notice it was gone in all that time?"

"No, with everything that's happened over the past 48 hours, including spending most of last evening in your precinct and waking up to find Aden had been kidnapped, I haven't given any thought to the whereabouts of my guitar." He struggled to maintain his composure.

"The man inside the house, do you know him?"

"Not really." Prompted by the Sheriff's raised eyebrows, he continued. "He approached me at the café' on the square, asked to sit at my table because it was crowded. We chatted a bit. He said he was looking for an anniversary gift for his wife. I referred him to Aden at the jewelry store." The guilt was plain on his down-turned face.

"When was this?"

"Umm, I'll have to think about it…sorry, it's all sort of running together, and I haven't had much sleep."

"Had you seen or met him before that?"

"No, that was the only time I've laid eyes on him until today…Oh, but I did notice, well, the makeup that was coming off when we found him in the basement earlier." The Sheriff ignored that and continued.

"So did he go to the jewelry store while Aden was there?"

"Yes." He closed his eyes. "She sold him…earrings, I think it was, for his wife. We both thought he was just a friendly old man."

"When you entered the house today, Drew was with you?"

"Yes."

"And the male individual in the basement was already unconscious?"

"Yes, unconscious and chained to a chair and cement block."

"You said earlier that you'd seen him assault Aden?"

"When we first peeked into the house, through the door in the back. Drew and I both saw him hitting and kicking her, and Trey and Cadence were there. They heard him screaming at her."

"What did you do?"

"We went to try and find a way in, at first." The Sheriff waited. "We had to do something to make him stop. We didn't want to let him know we were coming, in case he did something…worse. Or try to take them and leave before you could get here. Then, Cadence suggested we distract him, get him away from the women for as long as we could…again, the plan was to just delay him until the cavalry could get here, but after we smashed the front windows, there was absolutely no response. Not a sound. Drew couldn't stand the thought of what could be happening. Well, I went with him, and we went inside the house. When we got to the basement, the door was open, and we found Julian on the floor."

"Julian?"

"Yes, he introduced himself as Julian Vinings, when I met him. Told Aden to call him Jules." He shivered involuntarily. "Of course, we found out there's no Vinings in town. That's what led us to Vintner and Kate and Liddell and this house."

"And how did you come across all that information?"

"Online, on our phones." The Sheriff exchanged a tired glance with Kim before sighing.

"Julian Vintner, Kate Vintner's son, died in 1991 or 1992." Maddox just stared back, digesting this piece of information.

"So who's that asshole in there?"

It was the Sheriff's turn to stare quietly before he turned to Kim and Max, behind him.

"Alright, you can take him home for now, but don't leave town." Before Kim could voice the ire that showed plainly on her face, the Sheriff abruptly walked away.

"So are there any theories about who this guy might be?" Max asked Kim.

"Not yet. Nobody on the force who's been down there so far has recognized him."

"Oh wait, the corpse," Maddox grimaced. "Who is...was that?"

"The Sheriff thinks it's Kate Vintner. He said she grew up in this house. When she got married, she moved to the house in town, had one son, Julian who inherited this house, but he died several years ago. Everyone assumed the place had been vacant since then."

"Looks like it was, until recently." Maddox looked toward the house. "So, can we go see Aden now?"

"Well, it may be a while before you can get in to see her, but yes, you can leave. I'll get somebody to drive you to your car and then drive Max home." Kim smiled at them both. "Give her a hug for me."

Maddox gave a nod and looked around impatiently for his ride.

"…then as Raylene, Shonda, and I were chaining Kray-Jay to the cinder block, Cindy had finally gotten the door open, and we heard what sounded like an explosion on the first floor, above us."

"Our diversion!" Cadence beamed.

"Well, we didn't know what was happening or who was up there, so we just got out as fast as we could. We went through the woods, and, well, I guess you've heard the rest." Aden tried to smile, but it still hurt. She was propped up in the hospital bed that was surrounded by her family and friends, crowded into the small room.

"I can't believe you call him Kray-Jay. That just cracks me up." Cadence smiled.

"Yeah, when Shonda first explained it to me, even in the middle of…well, I thought about you. How you'd probably love it." Aden chuckled, grabbing her tightly wrapped ribs with a grimace. "Okay, so you all promised that after I told you how we'd escaped, you'd tell *me* how you found us."

"I know you've heard some of it from the police." Janet squeezed her hand. She hadn't left Aden's room for the two days she'd been there.

"Yeah, the police are taking all the credit in the news interviews, but it was Maddox and Trey who found you," Drew said, nodding to the two of them, standing side by side on the opposite side of Aden's bed.

"Mostly Maddox, you mean." Trey nudged him with an elbow. "But you were there too, Drew."

"It was most definitely a group effort," Maddox said.

"He went up to your Special Spot and tried to contact you…you know." Cadence grinned. "So is the mental reception better up there?"

Aden inhaled sharply, looking around at all the smiling faces. "It's okay," Maddox assured her. "They all know I'm a freak."

"You're a hero," Drew corrected. "We wouldn't have found them if it wasn't for you."

Everyone began talking at once as they related the events of their search, each adding details to the others' stories. Aden sat quietly listening with a small smile. *A miracle. It's a miracle that they found me, I mean us. Thank you God, for your help, and thank you for my friends and family. Thank you, thank you.*

The next day, the doctors released Aden from the hospital. The building had been surrounded by news media from almost the minute Aden and the others had arrived, so they wheeled Aden to a side-entrance where Trey's car waited. The reporters had pegged Janet and Drew's vehicles, as well as Maddox's, filming and photographing their every move in and out of the hospital over the last few days.

Janet, Kim, and LeighAnn had gone ahead to prepare for Aden's homecoming leaving Drew, Natalie, Maddox, Trey, and Cadence to escort her home. A few hospital staff and a couple of police officers waited in the corridor by the exit. Nearby, a small cluster of people surrounded another patient in a wheelchair.

"Raylene!" Aden waved. "How are you?"

"Going home!" The woman beamed, with tears in her eyes. "Thanks to you. And your friends, I understand?"

"I didn't think it was public knowledge." Aden looked up at them.

"Word gets around." Raylene smiled. "I never did get to thank you all."

Aden had barely begun to nod when Raylene's husband, son, and several other family members came forward to greet, thank, shake hands, and hug the entire group.

"Well, I didn't do anything," Natalie kept repeating while greeting and hugging.

"I heard that Shonda and Cindy haven't been released yet," Aden said to Raylene as the families and friends spoke around them.

"Yeah, Cindy's arm isn't doing so well, and Shonda was there longer than any of us, immobile and malnourished, but they say they'll both be okay eventually." Aden nodded. "I got to meet Cindy's little boy yesterday. Her sister brought him by my room."

"Yeah, I met him too."

"I wonder what they'll tell him, how they'll explain…"

"I don't think there is an explanation," Aden said, just above a whisper.

"Are you gonna be okay?" Raylene asked, just as quietly. Aden grabbed her hand, nodding.

"You?"

"Yeah, I've got them." She nodded toward her family.

"Yeah, we're lucky." Aden smiled.

"Survivors." Raylene beamed. "And we're going home."

Sheriff Richey came through the door and strode up to them, smiling. "This is a happy day, ladies."

"It is. Thank you, Sheriff," Raylene answered.

"Yes, thank you," Aden chimed.

"Okay, we're going to escort you out quickly. The drivers of your vehicles have already been advised to pull out as safely, but quickly as possible."

"And I thought we were over all the drama." Aden rolled her eyes towards Raylene.

"Sorry, but you ladies are big news. Now, I know you've both requested privacy, so we're going to do everything we can to give you that. Just keep your head down and leave the rest to us."

"You take care." Raylene squeezed her hand one last time before the nurses pushing their chairs separated them.

"You, too." Maddox's hand replaced Raylene's as they walked slowly toward the exit. "Is it really crazy out there?" Aden sked him.

"No worries." He smiled. They stopped just inside the door, and Aden could hear a crowd of voices outside.

"Ok, here we go," the Sheriff said, pushing open the door.

Raylene and her family were the first outside, welcomed with a roar of questioning, demanding voices. As Raylene's group cleared the doorway and hurried to their vehicle, Aden got her first glimpse outside.

Despite the subterfuge they'd tried to employ, the media had caught on and were being held back by officers and police barricades on the opposite side of the waiting vehicles. Aden's chair was suddenly propelled forward toward Trey's car, back door open in readiness. Before she knew it, Maddox had half-lifted her into the back seat, dark as someone had hung towels on the back windows to block the view. She'd barely gotten settled on the seat before Maddox was beside her, closing the door.

"Go," he directed, and Trey hit the gas, leaving the noise behind. Cadence turned around from the front seat with a huge grin.

"So how does it feel to finally be sprung?"

"There just aren't words to describe it." Aden smiled briefly, then sobered. "I can only imagine how it feels for Raylene, or Shonda and Cindy, for that matter. Shonda was there since February! I don't know how she...how she did it." They were all quiet. "I was only there for what? Twelve hours? And I don't think I'll ever be the same..."

"No." Cadence shook her head slowly. "I think it's made you stronger. You escaped from an impossible situation, all by yourself. Just remember that."

"I wasn't alone." Aden stopped Cadence's interruption with a gesture and continued. "No, wait. I wasn't. I mean, I did knock out Kray-J, but I had the others there with me, cheering me on, and I had you guys outside, I just didn't know it." She smiled as Maddox squeezed her hand between them. "Actually, Maddox...I haven't had a chance to tell you...I mean, it's been so crazy the past few days."

"What?"

"I heard you. Or felt you. Or something." She turned to face him, wincing at the pain in her ribs. "When I woke up from the sedative, there were a couple of times...I swear I thought I knew you were nearby."

Cadence watched them, wide-eyed, and a tear slid down one cheek.

"I know how crazy that sounds." Aden searched his eyes, dark in the gloom of the covered windows.

"It's not crazy at all," he answered quietly, staring back at her. "I was screaming through heaven and earth, space and time, trying with everything I am to reach you, to find you."

"You did it. You found me." Tears were rolling down Aden's cheeks now as she saw moisture gleaming in his eyes.

"We found each other." He cleared his throat as Cadence sniffed loudly. "Seriously, I heard you too." At Aden's surprise, he continued. "Grapes. You sent me an image of grapes, and then you were thinking about...*his* face."

"You saw that?" She was incredulous.

He nodded. "I saw that. It's what led us to Julian Vinings, then to Vintner and Liddell and the house that was only a few hundred feet from where we were." He paused. "See? It really was all you."

"I can't believe it." She whispered. *A miracle.*

"Believe it. You did it, and here we are."

"Going home." Aden closed her eyes. It was quiet for another long moment when her eyes flew open. "Wait, where's Drew? And Natalie?"

"They're behind us. Don't worry," Maddox answered.

"Yeah, hope you're not too tired; there are a lot more people at your house waiting to welcome you home." Cadence smiled.

Aden nodded, though she wasn't really sure. She wasn't ready to talk about it again.

"It's okay; everybody's been told that we're not re-living…everything. We're focusing on today and the fact that you're home." Maddox assured her.

"Yeah, and your Mom set a strict time-limit for when we all have to leave," Cadence added. "It'll be short."

"Actually, it'll be just as short as you want it to be. Just let us know, and we'll shut the whole thing down," Maddox promised.

"I really just want to take the world's longest shower." Aden frowned.

"Then that's what you'll do," he confirmed.

She couldn't shake the dark, brooding feeling that had come over her. Then, she realized how dark it was inside the car with the towels covering the windows.

"These can come down now." She pulled down the towel from her window. "I've had enough of the dark for a while." Maddox took down the one on his side of the car. The bright sunlight helped, and she settled back with Maddox's arm around her shoulders and dozed.

"Welcome home, Aden." Trey smiled as they approached her driveway up ahead.

"Already? That was—" She inhaled sharply, leaning forward for a better view. Cars and news vans lined both shoulders of the highway for a quarter-mile before and after her driveway. A policeman stood in front of wooden sawhorse barricades at the end of her drive. "Holy hog muffins."

Cadence giggled. "Yeah, you made national headlines. Maybe international."

"It's a happy ending," Maddox interjected. "You all escaped."

"Except for Kate Vintner." Cadence frowned.

Oh God, please don't remind me. I don't want to think about seeing her. Aden closed her eyes again.

"Okay, enough of that. This is a happy occasion. We're celebrating," Trey said, slowing the car. He began to lower his window to speak to the officer at the end of the driveway, but she frantically waved him through, already having moved the barriers aside. There were people with cameras everywhere, surging toward the car as it made the turn into the driveway. Aden tried not to look directly at them.

"But why are they all *here*?" Aden wanted to know.

"Oh, they're all over town, interviewing anybody who pauses on the street. I'm sure there's just as big a circus at Raylene's house right now, too," Cadence said. "They were trying to keep your homecoming plans a secret, so the media just camped out here for the last couple days, waiting."

"Yeah, they've been trying to sneak into the hospital, too." Trey nodded.

"You could take your pick of the talk shows you might want to be interviewed by." Maddox frowned. "Your Mom has fielded so many calls from reporters and PR people she's un-plugged your phones. The phone company has agreed to change your phone number for free."

"I am *so* not doing interviews," she sputtered.

"Shhh, we know. Nobody's making you do anything you don't want to do," Maddox assured her.

There were cars lining one side of her driveway all the way up to her house. "Okay, we're here," Trey announced, cutting the engine. Aden took a deep breath, and they all waited for her cue, looking elsewhere.

"Okay," she let out the pent-up breath and opened her door.

"Hold on, I'm coming around." Maddox jumped out and met her, gently helping her stand. Trey and Cadence stood close by, too. "Do you really want a shower first thing?" Aden nodded, looking anxiously toward the kitchen door.

"I'll go let your Mom know." Cadence skipped off.

"What can I do?" Trey asked, taking her arm on the side opposite Maddox.

"Thank you so much for just, well being here and for all your help." Aden squeezed his arm. "I don't have words to express how much it helps, just having you all here with me right now."

"Whatever you need, just ask." Trey smiled down at her. Janet stepped through the door, followed by Kim.

"Welcome home, sweetheart!" Janet came to lightly hug Aden's shoulders, then gave big hugs to both the boys. "Before we go in, I know we talked about a small, quiet homecoming, but there were just so many people who really wanted to be here to show you their love and support…"

"It's okay, Mom. Thank you for handling it all."

"Cadence said that you want to shower first. I'm so sorry; I should have thought of that."

"It's just that—"

"You don't have to explain a thing. We're going straight through to my bathroom; you can just wave at everyone on your way by. Cadence is in there already picking out some clothes and putting them in my bathroom for you."

Aden just nodded. "Okay, then."

Janet walked with Aden into the house, where the hum of conversation suddenly ceased as everyone turned to look at them. Aden frantically searched for something to say to fill the void.

"Thank you all so much for coming." She couldn't believe the number of people crowding her house and the deck beyond. Practically everyone she'd ever known was here, grinning at her. Cadence's entire family, including Patience and some of her cronies, Mr. Keith, Mrs. McConnell, and Beverly from the store, fully half of her high school classmates, Billy Ray with his Dad, some of her teachers, and she spotted her aunt and uncle from Florida with her two cousins she hadn't seen in ages. Honestly, half the town was here. She was overwhelmed with the good will filling the room. It showed on all the happy faces of the people she knew, emanating outward to fill the spaces in between and forming a warm bubble of support. She blinked back sudden, happy tears. "This just…all of you…I'm truly touched." She smiled, sniffing. "Thank you from the bottom of my heart, for being here." She laughed and rolled her eyes at her own awkwardness, prompting warm laughter and cheers from the crowd.

"And if you'll excuse us, Aden's going to go freshen up a bit and settle in," Janet announced. "There's still a ton of food here; please help yourselves." Nodding politely at the people they passed, Janet quickly steered Aden through to the master bedroom with its attached bath. Cadence was already there, sitting on the bed.

"Okay, shower's running, water's hot. I've got your favorite jeans and that cute top you just bought set out in there," she said, bouncing up when they entered.

"Your bathroom is the guest bath that everybody's been using all day. We thought you'd have more privacy in here," Janet explained.

"Thanks, Mom." Aden hugged her.

"You take all the time you need, okay?" her Mom said. "You don't even have to come out if you don't want to. Climb in my bed and take a nap if that's what you want." Aden nodded. "I love you." With that, Janet slipped out the door, closing it firmly behind her.

"Do you want me to stay? Help?" Cadence offered.

"Thanks, but I think I can manage." Aden hugged her friend. "Thank you so much, Cadence, for everything." Cadence hugged her back, silent for once. "Now get out there and find Trey."

"If you're sure." Cadence pointed to Aden's cellphone lying on the bed. "It's charged, so text or call if you need anything." She nodded and Cadence left, however reluctantly.

She took a deep breath and looked around her mother's room. It was the first time she'd been alone since…well, for a while. The heavy drapes were pulled shut over the sliding doors to the deck, and she could hear voices outside there, as well as the loud hum from the main room she'd just left. But here, it was quiet. Nice. She turned toward the long-awaited shower.

CHAPTER 24
mordred

Hours later, Aden was ensconced in a cushioned lounge chair on the back deck with Maddox at her side. Drew and Natalie sat nearby, as did Cadence and Trey. Janet was inside with Max, LeighAnn, Kim, and Janet's brother and his wife. Their two daughters, Aden's pre-teen cousins, sat on the deck with the other young people and stared at Aden with awe.

"I can't believe the Leering Letch was here." Cadence glared.

"He was very polite and respectful," Aden said. "I think it was nice of him to want to be here, considering…well everything." She glanced at her young cousins meaningfully, so that the others wouldn't say too much.

"When Mr. Payne asked if they could come, he assured me that he'd be 'stuck to Billy Ray like glue' the entire time," Drew said, "But they both really wanted to be here."

"I overheard Mrs. McConnell, who works with you," Cadence said to Aden. "She was saying that Mr. Keith, your boss, had gone and bailed out both Beverly and Billy Ray in Spartanburg the other day."

"Really?" Aden frowned. "Why would Mr. Keith be the one—"

"I dunno. I didn't catch it all."

"Amazing that we all didn't hear it." Drew shrugged at Aden's admonishing look. "Sorry, but she's really loud."

"That's just…odd. I don't know why Mr. Keith would do that." Aden was perplexed. "And I was really surprised that Beverly was here today. She hates me."

"Why?" Cadence asked.

"I have no idea." She shrugged back tiredly. "She's been adversarial from the moment I met her, my first day at work."

"Well, even Patience was on her best behavior today," Cadence observed.

"I know! She hugged me!" Aden laughed. "Seriously, she was really nice to me."

"It's a miracle," Cadence muttered.

"There've been lots of miracles in my life lately." Aden squeezed Maddox's arm. He'd been quiet all evening.

"So I heard your Mom has another case? In…Wyoming, is it?" Natalie asked him.

Maddox sighed, nodding. "Yeah, heading out tomorrow."

"No rest for the weary, then?" Drew asked, frowning. Maddox met his frown with his own.

"That's the job." He turned to examine the darkness dripping deeper into the forest as they all looked from him to Aden. Aden examined his profile with a growing knot tightening her abdomen.

"So…" Cadence interjected, "I guess we should probably get going." She jabbed Trey's arm and stood abruptly. "You call me tomorrow, okay?" She bent and hugged Aden, who nodded.

"Drive carefully, you two." Aden smiled and waved. Trey squeezed her hand on his way by.

"We should go, too," Natalie said quietly to Drew.

"Guess this is good night, then." Drew stood, stretching.

"Good night guys, I'll see you soon." Natalie waved, then paused smiling at the two silent girls. "Have you two seen your Cousin Drew's drum set? I'll bet we can find some popsicles in his 'fridge too. Wanna come?" The girls looked at each other.

"I think they wanna be alone," the older one said to her sister.

"Do you really have popsicles?" the other asked Drew.

"Good night, you two!" Aden called, smiling. "Thanks for putting up with all the boring sitting around we've done all day." Waving, they followed Natalie inside.

"Good night," Drew said, pecking Aden on the head with a kiss on his way by. "Maddox, always good to have you here."

"Thanks." Maddox smiled back, bumping the fist that Drew held out. "Good night, Drew."

Aden sat back, listening to the river winding its way through the twilight as constant as ever. Without turning to face him, she spoke hesitantly.

"So. Wyoming."

"Yeah, that other case my Mom's been working on…there's a lead in Wyoming."

"Are you going with her?" Turning to face him, she held her breath.

Maddox searched her face, probing for something. "I hadn't decided."

"Hadn't decided?"

He thought for a moment before answering. "I wasn't sure if…you'd…" he sighed. "I wasn't sure if you'd want me around as a reminder…" he held up a hand to stop her response. "I overheard so many people today stumbling all over themselves so they wouldn't say the wrong thing, make you have to talk or think about what happened, and here I am, the biggest, flashing neon reminder. Everything escalated the very day I met you. Your life was normal before me…"

"Maddox Dixon." She glared. "My life hasn't been 'normal' for several years, and you know as well as I do that that…psychopath, whoever he turns out to be, apparently has been…stalking me for two years, or at least, longer than you've been here this summer." It was her turn to hold up a restraining hand. "No, wait. I know that you have something waiting for you back in Virginia, and you've helped your Mom with other cases. I just…" she took a deep breath and then rushed on. "I just hoped that you might be able to work it out to stay for a little while longer. At least a while, and—"

He stopped her rush of words with a smoldering kiss, his hands caressing either side of her head gently, to avoid the bruises. Pulling back with a smile, he touched her bruised cheekbone with a feather-light caress of his thumb.

"If you want me to, I'll stay," he whispered.

"I do," she choked out; it was all she could manage with his nearness burning away her consciousness of everything else. She frantically searched for something more to express what she was feeling. "But if you have…other…obligations…"

"Aden." He searched the depths of her eyes again, unhinging time and space. "I love you." Her breath caught in her throat as she froze, seeking to hold on to this moment. "I know it's crazy, we haven't known each other—"

"Shhh," she interrupted, eyes closed. His frown deepened in concern as he impatiently waited, enumerating the obstacles, the reasons why this couldn't— "Say it again." Her eyes opened, and he met her gaze questioningly. "Say it again, please."

His arms went around her back, drawing her close, and his hand held the back of her head gently as he leaned in with eyes of flame. "I love you, Aden."

Her eyes closed as his lips met hers, searing every nerve ending in her body. She gripped him, pulling him nearer with all her strength. He normally ended their kisses, but this time she pulled back first.

"I love you too," She almost panted, short of breath. "And I don't want you to go."

"Your wish is my—" He started, but she cut him off with a toe-curling kiss of her own. A few minutes later, they were still snuggled together watching the dark woods when the sliding door opened behind them.

"Maddox, we need to be going," Kim said, coming outside with Janet. "We're the last stragglers, and I really didn't mean to stay this long."

"I'm glad you stayed," Janet said.

"Well, the flight leaves just after 8:00 in the morning, and we've got so many things to wrap up here before we go." She looked questioningly at her son.

"I'm going to stay in Blackwater Falls for a while." He stood and helped Aden up. "If that's alright." He looked from his Mom to Janet. "Dad and LeighAnn already said I could stay with them."

Kim looked from Aden to Janet. "How would you feel about—"

"Maddox is welcome in our home anytime." Janet smiled at him.

"Well, I wouldn't say anytime. I know how my son feels about your daughter and—" Kim chuckled as Maddox interrupted her.

"I don't know about Aden, but I'm offended."

"Oh, stop. You know I'm only half serious." Kim waved him off.

"Then I guess I'm only half offended."

"Okay, so change of awkward subject." Aden turned to Kim. "Any news? Has the psycho talked yet? Do you know who he is? Anything?"

"There have been some developments." She hesitated, looking at Janet. "Sheriff Richey should be contacting you tomorrow. I've asked him to keep you all updated when they have confirmed news about your case."

"Can you tell us anything now? A hint?" Aden wheedled.

"It's late." Kim smiled. "I'd be here all night explaining, and the Sheriff promised to show you…besides, you need a good night's sleep. Take the night off from all of it. I'm sure he'll call you in the morning."

"Thank you again for everything." Janet hugged Kim. "Will you be able to visit again this summer?"

They led the way back inside, Aden and Maddox following.

"Yes, I hope so."

Maddox pulled the heavy door closed behind them, securing the thumb lock, and then went to lower the security bar on the other side.

"Mrs. Garrett, you need to be sure the door in your room is locked as well."

"The bad guy's in jail," Aden protested. "Do we really have to keep—"

"It's not a big deal," Maddox said. "Just a lock. Just because."

"Seriously, I was looking forward to getting back to some kind of normal—" Aden began.

"That door." He nodded to where the hole in the glass had been covered with thick layers of duct tape. "Who unlocked the security bar that night so it could be opened?"

"What?" Aden blinked.

"The night you were abducted. Did you or Cadence unlock that security bar on the floor?"

"You know we didn't. We've been over this twenty times with the police."

"Then who did?" Maddox asked quietly. "The guy got in here by cutting the glass and unlocking the thumb lock on the handle, but he wouldn't have been able to open the door unless the security bar was already up."

Aden shuddered. "Are you just trying to scare me?" she glared.

"No." He frowned back, then after a moment, he shrugged. "Maybe."

"They're coming tomorrow to fill the hole with some kind of epoxy. The new glass has been ordered, but it won't be ready for another week and a half." Janet frowned.

"Fine," Aden sighed heavily, rolling her eyes. "I'll lock every door I go through from now until eternity."

"As long as I'm not on the other side." Maddox smiled.

"On that note, we really do need to be going." Kim walked quickly through the kitchen, and Janet followed her outside, leaving the door open.

"Call you tomorrow?" Maddox asked, after a quick hug.

"You'd better." She pecked him on the cheek as they walked arm in arm to the door.

"Please be careful," he whispered. "I love you."

"I love you, too." She hugged him tight before he jogged to the car where his mother waited in the passenger seat.

"Okay, locking up." Janet waved her back inside the door as Maddox slowly turned the car around. He tapped the car horn as Janet shut the door and locked it.

Predictably, Aden slept late the next morning. She barely remembered changing into pajamas and climbing into her bed. She was just blinking and stretching when her mother lightly knocked on the door.

"Aden, you awake?"

"Yeah, Mom." Janet opened the door.

"The Sheriff called earlier. He's asked if we'll come to the hospital at 1:00 today. He says there's something he wants to share with all of you, the survivors...Shonda, Raylene, Cindy, and you."

408

"I didn't even hear the phone. So we're meeting at the hospital?"

"He called my cell. I had to unplug all the house phones."

"That's right. Maddox told me."

"We're going to the hospital because Cindy and Shonda haven't been released yet. He said you all have a right to see the video, but it's evidence, and he's only showing it once."

"Video?"

"I don't know any more than that." Janet shrugged. "So we'll leave around 12:30." Aden jumped up to shower and dress.

"Can Maddox come?"

"Oh, I don't know." She frowned. "The Sheriff still doesn't like him very much."

"So?" Aden challenged. "We like him, right? And he's got a right to see and hear whatever's going on there today."

"Let me text Kim and ask her opinion."

Later, after Aden had showered and dressed and grabbed a banana from the kitchen for breakfast, Janet came out of her own room.

"Kim said the Sheriff invited Maddox, too. Problem solved."

"Yeah, Maddox texted me a little while ago that he'd see us there."

"Okay, then. Drew's waiting outside. Are you ready?"

At the hospital, they were led into a room with a flatscreen TV on the wall and rows of folding chairs, where the other victims and their immediate families were gathering. Aden was enveloped by hugs and well wishes from the other three women and their families, commiserating over the media attention and recovering injuries, both physical and mental. Maddox and Drew were engaged in a tense conversation with Sheriff Richey in a corner of the room. She kept glancing over, but was unable to break free of the impromptu reunion.

Several minutes later, the Sheriff stood in front of the flat screen with hands raised and whistled shrilly for attention. It reminded Aden of her dad, who could produce loud whistles like that. The thought silenced her in mid-sentence, as the whistle silenced the rest of the room. She found a seat between her mother and Maddox, with Drew on his other side.

"Sorry to interrupt, folks, but I've got an ongoing investigation to get back to. We're committed to getting you some answers and to make sure justice is served that fits the barbarity of what you all endured." He paused. "We've confirmed the identity of the...alleged perpetrator. A family member has come forward, and it's been confirmed through preliminary DNA testing." He walked to the corner where shelves held a DVR and other multimedia equipment and picked up a remote. "I'm going to play part of the interview with the family member for you, at that individual's insistent request. Now, this is not only highly irregular; I'm bending several regulations and possibly a law or two." He looked as though he would say more, but he just sighed and pressed a button on the remote.

The screen flickered on to a paused image of an older lady sitting at a table, grasping a limp handkerchief. The image came to life with the sound of soft sobs.

"Please state your full name for the record." The Sheriff's voice, uncharacteristically gentle, came from off-camera. The old lady wiped her eyes with the handkerchief and took a deep breath.

"Abigail Rose Liddell Garner," she intoned.

"Thank you, Mrs. Garner, and you say you've come here today with information regarding the suspect in the recent abduction case, is that correct?"

"Yes." She nodded slowly. "I saw his picture on the television. I haven't seen him in...so many years, but I knew it was him."

"And who would that be?"

"His name is Jacob Mordred Liddell." She took a shuddering breath. "He's my nephew."

"Mrs. Garner, I'm somewhat familiar with your family here in Blackwater Falls. You have one sibling, your sister Katherine—"

"Pardon me Sheriff Richey, but I can save you the trouble of your questions. It'll be easier if I can just tell the story from the beginning." She paused as the Sheriff apparently gave silent consent.

"Kate...my sister, Katherine Liddell Vintner, didn't have an easy life. Her husband Louis...well, he was one mean son of a bitch." Aden and several of the others looked around in surprise at the choice of words from such a proper southern lady. "We didn't

410

know it at first, of course. She kept it to herself for many years, but it got worse after our father died. Louis was a drinker, and he abused Kate their whole married life. We'd almost talked her into leaving him once, but she found out she was expecting her first son, Julian. Louis was somewhat kinder to her for a couple of years. He doted on Julian, so proud to have a son, but it wasn't long before he was back at Kate; I would see the bruises. She'd have to stay at home for weeks while they healed, so no one would know. Kate sent Julian away to a school in Louisiana, to keep him away from his father. It was around that time we started hearing the rumors all over town. Louis was unfaithful. Apparently, he quite publicly flaunted his…flings. Kate was mortified, and she moved out of Louis' house here in town, went to live on the mountain, at our father's house we'd inherited." She took a sip from the cup sitting on the table in front of her, then cleared her throat daintily.

"It was while she lived on the mountain that she finally found love. She met a man, at the market she told me, though she never told me much else. His name was Paolo; she never told me his last name if she knew it. She introduced me to him only as Paolo. Italian he was; tall, dark, and devilish handsome. Kate glowed when she was around him. I've never seen her so happy." She paused to gently dab at the tears on her cheeks as her tentative smile fell. "But they weren't careful; she found herself expecting again, and Louis, of course, found out. He was…enraged. Vowed to kill them both." Another deep breath. "The police back then, well, it was another time; they looked the other way in 'family' matters such as that. I mean, they talked to Louis and told him he couldn't kill anybody, but that was about the extent of their involvement. I knew he would kill her; there was just no doubt in my mind. I hid her in my own house for a day or two, but my husband didn't want to be involved with all of it. I drove her myself down to Macon, to a Women's Home in the middle-of-nowhere-Georgia, and I never told anybody where she'd gone, until now." Another sip of water.

"Louis threatened to kill *me*, then. He used to follow me around town, glaring. He'd catch me off guard, when my husband wasn't around, and threaten and scream and pitch such fits…" She sat up straighter and raised her eyes from the table. "But I never told him a thing. Never told anybody. Kate had a boy, Jacob. He looked just like Paolo, absolutely the opposite of Kate and her husband, Louis. I went to Macon to visit her when he was born. She begged and begged me to ask my husband if we could adopt him, raise him as our own. Never telling anyone he was hers, of course, and I did try, but my husband well…

"Kate had to leave the Women's Home after the baby was born, and she stayed with our elderly aunt down in Anderson for almost a year. She found work at the college there, but when our aunt died, she hadn't saved enough money to support herself and the baby for long and had nowhere else to go. So I sneaked her back up to the mountain house with the baby late at night. It worked, for a while. I couldn't visit because I was so afraid someone would find out she was there and tell Louis…I don't know how it was that he found out. She would telephone occasionally when she thought my husband was at work, but the calls suddenly stopped. Louis had dragged her back to the house here in town, along with little Jacob. She never told me what she endured, what they both endured, at his hands before I learned she was back in that house with him, but when I went over there, demanding to see my sister, and he finally let me inside…he had beaten them both so badly…" she closed her wounded eyes.

"I realized he'd run off after he let me inside. He was the worst kind of coward. I called an ambulance, and Kate and her son were in the hospital for weeks. The police found Louis, put him in jail for all of three months. The day he got out, he found Kate back up at the house on the mountain, and he beat them both again. She got a restraining order against him, but it never did a lick o' good. He'd go up there in the middle of the night and he'd…abuse them both, but especially that little boy, in every way he could imagine to inflict pain…it was heinous, the blackest evil. I'd only know because I wouldn't have gotten my phone calls from Kate. The police would come, and he'd put on a show. And a grand actor he could've been, fallin' to his knees professing undying love for Kate. He never loved anyone. In all that time, he was paying off the police department. Oh yes, believe it." She nodded.

"He paid them and the hospital staff to never tell anybody about 'Kate's bastard.' That's the only thing I ever heard him call the boy, 'Kate's bastard.' Of course, people found out. Kate finally made the decision to give him up. She loved that boy beyond reason, and it took a long time to convince her that she couldn't protect him. During one of Louis' drying-up weekends in the county jail, I went with her to Charlotte…we left Jacob at an orphanage. Kate was never the same after that." Her voice hitched.

"How old was he then?" the Sheriff asked quietly.

"He was almost four years old." Her voice and her eyes were far away. "So tiny for his age, afraid of his own shadow…of course he had every reason…"

"Did you see him after that?"

"Yes, twice." She nodded, coming back to the present. "Kate kept regular correspondence with the orphanage whenever she could. They even sent her pictures once or twice."

"He wasn't adopted?"

"No, they described him as 'different' and later 'troubled'…he grew up at the orphanage, taking care of the younger children for a while. Then, they switched him to janitorial, kept him away from the others."

"Did you ever see him in person, while he was living at the orphanage?"

"Yes, Kate and I visited a couple of times over the years. The last time was right before he left there." She paused. "He was turning 18. Originally, the staff had promised him a job and a room above the barn, but…he'd been accused of…crimes. They told him he'd have to leave and contacted Kate."

"What kind of crimes?"

"He was always fighting with the other boys, but he got more aggressive as he grew older…they tried to keep him away from the boys." She looked down at the table once again and lowered her voice. "But then they started finding him with the girls…the little girls. Nothing was ever proven, but…" her voice broke on a sob. "It was just all he'd ever known…all he knew of men came from Kate's husband Louis." She took a deep breath and sat back upright, ramrod straight against the chair back.

"I don't mean that as any sort of excuse. There is no excuse for what he's done, and he should pay dearly. He is broken, Sheriff, an utterly broken soul, and he should be locked away, forever."

"So what happened? When he left the orphanage in Charlotte?" Sheriff Richey asked quietly.

"When the orphanage called Kate to explain the situation, we drove up the next day. Jacob was sulking in his room and wouldn't speak to us, while we were standing right there over his bed, mind you, trying to discuss his future. He wouldn't say a word. Kate informed him that she was taking him home. She told him she'd been living at the mountain house, and Louis wasn't comin' 'round anymore. He'd been living with some new woman, over in Greer. She told him that Julian was coming home for the summer in a few weeks, and as he'd never met his brother, they would all spend the summer together." She slowly shook her head.

"I could see it in his eyes, even if he wouldn't speak, he never had any intention of going back to that house with us. When we came to collect him, after Kate signed all the paperwork, he was gone. I never found out where he'd gone or how he's managed all the years since. Kate was devastated; she never gave up looking for him. Then, out of the blue, he showed up here in town a couple of years ago."

"You saw him?"

"No, he visited Kate. He'd found out that Louis and Julian were both dead. He never did meet Julian, so sad. Anyway, Kate said Jacob showed up at her door one day. He told her he'd looked for her at the mountain house, and then came to the house in town. She's lived in town since Louis died, you know." She paused, and Aden imagined the Sheriff nodding across the table from her.

"How long was the visit?"

"He stayed with Kate for a couple of days, then asked if he could stay at the mountain house. Kate told him it had been vacant for many years, but he was welcome to it. She'd signed over the deed to Julian when he came of age, and I don't know if she ever transferred it to Jacob or not, after Julian died, but she meant to. When she told me he was in town, we both went to visit, but he wasn't there. He would disappear for months at a time, popping up at Kate's door at odd hours…I never did actually see him." She sighed.

"By this time, Kate…well, life had taken its toll. She'd never been the same since leaving Jacob in Charlotte that first time. Learning what he'd grown into, well, that was another hit. Then Louis and Julian both dying within a few years of each other…her mind was…disconnected much of the time. She was capable in body, and took care of herself and her house, but she was…well, not really here, with us. Her mind was always somewhere else." She took another sip from the cup and folded her hands on the table. "I like to think she was with him, with Paolo, in her mind these last few years."

"What happened to Paolo?"

"I don't really know, but I have my suspicions." She frowned, her eyes far away again. "When I got home from Macon, from taking Kate to the Women's Home there, he was gone. He was supposed to have met up with Kate in Macon the following week, but he never made it. He'd left a suitcase of clothes and a hat in the boarding room where he'd been staying, but he never came back…I think Louis killed him."

"Do you have any proof of that?"

"No, but I'm telling you that Paolo was in love with my sister. He was over the moon about the baby, and he could hardly wait to get to Macon to be with her. He wouldn't have just left her; I'm sure of it."

They were both silent for a few moments.

"When was the last time you were in contact with your sister?"

"Several weeks ago. She called me to say that she was participating in a bake sale at church. She asked if I would make my peach cobbler and bring it along. She always liked my cobbler better than her own, though her cakes…well, I never did figure out what she did differently." The Sheriff politely cleared his throat, bringing her back to the present. "Oh, yes. We spoke for a few minutes about this and that, nothing important, and then, right before we said our goodbyes, she said that she was going to the mountain house for a few days, and she'd see me at the bake sale on Sunday." She frowned. "It was a little odd…I mean, she hadn't gone there for so many years, but I didn't really think too much of it."

"Did she mention Jacob? That he was back in town?"

"No, that would have been unusual, important news. She only said she was going to the house…that was the last time I spoke to her." She dabbed again at her silent tears. "When she didn't show up that Sunday, I went to her house here first, and there was no answer. I went home and phoned her several times that day. The next day, I drove up to the mountain house, but there was no answer there, either."

"What about her car? Did you see it at either house?"

"No, her car was missing, too, but I told you that when I filed the missing persons report that next day." She looked at him with an accusatory stare.

"Yes, you did."

"Have you found her car?"

"No, we haven't."

"Well, I suppose it doesn't really matter now anyway, does it?" She paused again, twisting the handkerchief in her hands. "You're recording this, right?"

"Yes."

"I want them to see it, to hear it, those girls he abducted. They deserve to hear the story of how the monster was made, and I want them to know…how very sorry I am. Truly, deeply sorry for everything. I only wish I'd known…the news kept saying they thought it was someone local, and I didn't know he was back in town…"

"Mrs. Garner, would you have suspected your nephew of those abductions…if you'd known he was in the area?"

She took a deep breath, closing her eyes against a new wave of tears and sobbed raggedly before answering in a whisper.

"I…I should have thought…with Kate missing, I should have come forward sooner." Releasing a long exhale, she continued. "I'm the only one who knew…how broken he is."

"Mrs. Garner—"

"You tell them, those girls. Apologies will never be enough, words…I'll never be able to make it right. Not if I lived to be a thousand years old, nothing I can do will ever change the evil he has done, but God can. Tell them to give it all to God. Forgive Jacob if they can, and forget. Put it behind them and move on. God in his mercy can help them to heal, and I will pray for them every day. Every day." The tears ran freely down her cheeks as she rolled her eyes upward to the ceiling. "May God have mercy on Jacob, and, dear God, please have mercy on my soul."

The video froze, and then the screen went dark again as the Sheriff rose. The room was silent for several long moments. Aden wiped her wet cheeks with a tissue she didn't remember having. Several others were doing the same. *Tragic*, she thought. *The whole story is just so tragic.* She wasn't sure how she was supposed to feel. When she thought of...*Jacob*, she still felt terror and rage and helplessness and humiliation and triumph—all stewed together in one un-nameable torment. Now, added to that was another layer of sadness and even pity. *I will not pity that bastard*, she told herself vehemently, but she was immediately repentant. Bastard was an identity that had haunted him his whole life.

"So," Sheriff Richey said, hands on hips. "At Mrs. Garner's request, you've seen her testimony."

"So his real name is Jacob?" Cindy asked timidly.

"Jacob Mordred Liddell," he nodded.

"Mordred?" Shonda grimaced.

"The name of King Arthur's illegitimate son." Aden frowned. "No wonder he took his brother's name."

"So why was he disguising himself to look older?" Cindy asked.

"And did he kill his mother? Or did she die of natural causes?" someone else asked.

The Sheriff held up his hands, "We don't have all the answers. We may never have answers for some of your questions. The investigation is continuing, and we'll keep you all updated when we have relevant information."

"Relevant? It's all relevant to us," Raylene's husband said.

"I have a question." Janet's voice surprised Aden. "This...Jacob claimed to have been involved in the accident that killed my husband. I met the driver of one of the vehicles, and his wife, the Simmons. They came to my husband's funeral. I was told that there was a couple in the third vehicle, and that their name was Valenti. I don't remember a Liddell, or a Vintner...or Vinings for that matter."

The Sheriff was nodding slowly. "We are looking into that as well. Look, I know you all have hundreds of questions, and we're going to find every last answer that can possibly be found, but at this point, we are very early into a large investigation. It's going to take some time to run down and verify all the evidence, possible witnesses, getting our perpetrator to talk…I can't answer all your questions today, but I promise to let you know when we do find answers."

"So that's it, then?" someone asked.

"For today." He nodded. "Thank you all for coming down here."

The ride home had been very quiet. Aden was alone in the Audi with Maddox as Janet was dropping Drew at the Paynes' garage on her way in to her new office for a couple of hours. Janet had agreed to Maddox hanging out at their house for the couple of hours until she and Drew could get home.

"Are you okay?" Maddox's glance was concerned as Aden considered her answer. "That was a lot to take in."

"Yeah, I'm alright," she decided aloud. As they approached her driveway, she saw that there were fewer news vans and people milling around than the day before. The policeman on duty at the end of her drive waved them through, and Maddox drove quickly away from the cameras. "I can't wait for them to find a new story, somewhere far away from here."

"They will. It's only been a few days."

"Seems longer."

"Come on, let's get inside and get you some lunch. You'll feel better when you've eaten something more than a banana."

"How would you know I've only had a banana?"

"I have my sources." His eyes sparkled as he flashed his perfectly-imperfect smile and caught her in a hug, careful of her many bruises. Aden smiled up at him, narrowing her eyes against the sun.

"And what else did Drew tell you today?"

"Oh, it wasn't Drew." He looked mysterious.

"Wait, you've been talking to my *mother* about me?"

"I don't know what you're talking about, and I can't reveal my sources, in any case," he teased, biting back a smile. Aden laughed outright, her first real laugh in days, as she opened the kitchen door.

Another smile, hidden just within the shadowy depths of the forest, spread in an evil rictus of intent as he watched the door close behind them.

Not yet, he thought with regret. *But very, very soon.*

He settled himself against the tree, where he'd wait and watch and listen. The exquisite contemplation and planning, red velvet anticipation wrapped around him in a titillating shroud…they thought it was over. He grinned in the sun-dappled shadows.

HE had just begun…

Melodee Lane
November, 2014
www.MelodeeLane.com

The story continues with the next installment of the *Blackwater Falls Series:* <u>Gemini Gate</u>, due out in May, 2015.

Read on for a sneak-peek excerpt, the Prelude and Chapter One of <u>Gemini Gate</u>, beginning on the next page!

You can follow along as the *Blackwater Falls Series* is being written. See photos of the actual Lake Jocassee, S.C. area, read inside-information about the characters, post your own comments, and more at the Blackwater Blog page at **<u>MelodeeLane. com</u>**. You can also follow the author on Facebook and Twitter to be the first to know about *Blackwater Falls* news and events.

Following is an excerpt from the second installment of the *Blackwater Falls Series*, Gemini Gate, scheduled for publication in May, 2015.

GEMINI GATE
A BLACKWATER FALLS STORY

Melodee Lane

PRELUDE

Damn, damn, damn it! I knew I should never have trusted Jacob; never should have second-guessed my first impression of him, so sweetly anxious, utterly insecure, and thoroughly deranged. Like a bull in a china shop. Wouldn't know subtlety if it came up and bit him. Freaking wedding dresses! What the -? For all four of them, too. Stupid, irrational, deluded idiot.

Only one of them was relevant. The other bitches were incidental, recreation. He SAID that he understood why each was chosen, but he didn't. Couldn't see past his own petty need for acceptance. They were just the warm-up, the dripping, glutinous rehearsal for the final triumph.

Aden. Such frost blue despondency emanates from her eyes, in stark contrast to the deep fiery shades of her hair. So much untapped pain and grief, held behind the pale wall of her existence just begging to be released in a torrent of tears and agony, terror and blood. Jacob thought to temper my ambition, to twist all my plans to his benefit, but nothing will stop me. Not the silly boy who now courts her vulnerability, or his bitch mother and her uniformed cohorts. No.

Jacob's done me one favor: they think the danger has been restrained. They think Aden is safe now. They think they're all safe. Pity, how little they know.

CHAPTER 1
solicitude

Aden stared at the newly-replaced glass in the oversized sliding door, the TV jangling on forgotten. It was only on for the background noise, to mask the intermittent and unknown creaks of the empty house and the faint rumbles of another distant summer storm.

The glass had been replaced just the week before, a complicated process involving many men and a couple of heavy-duty machines to lift the heavy plate into place. Her mother would have replaced it with bullet-proof glass or steel if they could have afforded it; anything to prevent a repeat of the night Aden had been taken.

Kidnapped. Abducted. Held. Attacked. Brutally assaulted. Physical and psychological trauma. All the words the media used to try and inject fact in a thin veneer of solicitude over the insatiable hunt for salacious details. *The world isn't interested in facts, they're interested in pain, the misery of others,* she thought, clenching her eyes shut against the memories but they came anyway. They always did. They lurked in the shadows of her conscious thoughts, waiting for any excuse to spring forward.

They played like a sadistic movie trailer in her mind, select scenes and snippets. Though she never saw it happen in real life, her mind showed her broken images of Jacob on the back deck of her house, cutting a hole in the door's plate glass, reaching through to unlock and slide the large door open as she slept on the couch mere feet away. Quick shot of a needle and syringe penetrating her neck mercilessly. Blurry, confused images of waking up in the dankness of the basement, pan right to the putrid rotting corpse watching over her in the darkness. That she *did* see in real life, and would never be able to forget. Rapid-fire flashes of a demented tea party, the other women's faces bleak and blank from the horrors they'd endured. Black evil seeping in rivulets down Jacob's face as he stood over her repeatedly kicking, punching, screaming. Chains. He kept them in chains, like animals. Worse than animals.

Swiping a hand through her hair, still wet from the shower, she opened her eyes and worked to focus on the green outside the big glass door. The deep summer forest

423

surrounded the house and the rock-strewn river behind it. Her architect father had designed and built the house with its clean, modern planes of wood, steel, and glass into the bedrock of the mountain overlooking the adjacent river's tumultuous route. The second floor had never been finished, following his death in a car accident almost three years before.

"Stop it." She stood, angry at her own lack of mental control. "Enough." Retrieving her cell phone from the coffee table, she paced to the door as she dialed. Tracking the spinning route of a tree branch between the river rocks below as she waited, she was finally rewarded with a formal, over-loud greeting on the line.

"Mrs. McConnell, this is Aden. Is Mr. –" She rolled her eyes at the inevitable interruption.

"Aden, dear, how are you? And your mother, bless her soul." Mrs. McConnell was a prim elderly lady who worked at the jewelry store on the small town square with Aden. Well versed in the quality, clarity, cut, and color of diamonds and other gemstones, she held her position at the store despite her predilection for gossip and the un-modulated volume of the hard-of-hearing.

"We're all well, thank you for asking. Is Mr. Keith avail–"

"I've been sitting with Abby Garner since…well. Mrs. Garner is shamed and broken-hearted that one of her family could do things so terrible."

"Yes, I received her letter –" Aden began, hesitantly.

"I helped her write it, you know. She sent one to the other three girls as well. Don't think she'll ever get past this."

Neither will we. Aden groaned inwardly. "I need to speak with Mr. Keith. Is he there?"

"Of course, dear. I'll just go tell him." Aden listened as she set the receiver down to go knock on Mr. Keith's office door in the back of the small store. The store phone included a 'hold' feature and an intercom that she could have used to transfer the call to his desk phone, but Mrs. McConnell refused every offer to learn their use. Just as adamantly as she refused the hearing aids suggested by so many. The phone clicked loudly as he lifted the receiver on his desk.

"Aden, so nice to hear from you. How are you?" She heard the surprised smile in his voice and worked to swallow her agitation at being asked that question a million times a day, lately.

"Just fine. Great I mean." Sighing inwardly she continued. "I was wondering if I might be able to come back to work earlier than planned."

"Oh?" It was his turn to flounder, with surprise. "Of course. I'm just working on a July schedule. When were you thinking?"

"Immediately. Tomorrow even. I mean, if that works...I would guess that Beverly and Mrs. McConnell might appreciate a break. They've been covering for me for weeks now." She hadn't heard Mrs. McConnell replace the receiver she'd answered in the showroom, she was probably hanging on every word.

"Tomorrow..." he hesitated.

"Or well, soon. I know you've already made out the schedule and I don't want to –"

"No, no, don't worry about that. Hold on one second...Mrs. McConnell?" he called, obviously away from the phone's receiver. Aden heard a loud click on the line. "I don't believe the receiver out there hung up properly, would you check?" she almost smiled at the now-quieter line. "Thank you...Okay." He said into the phone once again. "Sorry about that."

"No problem."

"She's been so worried about you. We all have." He added.

"I'm just –"

"Fine. Yes, you said. I know that can't really be true, though." Aden started to interject but he spoke over her. "In any case, I can understand how you might want to keep busy. Maybe break out of the fishbowl for a bit." She was stunned that he, of all people, would know that. "The media has mostly moved on, I don't see them lurking around anymore. There's still the stray, following up every now and again, but it's mostly quiet. You could hide in the back if one of them comes in. Beverly's working the morning shift tomorrow, why don't you come in then?"

"Really?"

"Yes, she's less likely to pump you for information than Mrs. McConnell would be." He said quietly.

"Thank you so much Mr. Keith. You don't know how much I appreciate it."

"No problem. See you tomorrow."

Ending the call, she focused on the river once more. The wayward tree branch was gone downstream, victim of the rowdy current. *Victim*. Another word the media used too often while re-telling the story of the Blackwater Falls abduction cases.

"Survivor." She muttered to the river, just as she'd corrected everyone after their escape from Jacob. She'd survived. The move from the city of Atlanta to the lethargic little town of Blackwater Falls, S.C.; the accident with the runaway eighteen-wheeler that had killed her father but spared her; the blank years since his death as she, her mother and brother struggled to cope; and the stalking and eventual abduction by a psychopathic stranger; she'd survived it all.

Watching a leaf spin helplessly downstream, it struck her that surviving no longer meant what it had that day. Things had changed. She had changed. Survival was okay, better than the alternative, but it was no longer enough. Now it was time for her to live.

"Are you sure?" Maddox asked again, his voice more guarded than before.

"For the very last time, yes." Aden groaned. "You've all got to back off. Seriously."

"We're just worried-"

"I know. I know. You're worried about me. Mom is worried about me. Drew is worried about me. Cadence, Grace, your whole family…Maddox, you're all driving me crazy."

"We just-"

"I KNOW!" she screamed into the phone. "I've heard you. All of you. Every single minute of every single day since- just back off. Please. I'm going back to work tomorrow in part to get away from all the concern. I'm drowning in concern."

"I was going to say love." He said quietly. "We love you."

"Fabulous. I'm drowning in love." She took a deep breath and let it out slowly. "I love you too." She said quietly.

"I do hear you, you know." He sounded hurt. *Damn it.* He was the last person she would want to hurt. "None of us will ever understand exactly how you feel, what you went through…but-"

"Maddox, stop. Please just stop."

"Aden-"

"No, shut up and listen to me. No, HEAR me. I don't want to talk about it. I don't want to think about it. I don't want any recognition of it at all. It's in the past, behind me, and I want to leave it there. Forever. But all of you constantly hovering, asking how I'm doing, questioning my every decision as if I were a five year old...it's got to stop. I mean it, I can't take it anymore."

"We just want to help." Still hurt. Sigh.

"You wanna know how you can help me? Go back to treating me like an intelligent human being. Like a person who's not made of glass; who doesn't need to be coddled and nurtured and second-guessed constantly." She huffed. "I'm still ME. I'm still the same girl that I was before. I just want you all to treat me like you used to."

"Before."

"Yes before!" she yelled. "I'm still ME. Nothing's changed."

"I love you." He said quietly, after a long pause.

"I love you, too." Her voice was still harsh from frustration.

"Can I drive you to work in the morning?"

"No." She sucked in a breath, "Drew's taking me." She felt instant regret, hearing her own tone of voice. "But we're still on for the movie with Cadence and Trey, right?"

"Completely up to you." *Crap.* He was really hurt.

"Maddox." She scowled at the ceiling as she clutched the phone tighter.

"I'll be outside the jewelry store when you get off work." He paused. "You can let me know then if you feel like being with people."

"Feel like being with people?" Instant rage.

"I didn't mean –"

"I've got to go." Aden ended the call, tossing her cell phone to the bottom of the bed. *What the hell was that? Feel like being with people? Did he really just say that?* She grabbed a pillow and, clenching it to her face as tightly as she clenched her eyelids shut, she screamed into it as long and loud as she could muster.

A soft knock drew her attention to the door of her bedroom. "Aden?"

"I'm fine Mom." She bit out between gritted teeth. Her mother paused for a long moment on the other side of the door before quietly leaving.

Regret flooded in immediately and hot tears rolled down even as she tried to decide if they were tears of anger or remorse.

"I'm sorry." She whispered, spluttering through sudden sobs, to no one in particular. To everyone. She did understand that they were just concerned. They had every reason to be concerned. She knew that, but the way they were treating her... the way the WORLD looked at her, every day, was maddening. Condescending. Pitying. Demeaning. She didn't need pity or assistance or concern; she just needed to move on. Normalcy. That's what she craved, to go back to being just a regular, normal person.

"Do you want me to drive you around to the back door, in the alley?" Drew asked the next morning as they neared the square, downtown. Her brother had always driven her to work prior to her meeting Maddox, and it felt nostalgic somehow, today.

"No, it's okay."

"I don't mind."

"I've never been in the back door of the store and I see no reason to start now."

"Alright then." He raised his eyebrows in annoyance. Aden opened her mouth to apologize, but closed it with a snap. What did she have to apologize for? A few minutes later, he broke the awkward silence. "So will I see you later at the garage or is Maddox picking you up?" He paused, shooting her a sidelong glance as he pulled up at the curb outside the front of the store. "We weren't sure."

"We??" she fixed him with a glare as he shrugged. "You've been talking to Maddox about me?" Drew met her glare head-on.

"Yes, I've talked to Maddox. It used to make you happy that your brother and your boyfriend got along so well. You've gotta stop treating us all like we're the enemy, Sis."

"Maybe when you all stop treating me like an invalid child."

"So we're all supposed to act like we just don't care about you? Is that what you want?"

"No, you idiot. That's not what I said."

"Fine." He huffed, eyes flashing. "Get out. I'm gonna be late for work."

Aden stepped out angrily and slammed the car door shut just as he sped away from the curb faster than was necessary. Crap! She sighed, turning to the store front and met Beverly's guarded scrutiny through the window. *Well, at least the mocking derision she's trying to hide behind that rictus of a smile is normal,* she thought to herself. *This is what I wanted. Back to normal.* Squaring her shoulders, she walked quickly into the small shop with her head held high.

"Welcome back." Beverly said flatly.

"Thanks." She half-smiled as she continued into the back of the store to put her purse away, registering the distinctive squeak of Mr. Keith's desk chair as she passed the door to his office.

"Hello Aden. It's good to have you back." He smiled, leaning against the door jamb as she turned back toward the store's front.

"Hello Mr. Keith." She fought to match his casually friendly tone while dreading the inevitable onslaught of questions and concern. "It's good to be back."

"I was hoping you might take a look at the cases and do another merchandise makeover for us." His smiled broadened as she smiled back with relief and gratitude.

"I'd love to." He just nodded and retreated into his office again.

Back out in the showroom, Beverly slumped with her elbows on the counter, staring out the front window. She didn't even blink as Aden walked slowly around the store, surveying the way the jewelry had been displayed in the cases.

"So you look like you're doin' okay." She finally stated, without looking at Aden.

"Doin' fine." Aden shrugged, her back to Beverly. "How are you?"

"Kinda bored today." She sighed, standing up straight. "It was exciting around here for a while with all the reporters and cameras hanging around. Did you see any of my interviews?"

"They interviewed you?" Aden froze, her back still turned.

"Well yeah. I'm a co-worker you know. I mean, school's out so they couldn't go there for interviews and your house was all barricaded, so I guess they came here." Aden silently turned and met her gaze. "You seriously didn't see any of that?"

"I wasn't watching much TV." Aden was quiet.

"Well you were all over the news. I mean, you and the other girls. Practically non-stop coverage."

"Thank God it's over now. We can all move on."

"You know, one thing they were all trying to find out about…nobody was ever really sure how you got out. There were different stories. Some said you escaped, some said you were rescued by police, then some said your friends were there…?" she waited, practically trembling with curiosity. Aden took a deep breath.

"Well, that's all sort of true." She grabbed a white towel and began furiously wiping fingerprints off the glass cases.

"So? How'd you get away?" There was a hesitancy in Beverly's voice, like she didn't want to ask, but couldn't help herself. Aden stopped wiping and searched Beverly's face. The usual derision was gone, she only saw hesitant curiosity. It was the hesitancy that made her decide to answer in a rushed monotone.

"I fought my way loose and knocked the bastard out with the same syringes of drugs he'd used on me. I freed the others and we walked through the woods where we ran into a search party that included some of my friends and the police, of course." *That was basically factual, anyway.*

Beverly stared. "Wow. A search party? And your friends were there, but you escaped on your own?"

"Yes." *Please let that be enough. Let this be over.*

"So Maddox came to your rescue? How'd he know where to find you?" *Of course she'd focus on Maddox.* Everybody in town was asking the same questions.

"They ALL came to my rescue."

"But how'd they find you?" This was the question everyone had been asking. Would be asking. Because she couldn't tell anyone the truth. *'Well see, Maddox and his Mom are sort of psychic. They see and hear things through other people's eyes, or their minds, so he saw me, saw the house…'* She smiled inwardly and outwardly told Beverly what they'd told the police and everyone else who'd asked that question.

"You were here when Jacob came in here, disguised as an elderly man."

"Yeah, I always thought that guy was creepy." Beverly nodded. "I said so in my interviews." Aden let that pass.

"Well Maddox was suspicious of him as well. He'd introduced himself to Maddox in the café over there before he came in here looking to 'buy an anniversary gift' for his non-existent wife."

"Oh yeah! I heard he gave those earrings you sold him to his mother?" Beverly chuckled.

"His *dead* mother. Yes." Aden shivered and inhaled deeply. "Anyway, after I was... kidnapped, some of my friends started researching 'Julian Vinings' online. They found property records online that eventually led to the house where we were being held."

"Wow. That's some story." Beverly stared. *You don't know the half of it,* Aden thought.

"And Aden and the others all lived happily ever after. The end." Mr. Keith stood in the hallway at the back of the store, his arms crossed. "Now please get back to work ladies." As Beverly scowled and turned away, he winked at Aden with a conspiratorial smile before turning back to his office.

"Dunno what he thinks we're NOT doing out here. It's not like there are any customers." Beverly groused quietly.

Morning passed into afternoon unheeded as Aden concentrated on the store's displays. Like many people in town, Beverly didn't try to hide her suspicion of Maddox, demonstrated by several quiet comments she would make in passing. Aden ignored her.

"I should apologize, ladies." Mr. Keith frowned, coming out of his office. "I've let the lunch hour come and go without making sure you both got a break."

"Beverly should go first. It's my first day back and she's covered for me for weeks." Aden offered.

"No, no, you should both go. Take as long as you'd like, too."

"But –"

"Don't worry. I can hold the fort while you're gone, I promise." He smiled. Beverly nodded, smiling as she bolted for her purse in the back room.

"Thank you. I won't be long, I want to finish these displays today." Aden assured him, following Beverly to retrieve her own purse.

"They're looking good so far. The displays have missed you too." He smiled. Knowing

Beverly would take offense to that, Aden didn't reply.

Beverly didn't say a word as they walked out the front door together and quickly turned the corner to where her car was parked and drove away. Aden sighed, looking around. She'd half-expected Maddox to be waiting, leaning against the side of the building as he so often did whenever she left work, but he was nowhere in sight. She acknowledged the wistful disappointment, replaying their last conversation in her head, as she walked to the café just down the street.

There weren't many people in the café at this hour of the afternoon, but every one of them stopped to stare as she walked self-consciously to the counter. She'd been out in public only a handful of times since the abduction had made her face so famous. No, worse, she was infamous. Not only was she one of the "victims" and salacious rumors ran wild of the atrocities they may have suffered, but she was Maddox's girlfriend. The man, the out-of-towner, who found them under mysterious circumstances. Everyone she met had so many questions crowding their accusatory gazes, and this was the first time she faced them alone.

Should have stayed in the store, she thought grimly. Taking a deep breath and purposefully meeting every gaze, she strode to the counter and somehow managed to order a sandwich and bottle of water without incident. She fought to un-curl her fisted hands and press them onto the edge of the counter, attempting a casual air. She hoped no one noticed the slight tremors or the methodical deep breaths she counted in an effort to fill the tense silence as she waited for her change.

The girl behind the counter took twice as long to make the sandwich as she couldn't pull her attention away from Aden. This was one of the same girls who'd giggled and jealousy ogled Maddox, the handsome new guy in town, when she was there with him on previous visits. But that was before. She was no longer enviable. No, now the kindest of sentiments she received was pity, and at the other extreme, a voracious watchfulness for her to do something, anything, that would confirm all the whispered accusations. Icy fingers of awareness scraped down Aden's spine, so she turned to deliberately meet the eyes that watched her with varying degrees of covertness.

"Okay…here 'ya go." The girl behind the counter said hesitantly, sliding a bag toward her. Aden could see the desperate search for a way to start a conversation; to get the first-hand account of all the horrifying details and to get answers to the questions and mysteries surrounding her life. So she was surprised when the girl smiled warmly. "I'm really glad to see you're okay."

"Um, thank you." Aden answered, a beat late. Mustering what she hoped was an answering smile, she took the bag and strode with carefully measured steps back out onto the sidewalk. Resisting the urge to glance through the window and see if they were all still watching, she pulled out her phone and checked it for messages. There were none, so she pulled up some old texts that hadn't been deleted yet and pretended to read them as she continued back toward the store.

This is crazy. I'm not going to hide from the world for the rest of my life. Get over yourself. Nobody's looking at you. But a cursory glance at the couple of people she could see out and about confirmed that they were, indeed, watching her. *Okay fine then. Hope you're all enjoying yourselves. Get a load of this fascinating behavior.* She pocketed her phone and crossed the square to sit on a bench in the small park across from the jewelry store. Though it sat in the deep shade of a massive old oak, the late summer heat shimmered off the concrete sidewalks and the humidity practically oozed from mid-air in the heavy atmosphere. Digging out her sandwich, Aden used one of the napkins tucked in the bag to blot her dripping forehead and the back of her neck. A couple jogging by actually stumbled into each other as they recognized her and gawked on their way past. Aden sighed.

Oh, aren't we in luck to observe in its natural habitat, the North American Abduction Victim. Note the pale skin and shadows under the eyes, the slight tremble of the hands as she takes her afternoon meal...Oh my God. I'm a moron. Finishing her sandwich quickly, she returned to work in less than half an hour.

Mr. Keith stood at one of the display counters with a customer, so Aden averted her head and quietly hurried past to stow her purse.

"Aden!" the voice stopped her in her tracks. "I didn't 'spect to see you here." She turned slowly to see his signature head-to-toe perusal of every woman he saw.

"Billy Ray. How are you?" she tried for the polite smile again. She had an uneasy history with him. Billy Ray Payne worked at his father's garage with her brother, Drew. His past attentions to Aden had not only made her uneasy, but his run-ins with her and her friends including one when he was armed with a gun, caused Cadence to dub him the Leering Letch, and the Sheriff and even Mr. Keith to warn him away from her.

"I'm good." His eyes darted from Mr. Keith to her and back, uneasily. "I thought you'd still be at home, you know, takin' it easy." Aden just smiled as he continued quickly. "Just dropped by to...um...say hello to your boss."

"I won't keep you then." Aden turned to go.

"It's good to see you, you know, out and about." Billy Ray called. Aden just waved without turning and continued out of sight. Swallowing the cowardice she felt, she stayed in the back until she heard the bell over the front door ring as he left. She met Mr. Keith in the small hallway outside his office as she headed for the showroom.

"I'm sorry about that. I didn't expect you back from your break so soon."

"It's not a problem. This is a public space after all."

"But I had barred him from the store, previously, as you know. I just wanted you to know we were settling a business matter and that he won't be back. He understands that he's not welcome here."

"Thank you." She felt so awkward. Though Billy Ray would never be her favorite person, he'd insisted on attending her welcome home party when she'd been released from the hospital and had been nothing but polite. Maybe he was turning over a new leaf. For his sake, she wished him well.

Having finished all her merchandising duties, and with Beverly finally returning from a very extended break (Mr. Keith *had* said to take their time, she supposed), Aden watched the last few minutes of her shift tick slowly by. It had been a very slow day, sales-wise, with almost all of the sparse customers just browsing on their way through town. Beverly had gone back to ignoring her following their lunch break, which was fine with Aden, except for the interminable silence that opened the door to Aden's ever-circling memories. Normally she combatted her most annoying cognition with dreams of Maddox, but he seemed so far away today. She knew it was due to the almost-fight they'd had during their last conversation, coupled with his absence for the entire day. That hadn't happened since…well, ever. From the day they'd met, she would see him or talk to him as often as they could arrange. Even during the horror-filled hours following her abduction, she could feel his concern for her. She'd never be able to explain it, but she absolutely heard him, felt his consciousness reach out to hers, as she'd laid chained in the dark; but she couldn't feel him now.

As the minutes ticked past, her apprehension grew into a nameless anxiety that she finally recognized as fear. Fear of losing him. Nothing had been the same between them since that night…would never, *could* never be the same again. They were different people than they'd been, living in a changed world.

"Your friends are waiting." Beverly's bored, flat tone brought her back to the present.

With a leap of excitement to see Maddox, talk to him, apologize, she followed Beverly's gaze through the front plate glass. Cadence and Trey grinned and waved. Her stomach dropped. She didn't see Maddox.

She waved and watched anxiously as the two of them leaned into each other out front, settling in to wait for her; without looking left or right to where anyone else might be waiting with them. *Crap. What if he wasn't even here?* Mr. Keith made an uncharacteristic appearance at the top of the hour.

"Aden, we're all so happy that you're back. I don't know if you saw if the printed schedule in the back, but I don't have you coming in again until Thursday. I hope a couple of extra days off won't be a problem?"

Aden was taken off guard, as preoccupied as her mind had been with the slowly ticking seconds; and Maddox's apparent absence. "Oh, sure. Sure, Mr. Keith. I know with everything that's happened...I mean, I appreciate everything that you've done for me. Just let me how I can begin to step back in. Whatever's helpful, I mean. I'll be here." Mr. Keith just nodded, smiling, with no further questions or commentary.

"We'll see you on Thursday then. 1:00?"

"Great. Thank you. See you then." Aden smiled dazedly as she went to retrieve her purse. *1:00 Thursday was too many hours away. So many hours to fill.*

"Hey there! So how was your first day back at work?" Cadence pounced as soon as Aden cleared the shop's doorway, wrapping her arm with her own.

"Um, fabulous." It really was nice to have been treated semi-normally for so many hours today. She glanced around quickly, looking for Maddox.

"He's waiting for us at the Café." Cadence smiled knowingly. "It was really crowded when we walked past, and he wanted to be able to save a good table." Cadence practically skipped along. "If that's okay." She slowed, surveying her friend with a frown.

"The café. Sure. Great." Aden threw out her best smile.

"Well, I mean, the movie doesn't start for another hour and we just thought – " Cadence's scowl deepened.

"No! No, that's fine. Great, I mean." Aden assured her, summoning her best smile. "I'm...pretty hungry."

"Okay then." Trey surveyed her dubiously as he held the Café's door open for her to enter.

"We don't have to do this." Cadence whispered, with a restraining hand on her arm as she moved to go through the door.

"I could call Maddox, have him meet us at the car – " Trey was saying.

"Stop! Calm down." Aden smiled in earnest. "It's not the first time I've been in here today." Taking a deep breath, she flung the heavy door aside and strode in, expecting a silence to descend as everyone turned to stare at her.

"There he is, back there." Cadence broke the tautness, stepping around Aden toward where Maddox sat alone in a back corner. Aden blinked; nobody had even looked up, let alone registered her presence.

She followed Cadence to a small table tucked in a corner between the counter seats and the swinging door to the kitchen. The table looked way too small to accommodate the extra chairs that had clearly been appropriated for their arrival. Aden realized that no one was looking at her…because they were all watching Maddox.

Crap.

Melodee Lane
www.MelodeeLane.com

Follow the author on Facebook and Twitter for updates about Gemini Gate and the *Blackwater Falls Series*!

www.ingramcontent.com/pod-product-compliance
Lightning Source LLC
Chambersburg PA
CBHW070346260626
47161CB00001B/34